Praise for Exiles

'A hunger for the possibility of freedom. The tumbling of borders and convention. The migrants of Mac Amhlaigh's *Exiles* fear the loss of home and its fixed reference points. Their voices swerve between two languages, two cultures, and two different ways of existing between the future and the past. A wonderful addition to Irish literature.'

Colum McCann,
National Book Award winner with *Let the Great World Spin*.

'Donall Mac Amhlaigh made a vitally important contribution to the literature of the Irish in Britain and indeed to the Irish diaspora worldwide. As with many working-class writers of his generation and writers of minority languages in particular, he didn't receive the recognition he deserved while alive. Mac Amhlaigh's *Exiles* demonstrates what the Irish and the migrant peoples of our day have always known – to be truly at home is not necessarily to sleep beneath a familiar roof. Home is not a particular place but is a community or a people and their sense of identity. I cannot stress strongly enough the importance of bringing this work to a wider readership.

Tony Murray,
Director, Irish Studies Centre, London Metropolitan University and author of *London Irish Fictions: Narrative Diaspora and Identity*

'Donall Mac Amhlaigh is the most perceptive and informed writer on the Irish in twentieth-century Britain. Mícheál Ó hAodha is to be congratulated for making this masterpiece… available to an English-reading audience. It deserves a wide readership to remind us what emigration and exile was like for the generation who left Ireland in the 1940s and 1950s.'

Professor Enda Delaney,
author of *The Irish in Post-War Britain*

'Mac Amhlaigh's novels and books have been rightly-praised for their exploration of the harsh lives of Irishmen who laboured to build up Britain again after the devastation of the two world wars. No less an achievement however, is his searing account of the lives and conditions of Irish women emigrants to Britain. Mac Amhlaigh's intimate evocation of the inner-most thoughts and aspirations of Nano Mháire Choilm, the novel's central female character, is on par with the masterful portrayals of this generation of Irish working-class women and their hopes and dreams by another great Irish writer, Máirtín Ó Cadhain.'

Máirín Seoighe,
documentary-maker and producer of the series
Imircigh Ban (Women Emigrants), 2015

'Despite the massive Irish emigration to the cities of England it is an experience little explored in literature. But Donall Mac Amhlaigh was its great chronicler. He was the best man for the job as he both lived the life and imagined that of his colleagues. This great novel is his best achievement, richly translated for the first time. It captures those times of hardship, of fun, of love and of spite perfectly, when the Irish were 'building up and tearing England down'. It is a story which appears to be documentary but is truly a sympathetic recreation through the imagination of what it was like for those hundreds of thousands of Irish who left our shores.'

Professor Alan Titley,
translator, *The Dirty Dust* (M Ó Cadhain), Yale University Press

'A valuable service [has been done by] Mícheál Ó hAodha… for the Irish Studies community worldwide, and especially for those of us who work on Irish immigrant culture in Britain. Although widely recognised as a classic of modern Irish-language fiction… [*Exiles* had remained] off limits to most Anglophone scholars because it [was] not available in English translation. In rectifying this discrepancy, [the translator] has produced a literary text worthy of the original, which deserves a wide readership not just nationally but globally.'

Dr Liam Harte,
Senior Lecturer, in Irish and Modern Literature, The University of Manchester and author of *The Literature of the Irish in Britain: Autobiography and Memoir, 1725–2001*

We have very few published first-hand accounts of the life of the Irish navvy and worthwhile works of fiction by authors who knew whereof they spoke, are as rare as hen's teeth. The books of Patrick MacGill, JM O'Neill, and Donal Mac Amhlaigh spring to mind. Mac Amhlaigh's novel, [*Exiles*], written in his declining years, has until now been inaccessible to readers unable to read work in the Irish language. It is greatly to his credit that Mícheál Ó hAodha has performed this labour of love… it [should] be enthusiastically received, not only by scholars of Irish migration history, but also by that general readership which undoubtedly exists for authentic artistic insights into that now-vanished world.'

Ultan Cowley,
The Men Who Built Britain: A History of the Irish Navvy

Exiles

Dónall Mac Amhlaigh

Translated from the Irish by
Mícheál Ó hAodha

PARTHIAN

PARTHIAN

CYNGOR LLYFRAU CYMRU
BOOKS COUNCIL of WALES

Co-funded by the
European Union

Creative
Europe
MEDIA

Co-funded by the Creative Europe Programme of
the European Union

Dónall Mac Amhlaigh (1926-1989) was one of the most important Irish-language writers of the 20th century. A native of County Galway, he is best known for his novels and short stories concerning the lives of the more than half-a-million Irish people who left Ireland for post-war Britain.

A prolific journalist and a committed socialist in the Christian Socialist tradition, Mac Amhlaigh, whose diaries and notebooks are held in the National Library of Ireland, was a member of the Connolly Association in Northampton and contributed regularly to newspapers such as the *Irish Press* and a range of journals on both sides of the water throughout the 1970s and 1980s often providing the perspectives of the Irish in Britain on issues such as class, economy, emigrant life in England, the conflict in Northern Ireland and civil rights-related issues.

Mícheál Ó hAodha is an Irish-language poet from Galway in the west of Ireland.

Parthian, Cardigan SA43 1ED
www.parthianbooks.com
First published as *Deoraithe* [Exiles]. Dublin: An Clóchomhar, 1986.
© Copyright The estate of © Dónall Mac Amhlaigh 1986
© This translation by Mícheál Ó hAodha 2020
ISBN: 978-1-912681-31-0 print
ISBN: 978-1-913640-15-6 ebook
Editor: Gwen Davies
Cover Image: November 1956: Finola O'Shannon and Paddy Bedford from
Dublin's Gate Theatre look for auditions in London. Paddy earns a living
working as a waiter in Soho and Finola models for artists. (Photo by Harry
Kerr/BIPs/Getty Images)
Cover design Marc Jennings @ The Undercard
Typeset by Elaine Sharples
Printed in the UK by 4edge Limited
Published with the financial support of the Welsh Books Council
Co-funded by the Creative Europe Programme of the European Union
British Library Cataloguing in Publication Data
A cataloguing record for this book is available from the British Library.

Dedicated to all my relatives in Leeds and Liverpool
and the Irish who took the boat across the water.
Mícheál

Chapter 1

On his way down to his train at Galway station, former soldier Niall O'Connell turned into the Philadelphia bar at the corner of Eyre Square. He set down his case and opened the packet of twelve Afton cigarettes he'd bought up in Renmore earlier. He had a good look around as the barman pulled his pint and took it all in – the baggage that most of the other customers had brought with them, the ancient advertisements for drink and tobacco, the rows of bottles that lined the shelves and radiated the wan, lonely light of the autumn sun, the damp, rust-coloured sawdust, cigarette-butts and ugly gobs of spit that littered the floor. It was more than three months since Niall O'Connell last stood in a pub.

Just as stupid an idea of ordering a drink was going back on the fags now, not that abstaining from them for a few months had diminished his love of them in any way. He had still been in two minds when he'd bought this packet in the canteen earlier. He wasn't sure whether he should smoke them at all – or, at least that's what he'd told himself, anyway! Truth is, they'd just been lying there in his pocket, secretly calling to him all the time, the same as a child promised a bag of sweets. The reason for him having given them up had gone, in any case: from now on, he could afford his own cigarettes and drink. Today was a significant day in his life. He could feel it. And it was a time for celebration. Still, his joy at returning his soldier's kit to the stores for the last time early that morning had been tinged with regret. Saying goodbye to the army forever and having the big iron gates of the barracks clanging shut behind him, a strange feeling had come over him, that of an old prisoner suddenly released after years in jail. A wave of sadness had coursed through Niall and a lump had formed in his throat.

He grabbed his pint and backed away from the counter, away from the other travellers who were pushing forward now and ordering drinks, left, right and centre. The two barmen were under pressure, flicking the tops off beer bottles and dishing out pints as quickly as they could. He couldn't remember seeing the Philly bar this crowded before, unless it was for the Galway Races. All the people in there were from Connemara: all speaking Irish, Irish, Irish. That sweet, melodious Irish that was music to Niall's ears; he'd miss it now that he was leaving Galway, as surely as he'd miss the army itself. Even downtown earlier, when he'd done a quick trot as far as the bridge, he'd been surprised at the huge crowds of Irish speakers – almost all of them on their way to England, no doubt. Not that there was anything unusual in the people of Connemara and the Aran Islands heading across the water. After all, that was where all his army comrades had gone once they'd completed their term in the army. But on this Saturday, in the autumn of 1950, you'd have been forgiven for thinking that the entire population of the Gaeltacht was migrating, lock, stock and barrel, over to England. Because the Connemara people were everywhere: congregated in groups on street corners, in the doorways of the shops or standing out in the middle of the path, unwittingly impeding the other passers-by. They were typical country people in town for the day – meeting up and chatting, and everyone friendly and relaxed. This crowd was a mixture, some of them shy and inoffensive: like fish out of water now that they were in the city. Others still had a real lively energy about them – as if they couldn't wait to go abroad. The majority were young people, men whom you could tell were powerful workers and swarthy-skinned girls – bright eyed and pretty – the type of girl whom Niall O'Connell had always found really attractive. It was really sad that so many young people had to emigrate like this, Connemara people especially. It was a disaster, Niall thought; of all the classes of people to be leaving the country! After all, this tribe of people were the real rightful heirs to the Irish nation! If there were any justice in the world....

If Niall had been running the country, he'd have tried his level best to keep these people at home – for the sake of the Irish language, as much as anything else. What was the point of all that talk they'd heard about independence – that blather about language and nation – if they were just going to let the wellspring of Irish culture disappear like this: thousands of people leaving forever on the immigrant boat! This was more than a catastrophe! It was a form of treachery to the ideals of the heroes of 1916 and the generations who'd come before them.

People were lashing into the drink heavily now, steeling themselves for the journey ahead. A few were already well-on-it and full of talk and bravado. Men leaned in on one another's shoulders in that familiar fashion of the country people when they came together for a drinking session. That tribal camraderie that combined clannishness with a veiled sense of threat. This race of people were a strange breed in the way their loyalty to one another could transform itself in an instant and break into argument: it was love/hate as two sides of the same coin. This was a peculiarly Gaelic trait Niall understood because he knew these people intimately, and recognised their ways. His connection to them resonated at his core. Their ways were his ways. Most of all, he loved their authenticity, the sense of humanity that defined them and was rooted in their language. And if he'd been able, he'd have memorised and recorded every single word and gesture of these people; he'd have transformed himself into some kind of a recording machine for these Irish-speakers and their culture, and salvaged their memory as best he could. Theirs was a unique culture, one that they'd somehow managed to salvage from ancient times; kept with them through the toughest of ordeals. Their history was important. Their story deserved to be told.

To the left of Niall was a middle-aged man was who drunk and ready to sing – if anyone'd listen to him, that is! The man suddenly threw his head back and shut his eyes, then began working his hands, winding himself up to reach for the words of his song. He was ready to sing and yet he was on-edge. He'd a prickly look about him – it wouldn't take much to start an argument with him.

'Neós, an chéad lá den mhí is den Fhómhar, sea chrochamar na seólta....'

'Well... now, on the first day of September, we hoisted our sails,', he sang at the top of his voice, as if daring anyone to interrupt him....

'Nár laga Dia thú!' (May God never weaken you) someone called out in a mocking voice and a few men looked over in disgust at him, much as to say that they resented this old-fashioned carry-on of his. These latter men were the types who'd already spent a season or two working over in England, Niall suspected, because they were the types who'd little patience with the latest wave of emigrants – such as this singer – whom Niall suspected was probably leaving home for the first time. The singer stopped suddenly and glanced around the room. His eyes settled on Niall and stared at him as if taking him in properly for the first time. He swayed drunkenly but the next moment assumed a confrontational pose, as if to challenge this unwelcome intruder to the proceeding

'Up Muicineach!' the man shouted out in challenge.

'Up Down!' Niall replied and someone skittered with laughter. Niall regretted his retort immediately. He knew how easily such smart-alec comments could start a row in a pub, and he'd never been fond of arguing or fighting. The man gave Niall another dizzy stare but then his attention shifted away. He began to whistle a reel. He'd an urge to dance now and so he drew his arms to his sides, pushed his two thumbs out in front of him and directed his eyes to a point somewhere at the far end of the room. Then he launched himself forward

drunkenly. Niall backed out of his way and tried to attune his ears to the conversations that were going on around him. What he heard disheartened him, however. All the talk related to England and to what life was like across the water. These people had already left Ireland behind in their minds....

> *No, you f**r, you change in Birmingham, you've no business going to Rugby....On the beet son, to Peterborough. That's where loads of the Mayo crowd go, those hoors are going there for years. And I don't need to tell you, Bartley, you're way better off with an English contractor. McAlpine or Wimpey or one of them. Let the Irish ones go to hell, those b**ds would kill you with work....Yep, the hoors, they were getting two pounds a day, seven days a week . Government work, son....*

Wasn't Niall lucky that he'd been thinking ahead and saving for this day – so that he didn't have to leave like these lot here?! That would be his absolute last resort. He'd prefer to stay in an army uniform for the rest of his life than have to leave Ireland forever and be reliant on the English for his livelihood

He must have some good stuff in him all the same, seeing as his plans had worked out and he'd managed to put a small bit of money aside lately. I mean, there were plenty of distractions that he could've blown it on, no bother. Hadn't Captain Delaney referred to him as 'the entrepreneur' – taking the piss out him? He was jealous because he knew that Niall was putting his weekly wages aside and saving it, whereas Delaney didn't have it in him to save a single penny! Every Wednesday, Niall had left a full two pounds of his wages sitting in the book and used the remainder to get him through the week. This had been no mean feat when you saw your comrades heading down to town of a night and having good craic while you were left hanging around the barracks, stretched out on your narrow bed and staring at the ceiling. It had been tough to hold out, but Niall had managed it despite everything. That's not to say that he hadn't often been sorely tempted to give up and head out on the lash....There'd been plenty of evenings when he'd been a right cranky b**ix because he was so sick to the teeth of staying in; he'd been at the end of his tether often enough: that desperate for even one pint of the black stuff. Never mind all the times he'd been dying for a smoke! He'd stuck to his plan all the same, and as the day of his release came closer, the temptation to break his strict regime had lessened and he'd sensed victory. And signs of it now – he'd a nice little stash of money set aside for himself. And he wasn't dependent for his money on anyone else – whether Irish or English – unlike this poor legion of the dispossessed here now, all of whom had had no option but to leave home so's they could earn a bit for themselves. Paddy Delaney could say whatever he wanted about him – but the joke was on him now!

Niall finished his drink and glanced up at the Fallers clock above the bar. He'd time for another drink. He didn't need to be at the station yet. Now that he'd the sweet taste of porter on his lips again he couldn't believe how he'd managed to stay off the drink as long as he had; he'd never have believed he had that much willpower in him. And as for the fags! The tobacco smoke worked its way down through him now in a wave of pleasure. It was just beautiful. Niall slammed his glass down on the counter and called another pint. He felt slightly dizzy now – between the cigarettes and the drink – but it was a nice dizzy, like a little dance of joy up and down his body. The crowd was pressing in on the bar and Niall backed out of the way, pint in hand. He was surrounded by people that would have stood out in any company. Even the way they dressed was distinctive – never mind their language and mannerisms. They had a wild half-subdued energy, something that distinguished them completely from people of other Irish regions. It was this same energy and dynamism that stood them in good stead over on the plains of England, where they tore into the work with great energy – eager to prove themselves. History and resilience was inscribed onto these faces of the west of Ireland. It was part of their Gaelic inheritance and make-up, and was passed on through generations. The men here were all style in their suits made to measure by the lame tailor down at the Long Wall, even if shop-suits were taking over in other parts of Ireland. Strangely enough, what was in for these lads was whatever fashion was on the wane elsewhere: the wide trousers, the long collars, the draped-shoulders look; and that wasn't counting all the other showy details – side-folds, big glitzy rings, multi-coloured ties, high-necked jumpers and zips. Many of them still wore caps even though that was going out of fashion with the younger crowd. Some of the lads sported a fountain pen or a comb in their jacket pocket, a flourish that the east Galway people would have regarded as showy or effeminate!

Niall himself wore a tweed suit and proudly sported a *fáinne*. After all, it was up to Irish people to buy their own home-produced products, he believed, and wasn't this as good an example of patriotism as any? Not that it was attracting too much attention right now! A little shiver of loneliness went through him once more. It'd have been nice had even one of the soldiers from the barracks – or indeed anyone he knew – happened to call in for a bit of a chat. All this, and the fact that he wouldn't get much chance to speak Irish from now on, made the years before him seem a humdrum prospect.

Niall looked around to where a young woman was sitting by herself next to the door, anxiously fingering her marriage ring, turning it around as if it might give her some insight. Judging by the loving glances she was throwing in his direction, it was her husband that was standing in front of her. He was swarthy and hawk eyed, a strapping young fellow who held himself ramrod straight. Handsome, with high cheekbones and piercing green eyes, this man sported a chequered cap perched rakishly on his head and a tie that was secured so tightly it looked like it'd choke him. He was as fine-looking a man as any in the Philadelphia bar that day, a true Westerner if ever there was one. A thick ring made from the corner-piece of a three-pence coin adorned his right hand, and around his wrist was a strip of leather.... Here is one of the rightest, hardest men as ever there was, Niall said to himself in a respectful tone. But for the amount of attention your man was paying his wife, she might as well have been a hundred miles away! That he was already three sheets to the wind was clear from the heat of the debate he was engaged in with two other sturdy looking bucks. Both of these sported blue gabardine coats and caps, the peaks of which they'd pulled backwards, as if to somehow make themselves look neater or more compact. The men were discussing some feud about seaweed that a gang called the Whites had taken over with them to England, a feud that was so bitter now, someone could be killed. The fellow that had red hair was going on about the fighting prowess of some man called Pete Willie, while the other two were contradicting him.

'Orah, God grant you luck,' he said to the others. Even the best of the Whites wouldn't last two seconds with Pete Willie, not two seconds, I'm telling you!'

'By Jaysus, but you might be wrong there, Trevor. Colm Pats White is some man – I'm telling you now!'

'Even if he's good, Peteen has a punch on him that'd knock a horse – sure, they say he gave Thornton himself plenty of it back in Doire Nia one day there a while back?'

'So they say.'

'That's what I heard, Coimín!'

'I find that hard to believe,' said the third man.

'There's two sides to every story.'

'There is, and seven sides! Any of the Whites would match Pete Willie, I'm not saying Máirtín Thornton.'

'I'm telling you now, Trevor, boy, there's *action* in that crowd you don't get in many.'

'And, damn it all sure? Did I say that there was no action in them?!

There's action in them alright but sure, plenty of men have action in them – that's not to say that any of them'd be able for Pete Willie.'

There wasn't much in the way of a hankering for home amongst these lads, anyway; if that's all that was bothering them now that they were leaving their native country! They were like a people that were blind to their own fate, Niall thought. And if that poor woman who looked like she was about to burst into tears was the big red-haired fellow's wife – and sure enough, she was – how come your man wouldn't spend his last few minutes with her now, instead of arguing like this about a crowd of idiots who were feuding with one another?

The same thought crossed Niall's mind again up at the train station later on when he watched the same man saying goodbye to his wife. She was weeping in a heartbroken manner by then and, once the engine roared to life, she snuggled herself into him and held onto him as if she'd never let go. This display of emotion on the part of his wife embarrassed the man more than anything else because he shoved her roughly to one side and hopped onto the train. She wasn't the only woman that was crying now, either, because everywhere you looked there were young women and their families in tears. One elderly man stood alone next to the edge of the platform and wiped his eyes with the corner of his bright Sunday bawneen as he shed copious tears. A young girl leaned her face against the carriage window, all the sadness of the world in her big tear-stained eyes. The same girl wound her handkerchief endlessly around her fingers as if she could squeeze her sorrow away in its folds. The sound of a woman's laughter came from one of the carriages just then, a laughter that was the other side of tears. The people tried their best to blot out the sadness of the moment. Crowding onto the train were pensive-looking men who'd left their women and children behind them earlier that morning back west, men who'd tasted the bitter cup of necessity and would have given anything not to leave home or family behind – if they'd only had a choice in the matter. Other men who were in a different mood took their seats now, fellows who were well-on-it already and whose sole concern now was dominating one another in conversation. The latter were the lucky ones, in a way, Niall O'Connell thought: emigration didn't bother them. And maybe they'd the right idea, really, seeing as they had to leave the country anyway. There wasn't really much point in getting down and mournful about it, was there? That's the way they saw it. Of course, Niall himself would've been making the same journey if it hadn't been for the plans he'd put in place already. The truth was that there were better men than him now left idle and unemployed in every town in Ireland and there was no sign of the situation improving.

Niall boarded the train and took his seat in the same carriage as the big red-haired man and his two friends. Opposite him sat a dark, russet-haired girl who was travelling alone. The big man chatted away loudly with his friends, still oblivious to his wife who stood outside on the platform, her eyes glued to her husband as if absorbing this last sight of him with every fibre of her being. Two young girls – sisters, by the looks of them, tucked themselves next to the group of men, and began a conversation with a solid-looking young fellow with black sideburns and a gold wrist-watch. The sisters had black curly hair and hazel eyes. They were no more than seventeen- or eighteen-years old. A small streak of dust marked the corner of one girl's eye – she'd been crying earlier. She'd recovered, however, judging by the way she was flirting with the buck with the sideburns. Niall had never found it easy to make casual conversation like this; he envied how easy conversation came to them.

It was a mortal sin, he thought, that such beautiful girls were being taken away across the water to a place where no-one would understand how unique and special they were. If the people running the country had been doing their national duty they'd have tried to keep all these people at home. The youngest of the sisters gave a heavy sigh as the train juddered and slipped slowly out of the station. A silence fell over the company. The big man looked over at his wife and signalled vaguely in her direction. He wasn't too bothered, by the looks of things. It was different for Niall. A shiver of loneliness coursed through him and the train gave a hollow echo as they clattered over the boards of Lough Atalia bridge. He stared fondly out over the blue tract of water and at Moneenageisha on the northern side, and then the fortress-like walls of Renmore Barracks. Over to the south the shoreline was dotted with the small blue-coloured thatched houses of Ballyloughane and the smaller villages round about, villages Niall'd come to love over the previous three years – Ardfry, Tamhain, and further on down to Kinvara and Ballyvaughan. Even though Niall was leaving Galway for a new stage in his life, the loneliness went through him in that moment like a cold wind. There was nowhere in the world that he loved more than Galway.

Once they'd passed Athenry, Niall felt a certain estrangement from the countryside. He was distracted by the russet-haired girl that sat opposite him, too. She was very pretty, he thought, a woman that it would've been easy to fall for; she was the type he'd have fancied himself – unless she was going out with someone else already.... The girl stared dead-eyed out the window as if intent on avoiding conversation with the other passengers. Every now and then however, she gave a flicker of a smile despite herself as she listened in on the conversation of the others. One of the gabardine coat brigade tried to make his way out into the aisle, giving Niall the chance to talk to her. He lifted her case onto the baggage-rack overhead and she thanked him politely. She told Niall that she was headed for a town called Norwold, a place that wasn't too far away from London, from what she could tell. She'd got a job in a hospital there and she was going to give it a go and see how she got on. It was only recently that she'd decided to leave Ireland. It wasn't that she'd any great hankering for England, she said, with a certain tinge of regret. There was a bit of a story behind this girl – she was someone who was emigrating almost against her will, Niall could tell. As if in recompense for this information, he told her that he was heading home to Kilkenny. He'd just completed his term-of-duty as a soldier in *An Chéad Chath*, the Irish-speaking battalion. Had he a job lined up back home, she asked Niall, and he told her about how he and Butler had plans to go into business together, something that'd keep the wolf from the door, God willing.

It was Kieran Butler, to give him his due, who'd ensured Niall hadn't gone off the rails, as Niall had been a bit wayward prior to this. They had been schoolmates – for as long as they'd stayed at school that is – and it was when Niall was home on leave in early-summer that they'd decided to go into partnership. Kieran had a job in the city graveyard. It wasn't the worse job in the world by any means, but – as Kieran'd say for a laugh – you'd be long enough there when you were dead – never mind spending all your days there when you were alive as well! There had to be other ways of making a living, he said, ones that didn't involve being under someone else's thumb all the time. You'd never get ahead in this life if you were always reliant on others for your weekly wage. It was lack of capital that was the biggest barrier to getting ahead, Kieran said. You just had to have a small bit to get off the ground first. If you had a bit of go in you and weren't afraid to take a chance….

Something had stirred in Niall as they'd chatted that afternoon in Bridge House, looking out over the river Nore, Kilkenny Castle and all the new-shorn trees. There and then, he'd decided to come home again and give it a go….

Kieran's plan was simple – put a small bit of money together and buy a horse-and-cart and timber cutting equipment, a two-handled saw, an axe and a wedge – and begin selling firewood around the town. Trees were cheap to buy, Kieran said. There were farmers around the place who'd as good as pay you to clear away fallen trees from their land and he'd a fair idea where they could get a horse and cart fairly cheaply too. 'The brave man never lost it,' said Butler, and – wasn't this the truth? – nothing ventured nothing gained. Two hours later and the deal was done. They'd save as much money as they could in the meantime – waiting until Niall was finished with the army – then they'd get going properly with the business. You had to start somewhere, and seeing as they were at the bottom, there was only one way they could go... and that was up. Anyway, who'd heard of a soldier or a graveyard worker who made big money?

Their plan made good sense, the russet-haired girl told Niall, and she wished him all the best with his new business. Anything was better than just going with the flow. It was up to everyone to find their own niche in life....

Definitely – there was something eating this girl, Niall thought. And she wasn't long divulging it to him, either. She was going out with a local lad back home and she mightn't stay too long across the water because of this. She'd see how things went.... Life was strange and you never knew what kind of turn it might take. Just when you thought things couldn't get any worse for you, there's be a sudden turn up for the books – or, at least, that's what the older people always said!

That other fellow must have been mad, Niall thought, because if he'd been going out with a lovely girl like her, there's no chance that he'd have let her slip through his fingers and disappear off to England like this; no more than he'd let Peg Dineen slip from him either, if he thought that he was still in with a chance there.... Sure, wasn't Peg one of the main reasons that he'd returned home in the first place – if she'd only realised it? Just thinking about her now sent a dart of longing coursing through Niall. Butler had already started working on the business. He'd bought a nice quiet-tempered pony already, as well as all the tackle and accoutrements; it wouldn't be long as Kieran had said in his last letter before they had their own yard and a big sign high-up over the gate: O'Connell and Butler, Fuel Merchants. Niall reached across and offered the girl a cigarette but she politely refused.

She never bothered with them, she told him. The two sisters didn't smoke either, by the looks of it. They were chatting away now to the black-haired lad with the watch, and the gabardine-coat men. Everyone at their ease with one another now. The sisters were heading for Huddersfield, as was the black-haired fellow; it was the first time over there for the women but your man had spent two years there already. It was a grand place to work, he assured them. There was lashings of work available and as many Connemara people around as you'd ever wish for.

There were times when you didn't need a word of English in the pubs or in the dance halls – that's how many Connemara people were living there now. You'd almost think you were back home, a lot of the time. It was an amazing country, really; there was as much work there as anyone wanted. One of the sisters was going for hospital work over there and the other was hopeful of getting a job on the buses. A girl from their village was already working as a clippy in Bradford and there was no telling how much money she was making – if you were to believe what people said....

Oh! There was big money to be made over there, alright... no word of a lie. That said, they worked ferociously long hours for it, the Mayo women and the Donegal women, especially. They were mad for overtime, the young man confirmed. Some of them never wanted a day off and just worked non-stop from Monday to Sunday; some sort of madness for work and money came over them the minute they crossed the water! Wasn't it a great thing too – to have the freedom to work as much as you wanted? – the younger of the sisters said. It beat working as a domestic for half-nothing back in Salthill, Galway, any day of the week! People were getting chances now that they'd never got before and they had to grab them with both hands.

The talk of England went on for a long time and only gradually petered out, as darkness fell. It was as if the loneliness of their leaving had usurped the moment again. Even the big red-haired fellow went silent and stared out of the window. They were passing through the countryside around Westmeath. The atmosphere was slightly awkward now that everyone had gone silent. It was as if all the energy and life had drained out of them as night drew in. What kind of a curse was on the Irish that they were driven out of their own land, generation after generation? Niall cursed to himself. Not only that, but they'd been an independent country a full thirty years since!

On an impulse, Niall blurted it out. Did it bother her that so many of the Irish were leaving home like this? The russet-haired girl stared at him momentarily as if confused by his question. It was a real failure, certainly, but there didn't seem to be any way out of it, she said.

And maybe there wasn't. either.... And yet this resigned and helpless attitude irritated Niall and made him angry at his own country and people. It couldn't be that God had pre-ordained matters in this way – that the Irish were always exiles – so that in the end, there was no-one whatsoever left living in Ireland. Now and then the train stopped at some small country station or other and voices reached them from the other carriages: a sudden screech of laughter or notes of music. Youngsters passed up and down the passageway outside their carriage, giddy young lads horsing around and burning up some of their pent-up energy.

Most of the youngsters emigrating had only a little English; in truth, it may prove that they would be the last flowering of the Gaels and their culture, really. Christ, Niall said to himself. Why in God's name was it that they always had to emigrate when it was all the anglicised bucks that were sitting pretty on the wealth of the country? It was enough to drive you mad and make you despair.

'Yes, you're probably right,' he replied to the girl who was on her way to Norwold – wherever that was. 'There's nothing that can be done about it.'

'We're nearly landed now, I'd say,' the girl said. She was right: the carriage was growing dark and filling with shadows. Scenes of the night outside were reflected through the windows, like ghosts of their own souls. A feeling of dejection came over Niall, for some reason: he was keen for this part of the journey to be over. He couldn't wait to be chugging along southwards from Kingsbridge.

A yellow-red glow hung over Dublin city, the street-lights sparkled on the Liffey as they crossed over the bridge towards Westland Row. Only a few people disembarked from the train there because most people were heading for the boat at Dun Laoghaire, and it occurred to Niall that he was the odd one out here; the only one not taking the boat across the water with all these other people.

'Well, I hope things work out well for you over there, sister', he said, and shook hands with the girl, feeling awkwardly formal. Niall felt a slight lump in his throat as a dart of loneliness went through him, an emotion he couldn't trace to its source.

Niall O'Connell had another pint in O'Mara's on Aston Quay and then got the bus that brought him out to Kingsbridge; as always, when he was on Liffey-side, he felt estranged from the big city streets and the crowds of people rushing along them. There was something about all those ancient buildings and tall dark hallways that depressed him, even if he couldn't explain why, exactly; there was something unsettling about these strange streets and faces. He wasn't at home here. In his heart of heart, he knew that this city didn't really belong to him at all.

His mood brightened again on the train southwards, however. There wasn't any word of Irish to be heard now but at least he felt an affinity of sorts with the other passengers in the carriage; they offered some sense of permanency: they weren't leaving their country forever. From now on, he'd have to make his own way in life as best he could, but who knew what the future held; maybe he could do his own small bit for the country? Even to keep living in Ireland now was an act of patriotism; it was some form of what the politicians referred to as 'practical patriotism', and it was now up to him and his like to offer their lives for Ireland, just as previous generations had once died on her behalf. Niall was glancing at a copy of the *Evening Mail* that he'd bought from a poor-looking ragamuffin boy on O'Connell Bridge when a small elderly man began to make conversation with him, and they continued chatting until they reached Carlow where the old man got off the train. It was nice to have had the company. A former hero of the Irish War of Independence, the man thought that Ireland was a great country now; life was improving every day, he maintained, they were building fine new houses instead of the miserable cabins that had been there when England ruled the roost; they had their own energy supply and their own industries, they had their own army and their own government (in most of the country anyway – and they'd have it all back sometime in the future); they were respected in the United Nations and in other foreign countries now as well. Normally, Niall wouldn't have bothered arguing with an elderly man but his smugness annoyed him, especially when Niall thought of all those fine Connemara people who'd be ploughing the waves across the Irish Sea tonight – and all because they didn't have any work in their own country. What about all the emigration, he asked the old man crankily? What about the way the countryside was left decimated as the nation haemorrhaged its own people? Was it a sign of progress that the pride of Ireland was leaving in droves every day? Niall asked. The man, who was sitting beneath an old smudged picture of Keimaneigh, gave a small understanding laugh but his eyes lit up all the same; there was nothing he seemed to like better than having a bit of debate with this assertive young lad.

No doubt about it, there was emigration and a lack of work but, then, it wouldn't always stay this way. After all, Rome wasn't built in a day. You had to walk before you could run, and we had to give the country a chance yet. We'd been under the British yoke for years and years; we'd been beaten down and destroyed by them – or nearly destroyed, anyway, he said. Those devils had never managed to quite get the better of us despite their best efforts. Look at how the embers of freedom had smouldered away within us for centuries and we'd had the courage to fight back again and achieve independence, even after long years of oppression. There was nothing that he wouldn't do to protect the freedom that we'd now achieved, the old man said. Nothing at all. No young hooligan of a British soldier would ever set foot on our land again, no way; he'd have to deal with him first! And it wasn't the end of the world either that there wasn't a man or woman in the country yet over the age of thirty who hadn't been born beneath the English flag. Hadn't he seen big changes, even in the short years since he'd been out with his gun himself, and nearly all of them for the better, too? Ardnacrusha, Bord na Móna, the beet factories – there hadn't been sight nor sign of any of those when the English were in charge; and there wouldn't be neither had the British still been here. Look at the way we'd remained neutral during the war! It was thanks to the Long Fellow, Dev, God bless him; he was the only person that could have brought us safely through that crisis, and in spite of Churchill and Hitler himself. The nation would be forever in Dev's debt for this. We needed to be patient, therefore, the elderly man said, in summary; if we were, we'd see the country thriving again one day, all the way from Rathlin Island down to the Blaskets. Niall hadn't it in him to contradict the man; he and his like weren't to blame for the bad state Ireland found herself in now either – whoever else *was* responsible for it. His generation had done their best when they'd had the chance – that was as much as you could ask for.

Yes, Niall had said to the old hero. There's a lot of truth in what you're saying, for sure. First there was Carlow, Bagenalstown, and then onto Gowran. As they came closer to his destination, Niall felt a little anxious. It must have been his longing for home again. He wanted to get going on his life as he'd planned it out. And he wanted to meet Peg Dinneen again if she was still around. A whole raft of different feelings coursed through him at once, leaving him with a vague uncertainty. He took a heavy drag on his cigarette as if trying to savour the full significance of the moment: this, his return home. One part of life had just ended; another was about to begin, and he needed to soak up every minute of it, draw it out for another while and prepare himself for whatever the future might hold; it beckoned to him as a veiled woman might signal in secret.

They were already crossing the bridge at Malogue, and the street lights at the edge of town winked one by one. The train slowed and came to a stop. Everything was as Niall remembered it the first day ever; for a moment, he imagined that he'd gone back into the past or that time had stood still. He stood for a moment at the door of the station and looked down the street. What he saw only added to his illusion of it being an unchangeable place. They were still there, the same group of men, all with their backs to the wall outside Ritzy Gorman's pub, silhouetted in a yellow streak of light. They all had the same lazy look; it seemed as though they'd never moved. Across the road from them, the lights of Saint John's Church illuminated the people coming and going in dribs and drabs from Confession, the elderly men lighting their pipes at the gate of the church, groups of women chatting together in groups. Down on High Street, the weak chimes of the City Clock announced time as the smell of turf fires wafted across the cool air of night. Niall took it all in again, and a warm familiar feeling came over him. The unease he'd felt earlier dissipated like a thin layer of fog beneath the sun's rays. He swung his small travel case and walked quickly down towards the town, whistling quietly to himself with contentment. He was home again.

Chapter 2

Norwold hospital was situated on the edge of the town. It had a nice area of land around it with a border of evergreen trees. Gravel walkways led to the hospital grounds from the main road, and into a large three-storey brick building covered in thick ivy. The place was very different from the way that Nano had imagined it. She'd pictured it as a grim place, empty, bare, cut off from the normal flow of the world and the eternal stream of traffic outside. It wasn't as she'd imagined it at all when she'd sent in her letter applying for the job as nurse assistant.... *Unqualified nurse assistants urgently required. Good pay and board. RC Church nearby. Address your correspondence to The Matron, Norwold Hospital, Norwold, England,* the advertisement in the *Connacht Tribune* went. Nano had, for a few weeks, mulled over whether to apply for the job before putting pen to paper. And, even then, she'd been unsure. She'd been in two minds until the very last minute, or at least that's what she'd told herself. Thinking back on it, however, Nano knew that she'd made up her mind the instant she read the advertisement: she'd already decided in her heart. She didn't have much of a choice, really, because if she'd stayed at home, she'd be in the way of her brother, and it was well past time for him to get married. Her only other choice was to leave, and hope that Máirtín would get a move on once she'd gone. But what were the chances of that, really? The truth was that Máirtín had no control over his situation – no more than she did. He was in a bind as much as any man had ever been.

It had been on the Sunday night after the ceilidh in Spiddal when they were cycling home together that she broached the question of the hospital job with Máirtín for the first time. She'd already put the letter in the post by then and this was probably the reason that she'd felt a bit out of sorts earlier that evening. She'd been in a strange and melancholy mood all evening, a feeling that she couldn't really pinpoint other it being down to her having already made her decision. It was as if she was seeing the old place and everyone in it properly for the first time ever – as though through someone else's eyes. She noticed things afresh, details that she'd never noticed properly before. It was as if change had crept up on the place, almost without her noticing. All those young and pretty fillies were turning into beautiful-looking young women before her very eyes, all the long-limbed youths transforming themselves into handsome men. Looking back on it, this was something that had frightened her: it was strange the way all the crowd she'd grown up with were getting old already, the fresh beauty of youth abandoning them like leaves on autumn trees. Combined with this mixture of sadness and regret that drifted over her then was the feeling that she should make her peace with certain people that she hadn't spoken to for a long time. She started chatting to Julie Phádraig Pheicse, a lump of a girl whom she hadn't had much time for since they'd had a row one day in the sock factory, a factory that was closed down now. She did the Stack of Barley with some tough young lad from a village back further west, a fellow who never shut up all the while they were dancing and kept asking could could he leave her home. It was as if she'd already left this place in her mind, there was no point in having a row with anyone because she was no longer part of this community. This feeling had stayed with her all night until the ceilidh came to an end and they played 'Amhrán na bhFiann' (The Soldier's Song).

It was when they'd negotiated the hill and were freewheeling down the other side that Nano raised the question of the hospital with Máirtín. The magical white gleam of the autumn sun illuminated the small rocky fields, it shone golden and smooth on the surface of the sea as the wheels of their bicycles whispered secretly on the tar road. This moment was beautiful; so too was the night, and it only bolstered the intimation that Nano had felt earlier; it was a reminder to them of life's fleeting nature. By this stage of their lives, they should not have been returning from a ceilidh; they should have been busy with their own lives, raising their own family in their own house.

'Guess what I did the other day, Máirtín?' she asked him half-quietly.

'What? I don't know, I swear!' A surge of anger enveloped Nano. How could Máirtín be so oblivious to the conflict that was going on inside her? She felt an urge to hurt him back, to pierce his complacency.

'I wrote to England, to Norwold, wherever that is, looking for a job in a hospital there. It was in the *Connacht* last week.'

Máirtín didn't reply: he was a man of few words at the best of times. Normally his silence wouldn't have bothered Nano in the slightest. Máirtín Bhid Antaine had never been much of a talker and anything he said was carefully weighed-up beforehand. He had a quiet confidence and he was a kind-hearted man, and if it wasn't for the fact that there were family issues preventing him, they'd have been married years ago.

'Looking for a job, is it?' he said, but Nano couldn't read anything into his deadpan tone. For a while, there was no sound in the world except for the whisper of the bicycle tyres along the gravel road. A little later, as they stood outside the gate of her house, Máirtín asked Nano to wait and see how things turned out.

'You'd be better off waiting a while so that we can see how things go, Nano,' he said, but despite herself, she reacted badly.

'See how things go, Máirtín? By God, but we're long enough waiting to see how things go – and we're not seeing anything!' She was tempted to add 'we're long enough looking at one another', but that would have been going too far. That would have been unfair to him, because the truth was that Máirtín wasn't to blame for their situation any more than she was herself.

Nano Mháire Choilm was twenty-six years of age and Máirtín Ó Spealáin was thirty. It was time for the pair to get their act together, but how? It was the old mother-in-law situation. Máire Bhid Antaine would never have welcomed a new bride onto her turf, no matter how fine and easy-going a person she might be. And Nano had no interest in forcing herself on her either. There were two women in that house already, in any case, even if Máire was counting the days until her sister Anna in Boston sent for her. And it wasn't as if Máire was standing in the way of Nano coming into the family either; she'd said as much to Nano often enough; she, more than anyone, would've loved to see Máirtín married. But Mammy was the problem, said Máire, adopting the English term and imbuing the word with a certain grandness, as was a habit of hers. Mammy was the boss, when it came down to it. Nano forgave Máire this little hint of grandeur because Máire was still young. And she'd plenty of good points about her too, to give her due; and anyway, her opinion didn't carry any weight. It wasn't true to say that Máirtín was completely under his mother's thumb either, even if this was the main reason that he wasn't married yet. It wasn't as simple as this, unfortunately. Bhid Antaine held an advantage over her son that was difficult to counter; she had a problem with her heart that meant Máirtín couldn't put too much stress on her. Nano knew full-well that Máirtín would go to England or anywhere else with her the next morning rather than waste any more of her life on her back here – if he'd only been allowed to. But he wasn't! He was completely trapped here and unable to move backwards or forwards, really. Because his mother's health was so bad, Máirtín couldn't take the chance of pushing her beyond her limits. His mother was a woman who hadn't had it easy, as Máirtín had explained to Nano: he couldn't just leave her there at home and entirely reliant on the neighbours, given that that she was so fragile and coming to the end of her days. But then, of course, he wouldn't have had to leave her at all had his mother just given in a little bit, had an ounce of understanding or had been less stubborn. The problem was that his mother didn't have any 'give' in her. And any time that Máirtín raised with her the question of marriage and bringing a woman into the house, Bhid Antaine's response to Máirtín was always the same – it wasn't the right time yet and she wouldn't be in their way much longer. In reality, the old woman was just using her heart problems as an excuse, Nano knew – and this was not to her credit! In truth, Máirtín's mother could probably still live on for years and if she had her way, there was no chance that they'd be married this Advent nor the following Advent, nor any other Advent for the next ten years. Meanwhile, they'd be getting older all the time, Máirtín and herself, the same as all the other couples who let the years pass them by until, by the time they finally got to the altar, they were nothing but a laughing stock. Wasn't it often said of youngsters who were itching to get married in that part of the country that they should go and 'get a room in Bohermore' – the new housing estate in Galway city – seeing as they'd be a long time waiting to get the home-place. And these younger couples were the more enthusiastic and go-ahead ones – or the ones lacking sense, whichever way you looked at it. Nano Keane would've preferred to move away from the countryside and into a housing-estate in the town, bad as it was, rather than this never-ending dance of courtship that herself and Máirtín had going on. But look it! Even that solution had been denied them!

'If I could get our Peadar to come home,' Máirtín always told Nano, 'I wouldn't spend another day in this place.' His repeating this mantra was by now like rubbing salt into the wound, however. It made no sense.

'Peadar? You know well that you won't get Peadar home, Mart! You can forget that one.' Peadar was over in Sheffield having the life of Riley, out carousing in the pubs and fighting and all the rest of it – or, at least that was the last report they'd had of him. And he was probably in some other part of the country by now anyway because he'd always had itchy feet; the same as many other Connemara lads over in England, he found it hard to settle down anywhere. Máirtín had sent word to him asking him to come home the previous year, but Peadar hadn't even bothered answering his letter! That's if he'd ever received it in the first place. And a man from Bohaun who'd met Peadar over there somewhere had reported back that he hadn't the slightest interest in that small scattered strip of a farm back home. 'He'd never go back' – he'd said, 'no way in hell.' He'd had enough of the place, tons of work for little reward, and the whole parish watching you all the time, watching your every bloody step. The work might be hard in England but at least it was well-paid and you'd a bit of comfort on top of that. A man could go to bed with a woman or go out on a bender for the night without everyone in the neighbourhood bellyaching. Máirtín should sort out his own situation – if he could, that is – but if he was expecting Peadar to come home again, he'd be waiting a long time, by dad, he sure would!

'But wouldn't you think,' Máirtín said, gauging his words slowly because he was at a loss to understand why your man across the water cared so little about his predicament – wouldn't you think that seeing as he isn't tied down and is just wandering from one place to the next, that he'd be as well off giving a chance to someone else, someone who wanted to make a go of things, wouldn't you?'

At least while the old lady was still alive anyway; after that he could do whatever he wanted. The reason Peadar hadn't a notion of coming back was simple – Nano wanted to tell Máirtín – he was having the life of Riley across the water – the life that neither of them had ever had. But what was the use in talking? Life wasn't fair for half the people anyway; many people never got their just rewards in this life; that was fate. Wasn't their Bartley in the same predicament? Nano's brother would be able to get married if she left home. But what would she stand to gain if she left home; that was the question Nora asked herself back then. Wasn't it an awful pity, she thought to herself, that people didn't figure out the best path while they were still fairly young – and not be left struggling blindly along like this in the dark?

'You never know, Nano,' said Máirtín with a false sense of hope, 'it won't be long now before Máire will be heading over to Boston and who knows what my mother might decide then?'

But his words only hurt Nano more, especially seeing as Máirtín didn't realise that he was saying the wrong thing. She kept what she really wanted to say to herself, however, and instead, she said, 'Your mother is the way she is and I don't see that this will change much, Mart; and anyway, I doubt if me and her would get on very well. She sighed gently and shook her head. 'God knows, Mart, but the more I think about it, the more obvious it seems to me that I'd be better off leaving – at least for a while, anyway. And as you say yourself, we'll see what happens after that.'

Máirtín was quiet again for a while but when he spoke next it was clear from the hesitation in his voice that he didn't really believe in what he was suggesting. 'Maybe if you didn't go any further than Galway… get something in there for a while?'

'Work as a skivvy in Salthill, is it?' she exploded angrily. Nano couldn't restrain herself now, despite her best efforts. She didn't care anymore if she broke Máirtín's heart because his helplessness was making her angrier and more bitter by the minute. 'If I ever up sticks, Máirtín, and you can bet that I will, it'll be over to England and to Norwold I'll be going, not working for the posh crowd over in Salthill, I can guarantee you that. And,' she added, her sarcasm increasing, 'what an awful pity that I didn't go off to America that time when our Babeen was asking me over.'

She couldn't help it, but she whimpered quietly to herself then and, next thing, Máirtín had his arm around her. She was so upset and emotional that she didn't care whether she lived or died, to be honest.

Because it was plain as day to her. There would never be anything for them at home – nothing.... All they'd get were constant barriers and one objection after another; all from a woman who was halfway to the grave (according to herself, anyway). And all the while, their lives would just pass them by. It was an awful situation to find yourself in and Nano had had enough of it....

She'd had enough. Máirtín soothed her gradually and she cuddled into him. A wave of longing went through her and she'd have given in to Máirtín and her own half-buried desires right there and then, if he'd wanted to go all the way.... Not that he did anything – nor would he have considered doing anything, not until he'd had the blessing of the church. Máirtín was exactly the same as her in that regard; she knew his way of thinking as well as she understood herself: he'd too much respect to take advantage of her like that. That's not to say that there hadn't been plenty of times when it'd crossed Nano's mind that maybe it was his fond, proprietorial and courteous attitude towards her on Máirtín's part that'd actually left them stuck in the rut they were in! Because weren't there many other couples whose need to be with each other fully in the physical sense (as well as in every other sense) had rushed them to the altar, and whose match hadn't done them a blind bit of harm in the end, either? There was a resolute tone to Máirtín's words this time that she hadn't heard before, however.

'OK, then, love; there's no way around this except that I talk to my mother tomorrow; she's long enough stringing us along anyway, and it's time for us to get this sorted one way or another. Come on, forget about it for now, darling: we'll see what happens tomorrow.'

That had been a fortnight ago exactly – to the day.

Chapter 3

Trevor Nee, or Trevor Bartley Billy as he was better-known, arrived off the Irish Mail into the smog-coloured station that was early-morning Euston, along with the hundreds of others who'd made the overnight journey from Ireland. Everyone crowded onto the platform with their baggage and made their way down towards the tall Doric columns at the main entrance to the station. He said goodbye to the other two men who'd been with him all the way over from Doire Leathan, Connemara, threw his battered old suitcase onto his shoulder and set off with a countryman's long strides in the direction of Camden Town. He turned up Eversholt Street and made straight for the underground station at Mornington Crescent. On arrival there, he put down his suitcase for a moment and lit a cigarette. Trevor Nee was a tall and striking-looking man. Powerfully built, he stood there, wide-shouldered, at the edge of the road. Dressed in his blue Sunday suit and an old peaked cap perching slightly askew on his big mess of red hair, Trevor was another member of that lively and energetic tribe. This ever-growing band wanderers was in great demand these days for digging, shovelling and all sorts of heavy work. It was these people that were rebuilding the cities of Britain after the Luftwaffe had near destroyed them. This was the era of re-construction and expansion, and tall buildings were appearing everywhere where there'd been massive bomb craters just recently. The arteries and sinews of all the big cities were being revived, and everywhere was a cacophony of noise as people threw themselves into the huge project of reconstruction. The Irish were to be found in large numbers wherever the highest pay was available. Trevor Nee might have been in exile but there was no way that he was sad about leaving home; the opposite was true, in fact. For Trevor, it was as though a weight had been lifted from his shoulders; he felt free from the ties of home and family. No-one could describe Trevor as a bundle of joy – he just wasn't that type, but he was someone satisfied with his lot. He felt at home in this vast and scattered city, even if the only familiar parts were those Irish areas that he and the other members of his class frequented, areas such as Finsbury Park, Kilburn, Cricklewood, the Elephant and Castle. And, of course, his destination on this particular morning: Camden Town. England was a great country, Trevor Nee thought, somewhere with freedoms and opportunities lacking back home. He'd spent a month at home this time and he'd been very glad to escape back to London again.

In truth, he had such little fondness for his place of birth that it wouldn't have bothered him in the slightest if he'd never set eyes on the place again. He knew that he couldn't cut all ties with home, however: he was trapped. Trevor flicked the butt of his cigarette away and took his case back onto his shoulder. It was so early that the streets had an abandoned look. The only signs of life were small groups of nurses making their way towards the early Mass on Arlington Road and the occasional street sweeper or policeman. It was difficult to believe, but before long, huge crowds would be milling about these same streets, and the pubs would be packed with his fellow-Irish – the big boys: the fellows earning big bucks in black or navy suits and bright white shirts, all of them laughing or posing, everybody enjoying life to the full in a way that they never could have at home. Back home, the same people would often have found themselves without a penny in their pockets of a Sunday: not so here. Trevor couldn't dream of a better set-up than he had over here. He had really fallen on his feet because this was the land of opportunity for those who sought it, a place where the only man who'd no money was the waster who couldn't get his act together and do some work. Men such as those lazy townies Trevor saw leaning against the wall at many a road-junction; all they needed was to ask for work and they'd have got it. There are bone idle men in this world, Trevor thought, who weren't worth wasting food on.

It is said that Camden Town is the furthest distance that the poor and exhausted traveller could carry their baggage from Euston Station on arrival from Ireland via the overnight ferry. This is the reason so many Irish chose to live in this area, or so they claimed. But this was only half the story, as the Gaeltacht people themselves could easily have attested to. Far more likely was that this area suited the working-classes, given its plentiful supply of cheap lodging-houses and cafés, never mind all the pubs, and the fact that every newly arrived immigrant immediately found themselves part of a large Irish community. It was to Camden Town also that the lorries of all the Irish employers came in a large fleet early each morning to pick up the strongest labourers, the men who were willing to take on the dirtiest and heaviest work – anything that involved heavy digging, dragging and shifting large quantities of soil, rock and concrete – and all the other work required for pipe-laying schemes and the installation of big energy cables. Over here in the vast metropolis, different races migrated towards the jobs that best suited their abilities and attributes, and the type of work that they were naturally associated with: the Greeks were in the restaurant trade, the Jews were involved in business, while the black people of the West Indies worked as conductors on the buses and trains. The English generally took the cleanest or the easiest jobs while the rural Irishman did the heaviest and roughest work of all, the tough life of the navvy. Tomorrow morning, Trevor'd be down amongst these men at the crossroads, along with hundreds of his other fellow Irishmen. And there wasn't one Irish company that would have hesitated to employ Trevor, either – Murphys, Mahers, McDonaghs, Kennedys, McNicholas', Fitzgeralds or McAlisters. Amongst the labourers, Trevor Bartley Billy had a name as one of the most powerful workers who'd ever come over here and this was no small reputation to have! His lodgings were a tall, narrow house at 147 Arlington Road where all the male lodgers were Irish. The woman who ran it was a Cockney of Irish background and she'd been so many years dealing with the Paddies, as she herself referred to them, that she was completely at home with them, even those men – a fair few – who had very little English. The door of number 147 was never locked at night, and all Trevor had to do was turn the key and let himself in as quietly and carefully as though he were opening his own front door back home. The kitchen and the dining room were located beneath the level of the road outside and even if the former was a little cramped, there was plenty of space in the latter, despite there being three tables each sitting six men. Unlike many of the other lodging-houses nearby, the rooms of which had been divided into small cells that functioned as bedsits, Number 147 was still laid out pretty much as it had been when the area housed wealthier and more genteel individuals. Mrs Madge Connolly had left the rooms of her house much as they were then, the only difference being that she'd crammed as many beds as possible into each room. Singles or doubles, whatever suited best: Madge got two pounds rent from each lodger every week, no matter whether he had a bed to himself or had to share. The men didn't seem to care either way. Truth be told, hardly any of them had had their own bed at home in any case.

Unlike many other landladies, Mrs Madge Connolly always gave her tenants plenty to eat; there was no shortage of meat in her place, even though it was still being rationed; signs on it too – wasn't there a path beaten to her door by would-be lodgers, and Madge could pick and choose which men she liked and who she turned away. Trevor was wetting a drop of tea for himself in the kitchen when the woman of the house came down from her room, her dressing gown half-undone and her hair up in a heap; she'd a copy of the *News of the World* in her hand and a fag in her mouth, and Trevor could tell that she'd had a good drink last night down in the *Brighton Castle* or in the *Hawley Arms*. And even if Madge was fond of her drink, especially at the weekends, she never let down any of her lodgers or let any man out to work in the morning without his breakfast, no matter how hungover she was. Mrs Madge Connolly was a grass widow whose husband had left her years ago without so much as a bye-your-leave. Not that Madge had any great regrets about this, by all accounts; most people thought that it must have been her choice to remain single. She wasn't half bad-looking for a woman pushing fifty, and there were many much younger men who'd have jumped the broom or even made an honest woman of her.

'You're back again Trevor,' said Madge, her hand to her face in a vain attempt at disguising her yawn. 'Luckily, I've a bed free for you above, a single bed; one of the lads went up the country working somewhere yesterday. 'Make me one, will you, like a good man?' She opened a box of *Players* and passed one over to Trevor. 'You're up above with Red Sweeney and Tom Joyce; you know which room; you've slept there before, I think: number seven. Trevor handed her a cup and she flopped down onto a chair again. 'I better get my skates on, a few of the boys'll be down soon; they're going out to Stonebridge Park this morning, working on the rails, I think.' She took a sip of the tea and a drag of her cigarette, then gave Trevor a quick glance. 'Did you have a good holiday, did you?' she asked casually, and Trevor's reply was just as indifferent.

'It was all right.'

Trevor was not a big talker in the presence of women at the best of times; he wouldn't initiate conversation with them, either, not without good reason. Neither had the term 'holiday' ever meant much to him. He'd never been on holidays and he'd no real interest in the concept either. Whenever he went home, it was an obligation – fat chance he had there of taking it easy! Schoolteachers, factory workers and the like – they went on holiday – not people like him! The only thing that Trevor understood by the term 'break' was spending part of the day drinking beer with the lads or sometimes throwing his jacket aside at the end of the night for a bit of boxing. That was the end of Madge's enquiries about his holiday. She'd little enough interest in the country, really, even if she did spend most of her life in the company of Irish people. She would've been the first to admit that she had no idea what the land of her ancestors was like; she could never bring a picture of it to her mind, even if she'd heard others chatting about it for years.

'I'll get your breakfast ready for you, Trevor. You're surely hungry after the journey,' said Madge, once she'd finished her cigarette and drank her tea. She piled her dark hair back high on her head and fixed it with a couple of pins, then washed her hands under the tap and began preparing the food. She chatted away to Trevor all the while, telling him all the local news. Trevor just sat there with not a peep out of him as she brought him up-to-speed. The barman down at the Bedford Arms had got a right hiding the night before last when he'd tried to throw out Hurley from Kerry (the lad with the glass eye, which was a shame for a lad as good-looking as him). And there'd been a ruckus another night when two groups – one of which was definitely from Southwark – had clashed. It was in the Elephant that this had happened, and one young lad – from Cornamona, a place she thought was Irish – had been stabbed in the middle of the melee. He'd had to have seventeen stitches in his hand, so they said, and was lucky he hadn't been stabbed somewhere more sensitive. What a shower of b**ds they were! From what Madge'd heard – because she didn't attend church or chapel, as Trevor knew – one of the priests below had given a thundering sermon the previous Sunday about the effects of this type of blackguardry. There were young scuts coming over from Ireland these days, the priests said, who were an awful shame to their country and their religion.

'Oh yes, and in case I forget, there was blue murder down in the

Gaillimheach pub the other night, and some poor girl got hurt during the fight – accidentally, of course, but it's all the same for her. She was pumping blood – the poor creature – when they brought her into the hospital, and the crowd responsible for the fight disappeared as soon as the police arrived. One of the doormen there, the Bully Walsh, had a big reputation as a 'hard man' and even he hadn't been able to get those f**rs under control!' Anyway, Madge said, placing Trevor's breakfast on the table in front of him, it was an awful pity to be giving them ammunition against the Irish. All the people of London wanted – well, most of them, anyway – was an excuse to put down the Irish. Trevor had a pretty good idea who that rough crowd was – a much better idea than he let on; he'd get the full story later, in any case, up in the Mother Black Cap or wherever he happened to find himself later that evening. He tore into the breakfast: egg, sausage, a slice of bacon and as much bread as you could eat. It wasn't in every English lodging-house that you got fare as good as this – especially in these early years since the war when food was still hard to come by.

'I might as well go up for a kip now. Staying up won't do me any good,' Trevor said to Madge after they'd smoked another cigarette together. He carried his case upstairs to where Tom Joyce and Red Sweeney were asleep in the double bed, though the single bed was made up from the previous day. Trevor threw his case down onto it, went over to the window, and unlatched it. He lowered it a couple of inches.

'All you crowd ever want is filth and stink, by the looks of it,' he said, in disgust. Tom Joyce was snoring away, probably still sleeping off a heavy night, while Red Sweeney was awake and blinking out from beneath the bedclothes. Trevor undressed and threw aside his clothes, except for the suit, which he hung up in the tall narrow wardrobe with a broken mirror. The two beds aside, the latter was the sole item of furniture. He took all the money he had in his pocket – three pound notes and a handful of change – and placed it carefully under his pillow. He got into bed and, only then, did he notice Sweeney watching him carefully with a hungry look. Red Sweeney stirred in the bed and gave Trevor a great welcome – he'd decided to seize his chance. 'You're very welcome, Trevor. Did you have a good time back home?'

'It was all right,' Trevor replied gruffly. Trevor knew quite well what was bugging Sweeney and he'd no time for his shite-talk now, no more than he'd much interest in listening to herself downstairs a few minutes earlier.

'How were things at home?' Sweeney repeated, a tad more urgently this time, afraid that Trevor would be asleep before he'd had a chance to get in his begging request.

'Same as it was, same as it always will be… a right shithole,' muttered Trevor roughly, pulling the blanket up over his chin and stretching his legs. He gave a long, slow yawn like a great cat and closed his eyes, while in the bed opposite him, Sweeney gingerly straightened up, leaning on one elbow.

'Listen Trevor, mate, I had a bad day on the horses yesterday. You wouldn't be able to spare me a few shillings would you?'

Trevor sighed with irritation and curled up against the wall. 'Go f**k yourself – you and your horses, Sweeney! You should have hung on to your money while you had it,' he said, and went to sleep.

Chapter 4

To get the miserable business out of the way as quickly as possible, Niall O'Connell made for the Labour Exchange nice and early on Monday morning. Despite the early hour, there was a fair crowd of people there already, all standing in a long straggly line that stretched out of the office door. Those shuffling in the queue, the majority of whom were poorly dressed, had the long suffering and beaten look about them of a people who've been waiting all their lives for something that will never happen. Niall cursed the length of the queue and lit up a fag, his last one for a while probably – unless he was able to get a few shillings somewhere. There was only one way of dealing with your worries, the lads in the First Battalion always said, and that was to rise above them, but how in Christ's name could you manage that, especially when you were as bitter as he was? Every time he thought about what'd happened to the money, the job, and all the plans he'd had, he fumed quietly to himself. Even if you were made of stone, you'd have to get angry at this balls-up – it was enough to make you explode with rage. What sort of bad luck was he cursed with, compared to other lads, that this sort of thing had happened to him?

Niall let out a tortured sigh and glanced around the place, dead eyed. He'd been tormented since last Saturday night just thinking about it – all those negative and angry thoughts endlessly circling his mind, all the 'what ifs' and 'how comes'. It was as though his mind was on a leash and couldn't escape all these bitter thoughts. However brave a face you put on it, he'd made a right hash of things. He'd been one happy son-of-a-gun getting off the train just two nights previously but, of course, he hadn't the slightest inkling then of how things were going to turn out!

A friend of his had been one of a group leaning against the gable-end of O'Gorman's pub, and as soon as he spotted Niall, he was by his side like a shot, his face lit up in a broad smile and rubbing the palms of his hands together in anticipation – the same as anyone who's just spotted his main chance. It was for the arrival of stragglers fresh off the train such as Niall that Mooney always looked out every afternoon, in the hope of receiving a bit of charity and quenching his thirst. To be fair, Nicholas Mooney was a good a man as ever grabbed hold of a shovel but his insatiable love of drink had proved his downfall. He only ever got the odd day's work now: casual labour down at the gasworks when one of the workers was absent or they had some other emergency. A big, heavy beast of a man, Mooney wore his hat low over his eyes, his scarf knotted at the throat and his thumbs jammed into his front trouser pockets, the image of a blackguard or corner-boy. He'd spent the best years of his life over in England and it was a common refrain of his that he'd be back there if he could only get enough money together for the fare.

'You're very welcome Niall! You're home again?'

'I am, Nick. I'm back for good now, I'm finished with the army.' Technically speaking, he wasn't fully done with the army, Niall had reminded himself, not yet, anyway; he still had a month where he could change his mind without breaking his official period of service, just in case he regretted leaving and wanted to return again for another term. The flipside of this arrangement was that he could still actually be called back to the army within the next month, for example in an emergency. It wasn't that uncommon either for former soldiers to return to their unit before the month was up, trooping back sheepishly like they were real losers because they hadn't been able to make it in the civilian world. When this happened, the lads who returned were routinely humiliated and made fun of, especially by officers such as Captain Delaney. Well, this was something that Niall didn't need to worry about, thank God! Because that wasn't going to happen – no chance!

'You won't see much in the way of improvement around here, I'm afraid,' said Nicholas Mooney. 'Things are only getting worse: they've never been this slack, there's no work going anywhere.'

'You wouldn't say no to a drink, I don't suppose?' Niall had asked; he never took any notice of Mooney's whining. Rich or poor, never the twain would meet, that's what they always said. There was no point in his entertaining Mooney's complaints now. It was his own bloody fault he didn't have an arse to his trousers. Some of these lads, they'd never have enough to scratch themselves with – and that was the beginning and the end of it. 'You're an absolute gent,' Mooney had said gratefully. 'I haven't been dying for a pint this badly since the day I was born! You're the boy, ye!'

'Come on down and we'll have a drink in Bridge House before I head home tonight.' They'd walked down John Street oblivous to the looks of the other corner boys, jealous that your man Mooney had got his hooks into this newly returned traveller so easily. It might have been Saturday night but there wasn't much going on, even if the shops were still open and trying to make whatever few pounds they could – especially off the country people as they tended to leave their weekly shopping until the last minute. The town had seen no change worth mentioning since Niall had last been home. The same crowd were still hanging around in their small, inoffensive groups on street corners, patient and quiet as ever, as if this were their eternal allotted station, and that all they had left in their lives was to enjoy the peaceful death that is the passing of time. Seeing all this all, Niall asked himself if there were something about this town – Kilkenny – as opposed to other places? During the three years that he'd spent in the army, he'd often recalled the lovely, relaxing evenings he'd spent on the banks of the Nore, the peaceful moonlit nights when the stars lit up the night sky, magical nights that seemed to go on forever. There'd been something otherworldly, almost, about the silence and peace that was to be found here, next to the old Ormond Castle, the evening light as silkily exotic as a dream. Mooney and Niall ambled down towards the town, past a series of small, poor shops, most of which had not been refurbished in years. They passed the doors of a good few pubs on their way, none of which had more than a handful of customers inside, down past the site of the lonely Protestant chapel and the dark, silent college that had housed the philosopher George Berkeley and the author Jonathan Swift at one time, on past the smog-covered window of the pawnshop that still held one of Niall's jackets – unless his period of credit had elapsed. They were just turning into the threshold of Bridge House when they heard a shout from behind them and the sound of running feet.

'Oh, Christ,' Mooney had said in disgust, 'you can't move in this place without someone knowing about it!'

'You made tracks, lads!' said a man who had caught up with them and was trying to catch his breath. 'I was coming down Maitland Street when I spotted you two. Any news, Niall?'

Bosco Sullivan was a tough and athletic lad who spent most of his days just arseing around. He was Mooney's next-door neighbour in Ormond Park, a poor, run-down suburb on the western side of the city. Sullivan's shirt was open to expose his chest, and an old Scout belt held up his trousers.

'I wouldn't put it past you,' Mooney had said grumpily, 'you don't miss a trick.' It would not have dawned on either man that they were actually foils to one another. Mooney used Sullivan all the time as a target on which to release his many irritations and frustrations; the flipside of this was that Sullivan took great pleasure in Mooney's constant bickering and unhappiness. 'Oh, shove it up your arse

Mooney, why don't you? Sure, it won't cost you anything, will it? You don't have anything in the first place!'

'Oh here, leave it go, will you? Sure, what's the price of a pint between friends, anyway?' Niall had said magnanimously, and they went inside. Bridge House was your regular Irish pub of the day, a wooden floor covered with a thin smattering of sawdust, a poky little snug secreted away just inside the entrance, a few tall barstools opposite the counter and a timber edging circling the walls, beneath which was a ring-board and a fireplace that was no longer in use. There were just three customers inside already – two farmers, for whom it was well past time for them to be gone home, judging by the cut of them – and one loner who was sitting dejectedly staring into his pint at the end of the counter. Niall O'Connell knew the latter well: Simon McCarthy, an old codger who had a name for talking shite and exaggerating whenever he was out on the piss. Simon would do the strangest and craziest things when out on the lash – harassing or insulting people who were always nice to him and who hadn't gone anywhere near him! Either that or winding people up and starting rows in places where better men than him would've beaten a hasty retreat. He was a great man too to spread a bit of scandal around; he'd a few juicy stories for the local townspeople and had a reputation for composing smart-alec retorts and witticisms that were repeated for years afterwards whenever people were out having the craic. Simon was one of the town's old timers and you needed to know your stuff if you fancied getting into an argument with him. Simon may have seemed eccentric but in fact there was a character like that in every town back then, so you had to make allowances for him.

It was all the same to Simon, however. As far as he was concerned, people could like it or lump it, because nothing would stop him from speaking his mind or winding people up – if he was in the mood for it. Tailoring was his trade, officially, at least. It'd been a long time since he'd done any work, however, and he lived with his sister who'd her work cut out for her trying to look after him.

The barman had been gazing in a bored fashion out the window when the three lads arrived. Only then did he perk up, because Pat Neary was no fool: it never took him more than a second to figure out who had dough on them.

'You're very welcome, Niall! You're back with us again for a while, are you?'

'I'm back here with you all again,' Niall had said proudly, placing his pound on the counter in a grand gesture that said: this is just small change to me. 'Three pints, there, please, Pat.'

'Three pints coming up,' said Pat Neary, siphoning a stream of lovely porter from the brass with a flourish. He performed the ritual with such aplomb that you'd have sworn he was dishing it out for free. 'So you're done with the army altogether, now, Niall, are you?' Pat said, handing him his change. Two men came in the door just at that moment but Pat didn't move a muscle. Chances were that their custom wasn't worth much. They'd most likely arrived just to pass the time. Pat could tell by the look of them. It was said of Neary that he could take someone's measure straight away, right down to the last shilling they had in their pocket. That didn't alter the fact that he was a very nice man, and sometimes, when there was a lock-in, Pat came out from behind his counter and had a few drinks with his customers. Niall liked this about him, and it was why he'd no objection to spending his drink money right here whenever he was home. In fact, it was because he held Pat in such high esteem that he couldn't wait to tell him about the new business venture with Power.

'Things are bad around here, Niall. It's not easy to get work.'

Niall couldn't restrain himself any longer: he just had to tell him. 'I won't be searching for a job right now, Pat. I'll be working for myself from now on – myself and another man – we're setting up a small business of our own, y'see.'

'May God grant you luck!' Pat had exclaimed. He gave Niall's hand a small squeeze and winked conspiratorially. They were both tradesmen now, weren't they? Wise men of the world. 'I'll be back in a minute!' Pat said and moved to serve his latest customers. Nicholas Mooney raised his pint to his lips as reverently as if he'd something sacred in his hands! He took a sip from his pint and wiped his mouth with the back of his hand. He gave a deep sigh of satisfaction. 'Christ, Niall, but I needed that badly!'

'Oh, down it if you're thirsty, boss; sure, what else are friends for?' Niall had responded expansively. He really couldn't remember the last time he'd been as happy as this. Things were definitely looking up; he felt blessed. He took the second packet of cigarettes he'd bought since that morning from his pocket and offered one to Mooney.

'Don't stay away so long next time! It's great to see you, lad!' Mooney had exclaimed, graciously accepting a cigarette. Mooney was a new man already, Niall could see. He was chilled-out now and as happy as the next man. Mooney loved porter so much, the story went that he'd drink it from a beggar's shoe, if he had to! If he'd ever come into money, he was bound to drink himself to death within a few months. Because drinking was Mooney's sole interest. There was nothing else in his life, really – just this constant need to satisfy his endless thirst. Niall had never even heard him talking about women.

Bosco Sullivan was a different sort of creature, though. In his case, drinking meant a bit of company, an excuse to come in off the street. He'd yet to take a sip from his drink, even, preoccupied as he'd been with collecting the rubber rings from the ring-board and getting ready for a new game. He had stepped back from the ring-board until his foot touched the wooden slat. He stood still momentarily and took his mark, his tongue jutting from the corner of his mouth, a model of concentration. His free hand gripped his jacket-lapel so that it didn't impede his throw. He leaned forward like a runner waiting for the off, and then flung the rings scatter-gun style, one after another at speed.

All five rings hit the board, each one landing on a separate hook. 'What do you say to that now, lads?' he'd boasted. Mooney winked at Niall and gave a deep belly-laugh. 'What can we say, eh? You have it, ya boy, ya, you know your stuff; you're the real deal!' Simon McCarthy straightened up on his stool and nodded. 'The real deal and the real boyo,' he announced happily. Bosco was back at the board again, getting ready for another go. 'There's some real tradesmen in here, alright, not that I see them making much,' McCarthy called sarcastically over his shoulder, and the men who had just come in tried to suppress their laughter. Two farmers looked up as if worried that they were the butt of someone's joke. The tailor stirred again and, as if speaking to no-one in particular, said, 'And there'd be no money about the place at all if we were relying on Ormond Park to generate business and the money for new suits! None of you here have bought a new suit within living memory: all you lot wear is hand-me-downs from St Vincent DePaul!' Someone gave a nervous laugh at this and an invisible tension had filled the air. Everyone looked away from their pints and over at Sullivan, who was retreating the required distance from the ring-board again. He took his mark again and flung the rings again.

'Yes Simon,' he'd said, 'no-one ever bought a second suit of yours, either, because once bitten twice shy!' Everyone laughed this time and the tension was broken.

McCarthy hid his head beneath his arm and mumbled something to himself.

'Knock that back,' Niall had said to Mooney with one eye on the barman who was whispering something to the farmers now.

Mooney wasn't one to let an opportunity slip, and he emptied the pint in one swallow and put down his glass. 'Sorry, Niall; remind me again; you were saying something to me there a minute ago,' Mooney said. 'Something about working for yourself?'

Niall had knocked back the rest of his drink before replying. He was in flying form now. It was like he was already drunk on the thrill of it alone. He might just stay till closing time and make a proper night of it. 'Arah, musha, just a little racket of our own that we're setting up. There'll be two of us; we'll get on OK. Myself and Ciarán Butler, do you know him? We'll be selling timber and sticks.'

'Is that the fella working up in the graveyard, Sikey Butler's son, the eejit who bought the tinker's horse?'

'The same man,' Niall replied. It was on the tip of Niall's tongue to tell Mooney that he shouldn't call anyone an idiot, let alone Kieran Butler, but he had held his counsel.

Bosco joined them and took a slug of his pint. 'What's this lads?' he said, but Mooney ignored him; he was looking oddly at Niall, as though his face were caving in.

'You won't be selling any timber with him, I'm afraid,' Mooney had said, deadpan.

Remembering it again later, Niall could kill himself for not having copped on earlier that something was wrong.

'Why not, Nick?' Niall had said, nodding in Pat Neary's direction.

Mooney raised a rough hand to his face and grimaced. 'Because he went to England the day before yesterday, himself and Tommy Fitz's daughter. Didn't I see them up at the station, sure?'

'He sure did,' Sullivan had confirmed. 'He's knocked her up, so they say.'

***

Niall sucked on the butt of his last cigarette, then flung it away in disgust. He'd no choice but to give them up now, anyway. For a moment, it seemed he'd gone back in time, as if he'd never left in the first place. Hadn't he left town precisely to escape all this idleness and unemployment? When the woollen mill he had been working in had closed, he'd decided to join the army. Little did he imagine then that he'd find himself back here again, standing in the Labour Exchange queue: right where he was now. He couldn't even countenance the possibility of returning to the army. He'd look a right fool and, worse still, he'd be classed as a total failure, especially given how loudly he'd proclaimed his faith in the benefits of self-employment before his departure. There was just no way that he could go back to the army because Delaney would torment him to the gates of hell and back.

'Here he comes, the entrepreneur; here comes the Gombeen man with his pockets as empty as ever. Broke again, is it, 07? You weren't long in the businessman game, now, were you?!' Delaney would've been made up taking the piss out of Niall; just the idea of getting to call him 07 again would set him off drooling. That would have been the ultimate humiliation. You'd have to be as dead as a piece of turf not to let that affect you.

'Hello Niall! You're back with us again!'

Niall was so shocked and broken by the news about Butler that it took him a few seconds to hear Nellie Moffat calling in his direction. This old grey-haired woman had a hump-back from years spent bent over a loom. This biddy was a gossip who loved winding people up and throwing in blue language for good measure. Niall had good reason to remember her sharp tongue, and he recoiled now from the sight of her.

'I am, Nellie,' he said, his face reddening.

'You're finished with the army, so, are you?'

People were turning around to stare at him, and Niall privately cursed this wagon of an old woman who wouldn't mind her own business.

'I am Nellie,' he said, praying that she'd just leave him alone. There was no fear of that however. Now that she'd an audience, there was no stopping her.

'The girls better watch out for themselves, so, boy; there's no-one can compete with a soldier when his stick is standing, isn't that what they say?'

If someone had prodded Niall with a needle just then, he wouldn't have bled a drop, he was that mortified. He cursed the old bitch again and hoped beyond hope that she'd just lay off. But Nellie was in full flow and smelt blood. A quiet, sullen-looking lump of a girl was standing next to old Nellie. Niall couldn't remember her name, even though she'd been working in the mill with him and Nellie, and many others who were queuing up now. Nellie poked the girl in the shoulder and announced at the top for her voice: 'Here he is, Biddy – just what you were looking for – a nice lad who's hot-to-trot and knows all the tricks in the book! What about it, girl?'

Biddy shook her head and tried to shuffle away a bit in the queue. Everyone was enjoying the show, however. They were all gawping at Niall as if he had two heads. For God's sake, you old streel of a woman, would you ever shut that dirty old trap of yours, Niall pleaded with her in his mind. But he was only wasting his time.

'She's a little bit shy, Niall but you wouldn't mind that. Of course, it's the quiet ones you have to watch!'

I hope you choke, you old bitch, said Niall to himself, but Nellie had the bit in her teeth.

'Be janey, you wouldn't know Niall, but she might be the one for you, Niall – if you're even half as likely or energetic as she is! Mind yourself, now, though, because this one here – she might just get the better of you, boy! It's the quiet ones that make hay, and I can guarantee you, lad, that this one will wipe the floor with you; she's all action!' Biddy drew away from the old wan a little bit and gave a gasp. Could it be, he asked himself, that the old scrubber had lost it altogether? 'She won't go out with you, Niall,' she screeched. 'She says that you can't trust a soldier. You're all charm and sweet talk,' she says. 'Be jakers, Biddy,' she addressed herself, 'you can't trust them, either, you can't trust any man until they're stretched out there cold on the death-slab!'

Niall's cheeks were burning in the heat of the crowd's derisive laughter. He was saved from further mockery, however, because just then Nicholas Mooney and Bosco Sullivan joined the queue. Mooney had his usual downbeat air but Bosco looked as happy as though he'd just won the Lottery. But as Mooney often said: wasn't it easy for Sullivan to look full of beans, given that the man hadn't an ounce of sense in his skull? As the Englishman says – where there's no sense, there's no responsibility. Wasn't it better to be simple yet happy than to be clever and tormented? That would be Sullivan's response to this one; 'It's not as if you're very clever, either, Mooney, and yet God knows you're always in bad form!' Sullivan greeted Niall with a big warm 'Hello', even if all Mooney did was nod grimly in his direction, glancing in disgust at all the people ahead of him in the queue. He rooted inside his breast-pocket and produced a small dried-out looking stub of Woodbine. He squeezed the small butt between his lips in a mixture of revulsion and resignation then lit a match by striking it between his thumb and forefinger.

'It's some hoor of a country when you haven't even got the price of a smoke on a Monday morning, isn't it?'

'This country's alright, there's nothing wrong with it, really, and if you don't like it, there's nothing stopping you leaving,' said Sullivan, enjoying his friend's recalcitrant mood. Mooney just grunted, while Bosco rubbed his hands together in playful fashion.

'You'd be better off giving them up, now, anyway, seeing as you can't afford it,' Bosco added and pointed to himself. 'You don't see this son of a gun here smoking, now, do you?'

'I don't, Bosco,' Mooney pretended to admit he saw the hidden humour of the situation. 'Many's the thing that we don't see you doing!'

'It's just as well,' said Bosco, adopting a boxer's stance and feinting as if to throw a punch in his direction.

Mooney cursed. 'Watch yourself now boy, that I don't make mincemeat of you.'

Sullivan's smile disappeared and he was quiet again for a moment. Nicholas Mooney was a contrary bugger at times and he'd once had a reputation as a fighting man. The dole office door had just opened and the unemployed began to push forward, shuffling slowly, almost reluctantly, in the queue.

Nellie Moffat looked back at Niall over her shoulder, still up for a bit of banter, but no-one took any notice now. She was done for the day on that score. From the outside, the Labour Exchange had a forbidding look and it was even more grim inside: all high ceilings and a sickly whitewash throughout. The only colour in the place – if you could call it that – was provided by the Social Welfare and Agriculture department advertisements that littered the walls. The floor was made of timber boards, while a high counter, like a protective fence, stood between the dole recipients and the office staff: just in case someone lost it and decided to go for one of the clerks behind the counter. There were two on duty: one middle-aged fellow who was always grumpy, and another, rugged-looking younger fellow who looked as though he used to play rugby. It was obvious from the dismissive look on this young man's face that he couldn't care less about anyone in this miserable queue of people that regularly appeared before him to sign their names, one after another; they disgusted him. Initially, most of the crowd shifted to the younger man's post but with a quick, arrogant sweep of his hand, he forced them over to the other window. A mood of despair permeated this place, a gloom that would've destroyed anyone's last spark of hope. Niall thought again of what had happened with Butler, and ground his teeth. He'd get his comeuppance, the dirty bastard! It was this air of defeat amongst the dole crowd that irritated the hell out of Niall, and he determined not to let it get to him. When it came to his turn, he leaned in over the counter eagerly, as if to say he had some priority in this place and that this should be acknowledged. If push came to shove, Niall would admit that this was a step down for him that he'd ever signed on here, and, should his application for work fail (and there was nothing more likely than that it would!) he'd have no option but apply for the dole. And in his heart of hearts, he viewed it as nothing but a form of beggary. It was ridiculous to try and convince yourself otherwise. And if he hadn't opened his big trap last Saturday night, no-one would have known about the whole shinanigans with Butler and the money. Niall was mortified because privately he was now convinced that he was a laughing stock.

'Well, man?'

McGlennon, the senior clerk, had never been known for his charm.

'I've just finished with the army,' Niall blurted as if the words would choke him. 'I suppose I have to sign on, do I?'

McGlennon tapped the end of his pencil impatiently on the counter-top in a manner that reminded Niall of a hen scratching corn on the floor of a country kitchen. 'It's up to yourself, you don't have to do anything you don't want: this is still a free country, you know?' the clerk said. Even though his clever-dick comments didn't surprise Niall, he was still surprised by his directness. He repressed his initial response. What he'd wanted to say was that if the country was still free, it was because of men such as himself who'd spent time in the army, and none McGlennon and his like with their cushy jobs.

'Well, I've no work anyway and I understand that I'm entitled to so much a week. That's unless you have a job to offer me, of course?'

It was difficult to tell whether it was surprise got the better of McGlennon or rather, annoyance. 'A job, you say! A *job* is it?' A dark look clouded his face and you'd have sworn Niall had asked him for his own job! Not that the clerk was Niall's biggest problem right now, because the other two lads – Mooney and Sullivan – were making the most of this situation. Mooney was bursting his arse laughing at this craic, and the other idiot was rubbing the palms of his hands furiously together. They were loving this whole pantomime. It was ridiculous: really ridiculous.

Wasn't it awful that someone couldn't go about their business without having the whole world smelling your every fart?

'What sort of a job had you in mind?' McGlennon asked dourly. He was a bit forward – this Niall O'Connell fellow... whoever he was. Maybe O'Connell was out to make a fool of him in front of everyone else, McGlennon thought. The clerk placed his elbow on the counter and assumed his 'don't mess with me' pose. He'd the look of a man who would not put up with insolence from anyone.

'Any job at all that's available, McGlennon. I'm not fussy,' Niall responded without batting an eyelid. This was the best approach to adopt, take this stupid game step-by-step and see what this clerk-fellow was made of and how far he'd go with it. God knows, the bastard had probably been humiliating defenceless people for years.

'You must think that there's plenty of jobs out there?' said the clerk in a voice that oozed disdain.

'You're the one who asked me what kind of a job I was looking for, McGlennon, and I'm telling you again: I'm not hard to please. Any job will do, man!'

If the clerk had been punched in the mouth by Niall, he couldn't have been more insulted. His jaw tightened with anger and his eyebrows twitched in irritation but he managed to keep his temper under control – just about. 'You're very innocent, son, if you think that you can just walk in here and get a job straight away when half the country is out of work,' he said crankily. He stared Niall down and slammed his pencil on the counter with authority. You can put your name down for Bord na Móna, they might need men up in Kildare to help with the turf come spring!'

'And there'll be jam tomorrow! With all due respect, McGlennon, I think you know where you can shove Kildare!' Niall hadn't meant to get this riled-up so quickly. Sullivan swayed gently from side to side, enjoying the show, while Mooney's smirk was hidden behind his fingers. The rest of the dole crowd were listening in on this exchange and a tense silence filled the room. As for McGlennon, he was temporarily lost for words.

'You'd better keep a civil tongue in your head when you come in here, boy. I'm not here to be insulted by the likes of you, I'll have you know!'

'And neither am I.' Niall said right back at him. 'And if you don't have any work available here, I'd be very grateful if you'd just hand me out whatever form I've got to sign.'

McGlennon gave Niall an evil stare and walked over to the shelf where the application forms were arranged in piles. He took one and slammed it down on the counter in front of Niall. 'Fill this out first! Have you got your severance document?'

'It hasn't been sent to me in the post, yet,' he replied, examining the form carefully, but before he'd a chance to write anything on it, the clerk swiped the form back from him as quickly again.

'That means you haven't officially left the Army yet. Are you trying to make a false claim here or what, sunshine' Come back here when you've received your severance form and you can sign on then, but not before. The likes of it..!'

Niall turned away from the counter and made for the door with the look of a beaten man. Outside on the street again, the lads were creasing themselves.

'Ah, Jaysus,' said Sullivan, breaking his arse laughing; 'that was better than any circus! Just to see the look on your man's face when you were talking to him like that; his eyes nearly fell out of his head! A job – be jaykers – you might as well be looking for a spot of God's Grace in a whore's purse!'

'Were you having a laugh?' Mooney asked. 'I mean, you didn't seriously think that was the best way to get a job?'

'Ask and you shall receive,' said Sullivan, exploding with laughter again.

They were passing the gate of Stephens Barracks now and could see right into the big empty square and the tricolour fluttering high above it. The Barracks was just an FCA training centre now unlike during the Emergency when hundreds of soldiers had been based there. Back then, the streets of the city were black with soldiers every evening, crowds of them ambling about in their sharp-shone boots and polished epaulettes. Even now, Niall thought – if he wanted to – all he'd have to do was walk into the office and he'd have been issued with a travel pass and returned to his Galway unit in double-quick time. But, just as quickly, Niall brought to mind the craic that someone like Paddy Delaney would have at Niall's expense were he to return. He smartly put this thought out of his mind.

'It can't be that bad, lads, there has to be a job somewhere if you go and ask for it?' said Niall, trying to play down his frustration.

'Where, then?' Mooney asked him with a challenge.

'What about those new houses they're building out at the Knoll; sure, that scheme isn't finished yet, is it?'

'It's as good as! They're letting people go up there these days, not looking for more workers.'

'You wouldn't get a job up there now, even if you'd a letter from the Pope himself,' said Sullivan authoritatively.

'Ah, indeed, sure, you wouldn't get a job these days if you'd a letter from the Son of God Himself, and that's the truth of it,' added Mooney in a disgruntled tone.

'Employers aren't exactly crying out for *you*, anyway, Mooney, are they?' Sullivan responded. 'But there's no demand for me neither, Niall. Chucks Phelan and Donie Comerton were let go only last Friday and there's more due to be let go this week,' said Sullivan, as though winning this argument made his position easier.

'Bosco knows a lot about work-stuff,' said Mooney, sarcastically.

'But surely there must be something available somewhere,' Niall said stubbornly.

'Have a look, so, and see for yourself,' replied Mooney, and that was the end of the discussion.

They sauntering aimlessly along John Street. As they neared Bridge House they spotted Pat Neary outside, pulling the shutters up for the day. Niall cursed himself under his breath. There was no way in the world that he wanted Pat to see him like this, wandering down from the Labour Exchange in the company of these two wasters; not after all the fine words of the other night – 'A little business of his own – for God's sake!' When he thought about it now, he was mortified – how well he hadn't had the cop-on to keep his trap shut until he really had something to blow about? But no! That would have been way too clever. It was true, what his mother always said, she always had it spot-on. Hadn't she said it this very morning, even, and wasn't she was always proved right in the end? He'd inherited his father's childish and naive ways, lock, stock and barrel, the same as his two brothers. It was all talk and no action with them. By the grace of God, the shutters were off by the time that they passed the pub, and Neary was back inside. Niall gave a quick sigh of relief. Wasn't there one hell of a difference between all the big talk and self-congratulation that'd gone on the previous Saturday evening and how things had turned out? From now on, he'd be doing well just to keep the wolf from the door, especially seeing as he'd be relying on the one pound, half-crown that he'd get in lieu of his daily pilgrimage to the Labour Exchange. Worse still, he'd have to become a regular butt of the jokes and insults of McGlennon and that other buck who worked there – all for one measly pound and one half-crown! He'd been getting twice as much in the army and had his lodgings to boot! You were a fool to trust any bastard in this life and yet who'd ever have thought that he would eventually be brought low by that bollix, Kieran Butler? His thirty lovely pounds all gone in one go, and as stupid as that! He'd have been as well off pissing it against the wall as losing it the way he had – never mind the three-month purgatory he'd endured to save all that money in the first place! You'd have to be someone completely devoid of emotion not to have gone mental and started tearing the place apart at what'd happened. Thirty pounds…! Three ten-pound notes! (Niall had never actually seen a ten-pound note in his life before!) six five-pound notes, ten one pound-and-twenty notes, three-score ten-shilling notes, half-crowns, florins, sixpences, tuppences, all those red penny-pieces – the whole lot passed before his mind's eye, tumbling to earth and disappearing as if in a great shower of autumn leaves! He could've screamed with frustration!

He didn't get much in the way of satisfaction from the Butlers, either, when he went around there after Mass the following Sunday. He might as well have been scratching his arse, for all the good it did him. What did the mother do but start crying straight away when she answered the door and he mentioned Kieran's name to her. And instead of her filling Niall in on what'd happened to make Kieran leave town so quickly, he'd ended up having to listen to her wailing and caterwauling – as much as to say that Niall was the one responsible for her son going to England!

What sort of curse has befallen poor little Kieran, she asked Niall tearfully, or what for the love of the dutiful Lord had come over him that he'd upped and left home so suddenly? Didn't he have a nice handy little number working down at the graveyard, never mind going off and buying a horse-and-cart? I mean: who'd put that ridiculous idea into his head anyway, the fool? Sure, what did he know about horses, a fellow who'd never had any involvement with them! He was always such a nice gentle son – the nicest that any mother could ever wish for – and didn't he have a nice handy life for himself here at home with her waiting on him, hand and foot. Always cooking his favourite food for him, the bit of lamb's liver for his dinner and the white pudding for breakfast; and his shirts always washed, and shoes cleaned – everything that anyone could wish for! She'd never have thought for a minute that he'd just up and leave like that, the creature. And, as if to rub salt into his wound, Kieran's dad, Sikey Butler, arrived then and brusquely asked Niall what he wanted. When Niall tried to explain the story, he'd just grunted ignorantly 'Takes one gobshite to know one'. If Niall had been stupid enough to give his money away so easily to that other gom – then, who cares? Neither would he countenance any mention of compensation. It was up to Kieran to follow that up, because hadn't Kieran sold his horse-and-cart for half-nothing to that idiot, 'Punch' Nugent, the feathers' dealer, who lived over on the Sion Road? The long and short of it was that Niall had nothing to show for his visit, except that – as Sikey'd said to him, turning inside from the door again, ignoring his wife who was snivelling miserably in the corner – if Niall found out the address of Kieran and if he happened to be writing to him, it might do no harm for him to mention to the idiot that Tommy Fitz was going to break every bone in his body once he got his hands on him for taking his daughter with him out of the country like that. Mary Fitz, Sikey spat derisively, a girl who looked like the back of a bus and who no other man in the county would've looked at twice, never mind spiriting her off to England like that!

Standing on the middle of the bridge, the three men stood together as one. First, they'd looked down at the water and over at the magnificent Norman keep that overlooked the river. The dark auburn and russet colours of the trees gave the scene a particular quality, even though some of the leaves were already falling from the tall trees at the edge of the river. It was the peculiar beauty of decay, the final rosy flourish one saw in the face of a young woman that tuberculosis had stolen away. Before long, those trees, that now had cascades of leaves falling red-yellow in the breeze, would be stripped bare. The river Nore was already darkening as winter drew in and because of all the rain, large bubbles of foam spun endlessly across its surface, binding and coming lose again in a kaleidoscope of shapes and patterns. For as long as Niall could remember, the smooth-flowing water of the Nore had always had a magic of its own. It had a mesmerising power over him: he loved to stare down at the rushing water. Sometimes, it seemed to him that if he allowed its special energy to wash over his mind, he might enter another realm and stumble into a new form of knowledge or insight. Even now, and despite how upset he was about everything that had happened recently, Niall took a great comfort in the eddying flow of the great river.

Mooney was keen to get moving, however. 'Let's get out of here, come on, we'll head up to the corner and see who's around,' he said, and Niall hated his friend in that moment for his total lack of motivation. Wasn't it a sad way to live out your days like this – just mooching around town every day hoping to meet someone – anyone – who'd throw the price of a pint in his direction! They crossed the bridge and passed up Rose Inn Street until they came to the corner of the Parade where the other unemployed lads hung around. They were already at their station, leaning against the wall, as usual. Khyber Brennan, Mikeo Linnane, the Sniveller Deniffe, Moscow Barry and a gangly fellow by the name of Packie Pugh.

Both Khyber Brennan and Mikeo Linnane had been in the British Army at one point, albeit at different times from one another. Brennan was getting older now but Mikeo was barely thirty years old, and the pair of them had a military bearing right down to the leather-shank trousers and the hard starched dicky that Khyber sported instead of a shirt. All the old gentry of the county – former British Army officers and the like – knew Khyber, and they never passed him on the street without giving him a military salute. If their memories did need jogging, Khyber wasn't beneath reminding them that he was always open to offers covering the price of a pint.

Khyber could reel off a list of Indian towns and regions: he was as familiar with those as he was with the names of his native county. He also spoke a patter of Hindustani – if it really was a form of Hindustani that he spouted and not some gibberish he'd made up! He regularly spouted this lingo, particularly when he'd a few drinks on him. The Sniveller was a small grubby-looking fellow, a half-boiled Communist whose nickname suited him perfectly. Packie Pugh, for his part, was an unashamed waster who'd praise to high heaven anyone who threw the slightest favour in his direction – the price of a glass of porter, a cigarette or even a red penny itself – and the corner crowd had little or no respect for him as a consequence, despite their own straitened and humble circumstances.

Niall and his two companions came to a stop opposite Brennan and the latter emitted a stream of Hindustani as if to officially welcome Niall to the miserable brotherhood of the unemployed.

Nicholas Mooney jammed his thumbs into the pockets of his trousers and spat drily out onto the road. 'Ah, Christ,' he said, 'but I'd kill for a pint, now, so I would!'

As for Bosco Sullivan: Niall could tell that he was on for a bit of messing; he was hyper, like someone who'd a bee in his bonnet, hopping from one foot to the other, furiously rubbing the palms of his hands together and calling out 'hello' to everyone who passed. He didn't let the chance go either when a very pretty, well-dressed young woman went by just then, her nose in the air, proud as a princess. Bosco put his fingers to his forehead and saluted her in mock-humble fashion. 'Miss Brophy!' he called out in a voice that was a peculiar mixture of pride and subservience. Miss Brophy didn't let on to have heard him. She ignored the lads completely. 'I wouldn't charge her for it, either,' Bosco flung a vulgar dart in her direction despite her being barely out of earshot, and a couple of the lads laughed.

Mooney wasn't one of them, however; he shifted his feet uncomfortably; he didn't like that craic at all. 'I don't know why you even bother talking to little bitches like her,' he said angrily, giving the leather belt around his waist a quick tug.

'As if you wouldn't knock a piece out of her yourself as well, if you got half a chance! By janey, I wouldn't like to leave her too long out in the middle of the woods with you, Mooney; you wouldn't be long sniffing around her, I'd say, son!' he said, rubbing his hands together with delight.

'I wouldn't let her ignore me out on the street like that, anyway: I wouldn't give her the satisfaction,' responded Mooney.

'Oh, she's more than welcome to it, it makes no odds to me,' said Bosco in an easy voice.

As frequently happened, it was a random statement such as Sullivan's now, that ignited a sudden feeling of lust in Niall. An image came to him of Anne Brophy all alone like that in the woods – her snootiness some sort of turn-on. The image was clear before his mind now and so was she… right there in front of him… momentarily transformed; in the dark woods she became a different woman altogether. The pair of them were out there all alone in his imagination and she abandoned all reserve and turned into a right slapper.

Niall dismissed this image from his mind and cursed whatever part of him incited such sexual thoughts – especially when surely the same thoughts wouldn't do anything for another man. Hadn't he more important things to worry about, anyway, between trying to find work, getting any news about Butler, and – more importantly still – making sure that he got some of his money back off him, if he could. Niall felt a great weight pressing down on him; it was as if a series of chains had wrapped themselves around him: psychological chains that were stronger than physical ones could ever be. Here he was, stuck in the exact same spot where the other men passed all their days. He was trapped, just like the other lads; if was as though it had beome perfectly normal that he too should spend all his waking hours with them, as idle and useless as they were.

Niall had to do something, and quickly. He turned to Mooney and made as if to go. 'I'm off to look for work, Nick. There must be something to be got somewhere – if you look hard enough.'

Mooney stared at him for a minute as if to say that he must be a bit of a simpleton, and spat on the ground again in disgust. 'There isn't a tap out there – not even if you stuck your arse out looking for it!'

'Do you see that bollix over there looking over at us,' said Bosco Sullivan, and Niall looked up at him in surprise.

'What are you on about, you fecker?' Niall asked.

'That c**t of a garda, Moriarty – who else?' said Bosco. 'He's a right bad egg, I'm telling you. He's the boyo who wouldn't think twice about giving you a proper hiding if he got half the chance.'

Niall looked across to where the officer was on traffic duty at the crossroads. A big block of a countryman, from Kerry, if he wasn't mistaken, Garda Moriarty didn't look as though he had the slightest interest in what they were doing. Sure, wasn't it inevitable that he'd glance in their direction now and then! He'd only be wasting his time trying to explain this to Sullivan or any of these other losers, however – even to somone like Moscow Barry who was bright and well-read. The way they went on, sometimes, you'd swear the guards had been founded with the express purpose of harassing men just like these lads on the corner.

A tractor and trailer loaded with beet passed Niall as he made his way through the streets. The city clock on High Street was striking, and it seemed to Niall that each chime sounded all the loneliness in the world. Over beneath the walls of the Castle, a scatter of leaves stirred in the breeze; they rose from the ground and fell again, like a flock of starlings swooping across the sky. The sky was was a dull grey colour now, so dead that you'd have thought it would never again see bright-blue. The steady, permanent nature of things which Niall had lauded earlier to himself now appeared hostile. He felt it engulf him, so that he was almost suffocated by the confines of that street corner.

'Oh, Christ,' he muttered to himself. 'Haven't I just made a total cockup!'

Chapter 5

Nano Mháire Coilm was very neat and particular about her work in the hospital. She didn't need anything explained to her more than once, and was always eager, an enthusiasm that was lacking among some of the younger local nurses. Some of them were so lazy and uninterested that Norwold Hospital was very lucky, Nano thought, that it wasn't entirely reliant on the English girls, but that plenty of immigrants worked there too. Some of these young local girls had the air of people who tried to get away without doing a stroke of work. Their attitude seemed to be that they were just in it for the money rather than for the job itself. There was so much work available – this might explain their indifferent attitude and a tendency to avoid paying heed to their supervisors. Unlike the *Connacht Tribune*, the local Norwold newspaper was chock-full of job advertisements every day. There were so many available that it seemed as though, before too long, local employers might have to go out into the streets offering work to people. Every business that you passed in Norwold – a town which was full of small shoemaking factories – had a sign up outside the gate listing vacancies, and it was the same in the large shops. All you had to do was call by and you could get a job behind the counter straight away. There was so much work around that it nearly made Nano greedy for more, and she was actually sorry that she couldn't take on a second post. If only her hours of duty in the hospital hadn't been so staggered, she'd definitely have looked for an additional job. This was so different from in Ireland where a shop assistant would have to have her feet well under the table before she'd be allowed even to serve behind the counter. And even then, the pay would be unbelievably low.

Whereas here in England, there were all sorts of jobs, including working on the buses, provided you put in the hours. God almighty, Irish people were earning up to ten pounds a week working as clippies, Nano'd heard. She'd seen many Irish clippies around the city centre, looking proud as punch of their jobs and spotless blue uniforms with the shiny silver buttons. Most of them were country girls, a class of people who'd been given the opportunity of having a proper job for the first time in their lives, and who, consequently, were naturally very pleased with themselves. Some of them were so officious in their duties that you'd have sworn they actually owned the buses, while others were always on the alert in case they overheard anyone saying something bad about them or their native country.

Sheila O'Dwyer, the Cork girl who was Nano's roommate, often slagged off these women. They were all big lumps from the country, she claimed, and half of them had never set foot in a city before they'd landed here. Their huge wages had gone to their heads, and they so enjoyed swanking about in their uniforms that they'd actually leave them on after work! Really, you could see them wearing them at the weekend, at the dances in Saint Bridget's Hall, the Catholic Club. From what she'd seen of it so far, Nano thought that England was a great country, no doubt about it! And if some of the fillies working with her here had ever done the brutal slave-work that Connemara women did on the bog or on the shore, back home, they certainly wouldn't have been moaning on about who'd filled the water jugs as they were right now; neither would they argue about who had to clean the toilet. Who had time to argue when nursing assistants had so much to do? Making up beds, sweeping, polishing, washing dishes and cutlery, never mind all that tending to patients, some of whom were very old and feeble. Still, it was fairly easy work, especially compared to what they'd have been doing back home. Also, you'd have to be really difficult or careless for there to be any suspicion of firing you. This was very different from Galway Hospital, where, according to what Nano heard the Connemara girls saying, you'd be out on your ear straight away just for looking sideways at the boss.

Nano could see the road from the section of Norwold Hospital that was the nurses' quarters. There were ten of these residential units, including the stores, the kitchen and the laundry, each one separated by a neat square of grass and a series of narrow tarmacadam paths. All told, it was a pleasant place to work, Nano thought; the countryside was right beside you and the city was just down the road as well. The Irish were the largest group in Norwold Hospital – even more numerous than the English – but many other immigrants were there too, including Italians, Poles and Germans, in addition to people from Eastern Europe countries that Nano had never heard of. Sheila O'Dwyer had her own take on the latter. She made out that you'd never understand their mentality: they were hardnosed, canny and careful with their money.

The English hadn't the slightest respect either for these displaced persons or DPs as they were called, Sheila claimed. Neither had the Irish, she said, even though they'd no reason to feel superior to any other immigrant, seeing as they'd no more claim on England than the others. Funnily enough, given the way that she distanced herself from some of the other Irish working in the hospital , you had to remind yourself that Sheila wasn't English! And she was wrong about the Eastern European girls, anyway, apart from anything else, Nano thought. Even a blind man could tell, from their polite and well-spoken behaviour, that they hadn't been brought up in old shacks. These weren't people who'd ever spent the day out on a rough red-clay ridge digging potatoes or up to their oxters out in the bay gathering seaweed. They had the look of people who'd been fairly well-off once but who'd come down in the world – and this wasn't even taking into account whatever had happened to them during the war. Indeed, Nano felt that these women were far more easy-going than were many of the Irish women working in the hospital, some of whom carried their Irishness about with them as though it were a challenge.

It was the English women whom Nano found strangest of all, however. She couldn't understand their childish ways and how they blathered on about ridiculous or insignificant matters. Every last one seemed to be cracked about some man or other. But whereas Irish girls would pretend to be uninterested in the men they had their eye on, these wore their hearts on their sleeves and told the whole world about their relationships and problems. All they had on their mind was their latest love interest and yet despite this (this is what floored Nano) it was very easy to turn their heads. Nano was shocked how some married women would arrive into work and openly describe affairs that they were having. Nano had thought she'd some notion of how different England was from back home, but she'd still been surprised at the level of personal independence here, and how that led to attitudes that were much more free and-easy. She couldn't get her head around it. Not that Nano sat in judgment on anyone else; she just found these differences strange. Most of the English people Nano had met so far were very relaxed – the nicest people you could meet – even if she knew that her compatriots at the hospital might be slow to admit it. It was the way that they'd ask you a question straight out that Nano found the oddest thing about her new English colleagues and it took her a while to get used to it.

On her first day in Norwold, Nano had found herself working in the elderly people's ward alongside an English girl who always went by her surname, Jackson. They were washing dishes after dinner when Jackson turned to her and asked whether she'd a man back home in Ireland.

'Oh, I do,' Nano said, and Jackson's eyes had lit up with interest.

'What's his name?' she had asked with such eagerness that one would have thought the Irish girl was about to reveal something of profound importance. Hilda Jackson was a big, ungainly looking girl who looked as if she'd been thrown together. Her hairstyle was a bit primitive; all in all, she was a bit of a state in Nano's eyes. Her overdone make-up and cheap Woolworths jewellery made her look a bit ridiculous; her fingers and arms were weighed down with tacky rings and bracelets, and on her neck she wore a silver chain with a cross.

'Máirtín's his name,' Nano had said, and Jackson repeated the name as if trying to form a picture of him in her mind.

'And his surname?'

'Spillane,' Nano had replied, giving the name a more English twang, and taking a handful of knives from Jackson to dry them. This girl was more of a hindrance than a help; all she'd done since lunchtime was gab.

'Martin Spillane,' repeated Jackson, slowly enunciating the words. 'The Irish have really nice names, don't they?'

'Oh, well, I don't know whether they do or not, really, love. Come on, get your act together or we'll have nothing to show for it!'

'Is he good-looking, Nano, your man?'

Work was the last thing on Jackson's mind, it seemed. Good-looking? Nano had thought this a somewhat strange question because she'd never considered that in relation to Máirtín. It was a person's nature and their personality that was the most important thing to her, and even had Máirtín been the best-looking man in the world, this wouldn't have been enough. 'Oh, I don't know, girl. Manners maketh the man. Isn't that what they say? He's a good man, I'll give him that.'

'What is he? Fair-haired or dark, Nano?'

'Oh, listen now, dear,' Nano laughed. 'He's somewhere in between. Here, do you want to do any work? Her upstairs will be down on us like a ton of bricks if we don't get this done soon.'

But Jackson was more interested in what this man – whom she'd never met – looked like, rather than in work.

'I like handsome-looking men, do you? I like men with black hair: my Ron is very handsome, he's like Rock Hudson.'

'Who's Rock Hudson?'

If Nano had asked her who Winston Churchill was, Hilda Jackson couldn't have been more surprised: she stared at Nano open-mouthed as if seeing her properly for the first time.

'You don't know who Rock Hudson is?'

'I don't know love, I swear!'

'He's the actor! Do you not go to the pictures?'

'Only now and then,' Nano had said, but in fact she'd only been to the pictures a couple of times in her life. Once had been in Galway town, and a couple of times at Spiddal College when the McFaddens had been showing their films. On their second visit, the projector had broken down and they hadn't been able to get it going again. To be honest, Nano wasn't particularly gone on films anyway; as far as she could see, they tended to involve people doing things that were fairly meaningless. She couldn't really understand why people were so keen.

'And are you in love with him?' Jackson asked her, putting down a plate that was only half-washed.

'That plate isn't washed, Hilda.'

'But are you really?'

'Oh, stop, you daft beggar; we just haven't got to that stage!'

'You're engaged to him, are you?'

'We're going out with one another.'

'You're in love him, then, of course you are!' Jackson had thought for a second then asked, 'But if you're in love, why did you leave him?'

'I didn't leave him, exactly.'

'But you left him back in Ireland.'

'It's not like that, girl. I can go home any time I want.'

But in her heart, Nano wasn't sure whether this was the true story. What business did she have with home, really, now that she was gone?

At home, things would be the same as before; in fact, it'd be more difficult to return there now, she thought.

'I wouldn't leave Ron for all the money in the world,' Jackson said, as if she didn't really get what Nano was saying. 'Beggars can't be choosers,' Nano had said, a slight strain coming into her voice now that she was thinking about home again.

It wasn't that Máirtín had let her down, exactly. But the upshot for her was the same no no matter how you looked at it – she'd been left in the lurch. Just as he'd promised her that night after the ceilidh in Spiddal, Máirtín had brought up the issue with his mother first thing the following morning. But rather than sorting out the situation finally, he'd ended up with hands more tightly tied than ever. Nano had been taking the cover off the baking tin, tongs in hand to check on the cake, when her father had arrived. There was some sort of a commotion going on in the house opposite, he'd said. He'd been down near the Drowned Field when Máirtín sped past him on his bicycle at such a rate that he'd barely even said 'hello'. There was something going on across the road where Máirtín lived, apparently: maybe his old lady wasn't well. She should go over there quick, he had said, as any good neighbour would have, and see what was up. Nano hadn't been too keen on calling in, however especially as she was afraid that something Máirtín'd said might have made his mother sick, if that's what'd happened. And it looked like that was probably it, because the next moment she spotted the doctor's car making its way down the boreen and going in the gate of Bid Antaine's house.

The doctor was inside for a half-an-hour exactly and Nano had been on edge until he'd left. She stared out of the window at Máirtín's house. She'd even burned the cake, she'd been that stressed about whatever had happened. The minute she saw the doctor leaving, she untied her apron, settled her hair in place and headed over there. It was Máirtín who'd opened the door, and she could see immediately what was up. His mother had taken a turn, he'd whispered to her. She was back in her room now, having a lie-down. She was still fairly weak, and Máire was keeping an eye on her even though Doctor Cooney had said that she'd recover this time if she made sure to take it easy, and provided no-one caused her any further upset. He had been responsible for that, probably, Máirtín had said, seeing as he'd raised the marriage issue with her that morning. He'd told his mother that he wanted to get married and didn't want to put it off any longer. She'd had her funny turn then. God, Nano, he'd said, a tear in his eye, but I thought that we'd lost her. It was at that moment that Nano Keane decided she was definitely leaving Ireland, whether she got a reply from Norwold Hospital or not. And the following day she'd received the reply in the post from England.

'But why did you have to leave?' Jackson had asked.

But Nano had had enough of this conversation.

'Oh, well, listen here now, dear,: it's a long story.'

She saw the disappointment in the other woman's eyes and so she gave Jackson a quick summary of the situation. That house wasn't big enough for two women: simple as that.

'Blimey, Nano, I do know what you mean! Our Diane, my eldest sister she moved into her mother-in-law's place after she got married to Bert and she had a dog's life there. The mother-in-law turned out to be a right bitch. She didn't stop nagging until the pair of them were at each other's throats!'

'That's an awful pity,' Nano had said, unplugging the sink, letting the water out then wiping it with a cloth.

But Jackson had shaken her head in disagreement. 'Uh-uh! It was the best thing that ever happened to her, Nano, to be honest. She started going out with an American soldier then – a white man – and they're married out in Michigan now. They've everything you can think of out there, a fine big house, a big car, a freezer and a pool in the back garden. Those Americans have plenty of money, and that's why all the girls are always after them.' Jackson had paused and then added, 'But I wouldn't give up my Ron, not for the richest American in the world.'

'What do you think? Will we do the toilets now?' Nano had asked Jackson. They'd been given a list of jobs to do earlier by the Ward Sister.

'Sure,' Jackson had answered in a bored tone. 'But Nano, couldn't you have stayed a little closer to him? Couldn't you get a job somewhere back in Ireland?'

'Oh, it's not at all easy to find work in Ireland' Nano had replied, 'not like in this country.'

It never occurred to Nano that she'd said something out-of-turn or that anyone could have read anything untoward into her innocent statement but, as she soon found out, she was wrong. Mary McDermott, one of the ward team, had come into the kitchen just then with a tray of water jugs ready for washing. She had been smiling as she came through the door – as though she'd something funny to tell them – but on hearing Nano's comment about unemployment in Ireland, she pursed her lips angrily and slammed the jugs down onto the table. She'd swept out the door again without a word to either girl, even though Jackson had invited her to join them for a quick coffee-break. Jackson didn't understand what had annoyed McDermott; nor did Nano – until she'd met McDermott near the linen store later that afternoon as they folded and stacked the sheets. There hadn't been a peep out of McDermott at first but suddenly she'd ruptured the silence as though she couldn't keep whatever it was to herself any longer.

'I've a question for you,' she'd said gruffly.

'A question?' Nano had said, confused.

'Were you saying to that divvy down the hall there a while ago that there was no work in Ireland?'

'What divvy? What are you on about?' Nano replied. She had absolutely no idea what McDermott was implying.

'You know full well what I mean! Jackson – that big looder of a woman. Didn't you tell her there wasn't any work in Ireland?' McDermott was really wound-up, so angry Nano thought there must be more to this than met the eye.

'I don't think so? Why?'

'Why? "Why", is it? Bloody *because*… that's why!'

If had Nano thought that this was a wind-up, then she was way off the mark. McDermott was furious.

'Because, you shouldn't say that to the likes of them!'

'To who? What are you talking about, anyway?' Nano still wasn't sure whether the other girl was playing some sort of a trick on her. Everyone had their own sense of humour: you couldn't always be sure what they were playing at.

But McDermott had not been joking.

'The English, I mean. You're not bloody thick, are you?'

Nano was stunned. 'Who are you talking to, girl? How dare you talk to me like that?'

'I've a perfect right, and what I want to know is this – why did you give that one the satisfaction of telling her there's no work back home?'

'Satisfaction? What are you on about?'

'Telling them there's no work in Ireland – that's the satisfaction! Have you any respect whatsoever for your own country?'

'Oh, for God's sake, don't you know as well as I do that there's no work at home, you fool? Isn't that the reason we're all working over here?' Nano had had enough of McDermott but the latter hadn't finished.

'Yeah, but why would you tell them that? Why would you give that shower the satisfaction? Even if there were twice as many of us working over here, you should still tell them there's plenty of work back home. Or maybe you're not Irish, after all?'

'By God, of course I am! I'm as Irish as *you*, at any rate. My Irish is better than my English; which is more than you can say!'

At least this riposte dumbfounded McDermott – temporarily. She recovered herself quickly enough.

'Well, if that's the case, then you really *should* be ashamed; you of all people should be looking out for your country's reputation.'

'Rubbish,' Nano had said brusquely. She had decided that McDermott didn't know what she was on about and that it was pointless arguing with her any more.

'You've a lot to learn, girl,' McDermott had said, as if she felt sorry for Nano. 'Wait till you've been here a bit longer, then you'll know what's rubbish. You're very innocent, my girl, I'm afraid!'

'If I'm innocent, then you're crazy! Mother Mary! Poor Jackson isn't the slightest bit interested in "Ireland's unemployment" or whatever; she was on a totally different track! And I'm warning you now; you listen to me or you'd better look out. I'm not some kind of idiot you can just push around like that!'

McDermott started to reply but then stopped, and they finished their work in silence. There was tension between them for the rest of the afternoon.

And that wasn't the end of it, either! Because when Nano went down for supper in the canteen later on, there was a group of Irish girls waiting to attack. A hint of what was ahead had come when the conversation ceased abruptly when she sat down at the table where the Irish always sat. Nano was soon at the receiving end of a string of filthy looks, silent as poison. Their supper that evening had been a strange mish-mash of cheese and onion; it was awful-looking stuff, a real dog's dinner, Nano thought, tasting it nervously. Nano wasn't a bit fussy when it came to food, and she'd been hungry since dinner-time when all they'd got was a tiny sliver of meat and a small bowl of watery soup, but her appetite had suddenly deserted her as she felt the hostility in the room. Everyone worked in teams when they were on-duty. Consequently, there were nearly ten women sitting at the this table, all of whom were Irish apart from one girl from

Eastern Europe, and this girl slipped away, sensing a row brewing. The noise the door had made as it closed behind her was ominous, Nano thought.

They were ready to go for her now, and McDermott was leader of the pack. 'We can tear strips off our own country now, girls; it's all the rage these days, apparently,' she had said.

'Is that so?,' said some small curly-haired dolly-bird, eyes wide in apparent shock.

'And who started this craic, anyways, Mary?' the dolly-bird asked, her gentle voice and lovely clear complexion belying the sarcasm of her tone. Sheila had already warned Nano that, despite appearances, this one was a right bitch.

'What do you think, girls? It definitely wasn't one of us, anyway. None of us have ever shown a trace of cowardice, that's for sure,' Mary McDermott had said, looking daggers at Nano.

'That's classy, isn't it? To do down your own country in front of the English!' said the dolly-bird, averting her eyes from Nano. She looked over at McDermott as though seeking her approval.

'You'd think we'd had enough scorn heaped on us already,' McDermott had added, 'without giving them a stick to beat us with as well! Or have some of us lost every ounce of pride that they ever had, I wonder?'

'Not an ounce left, it looks like! I wouldn't badmouth my country like that, even if someone threatened me with a shotgun! I wouldn't let anyone laugh at me, especially some big streel of an idiot like Jackson, with her big cheap earrings and war-paint!'

Struck by these comments, Nano had briefly been at a loss for words. But as she was about to respond, a girl from Mayo jumped up from her seat and let rip, 'For God's sake, will you grow up, the lot of you! You're worse than a bunch of kids, the way you're always bitching on at one another all the time! Listen to her, for God's sake, this girl isn't bothering you lot at all!' She had stormed out of the room.

Whether because of the way this woman had jumped to her defence or not, Nano had become convinced that she could stand up for herself and face down this crowd. She got to her feet and looked around at all the other girls, speaking in a careful and measured tone. 'That there is probably good advice for you lot,' she said, 'but in case it doesn't do the job, I'm telling you all now that if any one of you ever mocks me again, you'll be sorry! I didn't come all the way over here to starting asking permission from anybody to speak my own mind. And you'd better know right now that I will say whatever I want to whoever I want! You'd better remember that and don't cross me again!' Nano had left them, head held high as she strode out of the door. But as soon as she was she back in her room and perched on her narrow iron bed then she burst out crying. Sheila O'Dwyer had been sitting cross-legged on her own bed, painting her toenails. Happy-go-lucky Sheila with her black curly hair and bright dancing eyes. She was a bit younger than Nano but she'd already spent two years in England, which gave her a worldly-wise air. She set down the small bottle of nail polish and slipped her feet into a pair of bedroom slippers.

'What's wrong with you, in God's name?' she had asked Nano kindly.

'Nothing, Sheila, I'm okay.'

'If this is what "okay" looks like, I wouldn't like to see you when you're upset. Come on, now, tell your old aunty here what's wrong: you're homesick, are you?'

'Arah, it's nothing, Sheila. A bit of cop-on is what I need.' Nano had felt better straight away. Hadn't she been lucky not to be lumped in with one of that other crowd on her first day? Even if Sheila was a bit too talkative at times, she was kind and friendly, and that counted for something in a place like this where she felt like an outsider.

'What is it? Can't you see that curiosity's killing me? I won't be able to sleep tonight if you don't tell me!'

Nano had given in to Sheila's promptings and told her the story, even as she realised that the whole thing had been a storm in a teacup.

Sheila had nodded. 'Those bitches are cracked; a kick in the arse is what they need, McDermott especially. You're afraid to open your mouth when she's around. And as for that little hussy, Fidelma Byrne, from Carlow. She's like McDermott's bloody shadow, going around agreeing with every word she says – because she's afraid of her, I bet. As for the other one, that ditzy dolly-bird, she's a right dangerous piece of work, girl, a proper little madam! Don't you worry about them, Nano, because they're not worth it; they've chips on their shoulders as big as Nelson's pillar!'

Sheila had gone over to the mirror that had been placed on the wall between the end of the bed and the narrow metal locker where the pair kept their clothes. She removed the pin from her hair, let it hang loose then gave it a vigorous brushing. 'Poor Jackson!' she had said after a moment, referring to the English nurse. 'She wouldn't know the difference between Ireland and Timbuktu! She wouldn't say boo to a goose, whatever you said to her.'

'What the hell's wrong with talking about there being no work in Ireland, anyway?' Nano had asked, loosening the belt on her uniform and removing her small starched cap.

'Oh,' Sheila had countered, 'believe me, it's a major crime here to say anything that's not one hundred per cent good about Ireland: you have to praise the place constantly! It's like a madness that hits some people as soon as they get over here. If we didn't know better, you'd swear that they'd been living in the land of plenty all their lives and that it was the best country in the world. But you know, as I've often said – and some of the English would say the same to you too when you're talking to them in private – if things were so great back in Ireland, then why didn't they stay there? You'd swear every Irishman was God's gift, listening to those morons!' Sheila cocked her head and raised one finger in the air. 'Listen to this.' She opened

73

the door. The sound of music came to them from the nurses' recreation room at the end of the hallway. They were playing the same record over again, the one they'd been playing constantly since Nano had started work there. 'The Boys of Wexford': a tune that Nano had rarely heard before she'd got to Norwold. 'Listen to that now, girl,' Sheila'd said. 'That hoor of a tune is going, morning, noon and night. If it isn't that, it's *Kevin Barry* or *The Valley of Knockanure.*' She'd closed the door again and applied some lipstick, pursing her lips together and wiping around them with the tip of her handkerchief. 'I bet they do it mainly to annoy the English. It's like a mad-house around here sometimes.' Sheila looked at Nano in the mirror and said, 'You'd be better off coming out with me for a bit of craic this evening. You'll end up going grey if you stay in this room, and we can't go down to the parlour or you'll be listening to *Boolavogue* until bedtime! I'll show you around Norwold town tonight, and you can tell McDermott tomorrow that it's as fine a place as Galway any day of the week.'

'She'd have a face like a slapped arse!'

On her very first night in England, Sheila'd asked Nano out to a dance in the Catholic Club, but Nano'd excused herself. She'd been too tired and she'd be best staying in and writing a few letters home.

'What do you say, then, are you coming out with me? It's better than staying in here by yourself in this ghost town anyway.'

'Not tonight, anyway, Sheila, thanks all the same.'

Sheila was ready now. She'd a lovely silk-type dress on that reached down to her ankles; this was the New Look as it was known, even if it'd already been the in-look for a few years. Two plastic pearl bands encircled her neck and she'd a pair of high-heeled shoes on to compensate for her lack of height. She took a similar-length coat from her locker and tried it on.

'Well? Will I do, do you think?'

'You look beautiful,' Nano had said. 'Have you got a date?'

'I'm not that lucky! But you never know what kind of a smasher you might run into. You sure that you won't come?'

'Certain – thanks very much all the same. Some other night, maybe.' Sheila stood at the door, head to one side and gave Nano a peculiar beseeching look. 'Sure-sure?'

'Clear off, now will you, idiot! I've got things to do here.'

'Okay… then,' Sheila had said. 'Tooraloo!'

'Oh, Tooraloo yourself,' Nano had replied, laughing despite herself. As soon as Sheila had gone however, Nano gave a sigh of resignation. Their room was small and bare. There wasn't one picture decorating the walls, something that would've given the place a sense of being lived in. Sheila hated it and spent as little time there as possible. You couldn't blame her much on that score. Nano thought of how different her own home was. Back there, her father and brother would've had a big turf fire and there'd be food on the table, wholesome food like home-made bread and a drink of milk if you wanted it. And a big tasty dinner instead of the strange hotchpotch of stuff they got here. She thought of Máirtín; chances were that he was probably over visiting their house right now, discussing the ways of the world with her father and with Beartla. The truth was that she'd emigrated out of pride more than anything else, but on the other hand, there'd been no point in her staying on there either. She didn't know how long it'd be before she and Máirtín would be together again but something told her that his mother, Bid Antaine, would live on for a long time yet! Not that she was wishing anything else, God help us! She'd give it a year or the best part of a year here now before she'd even think of going back on a visit. People made fun of anyone who came running home almost straight after leaving. It was even more unlikely that Máirtín would be able to visit to her. Nano felt really alone: it was like she'd played the game and lost. The silence around her magnified until all she heard was the faint gurgle of the water in the heating pipes in the skirtings, and the occasional voice calling somewhere inside the building. It wasn't even nine o'clock yet but the rest of the night stretched out in front of her like an endless road. Nano gave a deep sigh and began to undress. She had nothing else to do. She might as well go to bed.

Chapter 6

It may well prove to be true, Niall thought: what Nicholas Mooney had said about there being no work available anywhere, no matter how hard you looked. Niall took a quick walk up to Grassmount where they were building the new council houses. He was hopeful that he might get some work there, unlikely as it was. Strangely, Niall had been in great form as he left the house that morning, whistling away happily to himself as was his habit – all those small nonsense ditties in his head; the ones he'd change the words of and make different, just for the craic....

Gamsa na ndoinín in arraí na geornan
An doinín gabóige chris sé a bhois....

The gabbit rance in the farley-bield
the grad daybourer grashed its boot....

Niall could never tell why these bouts of giddiness came over him; they just did; this was just the way he was. Often, back in the army barracks, even when he hadn't had the price of a cup of tea on him, never mind that of a cigarette, the same crazy mood would come over him and he'd feel the urge to let out a great exuberant roar. Maybe there was something wrong with the connections in his brain, as Captain Delaney had claimed. Delaney maintained that these moods were the first strains of madness – however long it took to kick in properly. In the end, Paddy Delaney said, Niall would most likely end up blathering away to himself – a nut job locked away in a padded cell somewhere. The barmy idiocy of the beggar, Delaney used to call these high jinks; it had come to his attention that for some reason, this strange condition seemed to affect people who hadn't a bean to their name. It must've had something to do with the crazy freedom of being dirt-poor or one of those innocent fools or tramps. This was the law of life, as far as Captain Delaney could make out; the rich always wanted to be richer so that it was easier to throw a few scraps to the poor. And, the way he saw it, every son-of-a-gun who was in his army unit was a tramp, a beggar or good-for-nothing shovel-man. It was just his bad luck to find himself in charge of the most pathetic and miserable bunch of losers he'd ever met in his life. Not that Niall or anyone else in the unit took much notice of Delaney's philosophy. To tell the truth, the man was always whining because he was stuck where he was and didn't have the drive to get ahead. It was a bit rich for poor Paddy Delaney to refer to other people as beggars when, half the time, he himself didn't have two pence to rub together himself. The poor Captain couldn't help himself however, no more than Niall could with this antsy mood of his right now. Even though he had lost that thirty pounds – and it was a massive amount of money to lose – it still wasn't worth getting down about. And, anyway, hopefully Butler wouldn't abandon him altogether; he'd surely send him on some money as soon as he got himself sorted, across the water. If England was as good as they made out, it shouldn't be too hard for Butler to do this. No sooner had Niall reached the building site than his good form deserted him, however. The first two workers he came across were powerful-looking fellows, shovelling stones and sand into the big, screeching cement mixer. These two fellows were bursting with muscle and the way they bent and lifted in such a relaxed fashion, you'd have sworn that labouring was a bit of a game to them. Two other men pushed wheelbarrows, overflowing with soft grey cement, up along a narrow platform that swayed beneath them, so rickety that it was a wonder they didn't go flying over it. There was a right racket with hammers and whining of machine saws everywhere. The labourers he passed were avoiding his eyes: they were so busy working that they were too afraid even to say 'hello' to you. He was probably wasting his time coming up here in the first place, Niall thought. The lads already working there probably didn't know from one day to the next when they'd be given the road themselves.

It was just eight o'clock now but Georgie Devlin, the builder, was already on-site, roaring instructions, the men scurrying here and there, busy to his command. Devlin was a big brute with a high colour and puffed-out cheeks; he reminded Niall of some cattle-dealer. He was known as a tough, merciless taskmaster, a man who'd fire a worker at a whim. And he was in a foul mood now, by the looks of it. Maybe it wasn't the best time to be asking him? Maybe he'd leave it for another day…. Suddenly Niall wanted to get the hell out of there.

Just at that moment, however, Devlin spotted him and gruffly asked him what he wanted.

'I was wondering whether you might have any work going, Mister Devlin?' Niall blurted nervously.

'Work, is it?'

The builder's intelligent little eyes narrowed, sizing him up. Was this fellow another one of those chancers, those clowns who came around just to waste people's time? Devlin grunted and gave a small laugh, laced with sarcasm. He had those dead-fish eyes that gave nothing away.

'The work here is as good as finished. Can't you see that for yourself? Where were you when there was plenty available, man?'

'I was in the army,' Niall replied but Georgie Devlin responded with a dismissive laugh. 'Doesn't seem to me as though you were doing much work in the army, anyway! Show me your hands, son.'

Niall didn't like this one bit but his own sharp retort surprised even himself: 'I'd sooner show you my arse, man. I came up here looking for work, not for a bloody medical exam: what are you driving at, in any case? Don't judge a book by its cover!' Unfortunately, this didn't even help Niall let off steam, as Devlin had turned his back on him and was roaring at a lorry driver who was backing in off the road and depositing a load of sand in the wrong place. Niall left the site again as quickly as he'd arrived. He was still hopeful that he'd get a job if he kept asking around and so he went straight down to Smithwicks Brewery down on the river. He got nowhere there either so he tried the new iron foundry over in the old fever hospital; from there, he went on to Ossory Mills in the shadow of the castle, on the southern side of the bridge. There was no point whatsoever in visiting the shoe factory. You needed to have your name down as soon as you left school before you had any chance of working there. Niall's brother, Maurice, had been there since he'd left school a couple of years previously. People were jealous of anyone who'd been lucky enough to get a job in the shoe factory; the pay was good there and it was a nice, clean and modern place to work. Even farmer's sons wouldn't have turned their noses up at a job in the Moccasin as it was known locally. The Ossory Mills looked like a prison; it was a tall grey stone building, tiny dark-rowed windows set high above ground. As it was surrounded by tall thick-leafed trees, it would be a wonder if any of the people inside had any daylight to work by. From previous experience he knew that, even on the brightest day, a series of lamps provided the only illumination inside those small narrow windows. A stranger could pass the Mills without even noticing, particularly in summer. The muffled drone of the machines, the wind in the trees and the movement of the river Nore all melded into one indistinct hum. The trees and the river conspired to hide that ugly view of the place from the world. When he got there, Niall crossed the small stone bridge, going down under the broken moss-covered arch and into a large round yard that was more like a farmer's haggard than it was a factory headquarters. The roar of the giant weaving machines deafened him. It was an unforgettable sound, unlike any other. Memories of the time he'd worked there flooded back to him and for the first time since his return home, the unpleasant realisation came to him that his world had been turned upside-down. The fact that he was back in this place again looking for a job was proof enough that all his plans had gone badly awry. This was his nightmare: to find himself back in the very woollen mills where he'd sweated his guts out before enlisting in the army. But then – to hell with it – which was worse? To have something or to have nothing at all? It was Hobson's Choice. He had no other, and so he walked nervously over to the office. But it didn't take him long to get his answer. There was no work available there, either.

***

Niall's family, the O'Connells, lived in Saint Canice's Row on the west side of the city. The houses here were small and old, and half of them didn't have any electricity. Damp and cramped, each house consisted of a tiny yard surrounded by a low stone-wall, an outside tap and privy. Some of the houses in the row were already abandoned, the residents moved up to the Grassy Knoll, an area that had far more space and was healthier. It was a place that the townies, particularly the older people, considered to be almost part of the countryside. The O'Connells had had their names down since the first sods on this new housing scheme had been turned, but all that time they'd been waiting to hear any word from the Corporation. Niall's mother was beside herself with worry by this stage, and was afraid that they might be left behind and have to live in that dump for many more years.

'We're like a group of hermits, now, abandoned here amongst the ruins and the pigeons,' Niall's mother would complain in her exaggerated fashion. She lived in fear of the possibility that tinkers might settle in one of the empty slums: having them as neighbours.

The 'new house' had been his mother's constant refrain since Niall's return home – as though they had already been allocated one. When would they hear about the new house; what was the delay? Could it be – God forbid – that their application had been forgotten about completely? Or, if they hadn't been chosen from amongst the long list of applicants, what a let-down that would be! It would be a disaster: a right kick in the teeth for their family. Mrs Kitty O'Connell was an anxious person, her outlook riddled with doubt and negativity. She often got the wrong end of the stick and sometimes took offence where none was intended. And the more that time passed and the construction work on the housing scheme drew to a close, the more worried she became. Wasn't it an awful state of affairs that there wasn't even one person on the council who'd speak up on their behalf? Not even McNeill – after all the money they'd spent at his shop down the years, even if it was mainly on the tab! (But then, realistically speaking: how could they pay the bills when they didn't have anything? They could never pay off McNeill, not without regular payments from Niall's father.) And what about the others who'd done nothing for them, a man like Paddy Lavelle who was always the model of decency, raising his hat to her whenever they passed in the street? Or Moss Hanberry who was from another county originally – the same as she was – and from whom you'd expect a bit of solidarity? How come none of them would put their case, even though some people were getting new ones when they didn't need a house half as badly as the O'Connells did? Of course, in the end, the Lord is just in all his ways, she knew that. And yet who knew what sort of behind-the-scenes deals, bribery and shenanigans were going on up there, behind officials' backs? You couldn't trust anyone, apparently – whatever had happened to basic courtesy and kindness? But while her disappointment in the Corporation went so far, what really riled her was her apparent abandonment by the highest powers of all: the saints – male and female – whom she'd besieged with prayer all her life! It was bad enough having no friends here on Earth, Niall's mother thought, but when there was none in the Heavens either, that might be explained by there being some hidden curse hanging over them. Had she herself done anything wrong? Could it be down to another family member's misdemeanor? She'd done the Novena of the nine Fridays three times in a row and she'd promised the world to Saint Anthony, Saint Philomena, Saint Anne – the mother of the Virgin Mary herself – and of course to the Sacred Heart – if they could only get their new house! Maybe they were testing her faith? Or were their motives more profound than this still? They could be letting her know, in their own subtle way, that the things of this world are not the most important, after all? But then she wasn't a big one for the things of this world in any case! I mean, she wasn't a materialistic person, was she? And how was it that this little hole of a house hadn't fallen in on top of them by now, anyway? Wasn't it well past time for them to get a proper place to live in? And what about Blessed Máirtín de Porres, just the man to ask things of, especially if you needed something badly (there was no end to the number of saints awaiting canonisation and the image of this black man was in every house in the city) – how come even he couldn't do something to help them out either?

Niall was sick to the teeth of this tune since his return. He wanted to tell his mother to put a lid on it. For God's sake, she was like a broken gramophone, the way she went on! And he'd have said it to her face, too, except that he was afraid she'd be even harder on him, and never shut up about his stupidity and the way he'd let such a large sum of money get away from him like that – 'without guarantee, without bond' – something that even a complete gobshite in from the mountains wouldn't have been stupid enough to do. Niall was annoyed with himself that he hadn't made up some story or other early enough to direct away from him her attention – and all the gripes she was surely storing up about him being such a big idiot. Needless to say, he'd been so flummoxed when he'd first heard what Butler had done that this had been the furthest thing from his mind, initially. And yet, despite the shock he'd got in Neary's pub the other evening, Niall had still slept as cosy as a hedgehog that night (there was nothing like a stomach-full of porter for an anaesthetic) and he was up again in the next morning before his two brothers.

Niall raised himself up gingerly in the bed and gave a reluctant glance around their narrow little bedroom, its plain wooden floorboards and tiny window that wouldn't open, the ancient faded wallpaper, like an elderly mottled face. The room was bare except for two beds, his own single and the old double that his two brothers were asleep in now. There was also a small rickety table in the corner, pockmarked with the melted remnants of so many candles that it resembled the exterior of a holy shrine or rustic blessed well. Two pictures hung from the wall. One was of Saint Anthony – another saint that never failed anyone, according to Niall's mother – and the other was Saint Patrick, Ireland's patron saint, standing ankle-deep amongst a horde of horrible-looking snakes that he was driving out of Ireland. Often, as a child, Niall had recoiled from this image of Patrick and the snakes, the hundreds and thousands of them spiralling around one another out of some filthy, dark place underground. All those horrible snakes, repulsive and filthy, coiled around one another, and defiant to the end, even if Saint Patrick had managed to drive them all across the sea eventually. A tiny skylight in the centre of the ceiling – jammed open with an old brush – was the only other light in the room, and it was through this tiny window that Niall watched the stars at night and reflected on the mysteries of eternity: the meaning of life. Not that he'd been doing much meditation that Saturday night when he'd been out on the lash! On getting home, he'd barely managed to get his clothes off and fall into bed before he'd fallen asleep. He'd slept the sleep of the dead. Very gently, because his stomach was churning from his rough night, Niall climbed to his feet. He sat down as quickly again on the edge of the bed, however, because he felt awful.

He dressed himself slowly and, as he leaned down to get one of his socks from the floor, he felt nausea rise up in him and he had to shut his mouth tightly again and force it down. A cold sweat broke out on his forehead and he went still for a moment, afraid he'd throw up.

After a minute or two, he took his jacket from one of the bedposts and went out to the kitchen to face the telling-off his mother would likely give him. The kitchen was as cramped and bare as the bedroom, a small soot-coloured stove for cooking on one side, a damp stone floor, and old press and a table and chairs. He'd forgotten how small the house was. He'd forgotten it all so quickly. Because sometimes, when he was away from home, Niall had imagined the place differently and almost convinced himself that things were better – that this house of theirs was spacious and laid out with proper furniture. The reality always came as a shock. Maybe Captain Delaney was right, after all, and he did have a screw loose. He'd definitely inherited his father's dreamy ways and stupidity, if his mother was to be believed – the crazy O'Connell gene, same as his brothers. Not one of them had inherited the cop-on that came with her own side of the family – or, that's what she feared. What good was it, she'd ask loudly, if the ship's captain was good but the rest of the crew weren't worth a fart between them?! Sometimes, when pushed beyond the limits of her endurance – because Mrs O'Connell was generally very reserved – she'd lose it altogether and come out with all this stuff; and who could blame her, really? The rest of the time she kept her feelings to herself, to a greater extent than most of the other women living on the row. The house smelled of that unique combination of turf-smoke and paraffin oil, and Niall's mother was kneeling in front of the stove, trying to get a few pieces of turf to light when he came in. Wherever the hell they were getting it, the turf they bought these days was cheap stuff and no good to light.

His mother gave him a spiteful look. He couldn't for the life of him remember whether she'd been up last night when he'd got home blind-drunk and without a steer under him.

'You didn't expect me to stay in bed?' Niall said, a bit touchy: he had enough to do right now keeping his nausea under control, never mind listening to herself now.

'Well, I'm surprised that you were able to get up at all given the state you were in last night, legless, like one of the rabble from Ormond Park just home from England.' A quick glance at the table influenced Niall's decision to keep any smart-alec comments to himself. He'd spotted a half-loaf of sweetbread left over from the night before; they'd obviously been waiting and had had a small party ready to welcome him.

'I'll get your breakfast ready for you, Niall,' his mother said, getting up from the fire that that was starting to catch in the grate. 'You must still be hungry after that long journey and nothing in your stomach except Pat Neary's porter.' Niall didn't give respond but went out to the small yard at the back of the house and splashed some water onto his face. Standing in the narrow noisy privy, he retched again but managed to get it under control after a few minutes and began to feel slightly better.

Niall's constitution was pretty impressive, no two ways about it. Many a man wouldn't have been able to face getting out of bed after a drinking session like the one they'd had the night before, and he'd bet the other lads were in a much worse state than him. He'd gone overboard with the drink, alright – but then you couldn't blame him for that, given what he'd just found out – all his money gone like that without a trace! He couldn't even come up with names vicious enough to describe Butler, he felt so bitter towards him. Niall yanked angrily on the rope that functioned as the chain of their toilet and the cistern gave a small splutter. He came out again, his legs weak as water, and gave a quick disapproving look around the yard. It was a right mess: the big pile of slack thrown in one corner and all the other bits and pieces scattered around. His old army bicycle stood rusting against the wall, same as it had been for years – he'd bought it ages ago for one pound. He'd brought it home from the barracks when the Emergency was over but neither Andrew nor Maurice had felt it was worth fixing. Niall couldn't remember it ever being in such a state; maybe his mother hated it so much by now that she couldn't bring herself to keep it tidy. Not only did she loathe the house but also the miserable street they lived on. And, more than anything else, she couldn't stand the pigeons that their former neighbours, the Synotts, had left behind – as if to spite her, or so she suspected, anyway. Those neighbours had already moved up to Grassmount, to a fine new house, and there was no room for such filth as birds up there; of course there wasn't! Those pigeons only felt at home with the likes of them, stuck behind in these poky little cabins. No way had Jackie Synnott abandoned the pigeons to spite Kitty, Niall kept explaining to his mother whenever she started going on about it. It was just in the nature of birds that they preferred to stay put in a familiar habitat. But trying to convince his mother was like talking to a brick wall. She was absolutely certain that the birds had been left there deliberately to annoy her. Added to which, she'd practically persuaded herself that the birds' ugly constant *hoo-hoo* was a way of mocking her.

The fire had become a red glow in the grate by the time Niall came back into the kitchen and saw that the kettle was on the boil. He sat down and sipped his tea as his mother prepared breakfast. The tension in the room was palpable but by the time his mother put his plate on the table in front of him, Niall had come to himself a bit and was able to eat the food fairly easily. There wasn't a gig from his mother as he ate, and the longer the awkward silence between them dragged on, the more wound-up Niall became. Normally, his mother's bad humour wouldn't have bothered him. But his anticipating how she'd go ballistic as soon as she heard of that balls-up with Butler and the money only made the silence more unbearable. How was it that a woman's tongue was always worse than a man's? He didn't care whenever some fellow tore strips off him during his time in the army, out on the barracks square. It was the opposite, to be honest. He'd just laugh quietly at the curses and insults they'd directed at him for his awkwardness as a soldier.

'You wouldn't have a drop of tea yourself, there, Mam?' he asked, trying to soften her up, but she just ignored him. She often undertook small extra mortifications such as going without tea in lieu of something that she was praying for: she had great faith in abstinence, fasting and mortification to secure favours from the saints. There was something else behind her silence this morning, however, Niall felt; something closer to sheer contrariness. The way that his mother was deliberately ignoring him annoyed the hell out of him, making his anxiety even worse. 'I was asking you there, Mam: would you not have a drop of tea?' His question was curter this time.

'I'm time enough,' his mother shot back, bristling. 'It's no harm to offer it up as a small restitution to the Sacred Heart for the sin of drunkenness.'

'No harm, I suppose,' said Niall, getting to his feet abruptly. 'And seeing as you're looking for something to have a row about, I might as well tell you that Kieran Butler is after fecking off to England with my money. That's what made me hit the drink so hard last night: I wish I'd just drunk every single penny of it in the first place instead of saving it up for months like I did when I was in the army!' Niall left the house, slamming the door behind him.

Chapter 7

No sooner was Trevor Bartley Billy awake – at half-six that Monday morning – but he was up and at it. He threw off his bedclothes and hopped onto the cold floor. His working clothes were still there in the suitcase where he'd packed them, his home-knitted jersey, corduroy trousers and heavy hobnail boots – Jordans, as the Connemara people called them. He emptied everything out of the case and dressed himself quickly, then grabbed the handful of change that he'd left beneath his pillow the night before and shoved it into the pockets of his trousers. Tom Joyce was awake too, stretching, yawning, and staring at those big shovel-like hands of his in the wan morning light as though he were noticing them for the first time.

'Is it time to get up?' he asked, scratching his chin. His partner in the bed, Red Sweeney, was still asleep, a gentle popping sound coming from his throat, not unlike someone smoking a pipe.

'You know full well it is!' replied Trevor who wasn't one for stupid questions at the best of times but especially not this early. 'Give that dirty f**r beside you a kick, will you? He made one hell of racket coming in last night from wherever the hell he was drinking. He hadn't so much as a red cent yesterday, or that's what the bastard told me....'

Joyce propped himself up on his elbow and gave the other man a good shake, then placed his mouth against his ear and bawled into it. 'Wake up Sweeney, you f**r! The first race has started.'

Sweeney jerked in the bed as though he'd just been shot, then drew up the bedcovers over his head. 'The curse of God Almighty on you,' he moaned. 'Can't you leave a man in peace this early in the morning? He turned sideways and jammed his head under the pillow.

'Ah, sure – let the bastard be,' said Trevor, disgusted. 'He has no intention of going to work anyway.'

'Of course not,' Joyce replied, reaching under the bed for his work things where he'd thrown them the day before.

'Any man who won't go out to work isn't worth a shit: he's not even worth feeding,' added Trevor, making for the toilet, a small towel hanging from his shoulder.

'Oh, feck it, I don't know, pal,' replied Tom Joyce, mournfully sifting through the meagre change he had left after another weekend on the beer. Trevor returned a moment later and drew a broken comb through his mop of rust-coloured hair. 'I was just saying that some of us might as well stay in bed for all the good it does us,' he added, tying his shoelaces. One of them snapped and Joyce cursed.

'Sure, you's to blame except yourself, if you've no money left at the end of the week? No-one's forcing you to waste it, are they?' Trevor replied impatiently and went down to his breakfast. There was never much conversation at breakfast in Madge Connolly's house. The men – the majority hailing from Connemara – would eat their food in silence, especially on Mondays when many were hungover. None of them were much interested in the radio or newspapers, and they'd always leave the minute they cleared their plates. Anyone who'd come across those same lads the previous night in the Laurel Tree or the Mother Black Cap or wherever – having the craic or in small groups whispering conspiratorially – wouldn't have believed they were the same people! Trevor left the table as soon as he was full, just like the other men did.

On his way down Arlington Road, Trevor's boots knocked sparks off the road. His shoulders thrown back, he sashayed proudly along in his bolshie way: a peculiar combination of shyness and pride. This walk of his was the hallmark of the Irish countryman in the city, and it was common for the latest Irish immigrants in London to imitate it, even when they'd become settled here. It was an attitude that city people from Dublin and Cork used to joke about amongst themselves. Trevor passed the Catholic Church – without so much as a thought of blessing himself – then turned down Parkway and made for the crossroads where the men gathered, waiting in groups every morning for the lorries that would take them out to work. It wasn't unusual for the men to travel fifty miles to whichever building site they were working on. There was a decent crowd there already – strong, tough-looking, well-built young lads, their shirts half-open – when Trevor arrived. A few of them even bore battle-scars from the previous night: scratches and bruises from a late-night fight outside one of the pubs.

Other men looked like fish-out-of-water here on foreign soil. Plenty of them were nearing middle age: men who'd sweated every day of their lives doing hard physical labour and who could do more work in a morning than others could in an entire day. Some must have been ready to find an easier way of making a living than navvying. Construction, for example, or work at the council: anything less brutal than this slavery, navvying for contractors who were their fellow countrymen. Some of these older labourers were marked by those years of heavy work: a plodding gait, bent posture, shoulders hunched from constant digging. Another ten years, and only the very strongest would be able to cope with this heavy labour and the terrible battering it gave their bodies. But by then it would be too late to learn a new trade.

None of these navvies carried a bag or a lunch box the way the Englishman did. Instead, they jammed a few slices of bread into their jacket pockets in the morning. If they found a café nearby, they might go there, or buy a loaf of bread and a few slices of meat at lunch time. For the most part, they wore hobnailed boots but those that didn't had the tops of their Wellingtons turned down as far as the ankles, a bit like pirates. The younger men were always joking and messing about, but the older ones were much quieter. The latter straddled both eras:

the present one, with plenty of cash and jobs available – even if you had to work very hard to make it – and the earlier period just before the war, much leaner times when you might get fired on the spot for as little as stopping work to light a quick cigarette. The major difference between the two age-groups was that the younger men couldn't imagine how hard life was back then for the older lot, because they'd arrived at a time when England was the best country in the world for emigrants apart from America.

The lorries were arriving every minute now, the workers eagerly climbing aboard, their hobnailed shoes skidding and scraping on the rough metal surface. Once everyone was in, one of them rapped his fist on the driver's cab, shouted, and they were off. There was no hanging around because they were all in a rush to get out to the building site as quickly as possible; it was as though the men were afraid to waste even one minute of their precious time. Many of the lorries were open at the back, with neither a covering nor a bench to sit upon, exposing its occupants to the elements. Back in the old days they'd travelled a lot more comfortably in the old buses run by Wimpey, McAlpine or Laing. For the men who gathered at dawn in the centre of Camden Town, comfort was one of the last things on their mind or they certainly wouldn't have been working for Irish employers.

Two lorries belonging to McAlpine pulled into the curb and Trevor climbed into the first one without even asking the man in charge for permission; Trevor was too proud for that. The truth is that Paddy McAlister wouldn't have thanked any ganger of his who refused Trevor Nee work, even though he had been absent for a month. He'd never have refused someone like him. Trevor sat down on the timber bench that skirted the area beneath the canvas covering and lit a cigarette. There was room on this bench for about thirty men; the rest either sat on the floor of the lorry or stood at the very back, braving the elements. Whenever the younger lads spotted a girl making her way to work at this early hour, they gave a wolf-whistle and a smile as the lorry sped past. There were at least twenty in the back of Trevor's lorry by then, all speaking Irish to each other. The younger lads were the liveliest in the mornings, chatting about the different dances they'd been to or the fights they'd witnessed around the pubs. The older crowd were much quieter; sometimes, they'd pass a copy of the *Daily Mirror* around between them. Most of them had eyes only for the racing pages. The majority never bothered with newspapers, however, unless it was their home newspaper, the *Connacht Tribune*: that was available to buy once a week in the church porch or at one of the newsagents round Camden Town. But it wasn't news, current affairs or politics they were keen on; nor books neither; their only interest was in following Gaelic football. When you got down to it, these were men who had left school at a very young age and who very rarely discussed anything that didn't relate directly to themselves or their lives. This habit was partly formed by the toughness of their daily labouring – and yet that didn't explain it all. On arriving over here, a different outlook had inculcated itself which represented a break from previous generations. They were like a people who'd had a sudden conversion to a new religion and had left the precepts of the old one behind forever. But even though they had adapted to a new life here, at the same time, their horizons had narrowed. Unlike the people back home – where the slower pace of life meant that they had more time to appreciate the world and take note of events happening in the outside world – the Korean war and the tension between the Russians and the Allies, for example – the lads over here weren't bothered about such issues that didn't impinge upon their daily lives. It was as though every man understood deep down that Ireland had failed him: each one had made a conscious decision to turn his back on his previous life at home – its simplicity, gossip and often overly relaxed attitudes. They were focussed now solely on their lives in the here-and-now – earning money, having the craic, earning the best pay possible and spending it as quickly again. This philosophy extended to Irish politics: for the most part the lads didn't care one way or the other whether Ireland was united or partitioned. What business did the Irish government have with the six counties anyway when they weren't even able to look after their own people properly as it was? That was the first question these men would have had for anyone spreading propaganda about the Troubles in the North. The way they saw it was that you were better off just minding your own business and leaving all that stuff to the hotheads who liked to get worked up about issues that were of no benefit to them one way or the other. None of these men would have shouted out 'Up Dev!' – either for the craic or to annoy others. The fact was that they'd lost faith in their own country and in the useless shower that were running it. Over here, most men were earning two pounds a day or even more, whereas if they'd been back home they wouldn't have had any work! And to top it all off, they'd a freedom and a scope in their lives here that they'd never had in Ireland.

Here on the vast plains of England a wholly new set of work values was in operation. Over here, there was nothing like the same deference towards the white-collared worker that you saw in Ireland. At home, people respected the person who was well connected in Irish society and who had wangled a cushy job for themselves: it was these types that people aspired to emulate. It was the opposite here, where the Irish navvy admired the man among them who could work harder than anyone else and who'd the strength and stamina to dig long trenches from half-seven in the morning until six in the evening and keep going forever – shovelling sand, cement and every other kind of heavy labour. No wonder, seeing as the average construction labourer over here earned more in a week than most schoolteachers and public servants did back home. All the talk and snobbery about education and qualifications meant nothing in this new world of theirs. You earned the respect of others in accordance with a different system altogether, one that ignored so-called educational qualifications in favour of whoever was able to roll up their sleeves and work hard.

And Trevor Nee couldn't wait to tear into work again now. He saw labour as a form of recreation in the same way that someone else might take a break from it, and the harder the work, the more satisfaction he got from it. Trevor had never played any sport, and he'd never had much interest in watching football or hurling either; if he enjoyed watching any sport, it would be wrestling or boxing. His only other outlet was in drinking sessions with the other lads. Their only topics of conversation when they went out drinking were work and everything related to it. This, and the regular bust-ups and fights that were a common feature of their lives. Who was making a name for himself as a fighter around the Irish areas of the city, who was throwing shapes and showing real *action* in the fighting stakes. Trevor didn't cling to memories of the past; he lived for the present moment and had a reputation as a powerful worker amongst his own people. Trevor's only other ambition – apart from protecting his reputation as a great worker – was to be rated as a renowned man of action among the Irish. It was within this milieu that Trevor Nee felt at home: as much so as any trout in a lake or a fox in the hills. He hadn't the least bit of homesickness this Monday morning as they passed through the labyrinth of London streets on the back of this lorry. He couldn't wait to get working again, since the month he'd spent at home in Doire Leathan had seemed like some sort of penitence. It wasn't that Trevor had become Anglicised: he knew barely ten sentences of English. It was just that he preferred life over here a thousand times more. For him, his home country symbolised dependence, poverty and restrictive attitudes; it was a place that was good for certain types whom he'd little fondness for and less in common with – the educated class and the gombeens, the clergy and the legal class. It wasn't a country for people like him, Trevor felt, and if it wasn't for his family ties there, he would be happy never again to darken the door of home.

McAllister's workmen were heading for a small town called Wingfield about forty miles and at least an hour's drive away. No sooner had they got to their destination than they all jumped out onto the road as though at God's command. This was the approach of employee and employer alike, to lash into the work immediately, attacking it as eagerly and vigorously as if they were taking on a wild animal. It would be scandalous for anyone to show the slightest laziness or reluctance; there was work to be done, and whoever didn't get straight down to it had no business being there. A long section of trench had already been dug next to the edge of the road and a big mound of red clay stretched along it. The support timbers stuck out from the ditch running along the road, like the teeth of a cavernous mouth. Next to them was a series of iron spikes around which a rope had been tied to warn passers-by about the trench. The red lamps that lit the ditch at night were being quenched, one at a time, by the elderly man who provided overnight security for the site. McAllister's were laying a water pipeline there, and every inch of trench had to be dug carefully by the men, using shovels and heavy digging forks. If they had been in the countryside, the company could have used a machine for digging, which would have been cheaper than employing all those labourers. However, because they were within city boundaries, using such machines presented too much risk of damaging gas or sewerage pipes. But then again, as Trevor and his compatriots liked to say, it was just as well that machines couldn't do all the work, as otherwise they wouldn't have had a job....

If you didn't know better and had spotted these men massing here in the early-morning light – the men rushing down from the lorries across the site to get shovels and tools – you'd have been forgiven for thinking that these were preparations for some great battle. And, indeed, such a comparison wouldn't have been too far off the mark. Because these men *were* going to war in a way, all battling against one another now to see how much work they could do in one day. There was no talk of taking it easy, and anyone who couldn't keep up with the others and bust a gut like them got no respect. At worst, your work-rate had to roughly reflect the others' by the close of play if you wanted to avoid a reputation as a slacker or a latchicoe, as the lazy ones were known. Virility was judged by the length of each man's trench and the speed at which it was dug: whoever failed to keep up would not be able to hold his head up as they headed home. The ganger was shouting and roaring at them already, chalk in hand, as he marked a length of rope for every ten yards of trench assigned to each man. It was up to them whether they wanted to work alone or not, but most worked in pairs, one man digging and his mate removing the soil and moving it aside. It made sense that the men who paired up were lads who worked well together, and it sometimes happened that they welcomed a third man, especially if the initial pair didn't gel that well. It was in the nature of the Irish lads – whether they were enjoying each other's company or falling out, being in favour or falling prey to factionalism, refusing to work with one or welcoming another – they were much more tribal and discriminating than the English. Such tensions and divisions were prone to simmer on-site during the week and to boil over into a right old fracas at weekends in the pub. Of course, there was no fear that Trevor Nee didn't get his choice of work partner, given his status as one of the best workers. Indeed, one man had already joined Trevor – a fellow from the second lorry. This was a swarthy-faced lump with a swollen eye and a bad cut on his mouth from coming out on the worst side of a fight that weekend. This young bloke was known to everyone as Seán Festy Junior, and this was the name everyone knew him by back in Ireland, even though Mullen was his surname and he'd been baptised Thomas. This fellow was always getting into fights which he seldom won. As the men said, he'd had more hidings than a tinker's donkey and he'd end up dead unless he started to show some sense and give up this fighting lark once and for all. But unfortunately, Mullen's fighting ability didn't live up to his courage nor his propensity to throw punches and get involved in scraps. Like many of the others, he worshipped all the best fist-fighters around – all those lads with a name in the pubs around the Irish areas such as the Laurel Tree in Camden Town or the Cock in Kilburn.

Seán Festy Junior smiled warmly in Trevor Nee's direction and gave him a big hearty welcome back. 'Ah, musha, Jaysus Trevor, it's great to see you again!' Here, let's us two work together, pal, I haven't seen you for ages.'

'Right-o then,' said Trevor, despite him not being Mullen's greatest fan. As far as Trevor was concerned, Mullen was a little eejiteen who wouldn't beat his own shadow. But the main thing here was that he was a very good worker. The tool box had been unlocked, and the men gathered around to choose the shovels, forks, pickaxes and other gear they needed or those that they preferred working with. The surface of the road had been broken already so that the men's first job was to remove the posts that marked the edges of the trench, and throw them to one side. They began digging and slowed only whenever they came across a big rock, when they switched to the pickaxe. Then they'd go back to the spade, shovel or graip (the latter was one hell of a powerful implement in the hands of the right man).

'I'll go first on the digging,' Trevor said, selecting a fork from the toolbox while Mullen grabbed a shovel. The Ganger, Mike Duffy, came down to their section of trench a few minutes later. Mike Dudley Stephen was over fifty, and, like others who'd managed to secure an easier way of making a living after many years of graft, he was determined to hang on to his soft job for as long as possible, no matter what it took. It made no odds to him whether he'd to lick up to someone or walk all over them, as long as he maintained his position. Duffy was very loyal to Paddy McAllister, even if his loyalty was of the twisted and cowardly variety, whereby the master always controlled his slaves. He was a clever operator and did whatever it took to keep his boss happy. However, he was also smart enough not to go too hard on some of those working under him. There were men in this work-gang who'd have jumped out of the trench and knocked him flat on his back with one punch, if he'd gone too far with that craic.

'Oh. Hello, Trevor. You're back here with us again, God bless you!' Mike Duffy said to Trevor even if – privately – he wasn't one bit happy that Trevor hadn't asked him for permission before hopping onto the lorry at Camden Town that morning. Duffy knew well enough not to show his disapproval, however, and he was all over Trevor now, with a big beaming smile that revealed a tooth that had been blackened from constantly chewing tobacco. Duffy sported a cap, the peak of which jutted sideways, country style. If Trevor had come to him at the passenger window of the lorry earlier that morning seeking permission to work, Trevor would have felt obliged to Duffy, but it hadn't worked out like that. 'Jump in there, you're more than welcome,' he'd have said to Trevor, 'you're exactly the type of man I need.' The independent streak in men like Trevor was something that really didn't sit well with Duffy. He remembered a time – not that long ago – when the best of men was down on his knees begging for work, and Duffy found it irritating now how forward this younger crowd was. There had been a time when you wouldn't have dared hop into the back of a lorry without permission: no way!

'You'll give me a sub this evening Mike? The tin is getting low,' Trevor said to him in a tone that was more demand than request, making Mike's opinion of Trevor fall even further.

'Sure I will, son, no problem,' he replied, and then, releasing his irritation on someone else, he let out a roar at a skinny young lad sauntering past, shovel on his shoulder, whistling softly to himself.

'Hurry up, Cooney, *for Christ's sake*, get a move on, will you, boy, or just fuck off home, can't you?'

Trevor spat onto the palms of his hands and rubbed them together, then grabbed the fork and slammed it into the ground with ferocity. The ground was so hard here, even on the surface, that many's the man that would have found using even a pickaxe hard-going. But Trevor was very strong and the fork was good enough for him. There wasn't a gig out of either man for the first few minutes – the silence was broken only by the sound of their digging. They took off their jackets, muscles bursting from their skin, jaws tight, as they slammed against the rocks strewn everywhere just beneath the surface of the soil. Any man who wasn't sporting a cap had a pocket handkerchief tied around his head, knotted on both sides to keep the soil out his eyes. Paddy's Helmet was the Cockneys' nickname for this makeshift cap, but – as was the case for many other habits of these immigrants which the locals found strange – there was method in this madness. Those knotted handkerchiefs offered good protection against all the dust and dirt that the wind blew onto them, and were a damn sight cleaner than those old-style caps that never got washed. Some of the men also wore clips to stop their trousers flapping. Others had metal studs called foot-irons on the heel of their digging foot to protect their shoes: they were proud as punch of these somewhat old-fashioned looking devices and the way they jangled like spurs on riding boots. Any onlooker could not fail to perceive how much pride and self-respect each labourer had, and how this arose from his knowing his own true value.

Trevor and Seán Festy had a good section of their twenty-foot trench dug before either of them spoke. Seán was the first to break the silence. This didn't surprise Trevor. He could tell, since they'd begun digging earlier, that his partner had something important to get off his chest. In truth, Trevor was not that bothered what Seán Junior might have to tell him. He wasn't a big man for talk anyway and he had little enough time for Seán, and even less for his conversation or opinions. Trevor could also tell that Mullen was secretly enjoying this brief anticipation in the same way that any gossipy idiot liked to sit on news and prolong the tension. However, Mullen had come to breaking point and couldn't keep the story to himself any more. Trevor could read him like a book. Nevertheless, he was kind of caught offguard by what Mullen had to tell him: 'Hey, Trevor, mate, you heard what happened, didn't you?' Mullen said, just as they were getting ready to go onto another few yards of trench.

'What happened? What sort of shite are you on about now, man?' Trevor responded gruffly. If this gobshite had something to say, Trevor thought, why didn't he just come straight out with it instead of going all round the houses? But Trevor's gruff response didn't bother Mullen in the slightest. He wouldn't have expected anything else; he was used to Trevor dismissing him – so much so, that he almost considered it normal. Mullen was the type of fellow who was just glad Trevor spoke to him at all. He look around momentarily, as if afraid someone else might overhear what he had to say, then bent down again over his shovel and said in a low voice, 'Your sister's husband's who I'm on about, Trevor. Walter Seán Jimmy. You sure you didn't hear anything?'

'What the hell would I hear, you f**r?' Trevor said, acting mightily pissed-off. 'Grow up and spit it out, won't you, for Christ's sake?'

'He got a bad beating last night,' announced Mullen, disappointed that he hadn't had the chance to put his own twist on the story and make it even more dramatic, 'in the Welsh Harp, down in the Elephant.'

'Bloody hell, did he?' said Trevor, and continued digging. He slammed his fork deep into the ground, down to the hilt. 'Tell us more, pal!'

Mullen hadn't witnessed the fight himself because by the time he'd called into the Welsh Harp, it had been over. Trevor's brother-in-law had gone home by then and Mullen had gone in for one last drink, having done a circuit of the other pubs in the area before heading up to the dance at the Shamrock. The news that there'd been a fight there earlier had come as a surprise to him. There'd been trouble earlier in the night up in the Grenadier alright but that was no big news; sure, everyone knew that the Kerry people were a right shower for fighting, and you wouldn't mind, but they weren't worth a shíte when it came to down to it!

'Ah, for Jaysus' sake, can you not just tell us the bloody story: what in hell is wrong with you, man? Tell me what happened straight out, you pleb, and stop talking shite, will you?'

'Sure, boss,' said Mullen, and described exactly what had happened just as he'd been told it....

It was that big animal, the Jackeen, who'd given Walter Seán Jimmy the hiding – the one who was related to Paddy McAllister's wife; a cousin of hers, apparently. From what Mullen had heard, Walter hadn't lasted even two minutes with the Jackeen – and Walter was no slouch when it came to using his fists.

'The Jackeen,' repeated Trevor, trying to bring this man to mind. He definitely remembered seeing him from a distance one evening, when he'd been late finishing work. He was certainly a stocky, tough-looking block of a man, and he had one of those tight, spiky haircuts that you'd see on some Americans or those posers they called the Teddies. Trevor hadn't paid much attention to the Jackeen that time even though he'd been a bit surprised to see him driving around in the car with Paddy McAllister, a man who never gave anything away that he didn't have to. That did prove that he must be somehow related to McAllister's wife. Paddy had obviously employed him as some kind of an office-man – just an excuse for a job, in Trevor's opinion. 'And he beat up Walter Seán Jimmy,' Trevor added, shaking his head as though he found it difficult to believe.

'He made mincemeat of him,' said Mullen and proceeded to describe the Jackeen's fighting prowess and reputation. His real name was Christy Power. 'He's a right bad yoke, that Jackeen. He hates people from the country, and especially Connemara people, so they say. *And* he's a trained boxer with a bit of a name for boxing in the British Army.'

'He might well be trained, but I'm still amazed Walter Jimmy didn't have a trick or two to floor him. That Jackeen must be pretty f**ing impressive if he beat Walter that easily,' said Trevor.

That rang true for Mullen. But while Walter Jimmy was indeed no slouch when it came to the fighting game, it was still hard to beat training, when all's said and done.

'He was in the British Army, you say?' Trevor was so shocked that he briefly put down his shovel. It wasn't that he felt sorry for his brother-in-law, exactly. It was more that by beating up his sister's husband, this Jackeen had as good as challenged Trevor himself.

'He left the army recently,' confirmed Mullen; 'that's how come he's going around now with Paddy as a timekeeper.'

'As his back,' said Trevor to himself. 'That'd suit him alright!'

'But, Christ, Trevor,' said Mullen. 'I'm telling you now, pal, if I'd been there and saw that bastard beating the shit out of your sister's husband like that, I wouldn't just stand there watching – no friggin' way, mate. Even if I had to use the bar stool itself as a weapon, I'd take the f**cker's head off with it, I swear!'

Trevor gave a Mullen a dismissive glance as much as to say that he hadn't done too well himself against whoever he'd been fighting the night before, never mind taking on an army boxer. He let it go this time, however, took hold of his fork and skewered the hard red earth with it, 'We'll have to look into this situation soon, I'm afraid!' he said.

That night after dinner, Trevor washed and shaved and put on his Sunday suit, then headed over to the Elephant and Castle where his sister Mainey and her husband, Walter Seán Jimmy, were living. This wasn't just a social call on his part, needless to say. He wanted to hear it from the horse's mouth. If it hadn't been for this, he wouldn't be in any great hurry to visit his sister. He'd likely have put it off as long as possible, as he hated visiting other people's homes and had never much enjoyed previous visits to his brother-in-law's house. Walter was too dull and boring for him, truth be told.

The underground was the most incredible of London's wonders, in the eyes of Trevor Bartley Billy. The way that the train arrived to pick you up without fail every few minutes, and how they just kept coming, one after the other; that, and the way that they constantly circled this noisy black subterranean world, madly screeching and roaring. The size and scope of the Tube were the most impressive aspects of all; it was hard to get your head around it. One thing, for sure, was that the men who'd built this massive system long ago must have been amazing men; how they'd excavated all those giant windy tunnels underground without the advantages of mechanisation. The same as with Trevor's own crowd; all that these people had laboured with had been the pickaxe and shovel. There must have been plenty of Irish in England at that time too, because only his countrymen would have been capable of the type of slave-work needed to build that monstrous underground system.

It wasn't just the physical layout of the underground that was the source of Trevor's admiration but also the people who travelled its lines each day. Sometimes, it seemed to him as if they weren't real people at all but an imaginary race of people from another world. Trevor was fascinated by the way that these large crowds would sit there, silent and dead-eyed, with their briefcases, newspapers, umbrellas and books. The students or clerks seemed barely alive at times; exhausted and half-asleep or whispering to one another in low voices. And the clerks looked like lost souls, dog-tired in their bowler hats and striped trousers. The white man, the black man, the Asian – all the skin-colours that God had created at the beginning of time. Even the best of them wasn't a real man in Trevor's eyes, it didn't matter whether they were black or white. When it came to work, he wouldn't have given two flying f**s for them, as Mike Dudley Stephen would say about the Dublin Jackeens. Trevor knew little enough about the various classes of people that he met on the underground. He knew nothing about their lives, really, and was always surprised that there was work available for so many of them. There was no knowing what kind of wealth was in this country – England, so that she could provide a living for all these different people. There was a hell of a difference between this place and where he'd left behind! You could be the most impressive worker ever back home and still only have a hand-to-mouth existence.

Was there any other country in the world that was so useless and lacking in opportunity? Trevor couldn't remember a time when he hadn't been keen to leave home; even when he'd still been at school, he couldn't wait to get out of Doire Leathan. At first, it was America that he'd always been thinking about – because his father had spent a good part of his life working there. At other times, Australia or New Zealand had come to mind. He had a certain image of America: it was a country full of other races and peoples, a place full of gangsters. But when he thought of Australia, he could never recall as vivid an image, and it was the same with New Zealand.

It was when he had been sixteen that Trevor had left home for the first time. He'd travelled eastwards to Caherlistrane, where he worked as a farm labourer for a while. He'd spent two years all told over that side of County Galway and returned home with the little amount of money he'd made working for the farmers there. After that, he'd enlisted in the Irish-speaking battalion, An Chéad Chath, in Renmore Barracks in Galway. Seeing as he wasn't eighteen yet, Trevor had been afraid that his father would arrive in from Doire Leathan any day and make him go home, whether he liked it or not. As the weeks passed and he didn't hear anything from home, however, Trevor knew that he'd be left to his own devices and it was up to him to make his own way in the world. And the question of how long he spent in the army was up to Trevor, ultimately. It wasn't as though he hadn't had the potential to make a good soldier, provided he could submit more easily to authority. Whenever they organised a guard-of-honour and needed their finest and best turned-out men, he'd been selected, and the same was true when it had come to any projects or other work.

Trevor had found it a doddle in the beginning, and the only issue he'd had with the army was the question of discipline and authority (after all, submission to authority was one of the principal aspects of military life). Initially, he'd found it very difficult to subjugate the streak of wildness that was in him by nature. And signs on it too, because one day he'd lost it and punched the OC after the man had mimicked his way of speaking English. This wasn't a crime that was easily forgiven in the army, and Trevor was tried and sentenced to three months imprisonment in the Glasshouse, in the Curragh, County Kildare. Once there, Trevor had discovered even more about the fickle nature of authority: he hadn't found it easy. If you as much as looked the wrong way at any of the Red Caps who were in charge of the Glasshouse, you were in big trouble and they had a whole series of petty rules and regulations, all of which were designed to catch you out at any point. Trevor was there barely two minutes when he realised that they were deliberately testing him or tormenting him in an attempt to impose their will on him and provoke him to fight back. Their tactics worked, as Trevor soon got into trouble again and they beat him up inside a cell one day after he'd tried to attack a sergeant who was making fun of him. One man beat the shit out of him while two others held him down. This had proved a particularly bitter pill for Trevor Nee to swallow, especially as he knew that not one of those men would have lasted a minute had they been playing fair.

From then on, however, Trevor had managed to keep his violent temper under wraps, and he'd served the rest of his prison term without further incident. His day would come, that's what he said to himself. And as it happened, his chance for revenge came around sooner than he'd anticipated. It was year later and just a few months after he'd left the army that Trevor had run into that same Red Cap who'd punched the living daylights out of him while he was downtown in Galway. This had happened purely by chance when Trevor walked into this dark poky little pub down in the Fish Market. This wasn't a pub that Trevor usually went into, but, for whatever reason, he had decided to go in there for a quick pint and was barely inside the door when he'd spotted the other man down at the far end of the bar. A silent rage had flooded Trevor, as had a powerful sense of impending vengeance. The Red Cap was incognito, in his civilian garb. and mulling over his pint, nice and relaxed; he was in Galway on leave. Initially, Trevor had pretended that he hadn't recognised him as he called for a bottle of porter. There was no way that the Red Cap hadn't recognised him, however, even if he hadn't put on any act. They'd stood there at opposite ends of the bar for a while as an invisible tension filled the air. Eventually, the Red Cap finished his drink and had plucked up the courage to make for the front door, passing right by where Trevor had been standing. 'The people always meet one another, but never the hills,' Trevor had muttered to himself in a low voice and had thrown back the last of his beer, then followed him out onto the street. The other man had already been running off in the direction of the bridge but Trevor had removed his old army cap, shoved it beneath the shoulder strap of his uniform, and set off in pursuit, his studded army boots knocking sparks off the road. The Red Cap had swung left at the end of the street and rushed in under the Spanish Arch but Trevor was still hot on his heels. A few seconds later and Trevor had caught him. He laid into him into him and left him lying there battered and bruised on the ground, his revenge complete. 'Now,' Trevor had said as he replaced his army cap, staring down at his enemy who was still on the ground and was staring back at him. 'Look here, pal, you tell those other two bastards that they'll get the same treatment if Bartley Billy's son ever catches up with them!'

Trevor had left the army the following week on pre-assigned leave. He was married by then and his wife Nora was expecting a baby.

Walter Seán Jimmy and his wife Mainey rented two rooms at basement level in a row of old houses that still retained a vague air of gentility about them. Trevor's sister opened the door to his knock and he could tell by her expression that she wasn't thrilled to see him; she knew damn well why he was there. Her cool welcome didn't bother Trevor in the slightest, however; women's ways never vexed him much.

'Don't wake the child,' Mainey warned him as he followed her into the living room. The same room had probably formed the kitchen in the old days when this part of the Elephant and Castle was a wealthy area and before the richer people had moved out to the more luxurious suburbs.

The child was asleep in an old high pram that must have been a nightmare to get up and down the narrow stairs, while Walter Seán Jimmy sat next to the fire in an old armchair that clearly belonged to an older, fancier era. Trevor could tell that he'd got a hell of a hammering the night before; his lip was all swollen and cut, his eye was black and one of his teeth had been knocked out. The fight mightn't have lasted too long but the Jackeen had been busy, that much was obvious.

'What happened to you?' Trevor said, grabbing a chair.

'As if you don't know! You can't fart in this town without everyone finding out!'

Trevor examined Walter's face more closely and gave a sardonic laugh. 'There must be action in that bastard, alright,' he said.

Walter Seán Jimmy didn't reply, and Mainey came over to the table where she'd been preparing sandwiches for her husband, getting them ready for work the following day.

'Don't bother bringing that up, Trevor,' she said. 'How's our father and mother keeping?'

'Not too bad,' replied Trevor, bored.

'"Not too bad". Is that all your news? God, it's like getting blood out of a stone!'

'Well, Jaysus, I said they're alright, didn't I? What else do you want me to say?' Mainey pursed her lips and shook her head in disgust. 'And do you mind me asking how are Nora and the kids?'

'They're alright,' said Trevor.

'It's about time you got them a place over here, somewhere in Camden Town. It's easy to get rooms there.'

She was obviously wound up about something other than what had just happened to her husband, but Trevor couldn't have cared less. The day that a man paid too much attention to what a gobby woman was going on about was a bad one, as far as he was concerned.

'Aren't they grand where they are? And anyway, this here is no place to bring up children.'

'And, are you just going to leave them at home until they're all grown-up? That's not much of a life for Nora back there, I'll have you know – not seeing you from one end of the year to the next. God knows, she must be one patient woman to put up with it, because I sure wouldn't.'

'Oh yeah! And what's it got to do with you, anyway? She's not that badly off at all. Don't I send her money home every single week? She's not lacking for anything. She's way better looked-after than plenty of other women whose husbands are back there with them all the time,' Trevor said in a tone that indicated this discussion was at an end, and turned back to his brother-in-law.

'What sort of fellow is this Jackeen anyway? What made him turn on you?'

Walter's head was bowed, avoiding Trevor's eyes.

'Make us a drop of tea there, will you, like a good woman,' he said to Mainey, offering Trevor a cigarette.

'Take your time, will you!' Mainey retorted, but she went over and filled the kettle all the same, then lit the gas ring beneath it.

'He's a man the same as any other,' Walter said, taking a quick drag on his cigarette. But he knew that this wouldn't be enough for Trevor.

'By Christ, Wattie, he must be really something, this fellow – or how could he leave you in that state, boy?'

A flaming ember fell out onto the hearth and Walter Jimmy bent down to replace it. He gave a short gasp of pain however, slumped back into his chair, and placed a hand gingerly on his lower chest. The ember singed away quietly on the hearth until Trevor bent down and threw it into the back of the grate. Walter gave another small gulp of pain and the baby began to cry.

'Didn't I tell you not to wake him?' said an annoyed Mainey as she rocked the baby back and forth and he settled again.

'Why don't you put him back in the bedroom?' said Trevor to Mainey over his shoulder.

Trevor had no interest in babies or in ogling this new nephew of his, even though he hadn't seen him since the day he'd been baptised, a few months earlier. The way Trevor saw it – it was only when they'd grown up that kids were worth sussing out; it was only then that you knew what they were really made of, anyway!

'He's alright there as long as you don't wake him again. God knows, I was awake half the night with him, never mind other people tossing and turning, and moaning with the pain,' Mainey said, rattling some cups.

'I hope that the little creature isn't coming down with anything; that's his second night crying like that. This flat is too narrow and crowded for a child, I'm telling you – I swear, Wattie. I'm telling you now, you better start looking for somewhere nicer for us.'

Her husband paid no heed to her. Trevor's questions about the fight was bothering him a lot more than anything Mainey was complaining about.

'Oh, musha, don't tell me he left you speechless as well as everything else.' Trevor said gruffly, getting back to the subject. 'What the hell happened? What drew him onto you – or was it that he came into the pub looking for you, or what?'

Walter cleared his throat and responded sheepishly.

'Arah, musha, it was nothing much. It was just one of those things.'

'"It was just one of those things"…?' said Mainey, from the other side of the table. 'If it was "nothing much", then how the hell did he leave you in that state?'

'What was "nothing much"?' Trevor said, ignoring Mainey's question.

'Well, I came across him first out in Watford,' said Walter hesitantly. He came around in the car with McAllister about a week ago when we were pulling the cables. I was at the drum releasing the cable from it...'

'Go on,' said Trevor impatiently.

'Well, anyway, I had the drum out on the side of the road and the kicker under the bolt, trying to turn it – you know, the way you've got to do it so you can turn it whichever way...'

'Oh, for God's sake, you'd swear that I never worked on the cables before? Will you just get on with it and stop blathering on about stuff like a child,' interrupted Trevor, who was fit to explode at this stage.

'Aren't I trying to tell you how it happened? I was after turning the drum sideways, facing the road, and there was only a small narrow space there but a car could make it through, no bother, if there was nothing in the way. Next thing, McAllister's car comes down the road. Paddy was driving, but the Jackeen has his elbow out the car window, as cocksure as if we were on his job. Well, the car stopped. There isn't a gig out of Paddy but this other fellow sticks his head out the window and says, "That yoke is in the way. Move it out of there now!"'

'Did he, by Christ?' said Trevor.

'It was the way he said it to me, y'know, ordering me around like that, as if I was working for him or something.'

'And what did you say to him?'

'What could I say to him? I wasn't going to let him get away with that. "If it's in your way, then it's up to you to move it," I says, and turned my back on him. I was putting the two jacks under the axle and in against the drum so's we could release the cable....' The withering look his brother-in-law gave him told Walter he'd better get to the point. 'Well, he said something to me then – the Jackeen, I mean; Paddy McAllister never opened his mouth to me one way or the other – and when I asked him what he'd said, can you believe the bastard told me to get the wax out of my ears!'

'Did he hell!'

'He did too, I swear!'

Trevor stared at Walter as though weighing him up on some imaginary pair of scales, as if he wasn't sure whether the other man was lacking in some way. He knew full well that Mainey's husband was a fairly good lad, plenty strong and handy with his hands but still, he felt something missing in him – that he could let certain things past him that like that, things that Trevor himself would never have let go. They'd both been down the pub on the Holloway Road one night when one of the Tipperary crowd – and there were loads of them down that side – had taken exception to their speaking Irish, as if to say (according to the fellow they were arguing with, anyway) that Trevor and Walter and their friends were talking about them behind their backs.

The problem wasn't that this English-speaking lot had objected to the Irish language, but more that Trevor wasn't willing to take any shit off them. If it hadn't been for Walter coming between them and explaining to the other crowd that they always spoke Irish together, Trevor would've floored that Tipperary fellow. To this day, Trevor was sorry that he hadn't clocked your man right there and then.

'And what did you say then?'

'I couldn't say anything because McAllister backed the car around suddenly, as if he was pissed off with the other fellow, and off they went. I didn't see him again until the other night in the Welsh Harp.'

'And was it him that came looking for you?'

'I doubt it. I don't go in there very often; he wasn't likely to have known where I was.'

'Does he live around here somewhere?'

'I don't know.'

'Hmm,' said Trevor in a dissatisfied tone, but before he could ask anything else, Mainey handed them two cups of tea and a plate of bread.

'Did you take any photos when you were back home?' she asked her brother but Trevor gave her a funny look. 'Nora took a few,' he said.

'And have you got them there with you?'

Like most women, Mainey was mad about photos and she never went home without bringing her old Kodak camera with her; she had a boxful of them already.

'Indeed I don't.' Trevor took a sip of tea and turned to Walter again. 'And did he go for you straight away?'

'Oh, for God's sake, will you let it go, the pair of you? All you talk about is fighting and trouble and that's it! It's not as if someone wouldn't have a go at this fellow here; he can be fiery enough himself at the best of times!' said Mainey, sitting next to them.

'Well?' said Trevor to his brother-in-law, ignoring Mainey again. 'I asked him what he was on about, and told him I'd got no wax at all in my ears this time,' replied Walter, as though this brought some small amount of satisfaction. 'I gave him a fair chance.'

'It looks like you did, alright,' said Trevor sarcastically. 'You'd have been better off punching him right there and then and never mind the chat.'

'Fighting and blackguarding, God knows but you lot are worse than children,' said Mainey.

'Did he punch you right then, or what?'

'The frig he did! He told me to go to hell and that he didn't give a shit about anyone that'd ever come out of Connemara.'

'Well, I'll be –,' said Trevor.

'I hit him then, or tried to, at least, but I might as well tell you that he's really fast; he's a very slippery customer... he had me down before I knew what'd happened.'

'Did you land any punches on him?' Trevor didn't disguise his put-down, and the barb had clearly hit home.

'I did, to be sure, course I did! I got him with one powerful belt, his jaw will know all about it today; I got him with one hell of a salamander, boy!'

'Did you see him today?'

'How the hell would I have seen him?' Walter asked, perplexed, but Mainey interrupted them again.

'Arah, sure he didn't go to work today,' she said, 'how could he go to work when he'd sore ribs; wasn't I awake half the night with all his twisting and turning?'

'And is your rib cage sore now?'

'You could tell by the way he said this that Trevor was a bit dubious whether Walter was as bad as he was making out. Not so for his wife, however. 'I told him to go the doctor's but sure, you might as well be talking to the wall. If he wasn't hurt, there's no way he'd have stayed away from work today,' said Mainey. 'God save us, but for all we know, maybe some of his ribs are broken.'

'You'd know about it if your ribs were broken, believe me,' said Trevor, doubtfully. Walter shifted uncomfortably on his chair; he couldn't wait for this conversation to end. 'And listen, Wattie, did he kick you?' Trevor added as though this thought had suddenly occurred to him.

'Kick him!' said Mainey in disgust. 'Now, isn't that just lovely?'

'He didn't kick me,' Walter said sheepishly. 'The likes of him doesn't need to.' He gave a deadpan laugh and shifted gingerly in his seat, wincing in pain. 'Well, I might as well be honest with you, Trevor; the bastard is dynamite! He's as slippery as an eel and he's got the strongest punch I've ever felt.'

'By George,' said Trevor solemnly.

'I think now, lads, that it's time for you to change the subject, or are you going to talk about this the whole night?' Mainey said, stamping the floor with her foot in disgust.

'Oh, musha, Jaysus, I can ask a question, can't I?' her brother exclaimed in exasperation.

'Asking a question isn't the same as doing a post-mortem on the whole bloody thing, is it? I can't understand for the life of me why the pair of you are interested in all this bullshit – arguing and fighting and murdering each other. It's nothing but the devil's work!'

'Leave it there, so,' said Trevor gruffly, offering Walter a cigarette.

'I will,' replied Mainey as though it had suddenly become obvious to her that she was getting nowhere, 'because we definitely should be talking about other things.'

'Trevor, it's about time that you brought that poor wife of yours over, seeing as you haven't a notion of going home yourself.'

'Back. Go back, is it? Sure, what would I do back there, in God's name? A spell working for the council on the roads, is it? What business would I have going back there, now? Good morra, Jack!'

'And isn't that exactly why you should bring Nora and the children over here with you? Isn't that what I'm saying? Or do you think it's fair for you to leave her over there by herself for the rest of your life? You have responsibilities now, boy, and you shouldn't be found wanting in them.'

'"Found wanting", is it? Four pounds I send home to her every single week; how's that shirking my responsibilities, tell me? You don't know what you're talking about, Mainey. Listen to me, now; I don't want to hear any more about it, okay? I'm telling you now.' Trevor turned back to his brother-in-law at this. 'We can't let him away with this, Wattie, can we, even if he's so much action in him,' he said.

'Oh, come on!' exclaimed Mainey.

Trevor got to his feet and put his cup down on the table. 'I'd better head off home now,' he said roughly.

'You'd have been better off not coming over, for all the good it did you. You've no news worth talking about and all you've gone on about since you got here is fighting and blackguarding.'

'It's getting late now, I better be off,' said Trevor, as if he hadn't heard her. Trevor did not head straight home, however. Instead he made for the Welsh Harp, a small old-fashioned pub that was about halfway towards the tube station. He had one drink there, standing at the counter, a watchful eye on the door all the while. There were only a few people there, and, if he was honest, Trevor couldn't say whether he'd have wanted Christy Power to come in then or not. If Power was as good a man as they made out, then you'd want to be ready for him, and you'd have to plank him mercilessly as soon as you got the chance. Trevor Bartley Billy knew that he'd one hell of a punch himself and he'd always been very proud of the fact that he wasn't afraid of anyone. This was something that he'd never been slow to remind his opponents at the beginning of any fight; he'd try and take them out with the first punch. Either that or he'd try his best to rock his opponent to the core at the beginning of every fight, rattle them so badly that they'd never recover properly – so that the fight would be as good as over. Fair play was all very well, provided you didn't stake your life on it.

On the journey back to Camden Town, the underground stations flew past: Lambeth North, Charing Cross, Leicester Square (all names that meant nothing to Trevor) and then the station that he knew best of all – Tottenham Court Road – where the Blarney was located. (This was the big Irish dance-hall where Peadar Michael Andrew had nearly fried himself working there once, when he'd struck an electrical cable with a pick-axe.) Next was Warren Street, where you met Connemara women in their droves, and after that again was Euston, a place that was always full of drunken Scotsman. Next up again was Mornington Crescent where all the Greeks lived, and then Camden Town. For the duration of the journey, Trevor's mind was only on one thing only, however: the Jackeen. It was the same when he went to bed later that night. In fact, the Jackeen was the last thought that came into his mind before he went to sleep. At some stage, he knew that he'd have to fight the Dublin man himself. He would have to fight him, but more importantly, he'd have to beat him; otherwise, he'd have no standing at all among his own people.

Chapter 8

Nano already knew it in her heart. Leaving home hadn't done a whole lot for her situation. Not that staying at home would have solved her problems one whit either. Even if she'd stayed at home, it wouldn't have done anything to speed up the chances of herself and Máirtín getting married. She'd have been in the way of her brother Bartley, too, just to make matters worse. The woman was always left in the halfpenny place; it was just how life ordained things. She remembered reading in some magazine, the *Far East*, maybe, that they'd throw newborn girls into the river out in China somewhere rather than feeding them; that's how little respect they had for women over there. Not that the so-called civilised countries were a whole lot better, sometimes, it seemed to her. She couldn't blame Máirtín, of course, as he'd no choice but to do what he was told; he was as constrained by circumstances as much as any other man. Máirtín was trapped, really, and he couldn't do anything. But then, this was even worse for her in a way because she didn't even have the satisfaction of venting her anger and frustration on him; it wasn't as if she could accuse him of being reluctant, or careless, or having an eye on other women, even. Even that opportunity to vent was denied her.

If Nano had any regrets about coming over to England it was that she hadn't gone somewhere else: in or around London where there were more of her own people – Connemara people – for company. It'd be nice to hear the odd bit of Irish spoken every now and then, and have the occasional conversation – nice and lively, in your own language, just as they had on the train that day to Dublin when they were on their way over. The Connemara people in London had a great life, from what she'd heard. You wouldn't be half as lonely if you were there; you'd have had some craic up there, maybe, and it'd be a lot less lonely than this place. She felt a bit like a fish-out-of-water here, as if she'd landed in some strange limbo-land. Everything about Norwold was so different; she found the life here completely alien to her, so that it was as if she'd no business being there. Then again, the refugees from Eastern Europe must have found it equally disorienting. Sometimes, it seemed to Nano that her life had taken a completely different turn from the one she'd originally planned; and this frightened her most of all. What if everyone's fate was ordained, and this was the road that had been laid out for her since the very beginning of time! Maybe there was no such thing as 'If only' or 'If it happened that': maybe things happened like this because they quite simply couldn't happen any other way. Weren't all of their lives – her own included – closely bound up with one another now: Sheila O' Dwyer's life, and Hilda Jackson's and Mary McDermott's and everyone else she'd come into contact with since her arrival in Norwold? Were all of their lives intimately linked together so that she was just another thread in the great pattern of being, that giant tapestry, so big that it was impossible to separate any one element from the whole? These thoughts frightened Nano and she did her best to push them aside and forget them whenever they came to mind. There'd been a good few nights recently when she'd gone to bed feeling down, something that wouldn't have happened if she'd stayed at home.

It was the work that proved her salvation; if it wasn't for working, she'd have gone mad. She flung herself into her work every day with great enthusiasm, even if it was only brushing the floor or collecting the cutlery or plates after patients' meals. Everything she did, she did as conscientiously and as thoroughly as she could; her work had taken on an almost ascetic aspect. Even the job that she hated most –

cleaning up and looking after the old people who had no control over their bodily functions anymore – Nano threw herself into it with great vigour and never gave the slightest hint that she hated some of her tasks, especially when in the presence of those elderly people. Instead, when she saw the look of shame in these patient's eyes, Nano felt a deep empathy for them. Nano's work was a regular reminder to her that there were plenty of other people in the world who were far worse off than she was. Neither was she always watching the clock as was the case with some of the other girls working with her, whose social lives were a lot livelier than hers. Most of them couldn't wait to finish work; and when everyone else was delighted to be going home, Nano would almost have preferred to stay on.

It was the same when it came to the holidays. The other girls never stopped going on about their holidays but whenever she got a day off, Nano would be awake as early as on any other day while her roommates in the nursing ward stayed in bed until midday, at least, Nano was different. She'd spend till lunchtime indoors doing various odd-jobs, washing or mending clothes, knitting things, or writing letters home. And this while the other women were playing records down in the recreation room; running in and out of each other's rooms and generally making a racket. In the afternoon, Nano usually went down into the town that was less than two miles away where she'd have a good look around the shops. Either that or she'd go out walking in the countryside, something that none of her other fellow countrywomen did.

Nano was fascinated by the English countryside, particularly how different it was to her own home-place. The fields here were all large and wide, even if they were stubble now that the harvest had been taken in, the crops all threshed and bagged by the big farm machines. Even the borders between the fields here were different to those in Ireland; here, the ditches were trimmed back as neatly and artistically as wattled baskets, and there were small russet-yellow copses that dotted the higher ground every few miles, as if in retreat from the machine and the plough. It amazed Nano how few thatched houses were left in the countryside here: the houses were posh, redbrick, two-storey buildings, the date that they were constructed inscribed just above the front door of each. It was true that there were smaller villages within a mile of the hospital where you found more thatched houses than you did even back in Cois Fharraige. But the difference here was that – unlike in Ireland – the gentry here seemed to live in the thatched houses. The small English country villages were different in other ways too: each had a tiny ancient stone chapel and graveyard at their heart, many of them situated on a slight rise, their stone slabs ivy-festooned and leaning this way and that, as if all the passing years had weighed heavily on them. Nano loved how neat and tidy the country villages here were kept; they looked so organised that you could have sworn there was no-one living in them anymore. And yet, despite this sense of order or perfection, Nano still felt that there was something missing here, some sort of lack in the landscape itself that she couldn't explain, something vaguely akin to death itself. It was as if the countryside here understood that its people had been forsaken, and that it had to fend for itself. She never saw many people going about their business during the day in the rural villages here, not as many as you'd have seen in her own rocky parish back in Ireland. Most of the rural people here now worked in satellite towns such as Norwold, Nano'd heard, and the farm-work that had once have been done by big groups of men was all done by machine. Sometimes it seemed that the soul had gone out of the countryside here as the people's links with it had faded. The countryside here was nearly as lonely and abandoned as when the human beings had first set foot on the earth. Did they know the names of the fields here anymore, Nano wondered, as they did back in Connemara – An Móinín Rua, Gort na Lachan, An Garraí Báite – and a thousand other names? Nano would have been surprised if there weren't names for every field and garden in this country too; it was a form of blindness to live in a place and yet not to know your own landscape intimately or to understand it. Nano thought back to the stranger who'd rented the bungalow down the boreen from themselves at one stage. She'd seen him wandering around alone, completely oblivious to the names of any of the fields he passed each day. She'd felt sorry for that man back then but now she was the one who was the object of pity.

Sometimes, when Nano looked at herself in the mirror, she thought that she could see herself getting old – aging right before her very own eyes – and she became frightened. Life was slipping away from her and she didn't know when she'd have her own share of it. She was like a prisoner waiting for parole, never knowing when the wait would be over. And so she followed the same routine every week, much as a prisoner would; even the weekends adopted a familiar pattern. Every Sunday seemed the same as the last; she'd go to Mass first thing in the morning before the rest of the day drifted into a similar routine. It was the same on holidays or days off; she never really took a proper holiday.

There were a few times that she'd nearly given in to Sheila O'Dwyer trying to entice her to out to the dances in Saint Bridget's Hall. Anything, Sheila said, was better than being stuck in there in the room by yourself every night of the week. The odd trip beyond the hospital quarters wouldn't do her any harm, the Cork girl said, not unless her boyfriend had forbidden her not to enjoy life before she settled down and got married. It wasn't as if she had to become a nun or anything, Sheila added, and spend all her evenings in their tiny cell of a room soul-searching; either that, or walking out around the countryside by herself like some kind of a crazy person. If Sheila's tongue was sharp at times, she still only meant the best for her, Nano knew. And the Cork woman didn't have any friends other than Nano among the Irish working in the hospital. But still, Nano wanted to plough her own furrow and she hadn't come over from Ireland for the craic, she reminded herself. For the most part, Nano eased her loneliness by writing letters home, long informative letters to Máirtín where she told him everything about Norwold and all the work that was available in England, and the fine pay that went with it, especially for men. She'd even sent him a copy of the *Norwold Herald* and marked the job advertisements in it, even if she knew perfectly well that Máirtín couldn't possibly go anywhere while his mother was still alive. And the longer their situation dragged on and they put it on the long finger, the more chance the whole thing would peter out. Would she still be as keen on Máirtín Bid Anthony after they'd had to endure a long period of separation? Recently, a few times, she'd felt as though her feelings for him might not be as strong as before; no sooner had this thought entered her mind, however, but she'd convince herself that this was just her imagination, and that she was still as fond of him as she'd ever been. Hilda Jackson had asked her one day whether she still wrote to Máirtín often and she told her that she did – or at least fairly often. The English girl told her that she thought this was very romantic – a couple separated from one another by an entire sea – and they exchanging letters each day.

'Oh stop, you old wagon, we don't write to each other that often,' Nano said, but Jackson wasn't listening. She'd read a love story one time, the Englishwoman said, a story so romantic that it'd brought tears to her eyes. This young couple had been living in some foreign country that she'd forgotten the name of, and they were so in love with one another that they'd decided to separate until death. They'd done this, just so as this love of theirs would never fade, as it would have done if they'd stayed together.

'Wasn't that a beautiful story?' Jackson asked Nano, 'wasn't it one of the most romantic things she'd ever heard?'

'They must have been a bit odd,' said Nano, laughing, but it wasn't as easy to get Sheila O'Dwyer to put a lid on it as it was Jackson.

'It's true,' Sheila had said to Nano one night as they were drinking cocoa, just before going to sleep. 'I wouldn't become a hermit for any man.'

'But we're promised to one another, Sheila, I can't go running around to dances all over the place now, can I?'

'Why can't you? It's not like you're married to him or anything, is it? And it's not as if you have some kind of date set either! As though you could say to yourself – "Well, I'll be getting married next year." I mean, he could string you along like this for the rest of your life.'

This hurt Nano but she let it go.

'I'm fine now as I am, Sheila,' she said, and Sheila shook her head.

'Well, for heaven's sake, how can you stand it, cooped up in here every night, staring at the walls? You know, Nano – I'd have gone completely mad by now if I were you. I'd be cuckoo!' said Sheila, cocking a finger to her forehead.

'You're cuckoo yourself already and it's not as if you stay in too many nights,' replied Nano, laughing.

'Watch yourself now, you cow,' said Sheila, grabbing a pillow and making as if to throw it at Nano. She went serious again the next moment. 'Listen now, my love, you'll come with me to the dance tomorrow night, won't you?'

'I won't,' said Nano.

'Ah, for pity's sake! Just one night, what harm can one night be? Máirtín isn't going to be after you for one night out, is he now; just a tiny part of one evening with a spot of dancing; sure, what's wrong with that?'

Nano gave in just to end the conversation and said that she'd go. 'Just the one night, mind you; I'm not going to make a habit of it.'

After ward-duty, Nano came back to the room and got ready to go, even if she was already privately regretted giving in so easily to Sheila. Máirtín wouldn't be out dancing this evening, that's for sure; he'd most probably be heading over to her family's house to spend a few hours chatting to her father and Bartley. Her name would surely be brought into the conversation at some stage, although Máirtín would never say anything much on that score. He was too reserved to hardly ever reveal his innermost thoughts, even to people like Nano's family whom he knew well. As if to salve her conscience about going out, Nano had promised herself that she'd write to Máirtín to tell him that she'd gone to the dance with her roommate. She just didn't have it in her not to tell him about it but, to give Máirtín his due, he wouldn't have been angry with her about it either way. Hadn't he actually said as much to her in the last letter she'd received from him? The other night, Nano had had a dream where she and Máirtín had broken up but in the confusion that was the dream, she'd felt a sense of relief mixed with heartbreak that it was all over. But Nano had woken to a slightly different feeling: shame at the cold indifference that had come over her during the dream.

Saint Bridget's was only a mile from the hospital and situated next to the Catholic Church that she'd read about in the ad for the job in the *Connacht Tribune*. But even though it wasn't far, Sheila insisted that they go on the bus.

'Is this how you lost your ability to walk when you came over here?' Nano asked as they waited at the bus-stop. 'A little walk won't do us any harm, you wagon, will it?'

'Haven't we walked ten miles since this morning, up and down that bitch of a hospital wing? We've done enough walking for one day!'

'You'll hardly be resting when you're inside at the dance,' retorted Nano. The ticket-collector on the bus was Irish, a fresh-faced young Kerry man who sported a Pioneer Total Abstinence pin on one lapel and a small tricolour badge on the other. He and Sheila chatted for the short duration of their journey.

'Hey, Sheila, he didn't take any money from us,' said Nano once they were off the bus.

'Of course, he didn't. The Irish never take any money from their own people – if they can avoid it,' Sheila replied. 'It drives some English people crazy.'

'Alright, but that's fairly dodgy, especially if the ticket inspector comes onto the bus, checking. Wouldn't you just die of shame if you got caught?'

'Would you heckers, like! All you'd have to say is that you had some very serious things on your mind and that, unfortunately, you just forgot about it.'

'Here, guess what we'll do; we're a little bit early for the dance so we'll go down to the Lord Nelson for a quick drink, eh?'

'Oh, stop, you biddy! Very likely: two girls like us, by ourselves in a pub?' Nano said, horrified.

Sheila placed her hand on her arm and adopted a beseeching tone. 'Ara, the only ones left in the hall are the sorry ones – Pioneers and anyone else who's too tight to spend money. Ara, for God's sake, you can just have a drop of lemonade or whatever – we won't be long in there, anyway. Come on, my love.'

It was on the tip of Nano's tongue to tell Sheila that she was far too fond of going out drinking, but she quickly thought the better of it. Sheila O'Dwyer was younger than her by a few years and she'd already been in England a good while longer; sometimes, though, it seemed to Nano that she was a bit too fond of the craic.

'You didn't mention the pub when you were asking me to come out with you,' she said as they made their way to the pub. The Lord Nelson was an ancient red-brick building with high narrow windows and a painting of the one-eyed man himself swinging above the door. Nano's pulse quickened on hearing the lively Irish music coming from inside; it was as good as anything she'd ever heard out at the ceilidh in Spiddal or in the Hangar in Salthill. Just as they approached the door, she had second thoughts, however. 'God knows, this is shameful, Sheila, two women like us going into a pub by ourselves. People will say that we're a right pair of rips…'

'Oh, "shameful"! You've "shameful" on the brain, you divvy. Would you have a ha'penny's worth of sense, woman, you're not back in Connemara now. This is 1950, for God's sake!'

The Holy Year, by all accounts, Nano said to herself. The parlour of the Lord Nelson was swimming in smoke and full of the noisy hum of punters. The sweet smell of the drink and the smoke formed a giddy perfume. Three musicians were sitting on a small stage in the corner furthest from the door. The pub manager, his wife, and a big lump of a woman with bleached hair and a protruding cleavage were filling pints and uncapping beer bottles to beat the band. The parlour and public bar were already crowded with people, and everyone was lashing back their drink and spending money like water.

'We won't get anywhere to sit here, I'm afraid,' said Sheila, raising her voice so that she could be heard above the din. 'You sure you won't have a thimbleful of something?'

'Well, don't get me anything stronger than a lemonade, will you?' Nano warned as they pushed their way through the crowd and up towards the bar.

'No fear, I'm not that rich,' Sheila called back over her shoulder.

'No-one will bother us here, anyway; there are plenty of women in here already,' Sheila said, glancing around.

'Yeah, and can't you see that half of them are slappers and that they'd be talking about us if we were back home. There's some freedom in this country, Nano, so there is.'

There sure was, Nano thought. Wasn't she herself as free as the wind – in theory, at least – for all the good it did her. What was she doing here, sitting in her new Marks and Spencer's dress? She'd have been better off back home, out at the ceilidh in Spiddal with Máirtín, or the pair of them sauntering along the road, nice and relaxed. There were some fine-looking men around her now, however, a few of whom were nodding and smiling in her direction; she was still pretty enough that she could have had her pick of anyone, but, of course that wasn't why she'd come out. The truth was that she felt completely out of place, here; it was all new and strange and she was sorry that she'd gone out with Sheila at all.

Over in the corner, the drummer struck up with a loud *cluc! cluc! cluc!* – like someone beating a set of old bones, and the other musicians struck up a reel, a nice, lively tune that Nano knew well. On hearing the music kick off, some of the men let out a wild whoop and began tapping their feet with joy.

'It's a pity that they don't have music as good as this here,' Sheila said as they arrived at Saint Bridget's Hall a short while later. Nano agreed. Sheila had downed three gin and oranges by then, but she might as well have been drinking water, for all the effect it had on her.

The only music they had in the hall was a record player and amplifier. A spotty-faced youth choosing the tunes was doing his damnedest to get the crowd up dancing. He roared loudly into the microphone, some blather that no-one could understand. He was just like one of those chancers that spouted gibberish on Radio Luxembourg. The floor of the hall was damp concrete with a series of arches running down it, against which dancers leaned whenever they needed a break. A small counter ran across the far end where they sold tea and soft drinks. Above it hung the Irish National flag and the yellow-and-white flag of the Pope, each criss-crossing the other. Above them again was a portrait of Éamon de Valera, grey and serious-looking, as well as a picture of the hall's patron saint – Bridget – her magic cloak spread out across the plains of Kildare. In between these two portraits hung a copy of the Easter Proclamation. There was no risk that anyone who frequented the place wouldn't understand these most respected symbols of Ireland. The person who ran the hall was Father Patrick Begley, a Fianna Fáil man to the core. The only Irish newspaper sold there – other than religious publications – was the *Irish Press*.

Father Begley – or the Big Priest as he was often known – was a big fan of rugby and boxing, and was well able to handle even the roughest of customers. A half-crown was the entrance fee to the dances there, and it was a constant refrain that Father Begley could have hired a proper band – at least now and then, given the profit he must've been taking. Not that the Big Priest kept a penny of it for himself: everything they got on the door went to benefit the parish and to spread the faith in pagan England. This was the Big Priest's only concern. There was nothing materialistic or worldly about Father Begley – otherwise how would you explain that old rusty bike he went around on? Even the priest's soutane was old and worn-out: so tatty, indeed, that the snobbier members of the Catholic community were embarrassed by him sometimes.

Nano and Sheila left their coats into the tiny cloakroom just inside the door, and made their way through the crowd to the far end, where there was room to sit near a timber platform skirting the wall. The place was already packed with sturdy country lads, handsomely turned-out in their dark navy suits, white shirts and starched collars. In essence, Saint Bridget's was a rural Irish country hall transferred lock-stock-and-barrel to this new country. The only difference was that some of the people here were hesitant and suspicious of one another compared to back home. This was mainly because – for the first time – they were coming across people from parts of Ireland that they weren't familiar with. Some of the women seemed wary, as though they were on the lookout for anyone that they didn't already know from home. The majority of the men, meanwhile – especially those grouped around the door – looked so animated that the slightest provocation was likely to kick off an argument among them. The most fashionable girls – those who'd visited Ireland recently – had on light, ankle-length summery dresses; a couple of them even sported wristwatches they'd acquired after months of saving up. The girls who'd moved to England more recently were less stylish-looking generally: their skirts shorter; their hairstyles, simpler; their heels, flatter. None wore trousers, apart from one woman still in her bus clippy's uniform, her leather satchel still hanging from her shoulder as though this were an essential element of her ensemble. This woman passed Nano and Sheila now as she made for the drinks counter and she didn't go unnoticed to Sheila.

'You wouldn't think by the look of her now that she was up to her ankles in cow-shit this time last year, would you?' Sheila said quietly. 'Look at her, proud as punch of her leather bag there, I bet she doesn't even take it off when she goes to bed at night!'

'Come on, show a bit of charity now, Sheila,' responded Nano.

'Ara, "charity"! Oh, look at these two coming over our way!' said Sheila quickly, extinguishing the butt of her cigarette under her shoe. The spotty-faced lad had just announced the quickstep and the couples were taking to the floor. Those women who hadn't been asked to dance disguised their disappointment with a few exaggerated laughs. Two handsome and well-built young men were making their way over to Nano and Sheila; the best-looking of them was all chat and smiles, while his companion looked a bit shy. It was obvious to Nano that Sheila knew both men, and the more gregarious and cheery one asked her onto the dancefloor. Nano agreed to dance with his friend, albeit reluctantly, because she didn't know many of the foreign dances yet. To be honest, they didn't even dance the waltz at the Spiddal ceilidh back home, unlike in other parts of Connemara.

'I'm no good at this dance, I'm afraid,' Nano excused herself to her partner as the pair of them spun around the dance floor at a cracking pace, a little too fast seeing as they hadn't the hang of the steps yet. A few seconds later, Nano was sorry that she'd said anything about her dancing; it was just that his silence had knocked her off her stride a bit.

'You're very quiet,' she told him when he still hadn't said a word to her, and the lad looked startled and began to say something.

His head jerked slightly, but he eventually managed to get the words out. 'I-I-I am, I suppose,' the lad said self-consciously and Nano realised that he had some sort of a stutter or speech impediment, and she was secretly angry with herself for saying anything. She'd have to try and get him to relax a bit more, to make up for being so blunt.

'Are you long here in Norwold?' she asked him, as nothing else came to mind. 'I'm Just Wild about Harry' was playing, and more couples were gathering to return to the floor, their faces all lit up from their exertions. A wild whoop of joy came up from the crowd near the door – a bunch of lads who'd no interest in dancing but preferred to slag off the dancers with smart-alec jibes or to horse around or shadow-box like a bunch of schoolboys. Sometimes this tipped over into a real fight, of course, but that never lasted long, given that the Big Priest was around and would never hesitate to eject the rowdies and trouble-makers.

'A couple of m-m-months, that's a-all; we came down here from D-Doncaster, m-myself and my m-mate.'

'Your mate?' Nano asked. She remembered Sheila mentioning some fellow called Mike whom she went out with from time to time. Nano suspected that Sheila had invited her out to make up a foursome.

'M-Mike, th-the other lad who's dancing with Sheila. H-How l-long since you came over here yourself… if-if y-you don't mind me a-asking?' Sheila and Mike flew past them, Sheila laughing at Mike's funny faces. He was a great dancer by the look of it.

'Oh sure, I've only just landed here, brother, I'm still giving off the smell of the sea!'

The man laughed so easily at this that one would never have imagined he'd anything wrong with his speech. It was an awful shame, Nano thought: a nice young man like him being saddled with such an impediment.

'Y-yes, I was thinking that I h-hadn't seen you here before,' he said, but before Nano could respond, the quickstep came to an end. She thanked him and went back to her seat. She'd barely sat down again than Sheila was beside her, eyes wide with excitement.

'Well?,' she asked Nano, eagerly.

Nano didn't really like being set up like this but she didn't let on.

'"Well" what? What are you on about, you fool?' she said.

'Well, how'd you get on?'

'Awkward enough, to be honest; neither of us would've won any prizes, I'm afraid!'

'Never mind that – how did you like him? Peter, I mean.'

'He's alright.'

'He's a really nice lad.'

'Do you think so?' Nano replied indifferently. She was annoyed with Sheila now.

'Seriously, Nano, he's a really nice lad.'

'Why don't you don't make a move yourself then, if you like him so much?'

Sheila pulled a face but quickly recovered. 'They'll take us home in a taxi, Nano – that's got to be better than walking, hasn't it?'

'I'll walk it, Sheila, you can do your own thing,' Nano said, and Sheila made another face at her.

'Alright. We'll both walk, then.'

They announced an old-style waltz next; it blared out loud through the speakers:

'Out you come now, boys and girls! Around the house and mind the dresser! You're great company, tonight, God bless you, and all in great shape! Out you come again, we've Jimmy Shand and 'The Lights of Old Aberdeen' now but don't let them blind you!'

'Would you listen to that loudmouth?' said Sheila. 'He's like a child with a new toy!' Mike had come back over but there was no sign of Peter, and Nano felt pleased. Or at least she was until she spotted a balding, middle-aged bull of a man coming her way. She didn't like the look of this fellow nor the reek of beer coming off him. Still, she was reluctant to refuse his request for a dance. He pulled her towards him into a rough and powerful hug but his sweaty hands disgusted her in a way that even the dirtiest patient in the hospital wouldn't have. He wasn't a bad dancer, however, and her opinion of him would have been less harsh had he not started bossing her about from the outset.

'You're new around here, aren't you?'

He held his head to one side, examining her in a way that would have been funny if it hadn't been downright rude. He ran his eyes up and down her body like a cattle dealer considering a purchase at the fair. Worse than that was how tightly he gripped her, shamelessly. You got the senset that this man hardly ever got the chance to put his arm around a woman.

'I *am* new here,' Nano replied brusquely.

Mike and Sheila came spinning past them, Sheila's head leaning into Mike's shoulder, his cheek close to hers. For some reason, the sight of the couple being happy together irritated Nano even more than the bald fellow she was dancing with. There was no sign of Peter anywhere.

'I knew that you were new,' said the bald man, squeezing her tighter. He was dressed in a teal suit that would have suited a much younger man, while his starched white shirt and collar looked as though it were pinching that big well-fed neck. He wore a pair of corn-coloured shoes and a green tie embroidered with a shamrock.

'Are you by any chance a bit of a ladies' man?' asked Nano sharply but he didn't rise to her bait.

'If you don't look, you don't find,' he said, staring at her lasciviously.

'Try not to break my back, please,' Nano responded cooly. From the corner of her eye, leaning against the wall opposite, she spotted Peter looking-down-in-the-mouth. Compared to this past-it beast of a bloke, Peter was the perfect gentleman. Nano was sorry that she'd agreed to dance this time. You had to be careful not to give in to other people too readily; it was better to follow your own gut-instinct. The man's fingers raked down her back, and he was pressing against her so hard that she couldn't wait for the dance to be over in order to get away from him.

'Have you got a lad?' he asked her but Nano gave no reply. 'What do you say to me taking you home later?' he asked, kneading the small of her back with his big fingers.

'Have you any manners at all, man!'

She had grown to hate the sight of this fellow so much that, were it not for the difficulty of escaping him right then, Nano would have walked off the dance-floor altogether.

'No offence, girl! How about I take you to a café afterwards? I'll buy you supper.'

'Why would you do that? Do you think I'm hungry or something?' Nano was in danger of losing it with this fellow and giving him a piece of her mind.

'Hospital women are always hungry. You're working in a hospital, I'd say, aren't you?' the man replied.

'Bring some bread to the dances, so, and divide it out amongst the women, why don't you?' muttered Nano gruffly, but the man nearly choked himself laughing.

'Good one!' he said. I like a woman with a bit of spunk!'

'You like women full-stop, I'd say.' said Nano, and it was on the tip of her tongue to tell him that he should put an ad into the *Ireland's Own* as was the habit for some older lads like him, fellows who were either a a bit desperate or randy old goats.

'A nice lady like you, you'll keep the last dance for me, won't you? I'll take you home then, I'll get you a taxi if you like.'

A lift home to Galway was what she really needed now, Nano thought ruefully. Between taxis and suppers, wasn't she having the life of Riley over here really!

'I think that really,' she said, trying to get the correct level of sarcasm into her voice, 'it's already past your bed-time.'

The insult was just water off a duck's back to him, though. Instead, he pretended that Nano was totally hilarious and gave another hearty laugh.

'Too old, is that what you mean? You'll find out if that's true, girl, if you give me a go, I swear. You'll get a ride you'll never forget!'

Nano had heard plenty of earthy talk back in Ireland over the years, especially living out the country, but she was still staggered by the vulgarity and directness of this man. She blushed and tried to force herself from his grip as the music came to an abrupt end.

'You won't forget now – keep the last dance for me now, won't you?' the man repeated, giving her a final squeeze before releasing her.

'Go to hell, won't you?' said Nano, as she slipped away.

Sheila gestured to her from over by the bar and Nano went over to her, still bulling about the dirty way the man had spoken to her.

Mike and Peter were at the counter next to Sheila. Mike had just bought four bottles of lemonade with straws for everyone. He reached out to hand Nano her bottle and Sheila jokingly made as if to swipe it from him.

'What a pity we didn't meet these fellows earlier because then they'd have had to stand us something stronger than this stuff,' Sheila laughed, looking over at Nano as though sizing up her up mood.

'Here Nano, say "hello" to Mike; and you know Peter already, don't you?'

'Hello,' said Mike and gave her a warm smile. You'd swear he'd known her for years.

There was no doubt about it: Mike had a presence that Peter did not. He oozed energy and self-confidence. He seemed like a fine man in every way, Nano thought, handsome, with a head of curly black hair; he was muscular and well-built to boot. He was a lad who thought plenty of himself too, she thought, unlike his friend Peter.

'You were doing well for yourself there a little while ago,' said Sheila blowing air down into her lemonade and making it bubble up.

'You don't know the half of it! He wanted to go home with me and all – if you don't mind.'

'It's a pity Peter here wasn't as sticky as him,' Sheila responded, but Nano pretended she hadn't heard her. The hall was packed by now, and many of the men looked well-on-it, particularly the ones who'd only just come in. Every minute or two, someone let out a shout and tension filled the hall, as palpable as the tobacco smoke billowing around. This was the stage of the night, Nano had heard, when old resentments from home were renewed between different groups, rows that could break out into ugly fights. Peter, with a stutter, offered Nano another bottle of lemonade, but she politely declined, and Sheila took the opportunity to propose her own plan of action.

'It's just as well for you lads that we didn't meet you down in the pub because we'd have a hole in your pockets by now, I can tell you! Nano, they were down at the Black Bull; pity we didn't know that, isn't it? We'll steer clear of those two pissheads. Sure, we'll see them up at Club Biddy's later on?' Sheila said, giving Peter a dig of her elbow. 'Isn't it true for me, Pete?'

Peter opened his mouth to say something but the words just wouldn't come out. It was an awful thing, a stutter like that, Nano thought. And she could have choked Sheila right now with all her blather implying they were a nice cosy, little foursome. 'Harvest Home' was announced next and the dancers lined up opposite one another in formation.

Mike let out a whoop and stamped his feet in anticipation, 'Ababa-baba-boo!' Nano remembered she'd heard some Castlegar people shouting that at ceilidhs at the Commercial in Galway.

'Let's see you out on the floor now, everyone!'

Peter asked Nano to dance again, and she couldn't really refuse him. Her mood wasn't really about refusing anyone a dance, anyway; it was more to do with her having to stand her ground later on when they'd all be getting a taxi home. It was another Scottish tune now, one by

Jimmy Sand, even if the music was nowhere near as lively now as it'd been earlier in the night down at the Lord Nelson. Peter surprised Nano by how good he was at this one, given how awkward he'd been earlier with the quickstep. He was like a different person completely now that he was free on the dance-floor; he wasn't a bit awkward but rather quite confident. But while Peter was good, he wasn't a patch on Mike. Mike knew every move and step perfectly, and his footwork was flawless. He held himself straight as a lathe, and when he came to swing Nano at one stage during the dance, he lifted her straight off her feet as though she were light as a feather. She'd felt the muscles in his arms beneath his jacket, as hard as a rock. Mike was as powerful a man as Nano had ever seen. However, although Peter may not have been so well-built, Peter was in some ways kinder and more courteous, as Nano later found out.

Suddenly and without warning, a fight broke out. Different men faced off and began belting each other. It all happened so quickly, and it spread throughout the hall. All you could hear, the next minute, was women screeching and men bellowing; everyone pushing, pulling and planking one another. In such a melee, it was impossible to work out who was fighting who or how many people were involved. God knows how he'd got himself into it, but the bald fellow Nano had danced with earlier was right in the middle, blood streaming from his nose. He and a younger, blond-haired man, were squaring up to each other. Just a few lines of people were still dancing at the far end, and the fellow in charge of the records was wailing into the microphone, 'Get the priest, get Father Patrick!'. As Nano looked on, the middle-aged man laid the younger fellow out with a hammer-blow to the jaw before being attacked himself by another man, a lad who slammed him in the mouth violently.

'Stand back and give them room, won't you,' Mike called out, enjoying every minute of the show, but the priest soon came onto the scene. Aided by two other men, he waded in amongst the warring parties. The priest took hold of one black curly-haired bruiser, grabbed him by the collar and shoved him out the door before returning again to the fray. This was the first time Nano had ever seen a priest fighting. He was right in the middle of it; he clobbered one man who swung a punch at him and knocked him to the ground, letting him collapse in a heap at the priest's feet. Nano was shocked to see any man raise his fist to a priest. She'd always heard that the hand that'd strike a priest would wither away but it was obvious that these lads had no qualms about that. And it wasn't just one man who'd the gumption to attack the priest either because another fellow went for him as well. Father Begley was too fast for him, however, and before he could land his punch, the priest had grabbed him by the arm and bundled him out the door too. One of the priest's helpers clocked the bald fellow with a haymaker of a punch that knocked him for six. The man nearly fell against Nano but Peter caught her and pulled her out of his way; seconds later, and he too had been bundled out of the door. The fighting was over almost as quickly as it had begun.

'Are you okay?' Peter asked Nano with no stutter, as though the urgency of the moment had overcome it for the briefest of seconds.

'I am, thanks very much. I'm alright.'

'The Soldier's Song' was now playing on a scratchy old record, and the people all stood to attention, though there was fear of everyone staying quiet. Father Begley climbed up onto the small stage next to the man playing the records. The priest looked very solemn. He waited there until the National Anthem was finished and then raised his hands in the air. The Big Priest was a fine-looking man, tall, strong and charismatic; he would have stood out in any company. When he spoke, it went so quiet you could have heard a cat walk by. 'Friends and fellow-countrymen,' he said authoritatively. 'Tonight, we saw another example of the blackguardry that's giving us and our country a bad reputation over here, never mind our faith also! Is it any wonder that those people outside say that drinking and fighting is the favourite pastime of the Irish? Well, people, we have a responsibility, and a very heavy one at that – even if I say so myself – with regards to our country and our faith, and I'm not going to put up with this business anymore.'

Father Begley went quiet and momentarily scanned his audience.

'Some of the crowd who are always fighting seem to think that to be a mighty man, you have to be a hero and handy with your fists. Well, I don't see any of them with medals or trophies, and I don't see their name up in lights as boxers either. But they're still very keen on fighting, by all accounts!' The priest gave a short rueful laugh and a ripple of laughter went through the hall.

'Well, if it's training they want, then they'll get plenty of it here from now on because as soon as a fight begins back home, I always hand them out the gloves and tell them to fight fair and square, the same as civilised people. We'll know pretty quick then who's any good and who has champion-potential in them! Good night, now, to you all, straight home everyone!'

On the way back to the hospital in the taxi, Nano couldn't help going over what had happened earlier. The memory of the bald fellow fighting, dripping blood from his nose and trading punches with a man young enough to be his own son. It was pathetic, really, to see a man at his stage of life – who should have been married years ago and had his family raised – being bundled outside head-first. She didn't understand why but she felt sympathy for the poor fool. Mike and Sheila were already smooching in the back seat; they didn't have the patience to wait until they were alone. Peter had withdrawn into himself, back into that shy world of his. There wasn't a peep out of him. It was only up the road, but the taxi journey seemed to take a long time. It stopped at the hospital gate to let them out. Nano was in a quandary. She didn't know what to do to get away from the other three; she'd have a stern word about this to Sheila later, that's for sure. She steeled herself to say goodbye to the others but Mike put a spanner in the works, and did it so smoothly that she was powerless. He told them to go ahead as he paid the taxi-man: 'You lads go on there, I'll be in after you, in a minute.' And as if seizing the moment, Peter placed his hand gently on Nano's elbow and said, 'I'll-I'll g-g-go, go go a bit of t-the w-w-way way with you, if you don't mind.'

'It's hardly worth it,' Nano said, but she let him accompany her along the gravel path all the same. The darkness cloaked them and Nano felt embarrassed and nervous at the same time. The other two were in no hurry to follow them in, by the looks of it. Sheila and Mike were standing in the middle of the path, beneath the streetlamp at the entrance, their arms around one another, kissing. This was the first night, since arriving in Norwold, that Nano had found herself out this late, and she felt strangely anxious. She needed to get a grip on herself, she knew; it wasn't as if she was one of these dippy, flighty types who was always on for a bit of a shift. They'd come as far as the door of the living quarters, and Nano hoped that Peter would take the hint.

'Thanks for coming in this far with me,' she said to him, secretly regretting that it wasn't out at the gate that she'd said goodbye.

'S-Sure, th-th-that was the l-l-least I c-c-could do,' Peter replied. Nano could feel his body close to hers; there was something physical there; she could tell that he was attracted to her and a wave of desire went through her too. But she was better-off leaving now; there was no point in her hanging around out with here with him.

'Well, I have to be going in,' she said, hesitantly. 'Your friend Mike'll be waiting for you by the road now in a minute, won't he?' But no sooner were the words out of her mouth but Nano knew she'd made a mistake.

This was all the chance that Peter needed. 'H-H-He w-won't b-be in f-f-for a w-w-while yet, I'd s-say!'

Nano felt the aching loneliness behind Peter's words, and his longing to keep her there for another while. Worse still, she also sensed herself weakening.

'J-J-Just h-hang on a-a-another second,' Peter pleaded as though sensing her hesitation.

'I can't, Peter, I have to be going.'

'Just a s-s-second!' He took a packet of cigarettes out of his pocket and offered her one.

'I don't smoke, thanks.'

'D-d-don't go yet,' he pleaded again. 'Just w-wait one m-more m-m-minute!'

'One minute, so, Peter,' Nano heard herself saying, as though her voice belonged to someone else.

'C-c-come h-here for a s-second,' Peter said gently, and, like someone in a trance, Nano left the path and went over with him to the hospital's brick-wall, where they both leaned into its shadow. There was no sign of Mike or Sheila; they may have turned back through the gate.

'I can't be much longer,' said Nano.

'Arah, o-o-one m-m-minute won't do any harm,' Peter said, slipping his arm around her somewhat awkwardly.

'Peter… I have a lad back home; I shouldn't be here with you at all really.'

'He's a very l-lucky m-m-man,' Peter stuttered.

His words went right to the heart of her. 'That's not what he'd think if he could see me now,' Nano said. Peter's cheek was against hers, and whatever shame she'd felt a few minutes ago about being here with him deserted her completely as another wave of desire coursed through her. Peter turned to her and held her in his arms, as gently as one would do a child. She couldn't control herself anymore. Nano cuddled into him and they kissed one another passionately.

Chapter 9

Niall could feel a change coming over him already, despite his best efforts. All the hope and enthusiasm for work and getting ahead that he'd returned with from the army had faded, and in its place had come the sluggishness of the dole-crowd. At one time, the sight of the lads making the daily trip to the Labour Exchange and all that boredom and hanging-around would have got to Niall. Had they no bit of manly pride or purpose left in them that they could waste their days like this, just hanging around town or leaning against the wall down at the Parade? There'd been a few times recently when he'd lost his cool and let the others know what he really thought of them and the lazy round of their lives – more to vent his frustration than anything else. Not that he'd made the slightest impression on any of the others – especially not Mooney or Sullivan.

'What's up with you – have you got a bee in your bonnet or something, you're that prickly?' Mooney had asked Niall; 'can't you just cool it, take it easy now and then?'

'It's not easy to relax, Nick, when you haven't a red cent in your pocket,' Niall retorted bitterly.

'Bosco hasn't a penny to his name and look how happy he is.'

'Bosco wouldn't stir from that corner if a bomb hit it,' Mooney replied, cocking his head in Sullivan's direction. Sullivan was rubbing his hands together vigorously as though in anticipation; he kept glancing up and down the road as though someone might appear any minute and brighten up his day.

'You're no different, Mooney,' said Bosco over his shoulder. 'I don't see you wearing out much shoe leather going around looking for work – no more than anyone else!'

'From what I can see, you lads wouldn't do a stroke of work if you could get away it,' was Niall's sarcastic retort.

'Oh, but where in hell is all this work you're on about?' Mooney asked in a long-suffering voice; he was bored with the subject by now.

Needless to say, the grim truth was that there was no work available anywhere – that was the long and short of it. Niall had tried every factory and building site in the town, and then asked up at the hospital and the gasworks – there was nothing to be had in either place – and if it hadn't been for the pay being almost as bad as the dole, he'd have taken the job as a yard-boy that was going in one of the big shops of Vicar Street, a shop that the country people always frequented. It wasn't the endless hanging-around and idleness that bothered Niall most but rather the sense of shame in being unemployed. Despite himself, he felt less equal or deserving of things as the crowd who had jobs, as though because he wasn't working, he wasn't less entitled than them to food and drink. Sometimes, someone would ask Niall if there were any sign of him landing a job – or whether he'd tried such-and-such-a-place – and the more they reminded him of his predicament, the worse he felt. The more they kept on about it, the more it riled him, as though he were somehow obliged to that person. It drove him crazy.

Sometimes, when he couldn't take it anymore, Niall would go for a walk out into the countryside. Sometimes, he'd just follow his nose and walk for maybe ten miles or more. Or he'd take out his old army bicycle and go out cycling, southwards to Thomastown, to Inistogue or up into the hills somewhere on the border between Kilkenny and Carlow counties. One day he'd gone into Carlow town and asked for a job in the beet factory there. This had proved a waste of time – needless to say – because even if he'd landed a job there, he'd have had to move all the way to Carlow. He'd never have been able to do that journey every day, not on that old squeaky heavy bicycle of his. Another day, he went even further from home – as far as Athy – to see if there was anything going there. But there was no work available there, indeed the whole area appeared to be dying on its feet. His journey home again that day was thirty miles, uphill, mostly until he hit Castlecomer and by the time he'd reached the Comer, he was longing for a pint of porter – so badly that he nearly asked someone to lend him fourpence to add to the sixpence he had in his pocket. Some other day, he travelled south to a place about halfway between Kilkenny city and Thomastown, where he left his bicycle against the wall and went into a field that had a small hill at its centre. Standing on this hill, he fondly took in the expanse of countryside all-around – the Blackstairs mountains, piling up blue against the horizon to the south, and the tall humpback of Slievenamon over towards the west. He felt right then like the rightful heir to this whole rich countryside, certaintly as entitled to it as any of the biggest farmers in the area. This land was as much a part of his inheritance as anyone else's. This encompassed all that was in his purview and all that was beyond. Even though he was unsure of their exact locations, the Gaelic names to all those places came to him as a litany from long ago – *Cois Bhearhbha, Tigh Mhoilinn, Gráig na Manach, Sceach an Mhaistín, Bearna na Gaoithe, Cupanach, Ceannanas Osraí, Callan, Cill Mhanach* and *Tullyroan*. This was Niall's native land: his most favourite place in the entire world. Why should he leave her behind to make a living?

Intimations of his history and his ancestors would come to Niall as he cycled through the countryside. He'd spot an old abandoned cabin, its empty frame poking through the rotten thatch like the bones of some forgotten ancient animal. Niall would remind himself that Irish was most likely the language that had been spoken in that ruined cottage at one time, a lively rural dialect that had disappeared forever, leaving only traces within the English spoke there today, like jewels scattered and lost in the mud of the road. And, God, how terrible that a language should be lost! Even if your country was free from Rathlin Island down to the Great Blasket and from Loop Head to Howth Head, it was hardly worth it if the Irish language was gone. The Irish were a wounded race in its absence, a people robbed of their own history and genealogy, a beaten tribe. Daydreaming along these lines, Niall would have given anything to be able to return to that area in the the old times, to listen to those earlier generations of Irish speakers, the people who'd disappeared from this world along with their own language. Would he have been able to understand their speech; what might their dialect have been like? Sometimes, Niall played tricks on himself, just for a bit of fun, pretending that he was back in the middle of the nineteenth century and that the Irish language was what everyone still spoke there. One day, he took this craic so far that he spoke Irish to an old woman he cycled past on the way to the town. Naturally, he felt immediately mortified at his ridiculous behaviour. It occurred to him that he himself was no better than those generations before him that had abandoned their language. He himself could quite easily have done more to encourage people to speak their native language. What he had done was to just go with the flow, the same as everyone else nowadays. No wonder the Irish language was on its last legs – when Irish speakers themselves weren't promoting it or passing it on. Wasn't it through forcing their own language on people that foreigners had spread English here in the first place?

The loss of Irish was just one of Niall's many worries. Everything in his life was falling asunder; all the objectives that he'd set himself just a few years earlier seemed more unrealistic and further away than ever. Look at the way that Butler had screwed him over by disappearing from Ireland overnight; he hadn't even had the decency to send him a letter of apology. There was the utter lack of work. And, to top it all off, there was no sign of Peg Dinneen anywhere: where had she gone?

Since he'd come home from the army, not one day – nor even part of a day – had gone by when Niall hadn't hoped to run into Peg. He was so keen on seeing her again that his eyes had deceived him once or twice and he'd thought he'd seen her at a distance downtown. But it proved not to be her after all – just another girl who looked very like her. He'd gone up to this woman, to see if it was Peg – his heart pounding with nerves – only to be disappointed. Surely he should have spotted her by now? She must have had some business bringing her into town by now, mustn't she? If Niall had gone around Redmondstown once, looking for her, he'd gone ten times. Maybe she had left for England, just like all those others who'd emigrated in recent months. Niall found that thought hard to countenance. That would mean utter disaster: for her to have left Ireland altogether. At the end of the day, wasn't it because of her – more than anyone else – that he'd returned to Kilkenny? After all, he wouldn't have been half as enthusiastic about Kieran Butler's plan hadn't his head been full of thoughts about Peg. She's been on his mind since they'd met for the very first time.

That had been when he was home on leave. That was early last summer on a glorious sunny day – the sky like a great beacon of sunny-blue – so hot that the sweet smell of melting tar filled the air. Niall had been at a loose end, unsure whether to spend an hour in the public library down on John's Quay or to go out into the countryside for a walk. He was just standing at the corner of the Parade when Peg had passed by, pushing a bicycle with a bag of groceries on its back-carrier. Their eyes had met, and Peg had given him a big inscrutable smile that had left his heart pounding. Niall was so taken with her mysterious smile and her beautiful dark eyes that he'd followed her right up the street, almost as if he was in a daze. He didn't say anything to the crowd on the corner because you couldn't stir without them knowing about it. He didn't care, and Peg must have guessed that he was following her because, rather than hopping back onto her bike, she continued walking until Niall'd caught up and begun chatting her up. Niall was very nervous initially, but instead of telling him to go to hell or asking him what he was playing at, Peg had responded to Niall's small-talk in a nice and friendly manner. Niall was on cloud nine because this girl was a stunner, someone who'd turn any man's head. In fact, she had a certain something that made him instantly crazy about her. They walked out past the edge of town together, Niall's heart pounding in his chest. He was almost delirious. The whole thing was like a beautiful dream with the magnificent summer countryside as its backdrop. If Peg and Niall had made any real conversation that day, Niall didn't remember now. Eventually, they'd come to the bend in the road near the old bridge, and Peg had stopped as if to say that she didn't want him to walk any further. They were hesitant and shy with one another for a while as they listened to the small stream wind its way musically beneath them and the breeze whispering in the trees overhead. Peg had one foot on her pedal and said something about going home because they were expecting her when Niall plucked up the courage to put his arm around her and kiss her. She leaned her bike against the wall of the bridge and kissed him back. They stood there smooching until Peg's bike slipped onto the ground. She straightened it again and turned back to Niall. His heart was pounding with excitement; this was almost too good to be true. It was pure bliss. They stood there and kissed one another tenderly until Peg reluctantly pulled herself away. She straightened her hair for a second and whispered to Niall in a throaty voice that she had to be going. One of her sisters would come out to look for her if she delayed any longer. She gave him a parting kiss and promised that she'd be at the bridge again at eight o'clock that night if he wanted to see her. Niall stood and watched her longingly until she disappeared from view. He was cracked about her, and that feeling lasted the rest of the afternoon.

Niall had waited at the bridge for more than an hour that night but the experience proved to be the longest and most torturous hour of his life. It was a total flop. She never showed up. He'd felt so anxious waiting for her that he smoked all the cigarettes he had left without really enjoying any. And even as he'd turned back in disappointment and made for home, Niall kept glancing over his shoulder in the hope that Peg might appear out of the gloom at any moment.

Although he'd no leave left at that stage, Niall had come close to not returning to his army unit in Galway at all. But then, a few days later again, Niall had received at his barracks a short letter from Peg. It was a short but loving note excusing herself for letting him down that evening. An aunt of hers had come from Knocktopher on an unexpected visit that evening and she hadn't been able to get away. She asked Niall to write back to her to reassure her that he wasn't angry for her having let him down. This note had seemed to be some wonderful gift in Niall's eyes, and he went around with it folded into the pocket of his uniform for weeks onwards – until it eventually fell apart. He'd sent a long, loving letter back to Peg on return, and his eyes remained peeled for every postal delivery to the barracks for days after that.

But it had all proved pointless; he'd never heard anything back from Peg again, despite sending her two further letters within the space of four weeks. Niall's efforts at pursuing her had come to naught. That same afternoon he'd met Butler in Bridge House to discuss their future plans, Niall had gone out walking near Redmondstown in the hope that he might run into Peg. Even now, Niall had to admit that he was still a bit confused about the whole thing. He couldn't understand how Peg could have been all over him one minute but have nothing to do with him the next. He'd replayed the scene that evening on the bridge so many times that he was almost dizzy. But instead of his love for Peg fading, his hankering had got stronger. She was on his mind day and night. She was the last person he thought about on going to bed at night, and the first one, on waking; she was like an obsession. He'd even scribbled her name on random scraps of paper like a teenager in love for the very first time. Once he'd scrawled it in big letters in the wet sand as he walked along the beach one afternoon. Peg was his ideal, his dream-woman – the only person in the world that he cared about. Any experience he'd had with any woman he'd ever met in Ireland was as nothing compared to the bliss of kissing her that day.

But where had she disappeared to? There was no sign of her anywhere! He couldn't ask after her or make enquiries about her without revealing to the other lads that he'd an eye on her – and there was no way he was going to do that. There was hardly any family within three miles of Kilkenny city that Bosco Sullivan wasn't familiar with, and it would be all over town within minutes if Niall were to give him even the slightest hint.

Niall had to remind himself that he didn't have much to offer a potential girlfriend. If you wanted to go out with a woman around here, you needed to be able to take her to the pictures or a dance fairly regularly. It wasn't as though Peg would be like some of those women he'd meet during his term of duty – women who were happy enough to spend half the night just wandering around the streets of Galway or going 'out to grass' – as they called it – for a smooch.

Every time Niall thought of his finances, it just reminded him of Butler's dishonesty again and the mess he'd left in him. Niall would then get even more annoyed and curse himself endlessly for being so foolish. His mother had been right; there wasn't a bigger idiot in Ireland than him. It seemed as if he'd no control over his life anymore, like an old stick someone had thrown into the river and had just drifted away. It was though there were some invisible barrier keeping him away from the world of work and those people who'd some sort of plan for their lives. Not only was he embarrassed that he had no job but also because the job situation was beyond his control. Whenever he passed a building site, Niall felt embarrassed seeing the men busy with their construction work. Then he would pull himself together again, throw back his shoulders and put a confident steer on himself again. And even then, he found himself making up excuses. Whenever people asked him about work, he'd tell them that he was looking around and had a couple different possibilities lined up – anything rather than admit he was at his lowest ebb and at his wits end regarding the job-front.

In all honesty, by now it was with the dole-heads that he felt most at home. At least with them, you didn't have to pretend nor feel embarrassed, because they were all in the same boat. That is not to say that they didn't annoy him quite often – they were so lost, lacking in motivation and liable to extinguish any hope you might entertain job-wise. The latter arose when they were reminded of their own failure. For instance, Niall emerged from the public library at John's Quay one day, having just read a story in one of the British Sunday papers. He'd gone over to Mooney straight away to get his opinion.

'I've just read a piece in the *Sunday People*, Nick,' Niall had said, excited. 'They're getting seventeen pounds a week in the BSA factory over in Coventry! Seventeen pounds, boy!'

'Rubbish,' Mooney had told him. 'Don't believe that old rubbish!'

'Oh – but sure, didn't I just read it now in the paper, Nick? Go down and read it yourself if you don't believe me.'

That'd be some wage for anybody, Niall had thought. He'd make up the money that Butler had stolen from him within a fortnight at that rate: seventeen pounds a week – that was £68 a month! A year across the water, and multiply that amount by two and you could get £500, once lodgings and everything else were accounted for. £500! Then you could come back home and set up some kind of business, something proper – forget about that hand-to-mouth existence with a horse-and-cart. You could buy a lorry for that kind of money, and then you'd never look back.

'So the newspaper's your Bible now, then?' Mooney had asked him sarcastically.

'Sure, it wouldn't be in the paper if it wasn't true; it's not like it's something that can't be confirmed or denied.'

'Seventeen pounds, is it?' Bosco Sullivan had asked, tightening the knot on the old tie that held up his trousers.

'There were men getting that when I was over there last.'

'Well, you weren't one of them, anyway,' said Mooney to Bosco cynically, trying to kill the BSA story. 'You didn't budge from the Hammersmith Broadway the whole time you were there! Stood there against the wall was where he was, Niall, the same as always. He would take the world by storm when he left here – going to "make a pile of money". You would've sworn he was heading for America, the way he went on. Going around all lonesome-like and shaking hands with everyone before he left....'

'You're so full of shit, Mooney! Don't bother listening to that coward, Niall, I didn't tell anyone that I was leaving before I went, even; I wouldn't go around telling everyone my business like that.'

'Sure, didn't twenty of them go across the water one weekend,' said Mooney, enjoying the memory. 'All of them wearing their George Wimpey labels on their coats, as big as saucers! They were like the crowd you see let out of the Mental Home for the day, out to thin turnips! That's the nearest thing they'd have reminded you of, I'm not joking!'

'Ara, shite!' Sullivan had responded.

'The fellow from Wimpey who was in charge of them, Niall, he was like a man driving cattle to the fair; all he was lacking was a blackthorn stick to drive them onto the train. And I wouldn't mind, but this fellow didn't do a stroke of work over there – even though he didn't have to spend a penny of his own money to get there! Leaning against the wall of the Hop Poles is how he spent his time over there, the same as if he was holding up the wall of Paddy's Pub right this minute!'

'You're a mine of information for a fellow who wasn't even there,' Bosco had replied sulkily.

'Oh, sure, doesn't the whole town know about it! Wasn't it all over the place? Just ask the Sniveller Deniffe!'

'The Sniveller Deniffe, is it? A man who never went a half-mile down the road from a cowpat! Sure, what the hell would he know about anything over there?'

'He knows as much as you do about it, and that's not saying much. And anyway, the story came back here, don't you worry! Sure, the whole town was in stitches laughing at you, man!'

'Let's get back to the BSA now, Nick, please,' Niall had said but he might as well have been talking to the wall – because Mooney was on a roll.'

'And that wasn't the half of it, Niall – wait'll you hear…! He only stayed over there three weeks, and the day he came home, he got a hackney from the station, a hackney to go up to Ormonde Park, if you don't mind! As if none of us had ever seen a car before! There he was with his head out the window as if he was an archbishop blessing the people or something and – you won't believe this, Niall… his head out the window, singing, "There's no place like home!"

'Bollocks,' Bosco had said, spitting onto the road.

'And apart from that,' Mooney had added, afraid that the craic had gone out of his story far too quickly, 'would you believe the bastard didn't have a ha'penny to rub together when he got home? His mother had to pay the hackney man's half-crown and there was a huge row afterwards because they hadn't a penny in the house!'

'Yeah,' said Sullivan with a grimace – and that's all that was killing you, Mooney – that I didn't bring back enough money to top up your supply of porter!'

'Not even one bloody pint,' Mooney had said in disgust.

'But lads – listen, wouldn't it be well worth heading over there if you can earn that kind of money? Seventeen pounds a week!' said Niall.

'Oh, but even if there is that kind of money to be had over there, it's the educated man who's getting it; they're not going to hand out that sort of cash to every Paddy that arrives off the boat! The Englishman isn't that soft, no way!'

'I knew men who were getting that in London,' Sullivan had responded, 'some of them were getting more than that, even!'

'You weren't one of them, anyway,' Mooney had said.

'I had my own ways of making money, don't you worry about that, Mooney,' Bosco had retorted.

'Sure you did – going around begging. The whole town knows that. "Bosco Sullivan's bumming fags over there in Hammersmith!"'

'I used to go to the greyhound racing,' said Bosco, 'down to the White City and out to Haringey! I often had twenty pounds in my pocket coming home.'

Bosco had stepped forward onto the path and imitated the signs that the tic-tac man made on the race-course.

'Get in out of that, and don't make a booby of yourself in front of the whole world,' Mooney had told him, but Bosco continued his signalling.

'I earned thirty pounds one night.'

'"Thirty" my shite!'

'I suppose there's no point in expecting a word of sense out any of you,' Niall had told Mooney in disgust.

'Oh, Christ, what do you expect?' Mooney had exclaimed. 'Didn't I just tell you that you wouldn't get that kind of money or nowhere near ten pounds if you went over. It's the men who are working their whole lives over there who get the big money, not the innocent little gobshites who've just arrived off the boat from Ireland!'

'Bad job, that,' Niall had said despondently.

'They have to take tax out of that – however much you make – not like here in Ireland,' Mooney had responded, as though he almost enjoyed taking the wind out of people's sails.

'That's true, income tax does have to be taken out of it,' Sullivan had confirmed in a serious tone.

'And lodgings,' Mooney had reminded him, unless you do what this layabout did when he was over there, which is sleep outside.'

'I never slept outside anywhere,' Sullivan had replied, deeply insulted. 'I had good lodgings in London – number ninety-eight Feningdale Crescent, WII. Run by a Scottish woman named Mrs Gillespie: you can write to her, Mooney, if you want to check it out!'

'I will write to her,' Mooney had said, deprecatingly, 'don't you worry!'

They went silent momentarily, their backs to the wall, each man more trapped and helpless than the next. Would they really go to England now anyway, even if they were taken over free of charge and given decent work as the Wimpey crowd had been that time? Or were they as as good as useless; unemployable now that they'd been out of work so long? Of the three of them, Mooney was in the best position, but what was the point in him going over there when all he'd do there – as likely as anything else – was go on the drink? Wouldn't he be better off staying at home somewhere where he wouldn't kill himself by going mad on the drink? As for Sullivan, he had laziness in his blood, of course, even if he was still fairly strong and athletic. That old man, the Sniveller Deniffe, was probably the worst waster among them, even on a good day. Niall couldn't remember the Sniveller ever doing any work – unless you counted going around all day at the fair or market carrying a sandwich-board or shaking a big brass bell advertising something around town. The Khyber Brennan was getting old, alright, but there was no excuse whatsoever, really, for the other former soldier, Mikeo Linnane: he was a big stack of a man who'd plenty of energy left in him, if he hadn't been so lazy.

As for Moscow Barry, he'd been left injured so that he lost the use of one hand after a bad row at the gate of the shoe factory during a strike more than ten years ago. His right-hand hung from his side without any feeling in it. Moscow Barry was one of the few who hadn't crossed the picket-line or given up on the strike when the factory manager had issued an ultimatum to the workers to return or lose their jobs. Barry had stood his ground that day, with the result that his arm had been badly broken. The bones in his hand had never healed properly and his arm had wasted away until there was little strength or muscle left in it. Moscow had compensated for this by strengthening his good hand, however, and he could still adapt and do a lot of jobs if the work in England was indeed as plentiful as they claimed. Wouldn't this have been better than him standing here every day on the corner, deafening people with his constant preaching about the Soviet Union – as he always called Russia – that, and forcing copies of the *Soviet Weekly* onto people who'd never read anything in their lives?

Niall had given a short sardonic laugh and shaken his head. Hadn't he himself changed a lot recently if he were now encouraging people to go over to England? Life was strange, no doubt about it!

'See that useless bollix over there; he has it in for us,' Mikeo Linnane had said, nodding in the direction of Garda Moriarty who was standing outside the Bank of Ireland even though there was little traffic on the road to keep him busy.

'Oh, isn't he the bollix himself to you lads?' Niall had said. 'I don't see that fellow bothering you lads in any way; why've you got it in for him?'

'He deserves it, the ugly mug,' Sullivan had said. 'He's a bad egg, if ever there was one!'

Mooney stirred himself momentarily and rubbed his palms together. 'Don't frighten the poor man anyway, whatever you do,' he'd said sarcastically. 'Big tough lads like yourselves!'

Niall realised that he was trapped inside an invisible maze, a labyrinth from which he could never break free.

Niall was at home, sitting in the kitchen drinking tea.

'They're forever talking about freedom,' said Niall's brother,

Andrew O'Connell, draining the last of the sugar from the bottom of his cup. 'But what use is it?'

Mrs O'Connell scowled in disgust but Niall's other brother, Maurice, took the bait. 'It's worth everything,' he said; 'there's nothing in the world as valuable as freedom!'

It was Saturday night and Maurice was washed and dressed, a big Windsor knot securing his tie, his hair swimming in hair oil. Andrew wasn't ready yet; he was still wearing his greasy dungarees, even though his mother had left out clean clothes for him. Andrew worked as a lorry helper for Texaco, although that wouldn't be for much longer; he'd be laid off as soon as he reached eighteen, when he became entitled to a pay rise. It was only recently that Andrew had got a bit contrary, refusing to take off his work clothes and constantly making a fool out of Maurice; irritating him whenever he could. It must have had something to do with his leaving his teenage years behind, but Andrew had become crankier recently, Niall thought; maybe this was becuase he hadn't managed to secure a better job than either of his two brothers, despite the fact that he'd spent two years longer than them at school.

'Well, what kind of freedoms have we now that we didn't have before, when England ruled us?' Andrew asked Maurice. It wasn't so much a question as a statement or wind-up.

'We've every freedom,' Maurice replied, stubbornly. 'You can hold your head up high in front of the whole world now; you can say that you're an Irishman and you're proud of it!'

'Sure, but that was true when England was in charge too,' said Andrew, so matter-of-factly that it annoyed Maurice more than if he'd come back to him really aggressively. This was a deliberate tactic of Andrew's, needless to say. 'But what use is it – this freedom? It won't put bread on the table, will it?'

'We didn't have much bread in England's time, either, did we – back when people were being evicted from their houses and the corn taken out of the country during the Famine. Did we now?'

'You're going back a long way now, Maurice,' Andrew said, as if he were speaking to a small child. 'All of that happened a long time ago. English rule was fairly easygoing and relaxed by the time that we got our freedom.'

'"Easygoing and relaxed"!' Maurice exploded. 'The death-cap, the gallows and the scourge. People dying on the side of the road and the corn leaving the country and being sent over to England? If that's a nice relaxed regime, boy, I wouldn't like to see a tough one, that's for sure!'

'Now, you're going back a hell of a long way,' said Andrew in the same ever-patient tone that he knew would annoy Maurice even more. 'England wasn't that bad for the last hundred years or so.'

'Really?! Isn't it less than a hundred years since O'Donovan-Rossa had his food thrown into him on the floor of his prison cell? Thrown onto the floor as if he was a dog! And sure, it's not even a hundred years since the Black and Tans were here torturing us!'

'Yeah, of course,' Andrew replied, again in his matter-of-fact voice. 'But these things happen during times of war and rebellion. Anything that the Tans did to us, we did to one another after that too, and the ancient Gaels were as able as the English when it came to attacking and killing one another, let me tell you. Freedom per se is what I mean, boy, and you didn't answer my question. What freedom do we have right now that we didn't have when the English were in charge? Can't you even give me one example?'

Niall had heard this same old argument plenty of times before down at the corner, and it was a refrain that was getting more frequent all the time, it seemed, the more that the country was going down the tubes, and the more England improved. The Irish people had a much better spirit about them during the war period, people said, even if they weren't sure whether England might attack them or not.

Maurice was stumped for a minute and went quiet momentarily but then retorted triumphantly. 'I can think of one freedom that you didn't have under English rule, and it's not even a hundred years ago or anything like it either. That's the freedom to write your name and address in Irish on your donkey-cart; now, that's something that you weren't allowed to do! – *"Lá aonaigh an Earraigh's mé ag taisteal go triopallach, trasna an droichid i Muileann na hAbhann"* – that song that we had at school, remember?' It looked like Maurice had won his case – he was so happy with this latest turn in the argument – but Andrew shook his head.

'I do remember,' he said. 'There was a court case about it, I think. It was Pearse who defended that man. I don't think it wasn't because his name was printed in Irish on his cart that the man was charged, though. It was because the Irish-language version wasn't compatible with the official one or whatever was written on his birth certificate. It was something to do with his official identity, little Maurice, and, most likely the man was trying to get one over on the local authorities, and they'd got wind of it.' Andrew gave a false yawn, adding to the insult of his earier mock-patience with Maurice. 'Anyway, that example doesn't relate to you or any of us either. You don't have a donkey-cart, Maurice, to be putting your name on – whether in Irish or English.' Andrew gave a small false cough and glanced over at Niall: 'Even people who should have donkey-carts or horses don't have them these days, never mind, the likes of you, who has no cause to have one anyway!'

'You've a sharp tongue on you, Andrew,' Mrs O'Connell declared.

Andrew's smart-alec comments carried no weight with Niall. All he was thinking about was how best to squeeze a few shillings out of his brother. Niall ignored half of what Andrew said to him, anyway; it was all bluster and nothing else.

As often happened, however, her son's blather had roused Mrs O'Connell to action. She got up from the table and began gathering the dishes. 'You're a great crowd altogether,' she said in an irritated voice. 'The house here is falling down around us and you couldn't care less, the lot of you! Instead of going down to talk to someone in the Town Hall about the new house, wouldn't you be better-off getting down on your knees in the church below and saying a prayer so that we don't have to stay here forever amongst the pigeons? Or is just rubbish talk that you're interested in? We've got Saint Joseph, the patron saint of the homeless, if you could actually be bothered to pray to him for help –'

'Saint Joseph, is it, Mam?' Andrew replied. 'He's no use, sure, wasn't he the one who failed even to get lodgings for himself and the Virgin, never mind getting a council house for us lot?'

Mrs O'Connell set down the tin basin that she used for washing the dishes and blessed herself solemnly; then she looked across at the picture of the Sacred Heart above the fireplace and prayed in a low voice – seeking reparation for Andrew's blasphemy – that's if she really believed that it was a form of blasphemy. Niall was familiar with these antics on his mother's part; you wouldn't know sometimes whether she actually secretly enjoyed these minor dramas…! The other day she'd come downstairs with an old copy of the *Soviet Weekly* that she'd found in a box under his bed; she'd held it away from her, between thumb and forefinger as though she were holding something diseased. She wouldn't have the Atheist's gospel under the roof of her house, she said. Now she knew why Niall's faith had waned. Andrew was punching his chest, enjoying this whole pantomime whether he'd won the argument or not. But it was on Niall that Mrs O'Connell now turned, as if he were the one responsible for Andrew's stupidity.

'Of course, it's no surprise that you've no respect for God or man, Niall, especially bearing in mind your state the other night: in at midnight and barely able to walk through the door properly, and you twisted-drunk for all the world to see!'

'A scandal, no doubt about it,' added Andrew quietly.

'We were all expecting you since eight o'clock – your tea ready there on the table for you – and none of us knew whether you were alive or dead until you fell in the door like some kind of a tinker. Is it any wonder that your brother has turned out the way he has – his work-clothes still on him on Saturday nights and no talk of him going to Confession or anything – like some kind of pagan or something!'

'A "scandal", is it Andrew?' she suddenly turned on him. 'It is a bloody scandal, it doesn't matter how much you joke about it!'

'In fairness, Mam, I think Andrew's problems go a lot further back than that,' Niall said, searching the depths of his pockets in the hope of finding a cigarette butt. I mean, I wasn't here for the last three years to give him scandal, was I?' Niall pulled closer to the fire and gave the cinders a poke. He didn't even have a fourpenny bit to his name, to go to the pictures, even, never mind the price of a smoke or a pint. The claustrophobia of this small house and his brother's shenanigans were getting on his nerves.

The taper on the paraffin lamp sputtered on, and the smell filled the kitchen. Andrew was at the door, rubbing his stubbly chin with his greasy fist.

'I'm going to head down to the Green, I think. Just to see who's around,' Niall announced.

'Like that, is it? Without a wash or anything? We might be living in a dump but that doesn't mean that you've to go out looking like a tramp,' said Mrs O'Connell. Just like her to somehow link everything back to the issue of the new house, Niall thought. 'I suppose,' she went on, pouring water from the kettle into a small basin, 'that it'd never occur to any of you that there's confession on Saturday night, or has Karl Max replaced Our Lord now for you two?'

Neither lad responded. Instead, Andrew glanced over at Niall and produced a half-crown from his dungaree pockets and flung it in the air towards him. Niall grabbed it in mid-air and gave Andrew a grateful wink. 'I suppose you'll be getting hammered again tonight, Niall?' said Mrs O'Connell, rattling whatever was in the basin.

'It's a long time since it was that cheap, Mam,' said Niall glancing over towards Maurice, who reluctantly threw another half-crown his way.

'Sound man,' Niall said, jumping to his feet. He put on his jacket and planted a kiss on his mother's cheek. 'Don't you worry, I'll be grand – it'll just be a few nice, quiet ones tonight – and a bit of a chat. That's all. I'll be home before twelve.'

'Like Cinderella,' said Andrew from the door. It was a really beautiful night out, the sky as clear as moonlight, one of those that raised your spirits and made you glad to be alive. The moon was a great orb in the sky, bright over the tops of the houses and Castle walls and out across the River Nore that sparkled in the dark. There was something almost divine about this moonlight. It radiated magnificently across this strange and ghostly country in such an exquisite manner that Niall felt an urge to stretch out his hands in its direction and reach up in a vain attempt to touch it. He longed to draw it all to himself, every fragment of its pagan essence, to drink it up into every fibre of his being so that he too could become pure spirit. The barriers that separated past and future would be no more, Niall imagined, the entire world crystallised forever in the quintessence of the moment as if eternity had revealed itself in all its magnificence. In that very moment, Niall became aware of a truth more fundamental to his nature than any other; all the wealth of the world was nothing compared to the ability to celebrate the magic and mystery that was this distilled moment in time – and to make of it a form of poetry.

Later that night, Niall had lit a cigarette and was leaning against the wall of the bridge over the river Nore. He stared down into water into the yellow-bright reflection of the moon. It was beautiful. Staring into the sparkling water, a series of exotic images and shapes sparkled in the water below. He could have stayed there forever. It had been nearly midnight when Paddy Neary had shown them out of Bridge House. Not that Niall had been in any hurry to get home. He was in great form and reluctant for the night to end; he felt at peace with himself and at one with the world around him. They'd had a great time in Paddy's – one of the best – he'd drunk five pints that he'd paid for himself and Paddy Neary had stood him another one out of respect. Not only that but Paddy had given him good advice about the failed project with Butler. He'd told him not to get too down about it, in the first place. These things happened to the best of people, Paddy said. He'd heard of the same thing happening to a man in the States, who'd lost way more money than Niall had. But that same man had built himself up from scratch again, Paddy confirmed. And Niall would recover too. The fellow in the States had determination and backbone; and if you'd these traits in you, you'd always come back again – in time. It wasn't that different to the crowd mentioned in the Bible, each of whom had been given a certain sum of money, but only one of whom had put their money to good use. And, in the heel of the hunt, and Sikey Butler's son would have no luck for what he'd done. Niall had welcomed Paddy's take on the situation, even if he couldn't tell him straight out. Stupidly, however – as if another person inside him had taken over momentarily – Niall had stupidly hinted to Pat that he might well be giving another business idea a go before long.

Niall flicked the butt of his cigarette into the bright whirl of the river and took stock of the unbelievable mess he'd made of things. That small butt of cigarette would float off with the current, disintegrating as it drifted closer and closer to the sea. The paper and the tobacco, tiny shreds becoming entangled in the sodden bits of branch and silt of the riverbed below; over time, they'd change shape and substance to become something else. At one time, that piece of paper had been the tiniest sliver of tree while the grains of tobacco had been a minute section of plant; and yet, it was in the nature of things that such matter could never be destroyed: it simply assumed a different form.

Niall knew this much from the little science he still retained from school. He was drawn to such philosophical musings now, as was often the case after he'd had his fill of porter – whatever the hell was in that stuff, it seemed to get his imagination going somehow.

'A concept,' Niall said to himself aloud, but then lowered his voice. It was the 'concept' that he wanted to bring to mind now – that particular feeling that lay somewhere between emotion and understanding. George Berkeley had spent part of his life as a visiting teacher in the local Protestant school in Kilkenny and he'd had a theory that this world was all in the mind and that nothing else existed beyond that or in the form of a concrete reality – or his theory went something like that, anyway! It was the mystery of the tobacco and those tiny flakes of paper that concerned him right now, however – those remnants of the Woodbine that would never coalesce together as one.

He sighed and lifted his head to take in the world around him: the noble silhouette of the castle outlined in the golden, heavenly light of the moon. He heard the sound of muted laughter and the rattle of a bicycle on its way across the bridge. There were two people – a man and a woman – and Niall saw them clearly as they passed. He saw the woman's face as clear as day. It was Peg Dinneen and a friend of hers. They were laughing together, and Peg was gazing up at him in as though he were the only man in the world.

Chapter 10

Trevor's wages were two pounds, one crown a day. This was one crown a day more than the majority of the men working in his work-gang were getting, and a half-sovereign more than the man who did the least work. From eight in the morning until six at night – travel-time excluded – were the normal hours of work between spring and early winter when the day got shorter and they finished at five o'clock instead. If there was anything unjust about this system of pay, there were never any disputes about it, unless they happened in the pub when the men were on the drink and jealousy reared its ugly head. The tribalism and sense of pride amongst the Irish were the main reasons that this system wasn't a much greater source of tension: the man earning two pounds never let on that he wasn't getting the highest rate, and the least well-paid were equally loathe to admit they were at the bottom of the heap. It was the custom on such jobs that each worker was handed his pay packet face-down so that none of the others got to know how much his neighbour was getting. It was only the Irish employers who utilised this system, which they'd devised in a spirit of cleverness and greed – and simply because they could get away with it. In this way, they made certain that all their men were always competing with one another, and it actually created a mindset that was detrimental to the workers. If there was a certain degree of arrogance about the Irish employers, it wasn't the English type arrogance whereby the contractor held himself aloof from his men but rather the snobbery of the countryman, a strange mixture of camaraderie and subjugation. Often, especially at the beginning of a job, the boss would appear on-site on the first day to make sure that everything was going smoothly and to speed up the work if necessary. On a day when they might have got the trenches dug and been ready to lay the cables, for example, many of the bosses wouldn't hesitate to jump down into a trench alongside their men – even in their Sunday best – and give a helping hand. Signs on it too! Such gestures lent the contractors even greater status, especially given the wealth they'd already accumulated.

'That's the boy that's not afraid to get his hands dirty or get up to his ankles in shit.' That was the tribute that McAllister and his like were given when the men discussed work amongst themselves over a few pints down in the Mother Black Cap or the Bedford Arms in Camden Town.

Not to say that all the men held their employers in such high regard – needless to say. The more naïve lads might have thought that way, but there were others who saw through their employers' clever ways and privately hated them. Those would say about Paddy McAllister that he would embarrass workers. Even wind them up on the day that they were laying cable, say, or some other big job was going on, calling out with a 'Hey, you crowd that are on the big money, up here to the front!' Hardly anyone hung back then, their pride ensuring they put a good face on the money side of things! There was no talk whatsoever among the navvies of solidarity when it came to their rights, and no chance whatsoever that they'd join a union. They'd argue that there was so much work going in England, that if you didn't like a job, you could simply leave and go elsewhere. *Don't stay if it doesn't suit you* was their motto – it really was just a waste of time for the union crowd to try and argue for their rights! The reason that these men were so reluctant to join wasn't that they lacked courage or were too shy to argue their case. Rather, they didn't see any need for these organisations: why bother with negotiations, regulations or unions?

Or with going on strike – an even stupider idea – when there was so much work around? You wouldn't be idle for as long as two days if you left your job. For these men, this emphasis on individual rights was even worse than group agitation. Wasn't the man who left his job on the grounds of poor pay and conditions only improving matters for his replacement?

As a rule, on any given day, Trevor Nee and Thomas Mullen would have dug well over twenty yards trench of around five feet depth and over two feet width. Additionally, they'd refill the trench once the pipes had been laid and then firm down the soil again with that noisy, unwieldy contraption they called the Jumping Jenny. Trevor and Mullen had been doing just that when Paddy McAllister came on-site, the Jackeen beside him in the car. Trevor had been shovelling away as fast as Billy-oh, with Seán Festy's son coming behind him with the machine, pounding the ground with a powerful *bum-bump! bum-bump!* The Jumping Jenny came to a sudden halt and Mullen had whistled at his work comrade.

'Look out Trevor! Look who's here!' Trevor straightened his back as Paddy McAllister's car approached. McAllister was at the wheel but Trevor couldn't clearly see the man next to him. 'That there is the bastard that beat Walter Seán Jimmy,' Mullen went on, starting up the Jumping Jenny again.

'Is that him, by Christ?' asked Trevor between his teeth. The car snaked slowly towards them. As was his habit, McAllister was there to have a good look at how the work was going, but Trevor still couldn't see who was sitting next to him, blinded as he was by the sun's reflection on the windscreen. The car came to a stop and McAllister got out. He walked up to the top end of the trench, where the ganger Mike Dudley Stephen was overseeing two men who were attaching a fitting to the end of a water pipe. The Jackeen stayed put in the car, the window down and his elbow jutting out. 'That's him now, is it?' Trevor repeated, putting down his shovel for a second.

'That's him the bollocks, Trevor.'

'I might as well go and see this bastard for myself, so,' said Trevor, walking slowly in the direction of the car, nice and casual. The Jackeen didn't pay the slightest attention to this man who was heading his way, not until Trevor was right next to him. He was a big sturdy-looking stack of a man, a skinhead who oozed pride and self-regard from every pore. If he sensed anything or was the slightest bit nervous about Trevor, you certainly wouldn't have thought it from his expression or the way he went on sitting there. Trevor peered in at the Jackeen, and the Dubliner stared back at him just as aggressively. Then, as though it had dawned on him who this man was, the Jackeen went for the door. Trevor was too quick for him and grabbed the handle, jamming it upwards. The man inside tried his damnedest to get the door open but Trevor gave a snarling laugh and pressed against it in an iron grip. The two men stared one another down and the Jackeen's face reddened as he strained against the door, trying to force it open. The muscles in Trevor's arms tautened as he leaned his weight against it from outside. Christy Power was trapped inside this car, and unless he made a break for the passenger door – which would be tantamount to admitting his strength had failed him – he was screwed. Neither man said a word, but even if the Jackeen couldn't be sure exactly why the big red-haired man outside was after him, he did know that the culchies were a clannish tribe and that this must be retribution for him having beaten up one of their crowd. He redoubled his efforts to force the door open but Trevor held his ground and pushed even harder on the handle, jamming him inside. The pair continued staring at each other with pure venom.

Trevor was the first to speak. 'Hey there young lad,' he said dismissively as though he were addressing some miserable beggar he'd just come across. 'I heard that you were fighting in the Welsh Harp the other night?'

'Did you now?' replied the Jackeen unperturbed, still looking daggers.

'There was little fear of you, lad,' Trevor scoffed. This tactic Trevor habitually used to catch his opponent off-guard. It didn't have much effect this time, however.

'Fear?' said the Jackeen. 'I didn't meet anyone in the Welsh Harp who would've frightened me.'

'You didn't meet the right man, so.'

The Jackeen grunted dismissively and redoubled his efforts with the door-handle. 'You're the big man are you,' he joked.

'I am surely,' replied Trevor.

'Release the door, so, and we'll see how good you are!'

'You've a right to get out of the car first – if you're able to,' Trevor replied. 'Put your shoulder to the door now, good lad, let's see if your arms are strong enough.' Trevor had developed an instant dislike for the younger fellow; every ounce of hatred and anger he'd ever felt towards anyone had coalesced into the shape of Christy Power. Manifest here was all the natural mistrust of the countryman towards the city slicker – and vice versa. It didn't bother Trevor in the slightest that the Jackeen had just left the British Army; indeed this made him hate him even more. For Trevor, it was as though the centuries of treachery that the Irish associated with the Anglicised people of the garrison towns were encapsulated in this Jackeen. Strangely enough, while men like Trevor never got too bothered by an English accent, a Dublin one was a wholly different ball game. If someone had asked Trevor right then where the roots of this hostility towards the man lay, Trevor wouldn't have been able to reply. This in no way diminished his loathing towards the younger buck. He was absolutely on fire, ready to explode. His was a calculated or controlled rage, however. He leaned in closer to the passenger window to take in the Jackeen's bearings more clearly and – as if sensing what Trevor was at – the former suddenly released his grip on the door inside.

'Back off there now – unless you're afraid? – and I'll be out this second,' the younger man said in a tone that conveyed both insult and indifference.

The compactor had stopped its racket, and Mullen made his way over to McAllister's car, curiosity written all over his face.

'Let that shit out, so that we can kill him, Trevor!'

Mullen was strutted like a cockerel on a dung-heap, as though he couldn't wait to have a go himself at the Jackeen.

'It's alright, Mullen. Clear off, will you?' Trevor told him tersely. Power glanced in Mullen's direction then grabbed the handle again suddenly and gave it a powerful push.

'Let the swine out, Trevor,' Mullen shouted, adopting a fighting stance, but the Jackeen just burst out laughing.

'Frig off Mullen, will you, this has nothing to do with you,' Trevor repeated without taking his eyes off the man in the car. But Mullen wasn't budging. He'd obviously convinced himself that he was more than a match for the Dubliner, and couldn't wait to fight him.

'Ara, why wouldn't it be my business, Trevor?' Mullen responded in Irish. 'Sure, aren't we all the one crowd? Let the bolloxs out now so that we can make shit of him!'

If he'd been close enough to him right then – and his hands had been free – Trevor wouldn't have hesitated to make shit of Mullen – he was that pissed off by his antics; he'd enough on his plate now without this gobshite annoying him as well!

'Who's the idiot with no English?' said the Jackeen to Trevor contemptously, but Trevor ignored him. Maintaining a poisonous grin, his eyes bored into the Dubliner's.

'You've no strength in your hands, Jack, by the looks of it,' Trevor scoffed.

'Back off, so, and we'll see,' retorted the Jackeen but his face reddened in a mixture of anger and embarrassment as he gave another lunge against the door.

'You must be getting soft, driving around in a car all the time; you should do a bit of work every now and then; if you're able, that is,' replied Trevor.

Still speaking in Irish, Mullen said, 'Ara, let the slob out and we'll see what he's made of,' said Mullen, starting to get annoyed with Trevor. 'What's the point of keeping him trapped inside like a pig in his pen?'

'What's he saying?' the Jackeen asked Trevor.

'He says you're a like a pig cooped up in his sty, Jack.' Trevor said with a dirty laugh. This made the Jackeen go totally ballistic; his face drained of colour and he whammed his shoulder against the door.

Just as Trevor was about to release him – so that things could really kick off – who should rush over to them but Paddy McAllister and Mike Dudley Stephen? The pair couldn't understand what all the commotion was about and why all the workers had suddenly downed tools and started congregating around the car.

'Hey, what's going on here, lads? Stop the chat and get back to work, the lot of you. What the hell's wrong with you all?' Mike Dudley shouted as if to reassure McAllister. It was obvious to everyone that Trevor and the Jackeen weren't exactly exchanging pleasantries. Neither Trevor nor Mullen responded to the ganger but Trevor removed his hand from the handle and said in a measured voice, 'You can come out now if you like.'

'Lucky for you that you didn't say that a short while ago,' the Jackeen sneered at Trevor fearlessly. 'But, don't worry, man,' he added, 'I'll be seeing you again sooner than you think.'

McAllister approached them with a perplexed glare. 'What's going on here?' he asked gruffly.

'Nothing at all, Paddy. This is between ourselves, is all.' said Trevor in a relaxed tone.

'Well, you'd think you'd have all night to sort these things out, and not be wasting my time here in the middle of the day. This isn't what I pay you for,' said their employer reaching his car

'Don't you worry about that, Paddy, you're not wasting a penny on us here today – not like some people,' replied Trevor, glancing maliciously at the Jackeen. Paddy McAllister stalled at the side of his car as if unsure whether he should let his employee get away with this. He pursed his lips and got in, Trevor and the Jackeen eyeballing one another all the while.

As the car pulled away, the Jackeen stuck his head out of the window and called over to the Connemara-man. 'We'll meet one another again soon, don't you worry, culchie, and you'll have changed your tune then, I can promise you that,' he said. The car shot off in a movement that reflected its driver's irritation.

When Trevor got back to his lodgings that evening there was a letter waiting for him. He ate his dinner and took the letter up to his room so that Red Sweeney could read it for him. Sweeney was stretched out on the bed with his usual depressed look of having run out of money.

'Here, Sweeney, read that for me like a good man, will you? Herself always writes to me in Irish and – you know – I can't read Irish.'

'Sure, Trevor,' Sweeney replied enthusiastically. He knew it made no odds to Trevor in which language the letter was, but that Sweeny himself was always rewarded for his reading and writing services. The more letters that came, the better he liked it. Trevor's wife's writing was childish and easy to read, and Sweeney got its gist straight away. Sweeney had a habit of speed-reading Trevor's letters and made sure to tone down any tension or problems they conveyed so that Trevor wouldn't get too angry. As he read on, it became clear that there was plenty in this letter that would to irritate him, and so Sweeney began shaping an alternative one in his mind that would be more palatable.

Trevor was quick enough to challenge his hesitancy, however. 'Oh, will you just read it, for Christ's sake and don't be staring at the damn thing like it was a whore or something!' he said roughly.

Sweeney read the letter out:

Dear Trevor,

I hope you are well, just as we are ourselves here. Dara hasn't stopped asking for his daddy since you left. And – ah, I'm as bad myself, Trevor, God knows. I don't know how I got home the day that you left on the train. It was like a knife going through my heart, Trevor. I've only one thing to say to you now and, Trevor, I hope you won't hold it against me. I'm not staying here any longer in Doire Leathan, Trevor. You have to find a place for me and the kids with you over there. Aren't you my husband, Trevor, do you understand that at all? It's a long time now since you promised me that you'd get us a place, Trevor; even if it's only one room, it'll do fine. If you don't get us a place in London, Trevor, I'll bring the children with me whether you like it or not. Send me some news without delay, love, and we'll arrange everything. Wouldn't it be better for me to be over there with you, looking after you, anyway? All of your family are well, as are Dara and Little Bartley, everyone under the protection of God and his Blessed Virgin.

From your wife Nora.

The tone of the letter was actually quite a bit stronger than this and Red Sweeney would have censored it even more – except that he was afraid. Because, unlike any other man, Trevor didn't throw his letters out or tear them up; he kept them all under the bed, as if for future reference, Sweeney would say to himself sarcastically, in private. There wasn't a peep out of Trevor as Sweeney was reading the letter out to him and for a short while afterwards. He just lay on the bed, chin in hand, tapping his foot on the floor. He reminded Sweeney of a giant cat sweeping its tail in irritation. Sweeney hoped that Trevor would respond to this letter immediately because he needed a few shillings badly: that bloody mule, Flying Colours, had wiped him out down at the racing in Wincanton.

Trevor gave a low moan under his breath and his jaw went rigid. 'Have you a paper and pencil?' he asked brusquely.

'I have indeed,' Sweeney replied, jumping up and pulling his old suitcase out from under the bed and placing it on the bed as his writing-table. He took a notebook out and produced a pencil from his jacket-pocket. 'Fire away now, Trevor.'

'Right,' Trevor said, and then without the slightest by-your-leave, launched into it.

'Tell her that I got her letter. And that I've sent her money back to Madge. It's not so easy to get rooms over here in London, tell her, there's thousands of people looking for them or does she not know that half the country was destroyed in the war? Does she not realise that there was a war here not so long ago, ask her, or did she ever hear tell of Hitler? Tell her this isn't a good place for children and what the hell is she thinking? Isn't she fine getting the four pounds sent back to her every week – and what's wrong with that? There are men working on the council back in the west who don't earn that much, tell her. Or, has she any smidgen of sense, ask her? The people who rent out rooms are mad against children and I've to go out to work every day – or does she think that I'm over here just touring around the building sites or something?

'Did you get all that down?'

Just like many others who can't read or write, Trevor couldn't understand how the other man didn't note down every word as soon as it was out of his mouth. Trevor didn't realise either that Sweeney only ever wrote down the bare bones of any story.

'I've got every single word down, no bother,' Sweeney confirmed, and Trevor continued dictating.

'Tell her I've more to be doing than running around looking for rooms, or does she think I spend my day leaning against the walls over here like the Dublin crowd, ask her? Anyway, it's a far healthier place for children back west, tell her. Trevor went quiet for a moment and gave an unhappy glance in Sweeney's direction, almost as though he were the one responsible for the situation.

Trevor was sick to the teeth of the whole thing. It was time to finish up this bloody letter.

'Look, you can tell her that I'm haven't forgotten her. Tell her I'll find a place as soon as I can and I'll send her word as soon as I see a suitable room. Tell her too that I hope herself and the children are all well.'

'Have you got that?'

'I have indeed!'

'Have you an envelope?'

'I have one in my suitcase here, I think.'

'Good. And you have the address, don't you? You've written it down often enough, anyway.'

'I do, mate!'

Trevor got up off the bed. Now that the letter was out of the way, he felt as if a load had been lifted from his shoulders. It was no exaggeration to say that dictating that letter had taken more out of him than all the digging and dragging he'd done since morning. He put his hand into his trouser pocket, took out two half-crown coins and threw them over to Red Sweeney.

'You'll put that in the post for me tomorrow now like a good man, won't you?'

'Of course I will, Trevor!' said Sweeney, putting the letter in an envelope and sealing it. He left the room a happy man with the two half-crowns in his pocket. Trevor sat down again and untied his shoes. If he was happy that the letter was out of the way, he was still pissed off with Nora. If he were honest, he would acknowledge that those few words of a letter weren't good enough. But then no letter could ever do the job. Nora was determined to come over to be with him. She'd never stopped going on about it during the month he'd spent at home, and the chances were that this was exactly what she'd do eventually, whether he liked it or not. Did the divvy have any sense, though? He regretted now that he'd ever put a ring on her finger that first day, or on any woman, come to that. But then if Nora Condon – or Nora Eamonn as she was known back home – hadn't been pregnant,

Trevor wouldn't have married her in the first place, no way! And the truth was that if she had been over here in England, he most likely wouldn't have married her. But this was a different place compared to back home; back in Ireland, people were tied down by convention, and if you didn't do what was expected of you, everyone in the community never let up or stopped bad-mouthing you. There was a certain protocol back home, added to which a brother of Nora's had been in the same army company as Trevor's in Renmore; and it wouldn't have been easy for Trevor to ignore his wishes, especially if he'd tried to deny that he'd got Nora pregnant. She'd yet another brother back home and, from what he'd heard, he wasn't someone to get on the wrong side of, either. Apart from anything else, he wouldn't get a moment's peace from his own family if he'd let Nora down. To give Nora her due, she hadn't pressurised him into marrying her when she'd told him tearfully that she was 'up the duff' as she'd put it in a frightened voice that night back then when they'd been walking along High Street in Galway city.

'Well, there's nothing to be done, then, except get married,' Trevor had said unhappily. And yet he might have agreed to marriage, but that didn't mean he had the slightest intention of letting his new spouse turn his life upside-down or force him to change the way he wanted to live his life. He'd had his mind made up well before he'd come out of the army that he didn't plan on hanging around back at the home-place either. He had the excuse that there was no work available in Connemara and anyway, there wasn't enough room for them back in his father's house or on the land there. He'd head for England, he told Nora as every go-ahead man did these days and, once he was over there and knew the ropes fairly well, he'd send for her and the child. If Trevor had ever really had any intention of fulfilling his promise, it hadn't taken him long to forget about it once he was set up across the water.

Initially, he'd worked on a beet-harvesting scheme in a gang who'd gone down to the smooth plains of East Anglia in the winter of 1947.

As it happens, that had been a very bad winter with heavy snow and frost, plus the scarcity that followed just after the war. When he'd finished the seasonal work there he'd headed for London rather than returning home as originally planned. England was starting to really blossom and develop again economically, especially in those cities destroyed in the Blitz. The country was being rebuilt again gradually and with all this renovation came a tremendous amount of work – gasworks, water schemes, electricity – everything that was needed to get the country up and running again. There was so much re-building work happening, and of course there was no better man for this type of work than the Irishman. The war had been long and brutal but at least a lot of work had become necessary in its aftermath. Where the money had come from was a big mystery, given that there were two million people unemployed in Britain during the Thirties. 'It was Adolf who made a real country of her,' the Irish used to say amongst themselves (and to the English sometimes also, just to annoy them!). 'It's a good war that creates lots of work afterwards.' There was a ton of work available by then and there were few jobs that the Irish weren't at the front of the queue for – even if you still saw the odd advertisement here and there banning them from certain jobs or lodgings.

The reality was that for the amount of interaction that Trevor and the other lads had with English people, they may as well have been living at home in Ireland. In truth, England was a place that suited Trevor Bartley Billy very well, even if he'd previously had little enough knowledge or understanding of the country or its people. He'd gone straight up to Camden Town from Peterborough when he'd finished the job there and got lodgings the minute he set foot in the place. That was exactly two-and-a-half years ago, and Trevor had only visited home twice since. The first time was for the birth of the new baby – a son they'd baptised Bartley in honour of Trevor's father – and there was a good chance that they'd have another addition to the family after

Trevor's most recent visit home. Another consequence of those two trips back to Ireland was that Trevor's dislike of it had increased. He hated the place even more, especially that he was now bound to it forever through marriage! Worse still was that last time he'd been back, Nora hadn't shut up about coming over with the children to be with him. She'd kept on and on about it so that eventually Trevor told her one day to shut her trap and that if he heard any more about it, she'd be sorry.

Trevor threw off his hobnail shoes and stretched out on the bed, hands folded behind his head. Was she right in the head was the vexed question he asked himself. God knows, the last time he'd been home, she'd said plenty of things to him that made him wonder whether she was the full shilling! In truth, Trevor knew very little about Nora's people or the place she came from: a small village from way up in the hills. It wasn't as though he'd married someone from his own village whose genealogy and bloodline he could trace back as far as you could go. For all he knew, there might be an odd strain in her family running back through the generations! It was at night that she was at her worst, just when he was dying to go to sleep. Why she wasn't happy just to do the business and then go to sleep afterwards was beyond him…! Instead, she'd start kissing and caressing him and whispering constant endearments into his ear as if they were still a courting couple all over again – constant blathering half the night!

'Why in hell do you have this incessant need to talk? Why can't you just go to sleep the same as everyone else?' Trevor had asked her crankily one night, after she'd woken him up. And whatever she'd said to him in reply was so off-the-wall that he'd nearly told her that she should be locked up in Ballinasloe.

'Oh, musha, Trevor,' she said, giving it a nibble. 'Don't start, please – sure, don't I talk to you every single day of the year, even though you're not here beside me?'

Yeah, and that was the least of it; some of the other rubbish she came out with was way worse – including her hatred of the sea, for example! Nora Eamonn had no experience whatsoever of the it or the type of work associated with the shoreline. In fact, you couldn't even see the seaside properly from the place she came from; you had to climb up to the very highest point in her parish, Corrán na Minsí, before you even set eyes on it. But who the hell ever heard of anyone spouting that kind of rubbish – that they were afraid of the ocean – especially someone who'd never even had to set foot in the water! Nora told Trevor that she hated every single day that she had to spend at the seaside and repeated this refrain when pleading with Trevor to let her and her sons return with him to England when his month at home came to an end. Even when she'd been working as a nanny, she'd hated the sight of the water, and whenever she had to take the mistress' baby for a walk in her pram to Salthill beach – and this was a place where there were hundreds swimming, diving and paddling happily in the water – a fear of the sea had always engulfed her. And it hadn't been long since she'd moved to Derrylahan – just after Trevor had gone to England – that Nora had got it into her head that the sea was her enemy, a calculating and malevolent force that was linked in some strange way to her own uncertain fate. 'It's the loneliness, Trevor,' she'd said. 'It's the loneliness that drives you mad here, God knows!'

Loneliness – what loneliness! – didn't they have a whole houseful of them: his mother, father, the children and his brother Briocán, who spent his life out fishing? She just spent too much time thinking about herself, that was the root-cause of all this stupidity. If she'd had to carry a big heavy creel-basket on her back as many a Connemara women had done for generations, she wouldn't have had time to feel sorry for herself. Not at all! And didn't they always say that idleness led to a whole host of other problems? That was only the half of it. As far as Trevor could make out, Nora felt as if the sea itself were watching her – so that she couldn't even go to the well for a bucket of water or spread clothes out on the hedge to dry – or anything else – without her imagining this hostile creature looking on. Some days, when the it was quiet and calm as a painting, she would say that that her enemy was playing tricks on her, lulling her into a false sense of security; drawing her in. 'Sure,' she'd tell Trevor – after he'd given her a piece of his mind, 'sure, it's my nerves at me. Didn't the priest say as much? If that's what he thinks, then that's good enough for me. Sure, it's obvious really.'

'The priest!' Trevor had asked her, in a mixture of anger and surprise. 'Ah no, you idiot, don't tell me that you went to the priest and told him all that shite? What business did you have going to the priest about that?'

'I had to, Trevor; I had a talk with him in Confession about it,' she said. 'Father Keenan is a very kind and helpful man – he's not at all like the parish priest. He's the type of person you can talk to and you can tell him about things that are bothering you.'

'You don't need to tell him anything other than your sins and even then, only if you feel like it. I don't bother with that caper, no bloody fear of it!' Trevor had replied, disgruntled. But Nora hadn't been listening, she was just blathering on as if she needed to get every little thing that had ever worried her off her chest now she'd the chance. It was after Trevor had gone back to England that first year – that had been the worst time of all,' she'd said. 'You couldn't step outside the door that year, the weather was so bad: it was constant rain and the winds whipping in and howling around the place like a crazy beast. The rain lashing down and constantly hammering against the windows, and the sea, a giant disturbed mass of water. She'd come to the end or her tether that winter, the new baby constantly crying, the uneasiness of her father-in-law who spent one day padding from the window to the door and back again, waiting for the weather to ease up. Worse still, Nora said that she was tormented by her sexual needs and the desires that had been awakened again with a vengeance when Trevor came home – and there was only one release from that – and it wasn't anything of the sort, so Nora said. And to top it all off, that was a sin too. The day that the storm finally calmed, the last streaks of cloud had cleared from the horizon and the sky had been dull and completely spent, as if exhausted from the constant rain, so Nora told him. It had been that day, more than any other, that she'd nearly gone utterly mad, Nora said. She'd been falling apart, so much so that she'd put little Dara in his pram and headed off down the boreen, in the direction of Cnoc an Asail, a place where she had no no sight of the sea. She'd imagined that she'd be safe there where the sea would have no power over her anymore; once she'd crossed over the hills, she'd feel better in herself again, she'd told herself. Trevor had told her angrily to shut up and go back to sleep. Nora had been silent for a minute or two, but then she was back to her favourite topic.

'Father Keenan told me that it isn't right or natural that we should be living apart from one another like this, especially as you've no intention of returning home, Trevor,' she'd said to him another night just after they'd made love. It was always then that the urge to talk seemed to come over her, much to Trevor's irritation.

'Father Keenan should keep his nose out of other people's business,' Trevor had said bluntly.

Wasn't he lucky, really, that he'd got the hell out of the place when he had, Trevor thought. There was no way he'd have lasted much longer back home with all that blather and gossip – between clergy neighbours and everyone watching everyone else like hawks, from cradle to grave. The whole thing was a bloody nightmare!

'What the hell were you doing bringing up our business with him anyway?' Trevor had asked Nora. 'Isn't it enough for you to go to Confession, if you had to go, and not be discussing these things with him. What sort of a divvy are you, for God's sake?'

It was because she'd gone to Confession that she'd ended up talking about it with the priest, Nora had told him. After all, she had to tell her sins to the priest, hadn't she? And the priest had told her that it was an awful thing for a woman to be denied her conjugal rights: that it was a form of abuse, really. It was neither good nor healthy to constantly live your life in the shadow of sexual temptation; human nature wasn't strong enough to resist it.

There was nothing surer than that Nora would get her way – sooner or later – and he'd have no choice but to bring her and the children over, Trevor knew. She'd come over to England with his permission or without it, unfortunately, it seemed. Wasn't it always said that a woman would get the better of the devil himself? He'd have to get a room or two somewhere for them then, a bloody hole of a place like the one Mainey and her husband had. Then he'd have to listen to children crying and women screaming and roaring for the rest of his days! But at least he'd have the comfort of having someone in his bed and things would be better in the sex department, he thought. And that in itself was no small thing. Sometimes, when travelling on the underground or walking along the road, Trevor would see a fine-looking filly and he'd get really randy and start imagining what he'd get up to with her if he had the chance – in the right place and at the right time. Trevor knew that the priest was right, really. It was too much of a burden for anyone, whether married or single; the desires of the flesh were a constant torment. And it wasn't as if Trevor hadn't had the odd fling himself every now and then in the last few years either.... There had been that big blonde one from Roscommon he'd picked up in the Blarney on Tottenham Court Road one night. Even if she hadn't been able to dance for toffee, she'd been dynamite in the sack! She'd known tricks in bed that Nora wouldn't have thought of in a million years! He'd never met her again; she didn't want to go steady with any man, she'd said. And what about that other ride, the one from Tipperary who'd an English accent mixed in with her Irish one. She'd been well able to go too – even if she hadn't wanted to get tied down with anyone either.

The curse of God on you anyway, Nora, Trevor said to himself as he felt a wave of lust course through him. He hopped up off the bed and went to the bathroom for a shave. He'd go out for a pint later even if he never really had that much interest in drinking during the week. Sure, he couldn't just stay indoors staring at the walls all evening, could he? And who knows – maybe the Jackeen would be around. It would be a big feather in his cap if he took him out, no doubt about it. His name would be sung far and wide, from Camden Town to Kilburn and from the Elephant to Shepherd's Bush – basically anywhere that the lads congregated. Out on the sites or down the pub, in the dance halls, wherever: they'd all have the same story. Trevor Bartley Billy was a mighty man – the way he'd put that Christy Power, the army boxer, in his place.

Chapter 11

It was Bosco Sullivan who'd told Niall what he could have found out a lot earlier if he'd asked around – what had happened to Peg. Niall had been in a right state since that night when she'd passed him on John's Bridge with the man in the cap, a countryman who looked a good deal older than her, unless Niall had been mistaken. Niall had slept soundly enough on getting home that night; the drink always worked well on that score. It was a different story the next morning, however; he felt like someone had kicked him in the gut when he woke up and remembered. His world had been turned upside-down in an instant! He couldn't understand what had happened. He couldn't make any sense of it. The more he thought about it, the more ridiculous the whole thing seemed. How long had she been going out with this other man? That's if she really was going out with him and there wasn't some other explanation for what he'd seen that night, the pair of them cycling home together like that. Or how could Peg have been so all over him that time if she wasn't really into him? Despite himself, Niall found himself asking Bosco the next day whether he knew anything about Peg or her family.

'Pat Dineen's daughter from Redmondstown, is it? Why wouldn't I know her?' Bosco had replied with a smirk that Niall didn't like one bit.

'Ara, no reason – just that I saw her with a man the other night, a fellow who was a lot older than her, I'd say. She's a good-looking girl,' Niall said, in as casual a tone as he could muster.

'She's a bit on the skinny side for me,' said Bosco. 'I wouldn't say no to her all the same though!' Niall felt like telling him to shut it, but if he'd done that, the cat would've been out of the bag. Sullivan would know that he was more interested in Peg than he was letting on and he'd be rightly screwed! They were on their way back from the Labour Exchange and Mooney was with them – not that he'd the slightest interest in this subject. 'She's been going out with Muldowney for a long time: he's from the village next to hers,' Bosco added.

'For a long time?' siad Niall in a tone that as good as gave the game away – despite his best efforts at disguising his disappointment.

'For three or four years anyway, I'd say. They'll be getting married; he's a place coming to him, that Muldowney.'

Niall was stunned but Mooney broke in, 'You're a right old biddy, Bosco, the way you know everyone's business, do you know that? You should have a skirt on, man, instead of trousers!'

'Kiss my arse, Nick,' said Bosco, but in a voice so gentle that you'd have sworn he'd said 'Hello, how it's going?' to him instead. They'd reached the bridge now and were staring down into the depths of the river Nore as they often did. The trees skirting the bank had been stripped bare in the previous week, they looked pathetic and miserable, lined up along it like a series of skeletons. Smithwick's Brewery and all the other building down as far as old Chandler's Mill were plain for all the world to see, bereft of their lush green summertime protection. Niall thought back to that beautiful summer's day when he'd walked along the road with Peg and they'd kissed and cuddled so passionately. He felt a gaping, invisible wound in his side; as though his guts had been torn out of him. What Bosco had said must be true, of course: Bosco was rarely wrong about that sort of thing. But why in God's faithful name had she kissed him so lovingly back then? Why had she kissed him at all if she was going out with another man all the time? She couldn't have been pretending: Niall could've sworn on it. Peg had liked him just as much as he'd liked her, and hadn't she sent him a letter with a series of kisses following her signature? Of course, she hadn't replied to any of his letters, but then maybe there was some other explanation for that too? Maybe she'd broken up with Muldowney the day she'd met him, or perhaps they'd got back together after she'd threatened to finish with him?

'You shifted her, didn't you, you fecker?' Bosco mocked, and – like the little bloody gobshite that he was – Niall denied that he knew anything about Peg, his cheeks burning in mortification.

'Well, let me tell you something about her now,' said Bosco, really enjoying himself. 'She's hot-to-trot, boy!'

'Ara, don't mind that frigger, what the hell would he know?' interrupted Mooney but he might as well not have spoken for all that Niall heard him. His heart froze inside him; he felt like dying.

'I know that for a fact,' Sullivan continued. 'I know a lad who met her down at the corra there once; a couple of years back, but anyway… he grabbed hold of her, you know… just having the craic, like… and what do you know but didn't she tear into him, and shifted him right there on the spot, not a bother. That's the pure truth boy, I'm telling you!'

'Who was your man, so?' Mooney challenged, and it was just as well. 'Do you think that I'm making this up, Mooney? Chucks Phelan is the fellow I mean and he wasn't making it up either!'

'Chucks Phelan is as big a liar as you are, Bosco! I wouldn't believe a word he says,' retorted Mooney, spitting down into the Nore scornfully. Niall believed Sullivan, however; his story had the ring of truth about it, unfortunately.

'Here lads; let's go back up the corner. And let's not all be blathering about women all the time either,' said Mooney, suddenly sick of this conversation.

'We might as well go on up, I suppose,' replied Niall.

A few nights later, as if it had been so ordained, the death knell sounded on the dream of Peg Dineen. Niall had gone out with another woman he'd met at the cinema. It was a waste of time to be carrying a torch for Peg any longer. For months, he'd been taking her to bed with him every night in his mind and treating her memory with an almost saintly reverence. Not only that but he'd been scribbling 'Peg Dineen' on the margins of old newspapers at home and repeating her name to himself as though it were some strange charm. He'd never even desecrated her image with lustful thoughts, unlike those of other women, which regularly came to mind when he was engaged in that dirty deed one engaged in alone. She'd been too unique and beautiful to have even dreamed of doing that. It was different now, however. He had to face facts. Peg Dineen just didn't love him in the way that he'd loved her; otherwise, she wouldn't be marrying another man, especially not one who was a good deal older than her.

Niall had been sitting in the thrupenny section of the cinema, lighting up a cigarette; when this new girl had sat down next to him. It was Friday night and Niall had still been flush with the dole money that he'd collected from the Labour Exchange that morning – minus the ten-shilling note he always gave his mother for housekeeping.

'Have you a match, by any chance?' the girl had asked, leaning into him with the cigarette already between her lips. While Niall sparked her cigarette, he'd given her the once-over. She wasn't too bad looking, even if she had an Ulster accent that he couldn't place exactly. She had that open and direct nature that some people consider overly forward but which was actually a form of honesty. She'd thanked Niall and sucked greedily on her cigarette, then exhaled a stream of smoke that wafted up in the direction of the projector light. A news excerpt from the *Pathé Gazette* had been showing, the clipped, crackly voice of the British announcer describing the war in Korea and the slaughter that the Communists were engaged in. The girl had shifted giddily in her seat and whispered to Niall, 'I don't like news – do you?'

'No,' Niall had replied quietly, his heart skipping a beat. As the people back West would say, 'You never quite know where you might catch a lobster', as, unless he was badly mistaken, he'd caught a good one here.

'I don't know why they bother with the news, no-one wants it,' the girl had added.

'You're right,' Niall had said. The truth is that he'd have agreed with anything this girl said just then, even if it was that the moon was made of cheese or the sea, of buttermilk. The *Pathé Gazette* presentation had finished, the on-screen cockerel flapping its wings and the globe beneath its talons giving a spin; this had been followed by a short skit with the Three Stooges, at which the girl had clapped her hands together joyfully like a child. 'I love these, they're brilliant! The curly-haired fellow is a real dote!'

Niall had glanced at her from the corner of his eye to try and make out whether she was joking; after all, people were entitled to their own opinion, but how could anyone call that stupid clown a '*dote*', in all fairness? The antics of the trio had become even crazier, and there wasn't one bit of slapstick the girl hadn't respond to with a loud roar of laughter or a poke to Niall's side. Her laugh was absolutely unreserved, not like the town girls' manner. She would give a loud raucous screech that reached the back of the hall. Her country-bumpkin ways had embarrassed Niall and he couldn't wait for the three idiots to leave the screen.

'I've seen the main film here before,' the girl had said, snuggling in to Niall. 'Any film that I like, I see it twice. I saw *The Bells of St Mary's* three times; have you seen that one?'

'I have,' Niall had said in a low voice. The girl had opened her coat and Niall could feel her sturdy thigh press against his, together with the heat of her body coming through the thin fabric of her dress. Slowly and carefully, he had slipped his right arm around the back of the timber bench until his fingers were on the girl's shoulder. If she'd felt his hand there, she hadn't let on, and she hadn't said anything either.

'Bing Crosby is a right dote,' she'd said, releasing another wave of smoke into the air.

Then, just as Niall'd feared from the beginning, she'd started chattering out loud, and someone behind them had told them to keep quiet. But this admonition hadn't affected her one bit, however.

'Some people round here think they own the place, as if we haven't paid our thrupenny bit the same as them!' she'd said, loud enough to be heard a good few rows further back. The main film had begun but Niall had lost interest, so stressed was he by the prospect of this girl's constant chatter annoying the neighbours. He hated any show or embarrassment. 'That's Alice Faye,' the girl had said, pointing at the screen. 'We have her on the gramophone at home.' Niall had handed her another cigarette in the hope that this would get her to button it. The crowd behind them had become worked up again, complaining among themselves about people talking and making too much noise. The girl had dragged happily on her cigarette then glanced over at Niall as if taking him in properly for the first time. 'Do you go to the pictures often?' she had asked.

'Yes,' Niall had whispered.

'I do too. I just live for the pictures,' the girl had continued.

'Whisht!' a voice had come from behind them. 'We can't hear the picture because of you two!'

The girl might be good looking, Niall had thought, but if she didn't know when to keep her trap shut.... Niall had been burning with shame but the next thing, she was looking around over her shoulder and saying in a disgusted tone, 'Have you ever heard the likes of it!'

It was now or never, Niall had thought. He who dares wins: better get in there now or never. 'Maybe,' he'd told her quietly, 'seeing as you've seen it before, you might like to come out for a walk with me instead?'

'We might as well,' the girl had replied. 'Better than staying here, anyway!'

Under the street-lights outside, Niall had realised that this girl was even better looking than he'd first thought. She was one of those well put-together country girls who wore low-heeled shoes and no stockings. There wasn't a small town or village anywhere in Ireland without a girl like her; lots of them worked in hospitals, the houses of wealthy people or those laundries run by nuns. She was his type: easy-going and modest, one of those 'salt-of-the-earth' women who never aspired to any great things in life nor expected life to give them much in return. She would be the sort of girl who'd share her last cigarette with a soldier, while her snootier friends wouldn't give him a second glance.

They had headed uptown along the half-empty evening streets, Niall walking at the girl's pace, matching his short army steps to her long country strides. She was from Letterkenny, she'd said, naming the nearest big town to her home-place. Kathleen Brouder, as she was called, had been working in Kilkenny for nearly three months and still didn't like the city or find the people as friendly as those back in Donegal. The people here were a bit full of themselves and domineering, she thought. Dublin was way better. There were any amount of cinemas in Dublin and plenty of people from back home working there, whereas she didn't know anyone in Kilkenny.

Kathleen was in-service at one of the posh houses up beyond the castle but Niall was loathe to walk her straight home; instead, he'd decided to take her for a wander up around Patrick Street and down Archer's Lane. It had been a nice night for walking, the mild, damp air perfumed by turf-smoke as the dark enveloped them. Coming across a small sweet shop that was still open, Kathleen had stopped to stare at the packets on display – love hearts, lollipops, aniseed, sherbet and all the rest.

'Oh, I love sweets. Don't you?'

'Look at those love hearts there; I could eat them until they came out my ears!'

Niall had gone into the shop and bought a quarter-pound of love hearts, petrified that someone would come in and catch him in such a soppy act.

'Ah lovely, you're a right dote!' Kathleen had told him when he'd returned with the sweets and they'd kept on walking. 'Don't you like sweets?' she'd continued when he wouldn't take any himself. As she took out each one – with a silly message written on it –from its bag, she would read out every single one, in the light of lamp-posts along the way. '"Kiss me now!" "You are my one true love",' Kathleen would say with a screech of delight. The advice given on the sweet was enough for him, Niall told her, requesting one, but Kathleen had exploded with laughter again, as though that was the funniest thing she'd ever heard. She was chattering away as they walked along, while Niall was only half-listening, mostly, and only got the odd word in. Talking must have provided some sort of outlet for Kathleen, because she rambled on constantly like a little girl whom the adults had always ignored. That was Niall's take on it. He could tell that she was lonely even though she told him that the people she worked for were nice and treated her as if she was one of their own.

The house Kathleen worked at was located at the end of a narrow secluded avenue, and was an ideal spot for courting, Niall had thought. The only chance that someone might notice them would have been had a car turned in there suddenly, with its headlights picking them out. They'd stood against a wall covered in a thick mass of ivy where Niall took his cigarettes out again. He was at that point far keener on having a kiss and cuddle than on having a smoke but patience was the best tack in this situation. Despite all her antics and talk, he'd sensed an innocence in her; as if her appearance and behaviour didn't match up. He knew he shouldn't frighten her away by going for the shift too quickly.

'I'm cracked about fags,' Kathleen had said, taking a long drag on her Woodbine. Niall had smoked another two cigarettes before he slipped his arm back around her, inside her coat this time. If she'd anything beneath that light dress of hers – a singlet or vest or whatever – Niall certainly couldn't feel it. The only thing beneath that coat and dress was her young smooth body, her skin soft and sensuous. A dart of desire went through Niall but Kathleen had started at his touch, jolting as though she'd come into contact with a sliver of ice.

'Oh, I'm ticklish!' she'd exclaimed.

'Ticklish?'

'I'm so ticklish; are you like that too? Just touch my skin sometimes and that's enough,' Kathleen had continued.

Niall had cursed under his breath. Wouldn't it be a right pain in the arse if she turned out to be one of those dippy types – as Captain Delaney called them – the kind you couldn't lay a finger on without her wriggling and squirming like a year-old mare? He wouldn't have minded if she'd been one of those wasted-looking skinny-malinks who wouldn't have set a corpse's pulse racing, but this girl was a nice, curvy bit of stuff. As gently and sensitively as though she were asleep, Niall had placed his fingertips in the small of her back – light as a feather – but Kathleen had shuddered even more violently this time.

'Stop it, I said. You're making me ticklish again!'

'Well, you *are* ticklish, Kathleen, that's for sure,' Niall had said, annoyed. Yep, unfortunately she was one of those dizzy girls who'd as much interest in a bit of a feel-up as a bloody plank of wood.

According to Captain Delaney, tons of Irish women were like that: whatever bit of 'go' that had been in them originally had been rendered completely frigid by their upbringing and the constant warnings of priests and parents. If Captain Delaney were to be believed, the French were hotter and more ready-for-action than even the wildest and most uncontrollable women here. This was some statement from a fellow who'd never been abroad. Even the limited experience Niall had had so far with women seemed to indicate that there was a lot of truth in what he said. In his private moments, Niall sometimes imagined the wild and unrestrained woman that had Paddy Delaney called to mind, a big horny bitch without the slightest hint of shame or inhibition, one of those untamed types who'd give you the ride of your life. Niall had yet to meet any himself but they were definitely out there; it was just a question of luck whether you came across one!

Niall had managed to put his arm around Kathleen on his third attempt, but she was still as flighty as hell. No sooner had Niall been thinking about moving in for a kiss on the lips and a bit of a snog than she started rabbiting on about Little Nuala – one of the kids that she was minding – and how she would trot out some strange version of the Lord's Prayer. Niall tried a different tack and had gone for a nibble on the neck, a move that Paddy Delaney assured him drove French women mad with desire. This move did sweet Fanny Adams for Kathleen however, except to make her ticklish again and give her goose-bumps! Niall had been forced to give up on that one fairly quickly too.

'I'd say you haven't much experience with the lads, Kathleen, have you?' Niall had said, grumpily.

It was obvious that for one who'd gone off with him so readily with him, she wasn't experienced, and yet she'd seemed stung by this.

'Of course I have experience of lads,' Kathleen had responded, 'why d'you think that?' I had a very nice lad back in Donegal, a shopkeeper's son named Hiudy Gallagher, sure, he was cracked about me!'

She'd stayed quiet for a moment and then – in a hurt voice – Kathleen had repeated, 'Why would you say that, anyway?'

'Oh musha, no reason, girl, I was only joking you!'

He'd made a balls of that, Niall had thought. He'd pissed her off too easily with his stupid comments. He'd have to try and butter her up again. Otherwise, he might as well give up altogether. 'Come on, Kathleen,' he'd said in the most charming voice he could muster. 'Give us a wee kiss!'

'All you care about is snogging! Hiudy Gallagher was a real gentleman with me; he used to bring me everywhere, to the pictures and everything. He brought me to Sligo once in his father's car and out to Bundoran another day.'

'A lively buck by all accounts,' Niall had responded, but his sarcasm was lost on Kathleen.

'He was going to bring me to Derry another day if I'd still been at home. A real gentleman, Hiudie, if ever there was one.'

'I'm sure that's true,' Niall had agreed. What jinx was on him that he hadn't had the sense to move away from this one when she'd first sat next to him? He could've still been back there getting an eyeful of Alice Faye! Instead, here he was, stuck here with this Kathleen.... What a dope! This was nearly as bad as being invited to a meal, only to find that there was nothing to eat. And how the hell could a girl be so clueless about the nature of men? He thought back to that lively one he'd pulled back in Galway one night a while ago, on Lower Dominick Street. He'd gone back up High Street with that frisky little bird and she'd gone with him down one of the grassy lanes and over a ditch, as eager as hell. Mind you, she'd let on that she was as hot for a bit of action as he was – but then, when he'd tried it on, he got nowhere, the same as now. Not so much as a feel…for his troubles. They'd only had a smooch at the end of the night – a quick kiss and that was it! It was hard to credit it. Unlike Kathleen Brouder, however, that girl had been great craic, and she'd spoken lovely rich Irish to boot! Her Irish was so beautiful he could've stayed there all night just listening to her talk – never mind the fact that he was really hot for her.

And that girl had done something – completely innocently, he was sure of it – that'd left him speechless with desire. She'd reached inside her blouse and taken out a packet of cigarettes and she'd placed one into his mouth and the other into hers, as gently as if she were handing a soother to a child to relax it. 'Which of us'll light the match, you or me?' she'd asked Niall and he'd lit their fags very carefully, as though they'd only had the one match and couldn't afford for it to go out. And that hadn't been the end of it, either, because a little while later she'd done another trick that left him completely wild with lust. She'd jumped up suddenly, thrown off her shoes and rucked up the bottom of her dress in beneath the elastic of her drawers, then began dancing around the place like a happy little fairy.

This had been such a harmless and innocent gesture and yet it had awakened some hidden longing in Niall, something indefinable that went all the way back to his early youth, when he'd felt the first-ever stirrings of desire. He was under that girl's spell in that moment; there had been something so sensous and pagan in that one simple act that he'd felt like throwing off his own clothes and dancing around the place with her, as free and unrestrained as a bird. Dancing and flitting around the place all the while, this girl had sung a short nonsense ditty that was common to Gaeltacht children of the era.

As soon as she'd finished, she'd rearranged her clothes as quickly again, stopped dancing and sat down on the grass beside him, completely oblivious to how her capers had left Niall completely wild with love and longing....

'And did Hiudie Gallagher never try to kiss you, Kathleen?'

'What's that got to do with you, anyway? Hiudie knew his manners, I'll have you know.'

He must have been a total saint, Niall had thought, to have been able to keep his hands off Kathleen. Niall had gone for it then; put his arm around her and given her a quick kiss. He might as well have been kissing a statue for all the good it did him, however, and he'd released her again and taken his cigarettes out of his jacket.

'Maybe,' Kathleen had said, 'you have a girlfriend of your own, have you?' Pity, I don't. If I did, I wouldn't be here with you, you divvy, Niall had thought but kept to himself.

'A girlfriend, yeah, sure!'

'Do you really mean it?'

'Absolutely!'

He'd offered Kathleen a cigarette which she'd accepted gratefully. 'Thanks very much. That's very kind of you,' she'd said in a way that he hadn't been expecting. Her words pierced Niall's heart: he felt ashamed of the lustful thoughts he'd been harbouring.

How was it that he couldn't enjoy the company of a girl for its own sake, rather than constantly trying to have an old feel? he'd thought. This wasn't the first time that he'd had this regret. As regards his longing for a bit of action, it wasn't the sin itself that bothered him as much as the undue and unfair pressure it put on the woman who wasn't seeking it. As if a change of mind had come over her, Kathleen had placed her head on his shoulder and drew happily on the Woodbine.

'I was telling you lies there a while ago,' she'd said softly.

'You were, were you?' Niall had said, desire coursing through him again. She was about to confess something that would put a different cast on the night altogether; it appeared that there might be scope for a bit of action here, after all.

'I was. I was telling you that the Lynch family were very kind to me, but they're not. The children are nice; sure, little Nuala is a real dote, but herself is a right bitch, she never stops giving out to me, you couldn't keep her happy, whatever you did. As for himself, he doesn't even know that I'm in the house. The only time he ever talks to me is when he's smoking.'

'Oh,' Niall had said, disappointed that there wasn't anything in this revelation that he could turn to his advantage.

'She's as full of herself as anything, she hasn't the slightest respect for a domestic like me.'

'She doesn't?'

'She always making dirty digs at me.' She'd paused. 'What's your name, anyway?' Kathleen had asked out of the blue, anxiously. 'Jesus, I don't even know your name yet, do I?'

It was never smart to tell any woman your real name – Paddy Delaney always said when he was dishing out advice – not unless you wanted to keep going out with her. And neither should you give her your army number, he'd add sarcastically. A woman had come to the gates of the barracks one day, apparently, looking for a soldier named Murphy. 'Is it 65 Murphy you're looking for or 32 Murphy?' the policeman on the gate had asked of her jokily, but immediately the woman had retorted, 'It's neither of them. It's 69452 Murphy, please!'

'Niall O'Connell is my name,' Niall had heard himself say, against his instincts.

'Niall O'Connell,' Kathleen had intoned as if testing the name, '"Niall O'Connell and Kathleen Brouder": those two go nicely together, don't they?'

'Hmm,' Niall had replied, hesitantly circling his arm about her again.

'Guess what she said to me this afternoon, Niall?'

'I can't, Kathleen,' Niall had said, kneading her waist with his fingers, petrified that she'd start squirming with goosebumps again.

'When I was getting ready this afternoon, she told me to put some sort of shape on myself; not to be so tatty-looking leaving the house!'

'You're not tatty-looking at all, Kathleen,' Niall had replied, giving her a sympathetic squeeze.

'I'm not, am I?'

'Not at all!' Niall had said, pulling her closer and planting a small kiss on her cheek. There was an art to this seduction business, that's for sure; you couldn't be too abrupt in such matters.

'Are you sure that you don't have a girl somewhere?' Kathleen had repeated, and Niall had reassured her that he didn't. He nestled in closer still, his hands exploring the small of her back, and then down along the side of her waist towards her lovely thighs, his heart in his mouth all the while. He hadn't expected, by this stage, for her to be on for a bit of a feel. He'd kissed her again, with greater urgency, but just as he thought he was really getting somewhere, he'd stopped. There was something wrong. Oh Christ, Kathleen was crying, snivelling quietly to herself! Niall's pent-up lust had died instantly.

'What's wrong, Kathleen? Why are you crying?' he'd asked, disturbed at this sudden turn of events.

She took a moment to compose herself, then had pushed his arm away and said, 'You insulted me.'

'What?' Niall didn't know what in the name of God he was supposed to do about this. 'I insulted you… how do you mean? How did I insult you…?'

What sort of a curse was he under to have run into this one – given all the other birds that had been in the cinema that evening? The only thing now was to get the hell out of there as quickly as possible.

'You're all the same, you lot. All you want is one thing,' Kathleen had blubbed.

'If you'd any respect for me, you wouldn't treat me like this.'

Slowly now – yet warily – Niall had produced his cigarettes again. He'd offered Kathleen one but she shook her head. He'd lit up himself and gave an anguished sigh.

'Come on, I don't mean to insult you in the slightest. Sure, what's wrong with me trying to put my arm round you and kiss you? Here now, don't cry, good girl!'

Kathleen had dried her eyes and inched away from him slowly. 'I think I'll be going now,' she'd said in a subdued voice.

'Ara, don't! Isn't it a bit early to be heading off? I'll be quiet now, I swear!'

Niall hadn't really mean that: it had just been gentlemanly talk; an effort to stop her crying. He couldn't wait to get rid of her, to get as far away from her as possible. A peculiar mixture of guilt and self-loathing had engulfed him, along with a strong feeling of regret. Why the feck did he always have to be bloody fiddling around, anyway?

'I'm leaving now,' Kathleen had said. 'Good night to you.'

But she hadn't gone. It had been as if she were giving him the chance to make amends; maybe she'd wanted him to win her over with some kind words.

'Ara, don't leave now,' Niall had repeated, but she shook her head as much as to say that she didn't believe anything he said. She'd turned her back on him and walked towards the door of the house, ignoring the words that Niall unconvincingly called after her: 'So, maybe, I'll see you again'.

Niall had stayed where he was, leaning against the wall for a few minutes, as though he were a criminal lingering at the scene of his crime, when by rights, he should have disappeared as quickly as possible. He'd heard the door close behind her and had given a sigh of relief. He'd walked back down into town again, filled with a peculiar mixture of shame and regret. God, but that had been really awkward! If he could have melted into the ground there and then, he would gladly have done so, he felt so disgusted with himself. He felt dirty somehow, like he was some sort of pox-ridden creature, someone who ruined everything he touched, or made shit of it.

He cursed himself all the way to Bridge House. There were just three people inside: Simon McCarthy and two work-men, both of whom were well on it already, judging by the cut of them.

Simon half-smiled and nodded in Niall's direction, while Pat Neary gave him a great welcome.

'A pint there, please, Pat,' Niall said. 'God knows, I need one badly!'

Chapter 12

For a good while, Nano hadn't gone on another night out with Sheila after that fateful Sunday night. She was angry with herself – at her own stupidity and her lack of loyalty to Máirtín, above all. After they'd kissed that night, she'd pushed Peter away and run indoors quickly into the nurse's quarters, half-mortified with herself. Back in her room, Nano had felt an awful sense of regret. She was ashamed at her weakness and at how easily she had gone with a man whom she barely knew. God knows what exactly had come over her. And then she'd run off and left Peter standing there, stunned, and looking like a right fool.

It was only when she reached her room that Nano realised properly what had happened and began to feel really sorry. What had come over her; was she actually some kind of slut to have shifted a fellow she'd only met just an hour earlier? She was no better than those floozies – the town slappers – you got back home, really, wasn't she? Just like those brazen types who'd go off with anyone? She was a shameless rip and there was no point in her denying it or making excuses to herself about what'd happened. I mean, it wasn't as if she were one of those dizzy lasses who went off the rails the minute they found themselves in male company? She was a grown woman, for pity's sake – a decent one who should have had more sense. This was the first time that she'd ever done anything that she couldn't tell Máirtín about and she was unsure now whether she should hide or admit it. It was bad enough to give in to your feelings like that if you were single and without any ties, but there was no excuse for it at all in her case. To top it all off, Sheila had found the whole thing hilarious the following morning. What were you doing running in so suddenly like that and leaving poor Peter Sharkey standing against the wall out there like a big gom, she'd asked Nano first thing the next morning. What kind of a freak was she running off like that – as though she weren't safe with Peter or something? For God's sake!

'What's wrong with him anyway?' Sheila had asked after a while.

'Nothing,' Nano had said in a flat voice.

'Well, why did you run away from him like that, then?' Sheila had said as though trying her best not to laugh.

'Because I shouldn't have been out there with him in the first place, Sheila, that's why. And I wouldn't have been, either, if it wasn't for you!'

'Ah c'mon, Nano, show some sense, will you? Anyone would think that you'd spent the night with him or something? Honestly, you'd make the cat laugh, the way you're going on! I'm serious. It's just as well for you that you didn't spend an hour or two out against the wall with him or you'd have to go off on pilgrimage now to Lough Derg or something!'

'At least, I'd have reason to go, then!' Nano had said.

'Ara, have an ounce of sense, love; a small bit of shifting like that is nothing,' Sheila had replied, putting on her uniform

It mightn't be anything to Sheila or many others like her, maybe, Nano thought, but it was to her way of thinking. Sheila was a girl who wasn't happy unless she'd a glass in her hand and a man by her side – that's just the way she was. And it wouldn't have made so much difference had she been a young one out dancing and singing and tasting a bit of freedom for the first time in her life! But Sheila was more of an age now that she should have been thinking ahead and planning for the future.

'Anyway,' Sheila had said to her that morning, 'he wants to see you again.'

'He'll be waiting a long time, then,' Nano had replied, placing a hairpin in her cap and heading down for breakfast. She'd been in a foul mood all morning because of that. She'd nearly bitten the head off Fidelma Byrne earlier about something or other; and she must have been at it again, because sitting opposite Nano at the canteen-table was that Carlow-woman, staring wide-eyed and frightened at her like she was some sort of wierdo. Byrne was afraid of her that morning, seeing as she didn't have McDermott or Geraghty or any of that crowd with her for back-up.

'What're you looking at anyway, you scrubber? Or did McDermott let you off the leash for once?' Nano had asked her gruffly, and Byrne had gone out as quickly as she could.

Nano had thrown herself into her work to try and forget the whole night-out, but it was the best part of a week before she felt herself again. Unfortunately, the constant digs about that night went on for a while afterwards. There wasn't a night when, on Sheila's return from the dance at Saint Bridget's Hall, she didn't have a new message from Peter for her!

'He's mad about you, Nano! It's true, I swear! The poor fellow's in an awful state; he's looking out for you every night at the hall, so he is. You should go and see him anyway – or talk to him, at least.'

'Listen to me now, Sheila,' said Nano with as much patience as she could muster. 'I'm getting a little bit sick of this craic.'

'Oh, but aren't some of people getting fierce stand-offish and hoity-toity?' Sheila replied. Another night, Sheila accused her of being a bit odd when she refused to go to the dance with her and was clearly hurt by Nano's behaviour. The truth was that Sheila was the best friend there that Nano had – the only friend, really – other than Hilda Jackson, and Hilda was very scatter-brained and all over the place at the best of times. But then, friendship and loyalty took different forms, and Sheila should've understood that.

'I'm not odd at all, Sheila, God knows I'm not! I'm quite happy to go to town with you any time that we're free – or anything like that.'

'You mean go to the shops, is it?'

'You know full well that I can't be going out to dances or be make up foursomes, though.'

'Because of Máirtín, is it?'

'Exactly.'

'You're mad,' said Sheila.

'Am I?' said Nano, just about keeping a grip on herself.

She'd bought the wool for a woollen jersey down town and she'd begun knitting it for Máirtín in the evenings as a small reparation – if that's what it was. Wasn't that what she was doing now?

In all honesty, though, there had been times lately when Nano had wondered whether Sheila might be right, after all. Maybe Sheila sensed that she was getting through because now she shut the door and stood with her back to it.

'I'm going to say one thing to you now, Nano, and you won't take this the wrong way, I hope.'

'Fire away, sister, I know that you're going to say it anyway, so....'

'If I was you, Nano, I wouldn't feel tied down or under an obligation to any man, especially if he's not even in the same country as you.' It's not like there's anything settled properly between the two of you; I mean, you don't know – any more than I do – when you might be getting married! Aren't you better off enjoying life a bit while you have the chance?'

'I enjoy life plenty as it is, Sheila.'

'Oh, Nano, c'mon, you've no life at all, really! Sure, you'd have more fun in prison than you have here, working all day and in here by yourself at night. I wouldn't call that a life, girl.'

'It'll do me for the moment, anyway,' Nano replied tersely, and an irritated Sheila slammed the door slightly on her way out.

Nano sat there without moving, then laid the knitting aside and wrote a letter to Máirtín Spillane. Nano had written a couple of letters to him since the night of the dance and she'd been sorely tempted to tell him that she'd gone out that night. But she couldn't bring herself to tell him about the dance unless she told him the full story, and she wasn't able to do that even if it would have been a big relief to get it off her chest. To tell a white lie was far worse than telling the truth, and she found this nagging conscience was making her cranky. But why did she have to confess anything to Máirtín Bid Anthony, she'd ask herself then. After all, it wouldn't have happened in the first place if she hadn't been forced to leave home – seeing as he didn't have the guts or sense to sort out their situation? Hadn't she wasted enough of her life already on him – and what exactly had she got for her trouble? There was a lot of truth in what Sheila had said, if Nano could just admit it. It was the man who always had the upper hand in these matters, anyway.

But if Nano wouldn't admit her moment of weakness to Máirtín, she did so in confession. Father Holmes was a small relaxed Englishman who was Father Begley's curate. Father Holmes couldn't see that she'd done anything much wrong at all, and, in all honesty, Nano didn't get much satisfaction from the almost indifferent way he granted her forgiveness. It was easier to be honest with God himself, directly, than with another person in a case like this, and it was that sense of forgiveness that Nano was seeking most of all.

And yet, when it got down to it, Nano felt that she hadn't done badly by coming over to Norwold. She'd a regular income now, something that she hadn't really had when she was working at the knitting factory back home in Spiddal, and she had a degree of independence that she would find difficult to give up. If the food in the hospital was bad –very bad at times – it was enough to sustain you, and in any case she would treat herself to a drop of tea and a bit of sweet-cake in some café downtown whenever she was off work. You could buy fish and chips cheaply there too, even if you had to take them outside and eat them out of a newspaper on the street; this was something that most of the country girls wouldn't do out of embarrassment. It was alright for the city crowd who were used to that back in Ireland, and Sheila and her friends couldn't understand why the other women wouldn't eat their chips outside. But out in the Irish countryside, that was something that a young woman just didn't do: it was regarded as being inappropriate.

The biggest thing that bothered Nano about her new workplace was the tribalism; the way that different classes of people were so suspicious of one another. All the disagreements and conniving that her fellow-Irish indulged in drove her mad, sometimes. It was true that the Irish had some sort of standing in England, and were granted more respect than the displaced people of Eastern Europe, the Italians and – in certain cases – some of the English themselves; but this didn't mean that the English weren't distrustful of them. They saw the Irish as an unreliable people who were, on occasions, impenetrable. Many of the English still had a beef with the Irish and were suspicious of them because of Ireland's neutrality during the war, and there were also plenty who maintained that ancient and long-established suspicion of Catholicism. Now and again, someone might throw the odd jibe in the direction of Irish women about their faith; this would have been even more of a problem had the Irish not been so ready to defend their religion. For them, Catholicism and Nationalism were intimately linked and deserved the same respect as symbols such as 'The Soldier's Song', the shamrock and the Irish flag. There were Irish women who never bothered going to Mass or the sacraments but who'd fight back with fierce pride and indignation at the slightest sarcastic or demeaning reference to their religion, to Eamon de Valera, or to anything or anyone relating to Ireland. When the chips were down, both the Irish and the English knew in their hearts how things stood between them and why they had an historical suspicion of one another – even if they never voiced such sentiments openly. This was an ancestral feeling or understanding that had been passed down through the generations in both countries.

It was a complex relationship, an ambivalent mixture of love and hate that two neighbours might have for one another. This strange combination of familiarity and contempt meant that the Irish and English peoples identified with one another in a way that didn't apply to other communities and nationalities. It wasn't all bad between them; they had mutual empathy and understanding in addition to a sense of community that had developed over time as both peoples had learned to live and work alongside one another.

It was a strange phenomenon, and Nano wouldn't have bothered reflecting on those issues, except that circumstances dictated it. Sometimes, she longed to keep herself to herself, but there were others when this simply wasn't possible, because she had to stand up for herself. Mary McDermott wasn't always wrong; she often spoke sense, and the same went for Sheila herself. At times, Nano had found herself defending Sheila against some of the English girls that they got on really well with, girls that she liked a lot more than she did the Irish Mafia, as she called McDermott and her friends.

Nano was saving a little, without realising it, and whenever she heard other women describing the really good wages that Irishmen were on, Nano would think it an awful shame that Máirtín wasn't over here, so that he could have been earning that kind of money as well. According to Catherine Geraghty, it wasn't uncommon for some of the lads here – for example those working on harvesting or piecework for farmers – to earn up to twenty or even thirty pounds a week, incredible as such wages might seem! They were all Mayo people, needless to say, because there were no crowd like the Mayo lot for earning money, if what Catherine was saying was true! If Máirtín Bid Anthony had been over here, and the pair of them had been working, they wouldn't have been long putting together a tidy sum. They'd be well set-up in no time, and their lives would have been on a secure footing already.

Naturally, Nano didn't mention all of this in her letters home; she praised England to the high heavens whenever she wrote to Máirtín.

She'd told him all about the good pay rates and how the work was so plentiful. They were building houses everywhere these days and, on the outskirts of Norwold, you could buy a new house with as little as £100 deposit. Nano had easily saved £100 pounds in only one year, and there was no doubt that Máirtín would have earned top wages over here also, no matter what type of work he was doing. There wasn't a better man in the parish at home for doing any sort of physical work, cutting turf or anything. But what good was that when Máirtín was as tied to home as though chains were wrapped around him – and he would be like that until his mother died. Nano, for the first time in a long while, considered their situation as coldly and objectively as she could. She could certainly stand one year, two years or maybe even three, if she had to. She'd still be on the right side of thirty by then and many women older than that had got married and had a family. But who's to say that Máirtín's mother, Bid Antaine, wouldn't live on for another ten years or more? Many a sick person lives longer than a healthy one, and Nano was very doubtful that Máirtín's mother was half as ill as others were making out. There was no point in Nano avoiding the truth or trying to pull the wool over her own eyes any longer; it looked very likely that she wouldn't be able to marry for a long time yet, maybe ten years, and by then she'd be pushing forty....

'Don't hold it against me,' Sheila had said the night after she'd slammed the door on her way out. 'I'm only thinking of the best for you; and I do understand your situation – really, I do!'

'I thought you were trying to make a match for me with Peter Sharkey – was that what you were about?' Nano had asked, playing it down. Anyway, this was nothing but a phoney war, needless to say; there was no point in them falling out with one another about this sort of thing. Nano would do whatever she thought was for the best, irrespective of what Sheila thought, and Sheila would come around to her way of thinking, eventually.

'Ara, don't bother with Peter or any of those others if you don't want to, girl. Anyway, every woman has to look out for herself, or she's the one who'll get the worst end of the stick. I try them out for a while but I wouldn't ever like to be left relying on any one man.'

'But you will some day, Sheila – be relying on someone, I mean – you do want to get married someday, don't you?' It occurred to Nano how little she really knew about Sheila or her life. Now that she thought about it – even though Sheila was the chattiest and most outspoken of them all – Nano had revealed a lot more about herself to Sheila than the Cork girl had to her.

'I suppose I'll have to rely on them then, alright, when the time comes,' Sheila had said with a tinge of regret.

'That's unless you intend staying an old maid,' Nano had replied, laughing.

'I might live to be old, but it's a long time since I was a virgin,' said Sheila, and Nano went quiet with embarrassment. It wasn't that she was surprised at this fact but rather at the abrupt way that Sheila had revealed it. 'Oh, that's nothing,' Sheila had added, noting Nano's discomfort. 'They're not half as plentiful as people think!'

Nano hadn't known what to say.

Sheila threw her head back onto the pillow and smiled disarmingly, staring over at Nano as if taking her in carefully. 'Do you mind me asking you something, Nano…?'

'Of course not,' Nano said, her face reddening. If Sheila had asked her this question at any other time, she'd have told her to shut up straightaway. But for some reason that Nano couldn't readily explain, she was glad – almost grateful – of the other woman's curiosity. Her shyness prevented her from talking, so that Sheila pressed her again.

'Well?'

'I'm still intact, sister, if that's what you mean,' Nano had said, blanching at the awkwardness of the term, and the pair laughed.

'You were lucky, so,' Sheila had said, wiping her eyes with the edge of her pillow and bursting into laughter again.

'There's no luck about it. That has nothing to do with it, sister,' Nano had blurted out. Sheila had paused then said, 'And, you were never tempted?'

'As often as I have fingers.'

'I wouldn't call that too often, really,' Sheila had replied. 'I don't remember any time I wasn't tempted.'

'Well, you were the lucky one, then,' Nano had said, adopting a more serious tone.

'Yes,' Sheila had responded, thoughtfully. 'Everything's stacked against women in this life; the man can just head for the hills but the woman always has to pay the piper, I'm afraid.'

'It's up to the woman to keep control of herself, then, and not get herself into any trouble,' Nano had said as she began undressing for bed.

'But, it's not always that easy, is it?' Sheila had replied. Nano hadn't made a response but she'd have reason to recall Sheila's words at a later date.

Christmas drew closer, and the town of Norwold begin its preparations. The shops might have been bereft of many of the products that had been plentiful prior to the war but, despite the rationing, the shops were beautifully decorated with holly and little Christmas trees on tin stands flanking the doors. Their windows were festooned with tinsel, pretend-snow and frilly paper decorations. The streets were crowded with people on Saturdays – tough-looking young Teddy-boys with skinheads, sporting synthetic silk vests and dapper suits tapering narrowly at the ankles, posing and loudly larking about. Also hanging around street corners in giggly groups were the factory girls; they were all dressed up too, in loose jackets and stiletto heels, their hair perfectly coiffed.

You could feel the energy in the air, the dynamism of people enjoying a sense of liberation and money in their pockets for the first time. The hardships and unemployment endured by previous generations were just a bad memory, a miserable era that had gone, never to return. Everyone had work and the state was looking after this new generation in an unprecedented way. This generation of English people were very fortunate, Nano thought; their lives didn't involve the pain of having to emigrate to another country to earn a living. If Nano and Máirtín had happened to have been born here, they'd have had it much easier, been able to make a living and save money instead of wasting their lives like they were at present. There were times when Nano couldn't but agree with Sheila when she said that there was some kind of curse on Ireland. About a fortnight before Christmas, the pair found themselves off-duty on the same day and they'd gone into town and toured the big posh clothes shops, looking at outfits costing more than a month's wages. This didn't bother Sheila, who tried them all on, even if there wasn't a hope in hell that she could afford any.

'You're shameful, Sheila, trying on all these clothes!' Nano chided.

'But sure, they don't know whether I can afford them, and anyway, it's nice to see what they look like, even if it's just for a quick minute.'

'I know, but it's not right to be wasting their time if you haven't a notion of buying anything.'

'To hell with them,' retorted Sheila. 'Sure, isn't that their job?'

It was the same story when they went into Woolworths to have a cup of tea, and Sheila asked the girl in charge of the records section to put on her favourite songs, ones by Guy Mitchell and Johnny Ray, and people that Nano had never heard of.

'They must be sick of me coming in here, listening to their records and never buying any,' said Sheila.

The Christmas spirit had already begun to affect Nano, especially since they had put up decorations in the corridors of the hospital: coloured paper, pieces of mistletoe and balloons; even *Merry Xmas* written back-to-front across the windows. Even so, she would feel homesick now and then. Some of the girls were going home for the holiday and were on a high. All they talked about was being back home and going to dances; all the friends they'd meet up with again and the tasty meals they'd get to eat. One girl from County Clare, who'd been in Norwold less than a year, was so excited about that she could barely eat. Nano had posted her Christmas cards already as well as a few presents. She'd bought a fancy clay pipe for her father that had cost her the lion's share of a week's wages, and she'd knitted a zip-up cardigan for her brother Bartley. For Máirtín, she'd bought a shirt and tie, and had nearly finished knitting him a pullover. Nano had also written to her sister in the United States. Christmas Day was when the loneliness would really kick in, so it was probably just as well that Nano would be working right through the festive season.

'You'll be coming to the hospital dance, won't you, girl?' said Sheila as they made their way from the bus-stop to Norwold Hospital that afternoon. This annual event, held by Matron for her staff, had already been advertised for Boxing Day, but Nano hadn't even considered going.

'Why should I?' she asked Sheila. 'Sure, I haven't a notion of going.'

'It's nearly a law here that we all attend the Christmas dance unless you've got a good excuse not to. If you don't, you'll hear all about it.'

'I couldn't give a damn,' said Nano. 'I'm doing my work well, arn't I, and that's the only rule I have to follow, as far as I'm concerned.'

'It'll be a great night,' Sheila said. 'It's always the best part of Christmas here. And don't tell me that Máirtín would be upset if you went to some annual hospital dance!'

'Why would he, Sheila? But that's not the reason, anyway.'

'I'll have to go by myself, then I suppose,' said Sheila with mock regret.

'Oh, you'll have plenty of company, don't you worry about that at all,' was Nano's retort. They turned in at the hospital, and, as they approached their living quarters, Sheila placed her hand on Nano's elbow and winked at her. 'Come on, we'll have a chat with this fellow here,' she said, conspiratorially, referring to the gardener who was bent over pruning some rush bushes at the side of the entrance. He had his back to them and didn't realise that they were nearby until Sheila said 'Hi' to him. 'You're new here, aren't you?'

The man straightened and turned to them with a warm smile. He was one of the best-looking men Nano had ever laid eyes on: even though he wasn't very tall, he was well built and had curly blonde hair and piercing green eyes. He was one of the displaced persons. He was wearing blue dungarees tied with a leather belt and had on a pair of work-gloves to protect his hands from thorns. There was something else that Nano found very attractive in him, which she couldn't yet place. Her heart quietly skipped a beat.

'Hi,' he replied, ignoring Sheila's question. His eyes studied the women carefully and his gaze settled on Nano. His eyes fixed on hers momentarily and she felt her face flush with embarrassment. She didn't know where to look.

'Do you need a hand?' Sheila asked him, and the gardener handed her the pruning shears, half-joking. 'They're way too big,' she joked. 'I might take your head off with them; they're massive!'

'I'll take a chance on it,' the gardener said, revealing a perfect set of teeth. The man looked at Nano again and she felt her throat tighten with awkwardness. 'How about you? Don't you like working?'

'It's my day off, brother,' Nano replied, surprised at how easy the response came to her. 'I've enough work to keep me occupied for the rest of the week.'

Sheila had Nano by the sleeve and was pulling her away. 'Let's go, Matron is looking out at us and this man will get the road if we keep him away from his work!'

What Sheila said was true: Nano also spotted the matron behind her office window. There was an informal understanding at the hospital that nursing and administration staff should avoid contact. They walked on.

'What would you say to a bit of that, Nano? Handsome or what! He'd only have to wave his finger in my direction and I'd be off with him.'

'He's not bad, I suppose,' said Nano with as much indifference as she could muster. Sheila was more perceptive than she let on, however, because back in their room she threw her coat onto the bed and said, 'I'm jealous of you now, girl.'

'What rubbish are you on about now?' asked Nano.

'Because of your man there! The only one he could look at was you, daughter; he had no more interest in me than....'

Sure enough, the gardener was waiting for Nano near the front gate the following evening as she was going down to the post box nearest the hospital. Nano got a bit of a fright as his shadow suddenly appeared at the gate.

'Hi,' he said. 'We meet again.'

'If we do, it's not coincidence, by the looks of it,' said Nano, but immediately regretted it. It wasn't good to sound so sure of oneself and, for all she knew, the man might have been waiting for someone else.

'It's not coincidence,' the man replied, not sounding the least bit put out. 'I was hoping that you might be coming this way.'

Nano was slightly taken aback by the man's directness. 'You must've been waiting a while, so,' she said. 'How'd you know that I'd be out here?'

'I didn't, of course; I was just hoping that you'd come along, Nano.'

'Who told you my name?' Nano asked, thinking of Sheila immediately.

'I just asked around,' he said, gently. 'Julius is my name, Julius Kuzleikas.'

'Well,' Nano said, unsure what to say. 'Well, Julius, I don't know why you're freezing out here waiting for me.' She made as if to walk away.

'I was hoping to see you, that's why,' replied Julius as if this were the most normal thing in the world.

'Why?' Nano asked him straight out, her question belying a slight nervousness.

Up to then, she hadn't paid much attention to any of the lads that worked around the place, looking after the gardens or walking to and fro with barrows of cinders from the boiler-house. She hadn't seen anyone that had set her heart aflutter – not until now! During the last few days, however, every time she spotted someone crossing the hospital grounds her heart had begun racing in case it was him. Despite herself, she'd started becoming preoccupied with this handsome stranger; the more she tried to forget him, the more she thought found herself thinking about him. She was on a bit of a high and she couldn't help it.

'Why?' said Julius, throwing her question back at her. *Why wouldn't I want to see you again?* was what he really wanted to say.

'You're posting a letter,' Julius said, 'let me walk with you as far as the post box.' This was a request that Nano could not refuse as it was only a little way down the road.

'Well, if you want to walk down with me, so,' she said, in a guarded voice.

It was a beautiful night with a touch of frost in the air; the stars twinkled in the dark-blue firmament above, reminding Nano of home at this time of the year. If she had been alone, she'd probably have gone for a short walk after posting the letter, she calculated; it was too nice to go back indoors yet, in any case. Sheila had gone out somewhere and their room was as quiet as the grave. They walked along in silence together for a few minutes.

'How do you like the hospital?' Nano asked.

Julius didn't have a lot to say about that. He wasn't particularly fond of his job as a groundsman there, he told her. 'Do *you* like this place?' he asked.

'I do… I think,' Nano replied. 'There are plenty of worse jobs out there, I'm sure.'

'It'll do me for a while, I suppose,' said Julius, as though talking to himself. They had reached at the post box, where Nano checked over her letter before posting it. It was just as well that the letter couldn't talk, she thought, as it could tell a different story to Máirtín than the one it presently contained.

'Well, I'm going back now, Julius, seeing as my business here is done,' Nano said.

'Don't,' Julius said, gently placing his hand on her arm.

'What about having a drink with me down here – just one quick one?'

'I don't drink, thank you very much,' said Nano.

'Have a glass of anything at all – that won't do you any harm, will it?' Julius replied, seizing the moment.

'Of course, it wouldn't,' said Nano, surprised at her own eagerness. The Tudor Rose was a large mock-Tudor building, built before the war to serve the needs of a local suburban housing estate being constructed on the edge of the town. The people around there had ideas above their station, Nano had heard the other nurses in the canteen say. The girls would joke about the local people. They were the type who made great play of drinking just one glass of beer on a night out when an Irish person might have drunk a gallon of the stuff. They were a fairly tight with their money, by all accounts. The Tudor Rose was half-empty most days except for the occasional refugee down from the old Prison-of-War camp a mile north of the hospital.

The pub was divided into three sections, one of which was a long, bare empty bar with a flagstone floor and hard-backed wooden chairs. Another was a noisy games-room where people were playing skittles, and the third was the lounge, which displayed a number of hunting pictures. Big evergreen plants in tubs dotted the place and – on a perch above the bar – was a tough-talking parrot whose wisecracks were always a great source of amusement to the customers. They went into the lounge, Julius opening the door for her very politely. In here, a bespectacled man was playing a nice, soft tune on the piano – not that anyone was paying any attention to him.

Julius held out a chair for Nano and asked her what she liked to drink. He was clearly a man who didn't go out dressed any old way because he was wearing a fine blue, specially tailored suit, a bright white shirt with gold-coloured cufflinks, everything matching.

'I don't mind, really – orange or lemonade. I don't drink anything stronger than that,' she said.

Julius nodded and went to the bar and Nano sighed quietly to herself. For God's sake, whatever was she doing; what sort of a fool was she to be sitting here with a man she didn't even know? She'd have to keep an eye on the clock and not go over the half-hour she'd told him was her limit or God knows where this stupidity might lead. Wasn't she old enough to have a bit more cop-on? There were plenty of other women who wouldn't have been half as nice as she was to this bucko, and who'd have told him to take a run and a jump for himself.

Julius returned with the orange juice and placed it in front of her as grandly as if it were a bottle of champagne. He'd bought a bottle of beer for himself; maybe he wasn't into drinking in a big way either, Nano thought. His hands and nails were so clean that you wouldn't have known he worked as a gardener. Nano noticed this as he lit up a cigarette in a small cigarette-holder, after requested her permission to smoke. Nano thought of other men who went out socialising, with dirty nails and fingers burned black with tobacco.

'Your health,' said Julius, raising his glass of beer and repeating the word in his own language afterwards.

Nano asked him to say the word again, and then once more, until she was able to pronounce it properly herself. 'Sviekas,' she said to Julius and he nodded with approval.

'That's Lithuanian,' he explained. 'I'm Lithuanian.' Sheila was wrong about him then, even though she was always making out that she had the inside track on things. She had thought that he was Ukrainian and had even claimed that they were a crowd that couldn't be trusted. There were Ukrainians, Lithuanians, Poles and many other different nationalities living up at the camp all year round, Sheila had said. They'd have wild nights up there and big drinking sessions; fighting, as well.

'There are other Lithuanians at the hospital, aren't there?' Nano asked.

'They're everywhere now,' Julius replied, with a short inscrutable laugh, and asked whether this was her first time at the Tudor Rose.

'It is. I'd no business coming in here before.'

'You haven't told me your surname,' said Julius, and Nano laughed.

'You should ask whoever gave you my first name!'

'You tell me,' Julius said in that very direct way of his. But then, she thought, maybe that strong or authoritarian trait of his was what attracted her to him, quite apart from the fact that he was very handsome.

'What sort of a country is Lithuania?' Nano asked, even though she was really more curious about Julius himself than where he was from.

'It's a country like any other. Or, it was once, anyway. I wouldn't like to go back there again.'

All of those countries were controlled by others now – the Russians mainly – from what Nano'd heard in the hospital.... War was a terrible thing, and God help us but they were lucky back in Ireland, really, even if things were bad there at times. Éamonn de Valera – or the Long Fellow as Nano's father called him, had kept Ireland out of the war, she'd always heard. If it wasn't for the Long Fellow, the English would have walked all over them – either them or the Germans – and it would've been the same all over again: a master-servant relationship all over again!

'So you wouldn't like to move back home at some stage?' she asked Julius with a small laugh.

'I couldn't, Nano.'

Nano already felt empathy and a connection with this man, and the more they talked, the less shy she became of him. There was no doubt that it was a very sad thing for someone to be unable to return to their own country. Nano wanted to know more about Julius and his homeplace, and the people he came from.

'Do you have any photographs of home?' she asked. Julius hesitated momentarily and took out an old worn leather wallet from inside his jacket. The photos were old and faded, and Julius' mother and father were in one of them. They were country people, his father in a hat and a long-sleeved vest, exactly the same type as one would see back in Connemara; his mother was a short and stocky woman, her hair covered in a headscarf. Julius also had an old photo of himself, although Nano barely recognised him. He was dressed in a military uniform and was the spit – with his uniform and buzzcut – of those young men Nano saw coming home on leave from Renmore. The last photo had been taken in the countryside as well, and showed a group young people standing in front of a large haystack. Nano felt an ache of sadness. It reminded her of home. A much younger-looking Julius stood in the centre of this photo, a girl next to him on whose shoulder he'd placed a hand in gentlemanly fashion.

'Your girlfriend, is it?' Nano asked him but Julius gave an enigmatic laugh.

'We were at school together.'

'What was her name, Julius?' Nano asked, wondering quietly why she'd spoken of her in the past tense.

'Agnes Mitskis.'

'Agnes Mitskis,' repeated Nano as though she were tasting the words on her tongue. 'She was your girlfriend, I'd say!' she joked, but Julius' reply was solemn.

'A group of us used to go around together; we'd all just started in the same college but the war put an end to that.'

College... no wonder she'd sensed that there was something about him: how proper he was and how good his English was compared to the other refugees that were working in the hospital. There was a lot more to this Julius than met the eye, Nano thought. 'You aren't engaged to one another or anything?' she asked. Julius shook his head and laughed. 'Maybe you would be if it wasn't for the war?' she persisted.

'If it wasn't for –' repeated Julius, thoughtfully. 'I'm not so sure that such an idea as "if it wasn't for" even exists.' A familiar emotion coursed through Nano: she had thought exactly the same thing since moving to England. Everyone single one of us was in the hands of fate.

'Isn't that strange? I've often thought that myself, Julius, that everyone has to accept their lot in life and that it's pointless to imagine that things can work out differently. We have to accept whatever fate has set out for us, don't we?'

'You've the makings of a philosopher in you, yet,' Julius said, teasing her. Nano glanced over at the clock above the bar

'I've got to be getting back now,' she said. She thought that Julius might press her to stay on for a bit longer but he didn't.

'Are you sure?' was all he said, a small note of regret in his voice. 'I'll walk as far as the hospital with you, then.' They were quiet for a while as they walked back up the road, and the thought of that lonely, bare room she was returning to made Nano sorry that she had called such an abrupt end to the evening.

As if sensing how she felt, Julius placed his hand gently on her elbow. 'Come out with me some other night, Nano – to the pictures or wherever you want.'

'I can't Julius, thanks all the same,' Nano hesitantly replied.

'You can't or you won't: which is it, Nano?'

'They're one and the same,' Nano replied even though Julius was by now holding her by the hand. His closeness was starting to make her feel a bit anxious.

'No, they're not – they're not the same at all!' said Julius in that commanding tone of his.

'What's stopping you from coming out, Nano?'

'You didn't ever think that I might already have someone else, Julius, did you?'

'It's very likely, I'm sure. But he's not over here, is he?'

'How do you know?' They'd reached a stage of childish flirting, Nano thought; she might as well say goodnight to Julius right then and head inside. 'He's definitely not over here,' said Julius. 'I told you that I made enquiries!'

'Good for you,' replied Nano, unsure whether or not she liked this idea. 'Get away with you now, you and your enquiries, both!'

'What's stopping you, then? Can't you come out with me some other night, then?'

If she went out with him one night, chances were that she'd go out with him again – and then there'd be another night and another one – and slowly but surely, over time, she'd give in and betray Máirtín.

'I can't, Julius,' she said. 'I've a boyfriend at home and it wouldn't be right. Thanks very much for the drink and the company tonight, though – really!'

She began to walk away but Julius stopped her again. 'I'm on afternoon duty for the next few days in the boiler-house. But I'm free on Friday night, Nano, and I'd like you to come out with me that then, if possible.'

'I won't, Julius,' she said. 'Good night to you now.'

But Julius wasn't going to be fobbed off that easily. He placed his hand in hers and gave her a gentle, persuasive squeeze.

'I'll be here at the gate at nine o'clock, Nano, and I'll wait for you. Maybe you'll change your mind between now and Friday?'

'I doubt it,' said Nano as she hurried inside.

Chapter 13

From the first instant that Trevor Bartley Billy jammed his fork into the ground each morning until he returned it to the toolbox every evening, he barely took a moment's rest. Other than the two breaks they had for food, he never stopped working, digging and breaking up the ground without cease, like someone in a trance. If Trevor had ever considered the question in any detail, he'd have realised that Paddy McAllister was getting a better deal for the two pounds, one crown a day that he paid him; indeed, he was worth more than two of your average workers. He'd have had to pay the latter thirty shillings a day each, at the very least, and their daily output wouldn't have come anywhere close to Trevor's. But Trevor wasn't interested in such measures of production; he was getting well-paid for his work and that was enough for him. And he was by no means under-selling himself, according to his way of thinking. He wouldn't have been shy to ask for a pay increase, had he felt entitled. He was one of the few men working for McAllister who earned nearly thirteen guineas a week, and that was something. Anyway, he'd other things to worry about these days.

'I've some news for you,' Mullen said to him one morning just after they'd started work, and Trevor could tell that he was bursting to tell him and what it was about.

'Fire away,' Trevor said, in as uninterested a manner as he could muster, flinging a massive heap of clay aside with a flick of his fork.

'The Jackeen half-killed Babeen Tam Peggy's son in a fight last night!'

'Christ!' said Trevor, shocked.

The Connemara-man who'd got the hiding, and whose proper name was Patrick Costello, was famous from Cricklewood to Gravesend and from Shepherd's Bush to Dagenham for his prowess with his fists. Anywhere that the Irish were involved in construction work or wherever they congregated in large numbers – in the dance halls and the pubs – his name came up, usually in connection to his skills as a fighter. After all, this was a man whom no-one had ever beaten in a fight since he'd first set foot in England! Costello was as fine and powerfully built a man as any who'd ever come over on the emigrant boat.

A giant of a man, Costello was also one of the strongest and toughest labourers the Irish community had ever produced. As a boxer, he combined power and ability, and had a killer punch into the bargain. Trevor had seen Costello fighting only once before and that had been outside the Garryowen in Hammersmith more than a year earlier. That night, Costello had fought a big Kerryman by the name of Fitzgerald, and, privately, Trevor would have admitted that he wouldn't have taken on either of them – if he was being entirely honest about it. If the Jackeen had beaten them, then he wouldn't have much problem beating anyone else in London either.

'Are you sure about this, you bollix?'

'Jaysus– wasn't I there watching it, Trevor? I saw the whole thing! The Jackeen challenged Patrick outside the Banba as cocky as if he was challenging me now. And he didn't give a tupenny damn about anyone else – even if there were loads from Con there!'

'Jesus,' said Trevor, picturing the scene. The crowd gathering outside on the street in Kilburn, and Patrick Costello the giant standing head-and-shoulders above the lot of them; then the Jackeen calling him out for fair play.

'And, did he have any reason for calling him out?'

'No reason except that he wanted to make a name for himself. He must have heard talk of Patrick and wanted to try him out.'

'He's not afraid of anyone, this bastard, is he?' asked Trevor as though he were talking to himself. 'Unless he had backup, did he?'

'No, he didn't have any backup, brother; he's not the type to ask for any, I'd say – because the bastard's dynamite.'

This bothered Trevor but he didn't show it; instead, he spat on his palms and rubbed them together. 'Here, Mullen, let's get back to work, we can chat as we're going along,' he said, jamming the fork deep into the red dry earth, soil that had traces of black, like cinders, mixed through it. 'Was it just that he asked Patrick to have it out straight away, right there on the spot, like?'

The whole thing was hard to believe – if it had been anyone apart from Costello! The night that Costello had gone up against the Kerryman was still etched on his mind. The Kerryman had been as physically strong and heavy as anyone his Connemara counterpart had fought, but Costello had planked him in the end with one punch. One punch the sound of crunching metal, right on the button, was all it had taken Costello. All Costello had done afterwards was nod in the direction of the other man and ask him if he'd had enough. An intimation of menace came to Trevor suddenly, as if from nowhere. He'd taken a big risk that day when he'd teased and tormented the Jackeen in the car; this buck was a dangerous bastard, no question about it.

'He went up to him, son, and said to him – and let me be struck down dead if I tell one word of a lie! – "Hi, culchie," he says, "I hear that you're fairly useful with your fists!" As the Son of God is my judge now, Trevor, that's exactly what he said to him!'

'And what did Costello say to that?'

'Oh, it didn't knock a stir out of him; he just looked as if he was about to laugh. "What?" he asked the Jackeen, as if he was talking to a child. "Were you thinking of giving me a go, is it?"'

'And what did the big mullock say to that?' Trevor asked, still ploughing the ground ferociously. He'd get a full blow-by-blow account of what had what had happened later on from someone else – and if Mullen was exaggerating, then he'd be sorry.

"'I was thinking giving you a beating, that's all,'" said the Jackeen, "if I got fair play, like.'"

'He said that, by Christ!'

'Oh, there wasn't a hint of fear on the f**er's part, Trevor. No way. He might as well have walked up to him and said, "How are things?". He's a cool customer, this one. I'm telling you!'

'And what did Costello say to that?'

It was up to Costello to get the first punch in, in this situation, Trevor thought. The first punch was often the clincher.

'Oh, he told him that he'd get fair play, he guaranteed him that. "You're a stranger around here, Jack," he said, and "the only one who'll land a punch on you is me, you needn't worry about that at all!"'

'By dad,' said Trevor.

'Well, the crowd drew back out of the way then and the fight started, and I'll tell you the God's honest truth; I thought initially that Costello would do a job on him because he knocked him down a few times in the beginning.'

'By Jay, but that's not what happened at all, Trevor son; what did the Jackeen do but get up again and flatten Patrick completely.'

'How long did it last?' asked Trevor, shaking out something that was stuck in his graip. The story would be all over town that day, the Jackeen's name up in lights and everyone who knew him horrified that Costello had been beaten, especially considering all the men who'd had a shot at him over the years, none of whom had managed to take him out in fight before. Pete Willie, Colm Pats, White, or Comeen Séamus Larry who'd been back over in Ireland recently with Trevor; none of them would have beaten Costello – and yet the Jackeen had!

'Oh, it lasted a good while, a damned good while!'

'"A good while, a damned good while!" How long is that you gobshite?'

It was a pity that he hadn't been there himself to see the fight, Trevor thought. It would have been good to see the Jackeen fighting before he took him on himself. He'd no choice now. He had to get it on with this buck now – just as though Christy Power were standing there in front of him right this minute.

'I suppose it lasted about ten minutes, Trevor, but damn it – I've never seen such all-out war in my life. They were well-matched, the pair of them, until the end – when the Jackeen let go a vicious haymaker, and knocked Costello out cold!'

'He knocked him unconscious?' said Trevor, horrified.

'As good as, Trevor. They had to pick him up off the road. I was never as surprised in my life, to tell you the truth. I didn't think there was any man would beat Patrick Costello, apart from yourself, that is.'

'"Apart from myself"?' asked Trevor, unsure whether Mullen was half-taking the piss. But Mullen wasn't mocking him; instead, he was looking across at him in awe, as if he were the only man left – the last and the best fighting man in the world.

'Arah, you'd take him, Trevor, you'd beat him for sure. Wasn't he practically a shivering wreck the day that he couldn't get out of the car? There he was, going mad trying to force the door open and he couldn't manage it. He's not a patch on you, Trevor. You'll destroy him!'

'I hope you're right,' Trevor muttered.

But wasn't the Jackeen taking his time coming to look for him all the same? The previous weekend, Trevor had taken a quick trip around the pubs in Canning Town. He had gone from the Mother Black Cap down to the Brighton and from there onto the Bedford Arms; he'd tried the Crown and Anchor after that, and from there, he went onto the Wheatsheaf, the Dublin Castle, the Hawley Arms and eventually onto the Laurel Tree, the latter being the most popular pub of all with Connemara people. Trevor didn't drink much as he went around – only a small bottle of beer in every pub – so that he'd have his wits about him if he happened to come across him. But there was no sign of him anywhere! No-one had seen hide nor hair of the Dubliner recently, and by the end of the night, Trevor wasn't sure whether he really wanted to meet Christy Power and fight him.

It was strange – unnerving almost – that the Jackeen had avoided him this long. After all, any man who was able to knock out Patrick Costello outside the Banba in front of hundreds of people was hardly afraid to come down into Camden Town, was he? Difficult as it was to countenance it, maybe the truth was more bitter still? Perhaps the Jackeen had such little respect for Trevor that he wasn't even bothered about looking for him! A wave of anger and embarrassment arose in Trevor at this possibility, and he ground his teeth in frustration.

'Let that piece of shit come around here any time he wants, Mullen, I'll be ready for him, you can bet on it. I'll be ready for him!'

'You sure will, Trevor, and you'll kill the frigger! Sure, didn't I tell him that straight to his face!'

Trevor was rattled by this and stopped ploughing with the pitchfork. He pulled the fork from the ground, held it aloft as though it were a giant spear. 'What did you say to him, you idiot?'

'I said to him that he might have beaten Costello but that there was another man around he wouldn't take, and that he knew full well who I meant. Maybe that was why he was keeping out of Camden Town, I told him!'

'You did, by heck?'

'Straight up to his mug, brother, I said it. Mullen here wasn't the slightest bit afraid of him, I can tell you.'

'Fat chance,' said Trevor under his breath, giving Mullen a dirty look. He wedged his fork into the heavy soil again and paused. 'And what did he say to that, damn you?'

'He said the batterin' he gave Costello was nothing compared to what he'd give you!'

Trevor released a low groan from between his teeth, 'We'll see, Mullen,' he said, 'we'll see.'

There was more news waiting for Trevor when he got home that evening.

'There's another letter there for you, Trevor,' Madge Connelly said, placing his dinner in front of him on the table. 'It's marked "urgent". I hope it's not bad news.'

'It'll be grand,' Trevor muttered gruffly, even if he was inwardly cursing the letter and his wife. She must have feck-all for doing, the rip, to be sending him over letters on every little issue like this! It was a poor state of affairs when a man couldn't eat his dinner and relax after a day's work without having a pile of letters waiting for him the minute he got home! Trevor put the letter out of his mind until he'd finished eating and had gone up to his room. Then he threw it over to Red Sweeney.

'Here, Sweeney, read that bastard, for Christ's sake seeing as you're not capable of doing anything else!'

Sweeney was still in his best suit, even if he was in bed. It was obvious that he hadn't bothered going to work that day at all. He was flat broke again and grabbed the letter with a bit too much enthusiasm for Trevor's liking. Trevor threw himself back onto the bed in resignation. He didn't even bother to take off his shoes. Sweeney opened the letter and cleared his throat as if though he were gearing himself up for action.

'You haven't been struck dumb, have you?' said Trevor sharply and Sweeney began to read:

Dear Trevor

I received your letter and the money also. I wasn't complaining about money Trevor; you've always treated me well as regards sending money home to me. But that isn't it, Trevor; I want to be with you – myself and the kids. Trevor dear, I'm not going to beat about the bush with this any longer; you married me, Trevor, and seeing as we're married in the eyes of God it isn't right that we should be separated from one another like this always. There's no point in you promising things, Trevor, when you've no intention of coming good on those promises. I could be here forever, and Dara and Bartley started in school and you still wouldn't have a notion of finding us a place in London. Well, you've another choice now, Trevor, anyway; they've started work out in Gleann Coimín – a power-station or something like that, and they'll be looking for men to work there, from what I hear. It's only about twelve miles from here as you know yourself, Trevor, and you could get out there on the bicycle; and anyway, Father Keenan was saying to me that there will be a lorry coming around this way every single day to bring men out there. The work will last there for a couple of years easily, the priest said, and he'll write a letter on your behalf, asking for a job there. Trevor, wouldn't you be better off coming home now that you have the chance; if you don't, the children won't know you Trevor; you'll be a complete stranger to them. For God's sake, Trevor, and come home now; isn't that the proper thing for you to do now, love?

I have other news for you also; it looks as if we'll have a new addition to the family in the New Year; who knows, maybe it'll be a little girl this time, with the help of God and his Blessed Mother. I often think, Trevor that if you had a daughter you might be fonder of home, maybe…. Send me a letter, Trevor, if you are planning on coming home. Placing you under the protection of the Blessed Virgin.

Your wife Nora.

Sweeney folded the letter and placed it back into its envelope. Trevor hadn't said a word yet, he just stared at the ceiling as cold and dead-eyed as a statue.

'Do you want to reply to her?' Sweeney asked after a minute, but Trevor didn't respond. What sort of a reply could he send her or what could a man say to a divvy the likes of her, really? Asking him to move back home and work on some whore of a job out in Gleann Coimín that no-one would earn anything more than six pounds a week on! And even if there was big money in it, what sort of a life would someone have living back in Doire Leathan? Every single day he'd spent back there recently he'd found a real drag, and he couldn't wait to clear the hell out of there as quickly as possible. Having to go back to live there again would have killed him. It would've been a right nightmare. It would be hell to return to a place where everyone watched your every move from one end of the year to the next, and you were under the thumb of that bitch of a priest (wouldn't they all be much better off if they just minded their own business!) and the way that everyone would talk about you if you didn't go to Mass. If he'd no choice other than to take her over and get them a few rooms to live in, then that's what he'd have to do. But, by God, he wouldn't do that either; no way – he wasn't going to give in that easily – not until he absolutely had to! To hell with her, the scrubber! She wasn't going to put out Bartley's son like this.

'I'm going out to have a shave,' Trevor said, jumping to his feet and grabbing a towel, a razor, and a piece of soap. He took off his shirt and was heading for the door when Sweeney called him back. 'What's the story Trevor? Are you going to reply to her or not?'

Trevor stopped and looked at Sweeney. He had an anxious, distracted air about him, as though he were registering Sweeney's presence properly for the first time.

'I know what's bothering you, son,' he told Sweeney, 'there's some people who won't fart without looking to get paid for it. Okay, son, you write to her. I'll leave it up to you to sort it out! Tell her to get a grip on herself and to have a small bit of sense. Tell her I'd sooner cut my own throat than go back to that bitch of a place again. And look, Sweeney, tell her to tell that shaggin' priest to mind his own business! I'll find her a place here when it suits me, tell her, and not before then! She's to stay where she is until then!'

Trevor put his hand into his pocket and produced a two-shilling bit, then threw it over onto the bed to Sweeney.

'Do a good job of that now, you f**r, won't you? And make sure to post it to her tomorrow.'

'Too true, I will,' said Sweeney, picking up the coin.

Another week went by and there was still no sign of the Jackeen making a move. Even if Trevor wasn't exactly losing any sleep over it, it was still at the back of his mind. Worse still, he kept hearing rumours about the Jackeen that made him increasingly uncomfortable. Everywhere he went, people were talking about him: the Dublin-man's stock had gone up all over London since he'd beaten Costello. And, if the stories that were going around were to be believed, Christy Power had built up quite a reputation as a fighter before he'd even fought Costello. Mullen told Trevor that he met another Jackeen in a small café in Finsbury Park one day who told him that Christy Power had never been beaten in a street fight, even though he had suffered defeat in the boxing ring. This man had known the Jackeen when they were children in Dublin and maintained that it was his speed that was Power's strongest attribute. You'd be beaten three times over by Christy Power before you realised what had happened at all, this man claimed.

One evening, as Trevor was having a pint in the Mother Black Cap on his way home, a man from the Joyce Country had annoyed the hell out of him with all his blather about the Jackeen. This man was named Cóilín O'Malley and even if they barely knew one another, he'd made a beeline for Trevor the minute he'd spotted him. O'Malley was a big domineering man who oozed self-importance: back in Ireland, his family were quite well-off and owned a sizeable farm, one of the family was a priest and another a schoolteacher. And even if Cóilín didn't have some impressive job himself, he was still well-cocky, Trevor had thought.

'I hear that Paddy McAllister's Jackeen is going to beat the shite out of all the Connemara lads,' he had said, even before Trevor had tasted his pint.

'Is that so?' Trevor had said, gruffly.

'That's what they're saying, anyway. He gave Costello a right hammering, didn't he?'

'How would I know whether he did or not, man?'

'You know all about this stuff, apparently. Sure, if you're afraid of him, then just keep out of his way, why don't you?'

'He's not bothering me one way or the other: because it has nothing to do with me,' Cóilín had said. 'He doesn't even know that I exist. You're the one he's after, from what I hear – whenever he eventually shows up around these parts!'

'Well, it seems to be bothering you more than it's bothering me, by the looks of it. He has all the time in the world; if he wants to come around here and see me. I never turned my back on any man who wanted to fight, O'Malley, as you know full-well!

'Maybe you didn't, but, as I'm sure you've often heard – a good run is better than a bad stand.'

It was hard to know, from the way that Cóilín had said this, whether he was just curious or trying to wind Trevor up. One way or the other, his talk had irritated Trevor, although he just about managed to prevent it spilling over into anger.

'I don't know about you, but I prefer the bad stand, myself,' Trevor had replied, sipping his pint.

But how he would get on against the Jackeen was on Trevor's mind a lot these days, truth be told. This Christy Power had hellish speed, by all accounts and he had a ferocious punch on him, too. But then Trevor was fairly handy himself. People had often remarked on his punching speed, and he knew that he'd a knockout punch when he landed one. Hadn't he knocked out Big Barrett from Binghamstown – a giant of at least sixteen stone – in one fight? He'd beaten the Mayo man outside the Round Tower on Holloway Road, and Barrett himself had admitted afterwards that Trevor's punch was the most powerful salamander anyone had ever hit him with. The Jackeen wasn't as heavy as Paddy Barrett, by any means, but it stood to reason that the heavier the man, the more difficult it was to knock him out. On top of that, the Jackeen had science, to add to his arsenal: he was a trained boxer, and it was always hard to beat training and knowledge like that. Also, if what they were saying was true, the Jackeen had never been beaten in a street-fight before. Trevor often imagined how the fight would pan out, a fight where he emerged victorious. He saw himself beating the Jackeen after an unbelievably tough fight and heard ring the congratulating roars of all the Connemara people. It would be like music to his ears, all the men clapping him on the back and falling over themselves trying to shake his hand and sing his praises. 'Trevor, Bartley's son: may the son of God never weaken you!' 'I love you, you son of a gun, you're the champion of them all!' Someone might compose a song about him, maybe, as they'd done for Patrick Berry and all the other great heroes.

Sé Treabhar Bheartla Bhillí an fear is fearr le fáil…Throid sé fear as Baile Bhiongaim agus fear as Dún na nGall….

Trevor Bartley Billy is the best man around; he fought a man from Binghamstown and a man from Donegal.

Trevor had no great skill himself in composing songs but who's to say that some other man might not compose one for him? It was a really wonderful thing to have a song dedicated to you; it made you famous forever. But there wouldn't be any songs written about him if the Jackeen proved too good for him or if he knocked Trevor out or left him lying there on the road the same way he'd left Patrick Costello! They'd all make fun of him behind his back; those same lads who were full of awe and respect for him one day would be the very ones that would be giving him stick if he lost.

'Ara, he thought he was the brown-haired boy, didn't he? Good luck to you; sure, he hadn't a hope against the Jackeen, really? Sure, he's not in the same league as him at all – and he never will be either!'

Trevor would get all wound-up just thinking about this and he'd try and force such thoughts from his mind as best he could. And yet, despite his best efforts, and how hard he worked each day, it preyed on his mind constantly. Christy Power, the boxer – and the fight that awaited the pair of them soon enough. It's like an illness that's got into your bones and that you can't shake off, he said to himself one morning as he splashed water onto his face before breakfast. The sooner you meet this bastard, the better.

Chapter 14

Nano was all up-in-a-heap until Friday came around again. She didn't know what to do about meeting Julius and she kept changing her mind from one minute to the next. It was as if there were two different people wrestling inside her. One moment, her conscience was at her and she'd feel ashamed or embarrassed at her apparent waywardness or lack of self-control; a moment later however, the temptation to accept his invitation was so strong that she really wanted to give in to it. She was as well admitting it to herself – it was pointless denying it any further: she really wanted to see Julius Kuzleikas again; she wanted to see him again so badly that her mind was consumed with the idea every minute of the day. If she hadn't already been going out with Máirtín, she wouldn't have hesitated for a moment. But maybe it was ridiculous to agonise over his invitation? In a way, the question was reasonably straightforward. Sheila O'Dwyer was right: why should she make a nun of herself, cooped up in that little room from one end of the week to the next, instead of getting some enjoyment out of life? Wouldn't she be better off going out one night to the pictures with someone like Julius – who was as lonely as she was – or going down for the odd glass of lemonade to the Tudor Rose? Just for a bit of company, of course, that's all. People needed company, after all; it was as necessary as food – and she needed to get out of the room, sometimes, even if it was only for a quick walk down the road with Julius. If you go around by yourself all the time, you eventually go cracked, as Sheila said. To be honest, it wasn't as though Máirtín had put any constraints on her; it was the opposite really, to give him his due. Hadn't he admitted himself in a recent letter to her that he was probably wasting her life and that he felt really bad about it? Máirtín certainly wouldn't have wanted to make a prisoner of her; he hadn't asked her for any such commitment when she'd said goodbye to him in Galway. It wasn't a question of what Máirtín would allow her to do or not; it was what she wanted that was at issue. There was right and wrong, just and unjust, and all this agonising with herself was dishonest – shouldn't she just admit how things really were and be done with it? What was the point in fooling herself anymore? If she was going to be disloyal to the man who was still promised to her, she shouldn't be pretending to herself otherwise. She'd stay in and not bother going on the date and that was the end of it.

Nano's sense of relief was always short-lived, however. No sooner had she unburdened herself of all these conflicting thoughts and feelings but the same mixture of doubt and temptation would return to torment her again. But then, there was a sort of dreamy pleasure in all these exotic, meandering fantasies. In the privacy of her imagination, Nano was free to imagine all sorts of romantic possibilities. She really wasn't *herself* anymore, workwise; she was all over the place – dreamy and distracted – and it wasn't long before Sheila noticed that there was something going on.

'There's something up with you these days, girl' Sheila told her one evening as she was getting ready to go out and meet Mike Shiels.

'Something up? Sure, what would be up with me?' said Nano, her cheeks burning with embarrassment. For some reason that she still couldn't explain, she hadn't told Sheila that she and Julius had been to the Tudor Rose that night. Nano regretted this and had been on edge ever since. She was worried that Sheila would hear about it from someone else and be hurt that she hadn't told her.

'I don't know what it is – but there's definitely something's up,'

Sheila repeated, standing in front of the mirror, inserting a hair-pin into her thick, black shock of hair.

'Oh, damn you! Sure, I might as well tell you, anyway. Julius asked me to go out with him on Friday night,' Nano blurted out.

'Julius?' Sheila repeated, swinging around. 'The gardener fellow?'

'Yep, the same one.'

'Well, may God grant you luck, girl! Seriously?' Sheila asked, wide-eyed.

'You're surprised, are you?' Nano asked, but Sheila just shook her head as if this were a ridiculous question.

'When was he talking to you, Nano? Now, see – wasn't I right about him that day we met him at the gate?'

'He was out at the entrance the other night when I was walking down to post a letter and he walked me down as far as the post box.'

'And are you going to go out with him?' Sheila asked her, all excited.

'What should I do, Sheila?'

'If he asked *me* out, I'd be gone with him in a second, but you and me are two different people – and I'm not sure what you should do, Nano.'

'You were trying to set me up with Peter, before,' Nano reminded her, but Sheila shook her head.

'It isn't the same thing girl. It'd be easy to deal with Peter but it mightn't be so easy to deal with the likes of your man, now.'

'How do you mean?' Nano asked her, defensively. She was happy now that she'd told Sheila about it: it was nice to get it off her chest. She sensed a certain wariness of Julius on Sheila's part that bothered her, however.

'Well, they're a law unto themselves in a way, aren't they? They stick to a woman, don't they, Nano? It mightn't be so easy to get rid of him later on, maybe if it didn't work out?'

'Sure, I haven't even gone out with him yet,' Nano said. 'It's a bit early to be talking about getting rid of him, isn't it?'

'But you will go out with him, won't you?' Sheila asked, gazing at Nano intently.

'I don't know yet, Sheila.'

'Do you want to go out with him? I definitely would!'

'I do,' said Nano after a pause, 'that's the worst of it, you see. I wouldn't go out with any fellow just for the sake of it, but with *him*; well…it's different….'

'Don't tell me that you're in love with him!'

Nano stared at her a tad sheepishly. 'Maybe this is all just a crazy flight of fancy, sister. Sure, arn't I old enough to have a bit of sense, God knows….'

'Ara, "old enough" – what are saying? Don't be talking like that! That's not what you meant….'

'No,' Nano agreed. The way things were going, she wouldn't be able to tell the difference between black and white.

'Sure, you could go out with him for a night or two and see how it goes,' said Sheila, somewhat uncertainly. 'You know, until you know your mind a bit better.'

She could do this, of course, but what good would that be? Sooner or later, she'd have to make up her mind.

'Yeah, but if I wanted to carry on going out with Julius, Sheila, I'd have to write to Máirtín and break it off with him,' said Nano in something between a question and a statement.

'Oh, aren't you getting a bit ahead of yourself? Just go out with him first if you like him, and see how things go after that. You need to box clever in this life, Nano; do whatever suits you and make sure that you're not the one left in the lurch, whatever happens. There's no point in being left on the shelf when all is said and done.'

'You're a right calculating one, daughter, aren't you?' said Nano, laughing.

'Well? Are you going to see him again, so?' Sheila said, looking into the mirror again; she was in a hurry to go out.

'I don't know, Sheila, and that's the truth. I'm between two minds. I don't know what to do.'

But by the time Friday came around, things were even worse. Nano was so wound-up at work that morning that Mary McDermott had told her to take it easy. Then, as she was opening one of the windows, Nano had spotted Julius wheeling a barrow of manure over to the flower beds and she'd stood there staring out at him, as if in a daze. Then Hilda Jackson had called her over to help prop up a heavy elderly man in his bed. That was the first time she'd seen Julius since they'd said goodbye to one another at the gates that previous Monday night. Nano was anxious for the rest of the morning. Jackson may as well have been speaking French to her for all the attention she paid her.

Nano had the afternoon free – between one and five, after which she was back on-duty until eight o'clock that evening. After dinner, she returned to the room and got herself ready for a night out. She arranged her hair and laid out her new Marks and Spencer's dress and a pair of new nylon stockings. She gave herself a quick look in the mirror and tied her chestnut-coloured hair up in a bun. She untied her hair again and turned her head right and left, searching for the best look. Did she have any control over her life anymore or was her resistance to fate all but futile? Maybe, whatever happened would happen, irrespective of what she decided? It was as if she had become detached from herself and was looking in at someone else's circumstances; an observer of someone else's story.

Nano had a good chunk of the afternoon free, and an urge came over her to clear out of the place altogether for a while. The weather was really beautiful that afternoon, the sun high in the sky, even if it was still cold. There was a small hint of spring in the air. Nano knew that Mary McDermott had bought a new bicycle recently and so she went down to the ward where Mary was still on-duty and asked to borrow it for a couple of hours. She and Mary were getting on a lot better recently, and Nano decided to make the most of it.

'Oh, you're very welcome to take it,' was Mary's response. She was clearly delighted to make up for the hostility she'd initially shown Nano. This was the first time Nano had been on a bike since she'd left home and she hopped onto the saddle and made for the countryside as quickly as possible. She flew effortlessly along the road on this spanking-new Rudge bicycle, easily negotiated the hill to the north of the old prisoner-of-war camp and freewheeled downhill again at speed, the wheels humming gently against the road. She thought of home and all the countless days that she'd cycled into Galway town or up across the bog to Oughterard on the odd Sunday, accompanied by Máirtín, or the nights they'd cycled home together from the ceilidh in Spiddal, the moonlight radiating across the surface of the bay before the darkness engulfed them again like black velvet. Every now and then the sight of a buoy sparkling far out in the water for all the world like a fallen star.

Wasn't it strange how things had gone so wrong for herself and Máirtín, as compared with other couples? If they'd had any luck at all, they'd have been up-and-running with their lives long ago. Needless to say, there was no point in 'ifs and buts' and wondering whether things might have been different. Things were as they were, and that was the end of it. Obsessively analysing the situation or constantly complaining about how things had worked out was just a waste of time. It wouldn't solve anything. If she'd had Christmas holidays coming to her as Sheila had, or if she'd been long enough over here so that she could return home without everyone knowing about it or joking about her ('Over to see the clock is where she went!') Nano wouldn't have minded taking a quick trip back home. It would have been nice to go back even if it was only for a few days, so that she could better make up her mind about what she wanted from life. Who knows? A quick visit home might have made her mind up for her. Maybe she'd be even even more determined to break up with Máirtín if that's what had to be done in the end; or she might promise to wait for him for as long as it took, or until they were allowed to marry.

Nano's mind was racing with all these thoughts as she cycled along, passing through various red-brick villages, all with strange-sounding names: Manor Knebden, Lillingstone Parva, Abthorpe and Tingeweek. A ghostly silence had entered the day and a purity had come into the air. The weather was changing again. On arrival at the crossroads, Nano turned left to return to Norwold a different way. Unlike, back home in the west, it seemed that the farmers here worked the land all year round. Tractors were ploughing the fields next to the road; from a distance, they appeared to be insects winding their way up across the wide hills, turning the soil.

After cycling a few miles, Nano came to an old chapel covered in ivy and surrounded by an ancient churchyard. Curious, she leaned the bicycle against the gate post and walked up the path towards the small chapel, the door of which was unlocked. She went inside, albeit slightly hesitantly; it was her first time ever inside a Protestant church and she felt slightly nervous. The church was quiet as the grave but it wasn't the quiet that struck Nano, initially: it was loneliness. There was some sort of sadness here, an unspoken absence. The interior of the church looked very similar to most other churches that she'd ever been in, with an altar overlooked by a big plain cross, and a wooden pulpit for sermons. But there was no sanctuary lamp nor Stations of the Cross, nor were there any lighted candles.

Nano couldn't imagine the place packed with people as her own home church would be back in Cois Fharraige every Sunday, or indeed Saint Brigid's Church here in Norwold, and she felt relieved to go outside after a few minutes. It looked as though no-one had been interred in the tiny cemetery for a long while: the graves were overgrown and the inscriptions were so worn as to be eligible. *Jonathan Tibbs,* Nano read on one headstone, *dear wife Adeleine… children Beatrice and Sophie….* 1707 was the date inscribed on another but there were yet more that were older. In one corner was a stone tomb, the lid of which was broken and had nettles growing up through it. The wind rose and the sky darkened ominously. She could smell a storm coming. She needed to make tracks and get back to the hospital.

Nano started cycling furiously again. She went through another crossroads, climbed another hill and freewheeled down the other side. She worked the pedals fiercely and the hedges flew past. It got darker, and an eerie light drifted across the sky. The wind died down as soon as it had begun and an uneasy calm settled over the countryside. Suddenly, the sky opened and the rain poured down. Nano spotted a ramshackle lean-to shed near the entrance to a field and she hopped off her bike and ran for this shelter, her heels sinking in the soft muddy ground as the rain lashed down. She was drenched by the time she made it to the shed and pushed her way in against a big pile of hay. Her hair dripped into her eyes and her feet squelched. The rain increased in ferocity and hammered down onto the zinc roof. It formed little streams which rushed along the ridges of mud and grass then formed puddles. It had got very dark. What if the rain didn't stop? Nano thought anxiously. What if this deluge continued and she was late getting back on duty? Just as suddenly as the storm had started, the black clouds lifted and the rain eased. The shower was over and the rain gurgled and musicked beneath her feet as Nano clambered out in the direction of the gate again. The ditch next to the road was heavy with water as she dried the saddle of her bike with the tail of her coat and set off again.

She was very busy at work that afternoon, and it was just as well. She threw herself into the different jobs she'd been assigned as if to escape her own thoughts. She had to make a decision, and soon. At the back of her mind, she still had a sneaking hope that something would happen to take it out of her hands. In fact, she'd no sooner started work that afternoon than another enormous shower fell, one that seemed to go on forever, the rain so heavy it raised the prospect that no-one would be able to venture outside that night. But as the hands of the clock approached the time for her to sign off work for the day, the sky cleared and the stars came out and filled the night-sky. On her way back to her room, the image of Julius came to Nano's mind again. He was so handsome that she just had to see him again. Any last uncertainty as to whether she'd made the right decision disappeared when she went into supper and found a letter in her pigeon-hole waiting. It was a long, chatty letter from Máirtín, a lot longer than the usual ones. She read through it quickly, relishing every sentence – until she came towards the end. His last sentences were like a thorn entering her flesh.... *My mother is very well, thank God. In fact, I haven't seen her looking this well in a long time.*

Nano rose from the supper table without bothering to finish her food and ran quickly back to her room; her face was pale, her heart pounding. She felt breathless. She threw off her nurse's cap and put on the new organdie dress she'd bought, brushing her hair vigorously in silent fury. She put on her stockings and her high-heeled shoes and was taking her coat from the hanger when Sheila came in from her evening shift on the wards. She kicked off her shoes and plonked herself down on the bed, folding her legs beneath her.

'You're going to see him, so, Nano?'

'I am, sister! Sure, I might as well? Didn't you say it to me often enough y'know – not to be making a nun of myself, cooped up in here every single night!' There was a glint in Nano's eyes and a flush in her cheeks that Sheila hadn't seen previously.

'Turaloo, Sheila. I'll see you later,' Nano said, in a voice that that was taut with emotion, as she ran out through the door.

Chapter 15

It is strange sometimes, the way everything happens at once. Out of the blue, that Christmas week, Niall O'Connell received a letter from Kieran Butler, an envelope containing two crisp five-pound notes. Also, with the same post, a letter for Niall's mother from the city clerk telling her that she could collect the keys of their new house from City Hall whenever she wanted.

'Praise be to the God of Glory,' Mrs O'Connell said with tears in her eyes, going over to the picture of the Sacred Heart. She kissed the tips of her fingers, and placed them against the picture-frame as reverently as if it were a holy relic. She'd just returned from eight o'clock Mass in the Black Abbey. Andrew and Maurice had gone out to work an hour earlier and Niall had just sat down to his breakfast. It was a very frosty morning outside, the small puddles of water out in the yard covered in a thin film of ice.

Niall couldn't believe it when he saw the two big five-pound notes fall from the letter. This was the first time he'd ever touched a five-pound note, and, for a minute, he thought that it might be pretend-money he'd been sent as some kind of a joke. It didn't take long for his mother to set Niall right on that score however.

'They're two English five-pound notes,' she confirmed, examining the money. 'Maureen Flood had six of those last year; I saw them myself when she was down in the shop. You'll have to take them to the bank to exchange for proper Irish money.'

Butler's letter was only a page-and-a-half long. He apologised to

Niall for the dirty trick he'd played on him, and he promised to send him the remainder of the thirty pounds owed as soon as he could. He'd been wrong about the horse-and-cart idea, he admitted. No-one would ever make money from that scheme, he said. There were too many in the business already and in any case he'd had to get out of town quickly, both him and Mary Fitz, even if it had all proved a false alarm. She hadn't been pregnant after all. He couldn't see much wrong with England so far. Butler added there was any amount of work available there; even a one-legged man could get a job, never mind someone who was in their prime. As a parting shot, Kieran said that if Niall had any inclination to come over, he and Mary Fitz were renting a place where Niall was more than welcome to stay until he had work and lodgings of his own. Niall stared lovingly at the two big bank-notes for a while. Their arrival that morning – just when he needed them most – was a minor miracle! Niall couldn't wait to swan uptown full of pride and self-belief, this fine ten pounds nesting comfortably in his arse-pocket, as good as the best of them.

He gobbled up his breakfast and left the table without so much as a 'yea' or 'nea' to his mother's excited chatter about the new house and how she'd lay it all out. She'd have to get the new furniture down at McGreerys, the squares of lino for the living room first; the other rooms could be done later. Who knows? Maybe Niall would have work in the New Year, and Andrew and Maurice had both promised her a raise in their rent-money to help her buy new stuff. Wouldn't they be over the moon when they heard the news! Number Seven, Saint Máirtín de Porres Avenue, she kept repeating as though intoning a psalm. She had an inkling that it might be a corner house with a small boreen stretching down to its gable end; this would be way better because you'd get more privacy with no neighbours on either side. She hoped to God that they'd have nice neighbours! And thanks be to God, it'd be really something not to have the sound of those awful pigeons driving her mad all day from now on! Was there anything in the world more awful than the noise of those pigeons after a while?

'Well, even if it was twice as much, I suppose I'd still have to sign on,' Niall had said, placing one of the big white banknotes on the table, jamming the other into his trouser pocket and avoiding his mother's eyes.

'I'm not sure what business you have going downtown with that amount of money in your pocket, Niall,' his mother warned. 'I'll give you the price of a packet of fags, if you want.'

'Oh, sure, isn't it as well for me to break it down at the bank,' Niall replied, feigning a lack of interest.

'I was planning on buying a few small things with it anyway, a pair of socks and a shirt, maybe.' He was nearly out the door now when his mother called after him,

'You won't be long, will you? We've a big day ahead of us, what with shifting our stuff up there. Will you be sure and call at Lawrence Doheny's – to bring the furniture up in his donkey-and-cart? You'd be better off calling on him straight away and collecting the key on your way home!'

Niall cursed to himself, but his mother wasn't finished yet. 'And whatever you do, Niall, be sure not to let on anything to that shower below about the money – or you won't have a penny to your name by the time you get home!'

'I'm not a child, Mam,' Niall responded gruffly, slamming the door behind him.

'You're not, but you're a right idiot, sometimes,' was Mrs O'Connell's hesitant parting shot. Niall went uptown like a man walking on air.

Their lives had taken one of those sudden and unexpected turns for the better, by the looks of it – the good things happening around the same time – first the money and then the news about the house.

Everything was looking up, just as that old fellow on the train the other evening had predicted. They'd get a nice new house up in Grassmount, somewhere they wouldn't be ashamed to bring people home. Their lives would be different from now on; everything would work out fine. He'd find work somehow, he felt sure of it. And, to hell with it if he couldn't find anything here: couldn't he just head over to England and spend a year in London? If that country was half as good as they made out, then anyone who was clever with their money could soon put together a nice nest-egg and come home again, then set up a successful small business of their own. And he'd go about it properly this time; no way would he have to stay across the water for good.

The town seemed in tune with Niall's feelings; everything looked different, new and more exciting than before. The sun shone golden on the cockerel weathervane at the top of the Tholsel and the melting frost sparkled on the doorsteps all along High Street. It was as if the city were in harmony with him and his good fortune, and silently revelling in his newfound happiness. There wasn't a trace of the hostility or estrangement he'd felt in the the buildings on his initial return home from the army. Money was the thing; money made the world go round. If that's what it took to motivate you to look after your pennies, there was no harm in a bit of poverty. At the Parade, Niall took the steps of the Bank of Ireland two at a time. Inside, he placed one of the big white notes on the counter and requested five single pounds in exchange. He separated them out and put one pound into his back pocket for himself and the other four he hid deep inside his jacket. His mother was right, of course. If some Mooney type got his claws into him, there'd be hardly any left by the time he got home. *They'd eat me alive, they'd eat me, that's true! Hickety, mickety, bickety, boo!* he sang to himself softly going down Rosheen Street *Fasten to me like limpets, that's what they'd do! Nickety, rickety, lickety, loo!*

Niall paused on John's Bridge and looked down into the Nore, but he was too excited to hang around so moved on. Bridge House was open as he passed by and before he knew it, he'd turned and gone inside. Only the barman Pat Neary and Simon McCarthy were inside. The tailor McCarthy was perched up on one of the high stools, hunched over the counter, his hat at an angle over his eyes and his feet entwined beneath the stool. It was a close call whether or not he was awake. He had the shabby, frozen look of a man who'd slept outside all night, while Neary had stubble on his chin, which was unusual for him.

'Niall!' Neary said, surprised to see him so early in the morning.

'A pint please, Pat, and ten fags,' said Niall, flinging a pound note onto the counter somewhat ostentatiously.

'A pint it is, Niall' responded Neary, leaning on one of the big, heavy brass handles. He let the black stuff settle for a minute and walked over to the cigarette-shelf. 'Woodbines or Players?'

'Ara, gimme one of the beardy fellows,' said Niall. 'I'm sick of those other f**ers!'

It was as sweet a pint as Niall had ever tasted, and the fag was lovely too. Niall looked around at the fine slack fire burning in the grate and the fresh wood shavings dusting the floor. The pub looked nice and cosy and Niall felt a flicker of renewed joy travel through him – lovely little darts of happiness going up and down in his body. So what if this was the random exhilaration of the beggar-man. Wasn't this still another day, a new day of his life?

'You're signing at the moment, Niall?' Pat asked, leaning out over the counter towards him, his voice low and conspiratorial.

'Oh, damn it anyway, but I am Pat,' Niall said, 'for all it's worth!'

'But sure, why would you leave it in the hands of those other feckers anyway, the small bit that it is? I sure wouldn't, and not a ha'penny of it either, I can tell you that much,' Pat said, nodding sagely.

'Didn't you put up stamps for it anyway when you were working?'

'Since I left school, I did. You can say that alright!'

'You're only getting what's due to you then,' said Pat, respectfully.

The publican sighed and brushed his fingers against the stubble of his beard.

'It'll be a quiet Christmas, Niall, there's no money around this year.'

'By dad, I don't know about that, Pat,' Niall responded solemnly. 'I was down at the bank a little while ago and there was a nice crowd inside and most of them were withdrawing money, from what I could see.'

'The likes of yourself, is it?' said Pat, with a knowing grin.

'Oh, sure, you know yourself, Pat. I wouldn't be lodging money in the bank this time of year anyway, whatever next year brings,' Niall said with a fib. He didn't know whether to mention his big news. When he thought back on the whole thing later, it was as if his good news had crept out of him – as though he had no control over what he said. The more showy aspect of his nature had came to the fore even while he could hear that small voice at the back of his mind warning him not to lose the run of himself

'There's money in this country alright, Pat, but it's idle money.'

Niall was reminded of the ads he'd seen earlier down at the Bank of Ireland, confirming that the bank had eighteen million pounds in stocks and shares in their vaults, safe as houses.

'Now you're talking, Niall,' Pat said, giving his wrist a gentle squeeze. 'Money makes more money if it's put into circulation, that is. It doesn't do much good if it's left lying there under the pillow!'

'Or if it's left inside a bank vault either, Pat!'

Simon McCarthy stirred in the corner and mumbled to himself; no doubt, he was listening in on their conversation – not that Simon's opinions carried much weight with him....

It was time for Niall to be going about his business. He'd plenty of things to be getting on with after he was done signing on at the Labour Exchange. He had to get the key for the new house, and then call on Larry Doheny to see if he was available to move their stuff.

'I'm as well going now soon and giving those shites below my autograph, anyway,' said Niall. 'We're moving house today and there's a lot to do.'

'You're moving house! Well, I wish you all the luck and happiness in the world, Niall, and I hope everything works really great for you all!'

As if a blindfold had been removed from his eyes, Niall understood Pat. The barman had all the signs of someone who'd had a rough night on the drink. The bloodshot eyes, the stubble dotting his chin and the eagerness for company; suddenly it all made sense. A shiver went through Niall and he was dismayed. It was as if he'd just seen something scandalous, like a priest showing signs of drink! Sure, Niall had heard it said of bar-owners that they themselves often became addicted to drink when life went against them – but this wasn't something that he'd have associated with Neary. Strangely, he felt disappointed, as if Pat had let him down by revealing such a failing.

Maybe Pat himself wasn't doing too well these days? Maybe things weren't going his way? After all, he often had less than ten customers – and this over the course of an entire day. Niall's mind went back to that night a couple of years ago when a small group of them had stayed inside Bridge House after closing time; Pat had shut the door late and had a few bottles of beer in their company, out of sense of neighbourliness and friendship. He'd told them about the time he'd worked in America twenty years earlier at the time of the Wall Street Crash. He'd seen greed for money over there then and a lack of empathy with his fellow-men that was frightening. It was all hustle and work over there, Pat had said, and if the people in Ireland worked half as hard as those in the States did, then this country would turn out a lot better. Everyone had agreed with Pat's take on the States that night, apart from a labourer from Burnchurch who was half-steamed by then, anyway. He'd challenged Pat's opinion of what made America a great economy. The reason there was no holding back the States, he said, was because the workers got rewarded and properly paid for their work there, unlike in Ireland.

'Because there's no-one in Ireland,' this farm labourer had said, straight out, and not the least bit fearful of Pat, 'that has a dog's respect for the working-man and who pays him a fair wage as Christ ordained! Not the shopkeeper, not the farmer, nor the priest.'

Niall never forgot this exchange, and neither did he forget the way that Pat had responded to this claim in as nice and relaxed a manner as could be. 'Well, there's one shopkeeper here, Johnny,' Pat had said, 'and he's not able to pay himself a proper wage never mind pay somebody else.'

If things had been different, Niall thought, setting out for the Labour Exchange, and if there'd been work available for himself and his like, then life would have been a damn sight easier for nice, friendly folks – someone like Pat Neary – and the same went for other business-types too. If there had been money in circulation, then people like Pat might have been doing a bit better than they were. Wasn't it only by cooperation and solidarity with one another that any community managed to survive? There was no benefit in people hoarding their money for years as some of the farmers who came in from the countryside did. Those fellows in their long threadbare coats dating back to their parents' era – just sitting on a pile of cash.

The queue had reduced a good bit by the time Niall reached the Labour Exchange but he was still impatient at the sight of all the losers lined up ahead of him. Usually, Niall felt a strong empathy with the dole crowd but today was different. Today, they seemed like a lost and abandoned tribe with some contagious disease. They were a people mired in poverty who had been sentenced to a life of idleness and had nothing else to look forward to other than a life of constant beggary. He wouldn't allow their apathy and gloom to infect him however, Niall said to himself, lighting up a Players. No way!

Nellie Moffat gawped back over her shoulder at Niall in a way that would have annoyed the hell out of him at any other time. But all he did was wink in the old woman's direction, a gesture that caught her by surprise and made her stare even more. When his turn came at the counter, he wrote his name down on the attendance sheet as proudly as someone signing a cheque, looked Linnane straight in the eye, then hurried out to catch up with Mooney and Sullivan, both of whom had been ahead of him in the queue.

'You're in flying form this morning,' Mooney remarked, trying to wind Niall up as they passed the gates of the barracks where a Red-Cap was on duty inside. A small group of FCA lads were jumping down from a lorry inside on the barracks square, all looking awkward and ungainly in their ill-fitting uniforms. The taller lads looked a bit ridiculous with their pleated trousers that were too short for them, and Niall recalled the origins of his disdain towards these clumsy-looking amateurs, in his former life as a professional soldier. It wasn't that long ago and yet the army seemed so far way that it belonged to a different life. A promising, new future beckoned him in the New Year. His life was a clean slate, an exciting new story that he could write for himself.

'I'm in good form, Nick! I'm going to put some kind of a shape on myself after Christmas, and if I can't get anything here then I'm going to give it a go across the water.'

'You'll make a pile of money, so, the same as Nick did,' said Bosco Sullivan, sarcastically.

'Yep. He made loads over there, alright. He brought a big pile home with him – a big pile of shit, that is!'

'I mightn't have come home loaded, but at least I did something while I was over there, unlike yourself, who never laid hand on shovel in his life,' Mooney retorted.

This childish sniping no longer bothered Niall, however. It all went over his head. He had stuff to be getting on with, getting Doheny lined up for the move and calling at the Town Hall but then, hadn't he time enough for all that yet? Nearing Bridge House, Niall heard that small voice whisper inside him, the voice of reason and common sense that told him he shouldn't tempt fate in this way. But then there was the other voice, the one that he heard coming from his mouth as if the latter was a separate entity to the one that invited the other lads into Bridge House with him. 'I'd say you wouldn't say no to a pint, lads?' he asked, coming to a stop right outside the door.

'Would you ever go and f**k yourself?' was Nick's ignorant retort, assuming that Niall was joking them.

'A bit of manners now!' Niall replied, going inside. 'Come in if you want a drink, stay out if you don't!'

Unfortunately, it looked as if he really was a born gobshite, and that his mother had him well-sussed. This is what Niall said to himself later on, in a drunken stupor. He leaned dizzily sideways against the bridge and looked down at the streetlamps in the purple evening dusk radiating in the surface of the Nore below. Everything seemed to be going grand at the beginning, Niall recalled. It was all hunky-dory until he brought the other two in with him to Bridge House. He'd ordered three pints and was rewarded with Pat Neary's grateful 'Good man, Niall!'. Sullivan had gone straight over to the ring-board that was shaped like a shield. He was more interested in playing a few games of rings than going drinking – at the beginning, anyway. Pat had never stopped blathering all the while they were there: the pound that was kept under lock-and-key didn't do anything for anyone, he'd said. It was useless, really – nothing more than a piece of paper.

'That's exactly what I was thinking a bit earlier,' Niall had agreed, nodding in Pat's direction.

'That's what's ruining this nation,' Pat had replied. 'Idle money. I mean, there's no knowing how much is in this county, never mind in the whole country! If only it was used to everyone's benefit, as it should be.'

'Absolutely. Sure, even if an actual bag of gold was hidden away – sure, what good would that do anyone if none of it was spent?' Mooney had added wisely, sipping at his pint.

Mooney had already knocked back half of it and was wiping his face in satisfaction whereas Sullivan hadn't yet touched his own that had been left on the counter. Mooney was to be pitied, really, Niall thought, and the same was true of any man who was addicted to drink. This fondness for drink always left lads hungry and miserable in the end.

'Y'see, the Irishman is too scared to take chances with his money or go into business,' Pat had said, 'and that's what's left us lagging behind. There are men out in the States – and they're millionaires now – men who hadn't a penny to bless themselves with once. I myself know of one in New York who started out selling newspapers on the streets of Manhattan, and there's no end to his wealth today.'

'The man who's got a bit of go in him. You can't beat it.' At the end of the counter, Simon McCarthy had stirred on his stool like a scarecrow that had magically come to life. 'It's just as well for him,' he'd gone on, 'that he didn't start out selling them on the streets of Kilkenny – because he'd still be selling them there today!

Niall chuckled now on recalling Simon's intervention into the debate, then flicked the butt of his cigarette into the river. They had all laughed at Simon's comment at the time but that had not been the end of it. There was no way that Bosco would have let the chance for a bit of craic slip by.

'Dead right, Simon,' he'd called back to McCarthy, 'and the same goes for tailoring. Montague Burton started out with nothing but a scissors and a piece of thread to his name and he has clothes shops all over the world today. You had a scissors and thread, too, Simon, when you started out back in the time of the flood, didn't you? And today, you don't even have a pair of scissors!'

'I don't,' Simon had admitted, raising his head, 'but I can tell you one thing, Sullivan. Even on my worst day ever, I never ate Dev's meat, not like certain people not a hundred miles away from me right now!'

'Pity, it's not available still,' Bosco had said, 'because I could do with a nice big chunk of it right now!'

Neary had given an impatient sigh at the turn the conversation had taken and tried to steer things back to a more judicious path.

'Investment is the name of the game, Niall. Investment is the oil that makes the wheels turn!'

'And in your own country, too,' Niall had said, 'there's too much investment abroad these days.'

'I hope it's not the rent that you're investing in this here drink,' Bosco Sullivan had said, sipping from his pint, his eyes widening in surprise. 'Ora, Christ, would you look at who's in!'

That was the moment that everything had gone to pot and the bad luck started, Niall thought. A thin, weedy young fellow had come in, Packie Pugh hot on his heels and carrying his suitcase as though he were waiting on him. The new fellow was just back from England, judging by the small trilby hat perched on the back of his head, the long white scarf dangling from his neck, his cheap chequered jacket and his black-and-white golf shoes. The newcomer's stuff had been in a large suitcase that was light as a feather by the look of it. Packie had put the case down on the floor. He'd turned a wary eye on the lads at the bar, as if he half-expected them to try and take his gig away from him.

'Bobo McGinn down from the Cills,' Bosco had whispered. 'It's less than a year since he left.' McGinn had gone to the bar, his wallet wide-open so that everyone could clearly see it stuffed with banknotes.

McGinn had turned to Packie behind him, and asked what he'd have to drink; he'd called for a whiskey himself. Then, as an afterthought that Niall considered almost insulting, he'd called for a drink for everyone present.

'By God, we're away on a hack, here,' Mooney had said, knocking the remainder of his pint back in one greedy slug.

I should've left there and then, Niall admonished himself later as he stared down at the water. I could've stood another drink for whoever was there and I still wouldn't have had to break the second ten-shilling note. Or he could have left without ordering any more drinks. He could have pretended he had no money left and lots of jobs to do – all of which were true – it wasn't as if he'd have had to tell a white lie, even. Christ, but his mother would be fit to be tied by the time he got home! He'd never hear the end of it, now, and who could blame her in all honesty? Wasn't he one right stupid b**llix?

It was all the shite-talk and the blowing that had kept him in Pat's pub when he should have been well gone home. He should have got the key for the new house and the stuff moved up there hours ago as his mother had wanted. What had kept him there longer was the posing of that bloody idiot back from England and the fact that there was no way he was letting that fellow get one over on the rest of them. Khyber Brennan was the first of the lads to put his nose in the door of Neary's, whatever premonition he'd had that Bobo McGinn was in town. Right on Khyber's heels were the Sniveller Deniffe and Mikeo Linnane, every man of them straight up to McGinn telling him what a mighty man he was, praising him to high heaven and licking his arse big-time. There was no stopping them – telling McGinn how well-dressed he was and how well he'd done for himself over there; it was all the exact same old shite-talk that the corner boys said to every idiot who came home from with their scarves and trilbies and big wads of cash rolled-up inside their wallets for show; more often than not, the poor fool who was being worshipped was in any case claiming that he'd made twice as much money as he really had.

Mind you, Niall had come very close to leaving at one stage; it must have been around about midday, although he wasn't too sure of anything now. He'd drunk four or five pints by then and a feeling of guilt had consumed him as he remembered his mother, and how she'd been bursting with joy that morning about the new house, and the image of her waiting for him and expecting him home at any moment – the poor woman must have been on edge all day long.

It must have been around the same time that McGinn had

produced those pictures from the pocket of his jacket. Pat had gone down into the cellar and the fact that he was gone a few minutes must have given the newly returned Englishman the courage to show them the pictures. He'd three in all, and it was the same woman in each. She was completely naked in all of them, except for the garter that came up to just above her knees and a rose jutting from her wild mane of hair. They'd all gathered around quickly to have a look – except for Mooney who didn't like that sort of thing – and had a good gawk. The eyes of the Sniveller Deniffe had been practically popping out of his head but Khyber Brennan hadn't been as easy to impress; he'd made out that those pictures were nothing compared to the ones he'd seen over in Port Said once, images that would make your hair stand on end they were so shocking, and had had both men and women in them.

Strangely, the pictures hadn't incited any lust in Niall, not in the way that much less explicit thoughts or images would have – say, the sight of a woman's legs on a bicycle or the thought of a shapely pair of legs beneath a pair of smooth nylon stockings. The woman in those pictures was too naked, somehow, she seemed weak and powerless, like someone who'd been rushed out of bed during some kind of an emergency. But there was something else as well about McGinn's pictures that didn't really make sense. The female body didn't match what Niall's image of it was, or how he'd always heard and thought that it looked like. Whatever it was, the sight of this woman's nakedness just wasn't the same. It did nothing for him; nothing at all compared to the buzz he'd always felt at a brief glimpse of skirt suddenly raised in the wind.

'I went out with her,' McGinn had announced proudly. 'She works in a nightclub in London.' Niall gave a short, dry laugh now that he called it to mind again. Sure, those pictures were fifty years old if they were a day. Any idiot could have worked that much out just from the way the woman's hair was arranged, the big thick silk garters she wore and the heavy draped curtains that were in the background. Bosco wasn't far wrong when he said that Bobo McGinn was a gobshite!

'She's a fine-looking heifer,' Sullivan'd said, standing on Niall's foot secretly at the same time. 'What's her name, anyway, Bobo?'

'What's her name?' Bobo had repeated as if this were a stupid question. 'Blimey, boy, you don't ask women like that their names when you go with them, and they don't ask you yours, either!'

'And you went with the three of them, Willie?' Packie Pugh had said, as though he were jealous. 'Hey, but you're the right boyo, aren't you? Aren't you the right stud, too!'

'There isn't three of them here, that's just one woman,' Bobo had explained, as much as to say that such stupid comments had just put the kaibosh on the whole experience. 'Look at her face, Packie, will you? It's her fanny that you're staring at, you dope!'

He might not have spotted the pictures but Neary had not been long sussing out what was going on, because he'd appeared up out of the basement and ordered McGinn to get this filth out of their sight and not to show those pictures again as long as he were under his roof. Niall hadn't been able to help himself; he'd gone puce-red with embarrassment, and the worst of it was that he couldn't have left then even if he'd wanted to – in case Pat thought that he'd taken offence at the way he'd admonished them. It had been too late by then anyway because the drink had already kicked in, and whatever bit of cop-on still in Niall's possession had gone out of the window by then. He'd got the taste for more pints now, especially since the arrival of Ned Purcell, dying for a drink, his old fiddle tucked under his arm. Purcell was a small nervous bird of a man. He never went anywhere without a box of snuff whose constant use made his nostrils yellow as cheese. Even Purcell's most loyal friend would not have claimed that he had much talent as a musician, and the local wits used to say that they'd sooner pay him to keep quiet and away from their party than to hear the screeching of his bow on the fiddle. Not that there'd been any lack of welcome for him from the corner-boys that night. Bobo McGinn had ordered a pint for him immediately and made room for him near the lower bar where they'd been sitting so that he could play a tune for them.

Bobo McGinn had been so well-on-it that he asked Purcell to play a new tune for them, 'Good Night Irene'. That song would remind him of London and put him in mind of his lodgings in Chiswick and the factory he'd been working in. The English people were the nicest people anywhere in the world, Bobo had solemnly announced, and de Valera could go to hell!

Niall, at the river now, lit another cigarette and took a long, deep pull of it. The curse of the dutiful God on Purcell, Niall thought; it had to be him above all else that had brought bad luck with him. Purcell never played two notes back-to-back without doing a fierce amount of foostering around with the strings of his fiddle and it had been the same earlier with 'Good Night Irene'. The way he had gone on tightening and loosening his fiddle-strings; testing their timbre, you'd have sworn he was in the Hallé Orchestra! And then, after all that, the tune that he'd played had had very little connection with the one that McGinn had requested. Not that it mattered much; it had been close enough to satisfy the newly returned emigrant and, as a sign of his appreciation, he'd given a great roar, grabbed a hold of the Sniveller Deniffe and began waltzing around the floor. Everyone there had started whooping wildly; all except except Simon McCarthy, who woke up from his quiet snooze. 'High-jinks and blackguardry, that's what that is, and I wouldn't allow that carry-on in my house, Pat,' he'd called over to Neary.

Niall hadn't been so drunk at that stage that he missed the look that Neary gave in their direction, however. He could tell that Neary didn't like this kind of clowning-around and knew that it wouldn't do much for the reputation of his establishment, either. But Bobo McGinn had taken out his wallet again and was calling for another round of drinks. In the split-second that his wallet was open, Niall had noticed the way that McGinn had folded each individual pound note into one another. This was a common trick that the English crowd did when they returned home. It was around about then (Niall found it difficult now to remember exactly the sequence of events) that a few pounds had fallen from Bobo's wallet and slipped to the floor. As sly as a fox, Mikeo Linnane had put his foot over one of them to hide it. Bobo had bent down unsteadily to pick up the money but he'd probably have missed that pound altogether if it hadn't been for Mooney spilling the beans. 'Hey, you've another pound there on the floor, Willie, you missed it there,' Mooney had said, and Linnane had quickly slid his shoe off the money again. It was as though they'd secretly divided into two tiny factions: the crowd that Niall had brought in with him first and the lads that had come into the pub a bit later, with McGinn as their mutual prey. It was as though one group was scared stiff that the others would get one over on them.

'Yep,' Mooney had muttered, 'it's nice to see someone showing a bit of generosity every now and then; that Linnane wouldn't wet your whistle even if your tongue was stuck to your mouth with the thirst!'

Purcell had begun playing 'The Rambling Pitchfork', and whatever madness his music inspired, Niall had hopped out onto the floor dancing and stamping his feet in time with the tune as best he could. He'd rattled the floor with his heels loudly in the way that he'd learned from the Connemara boys when he was in the army, each step striking the timber as sweet and measured as a drum, then let a wild whoop of joy to finish off. The lads had roared and clapped and whistled in approval, but whatever happened next, Niall had lost the plot. Sure, you had to go a bit crazy at least once a year and go on a real tear, and so he'd got in anther round of drinks for everyone. It had been around then, Niall remembered, that the first of the lads had felt sick. McGinn had been the first of them to go down and next thing, he was running out to the toilet at the back, ready to puke.

'Seasickness,' most likely, Sullivan had said, in his element. 'The old *Princess Maud.*'

Linnane had also gone out fairly quickly on McGinn's heels, however, letting on he was worried about him, and Packie Pugh hadn't been far behind him.

'Get out there quick after him, you idiot,' Mooney had ordered Sullivan, 'in case he robs the poor bastard blind or have you any bit of cop-on left in you at all?'

Even Jesus Christ hadn't had it this bad, Mooney had said to Niall when Bosco'd left – and found himself stuck between two robbers. That poor idiot McGinn in the clutches of Linnane and Packie Pugh! He'd be lucky if he wasn't fleeced completely by the time he came back in.

McGinn's face had been as pale as death when he returned from the toilet, his feet unsteady, Linnane guiding him along and Packie Pugh wiping his face with a piece of old cloth. They'd plonked him down next to the bar as Linnane advised McGinn to try a drop of brandy, that there was nothing better than brandy to soothe the stomach. And, to give him his due, McGinn had recovered fairly well – for a skinny scrawns of a fellow like him. A quick sip of the brandy and he'd wanted to start singing. The day had seemed to be passing them by, and Niall couldn't by that stage remember whether he'd bought another round or not – or even how many pints he'd himself drunk by the time the row started. It was Khyber Brennan who'd kicked things off as usual: what did he do but insult Purcell, and for absolutely no reason at all! He'd advised Purcell to put down his fiddle for a while, that it was worse than the sound of a cat screeching at the night. Brennan'd no ear for music, Purcell had thrown right back at him, those small eyes of his nervous and darting all over the place How come no-one else was complaining about it?

An ear for music! Khyber had guffawed. He'd prefer to listen to an old wan piss in a bucket than listen to the awful racket Purcell made.

Next thing the two of them were going for one another and were wrestling onto the floor and had had to be separated. They'd only just been pulled apart when the tailor McCarthy had fallen off his stool and had to be helped back onto his perch. Unsurprisingly, Pat Neary's patience had worn thin by then, and when Linnane and Packie Pugh squared up to one another, he'd had enough and ordered the lot of them to get the hell out of there and go home. Even then, the barman was hard put to get them out. McGinn had got all bolshie and Neary had had to drag him out and onto the road outside, McGinn roaring all the while that he'd been in plenty of fancier establishments than Neary's over in London, that he wasn't some common blackguard that should be thrown onto the street! The town had been swathed in evening darkness as they'd walked down the road, Linnane carrying the newly returned emigrant's suitcase and Packie Pugh on hand to support him, just in case.

The six of them had disappeared unsteadily into the dusk: Brennan, Purcell, Mooney, Sullivan, and Niall himself – that band of idiots swaying against one another all along the road. Bobo had got a second wind now and was fine and happy again. They'd have another drink in Róisín Street, he'd promised them, and Pat Neary could go and take a running jump! Crossing John's Bridge, the spell of the beautiful Nore had enchanted Niall: the orbs of the streetlights gold and luminescent on the black waters, all the colours merging as one. Niall had fallen behind the other lads so he could embrace the secret energy of the night-river for himself. It was at times like this, when the alcohol heightened his deepest senses, that Niall grew more alert to his inner self and the meaning that lay therein. He'd experienced something similar many times when he'd been in the army. When he would return to the barracks at night with a good drop on-board, sometimes, he'd go into the wash-house and stand in front of the mirror, staring into himself as if searching for something within, an understanding of his own essence.

Niall was now standing half-dazed, entranced by the mystery of the river and had almost forgotten about the others until he heard the angry shouts coming from the other end of the bridge. He rushed over, splayfooted and unsteady to find them but got there to find McGinn lying in a heap on the ground and Khyber Brennan bent over him and trying his best to get him back onto his feet; Linnnane was over the other side of Róisín Street, travel case still in hand, while Mooney and Sullivan were involved in a heated argument with two members of the Garda Síochána. There was no sign of Ned Purcell at all. One of the guards (Moriarty, as Niall soon discovered) was agitated and asking Mooney for his name while the other guard stood next to him, relaxed and seemingly oblivious to the chaos around him. Maybe Moriarty was seizing his chance to get his own back on some of the lads, Niall thought. Maybe the corner-boys hadn't been as wrong about him as he'd thought.

'What do you want my name for? You won't get my name, man,' Mooney annouced defiantly.

'You were causing a disturbance and you were drunk, that's why,' said Garda Moriarty stiffly. 'Your name now, like a good man, and your address.'

'I won't: not to you and not to any other redneck from the arsehole of Ireland, either. I'm descended from the townspeople here, the same as everyone before me. So, go back to the bog now the pair of you and don't be annoying normal decent people the likes of us!' Mooney's temper was up now and Sullivan had the look of a man who was ready for a fight.

'I won't ask you your name again, now,' Moriarty threatened, jamming his cap down more firmly on his head as if he meant business.

'Don't hassle me again now, I'm telling you. Because you won't get my name, boy, and that's the end of it, how come you don't bother asking any of the big bucks around here their names? You're too afraid, that's why, you gobshite!'

Whether to placate him or in an attempt to arrest him, Moriarty placed his hand on Mooney's shoulder but got a right hook to the chin for his troubles. Moriarty staggered backwards and his cap rolled out across the road. The second guard clocked Mooney with a vicious belt to the mouth, but Mooney charged back at him with a roar and caught him brazenly with two punches before the guard had time to recover. Moriarty tackled Mooney, wrestling him to the ground in a rugby tackle.

The other guard had his baton out and lammed Mooney with it on top of his head, despite Sullivan's best efforts to prevent him. Mooney roared with pain and tried to climb back to his feet but Moriarty had twisted one of his arms behind his back and had him trapped. And, in case that didn't do the job, the other guard gave him a whack of his baton across the temple, and left him face-down on the road. Moving heavily and almost in slow-motion, Niall tried to grab hold of the baton but the guard brushed him aside, as if he were swatting a fly. Then, as if to add insult to injury, he belted Sullivan just below the ear and landed him on his backside. The guards had pulled Mooney to his feet and were dragging him down in the direction of the barracks, his right arm twisted behind him. Mooney'd lost his cap during the fracas and, drunk as he was, this was something of a revelation to Niall. He couldn't remember ever seeing Mooney without his headgear before: the man was as bald as a coot! Sullivan was stretched out motionless in a heap on the ground but the other lads had disappeared. It was a struggle but Niall lifted Bosco to his feet, placed his arm over his shoulders and the pair of them tottered slowly back along the path. Bosco stopped momentarily and puked over and again, retching up everything that was in his stomach.

It took more than an hour to get Sullivan home and up to the door of his house in Ormond Park. No doubt about it, Niall thought, he'd made a right hames of the day, whatever kind of a born idiot he was! He was too afraid to check how much of his five pounds he'd blown that evening, too afraid to count whatever few bits of change he'd left. And how he'd go home and face his mother after all this, God only knew!

After he'd helped Sullivan home, Niall stumbled his way slowly back to Saint Canice's Row. He couldn't understand at first why there was no light in the house but as he approached the front-door, the silence hit him like a wave. The door was open and he had to light a match to see into the hallway. Their small house was empty and silent. There wasn't a stick of furniture left in the kitchen except for the battered old dresser that wasn't worth bringing to the new house. The house was abandoned. Niall lit another match and climbed the stairs. His bed was gone but the old double bed that his brothers had slept in was still there, broken springs showing as clear as day. His mother had been busy since morning. She'd kill him once she got her hands on him!

Niall came downstairs again but on the very last step, he tripped and fell heavily onto the ground. He twisted his ankle and the pain went through him like a spear. He lay there on the ground, writhing in pain while the deadly loneliness of the house enveloped him. Once the pain had eased slightly, he sat on the bottom step of the stairs and took out a cigarette. He finished his smoke and climbed to his feet again slowly, then left their small house behind for the last time and hobbled gingerly up the road. He had a way to go yet in the dark, all the way up to the new house.

Chapter 16

Things never work out the way you hope – or so it seemed to Trevor. Just when you thought things were going fine, something would always come along and feck it all up on you! As Christmas Eve fell on the Sunday that year, the men were free till the following Tuesday, so they worked up until their usual finishing time on the Saturday. On returning to the lodgings that evening, Trevor received the news that really put the kaibosh on things and filled him with rage.

'A telegram came for you today, Trevor,' Madge Connolly announced in a slightly regretful tone, and he barely in the door.

'Because I was afraid that you might have bad news and that I'd have to send a message out to you at work, I opened it.' Madge said, telegram in hand. Sensing Trevor's hesitancy, she gave him the message straight. 'Your wife and kids are coming over to you. They'll be at Euston in the morning.'

'Christ,' said Trevor, in a dead tone.

Madge watched Trevor carefully, as if trying to read his mind and said, 'It won't be easy for you to get a place this close to Christmas, Trevor, but I'll have a room free from tonight. Peter Walsh has gone home and John Joe Cloherty is going up to Manchester to see his sister tonight. 'I could get that room ready for you, until you get Christmas over, if you like?'

Trevor was so stunned that he didn't respond at all. He ate his dinner in a daze, then went upstairs. His head was all over the place, he didn't know what to do. In a flash, his life had been turned upside-down and he was in the shit, if ever a man ever was. 'The curse of God on the wagon; had she completely lost the plot this time?' he hissed and threw himself onto the bed. He was furious. It was hard to believe that she'd have the stupidity and stubbornness – the bitch – to do something like this; what kind of a fool of a woman was she? To land over here like this on Christmas Eve with two children, and without the slightest warning! She must have lost it completely or else…. By God, she might be cracked but she still had the cleverness of the nutter: look at how she hadn't sent any letter beforehand or given a week's grace so's that he'd have the chance to stop her coming over? She was on her way over already, she was on the Dublin train right now probably, and he'd just one more night to himself and she'd be with him all the time after that. Bloody hell! Trevor felt like a man facing a long stretch in prison; he couldn't see what lay ahead of him or behind him anymore; damn it, but he was completely trapped! Every night, from now on, she'd be there when he came in from work and every morning she'd be lying there next to him in the bed and God – the Mayo fellow who'd said that there was space for only one head on any pillow had been right. There'd be a racket and the crying of children in his ears after work every day and he'd have to put up with Nora's moods into the bargain. And – oh Christ, but wasn't it awful embarrassing for any man to bring his wife and kids into a lodging house with him! Because he had no option but to accept Madge's offer; either that or he'd have to go and ask Mainey to take them in – and there's no way he was going do that, absolutely no way! He didn't know where he'd be able to look – in front of the other men – kids crying around the house and all the rest of it. He'd go half-mad! She'd have to eat her food in the kitchen with Madge, or up in the room; there was no way that he'd let eat her meals down amongst the men; he'd be the butt of all their jokes. And wasn't she some rip all the same! What the hell were the older people playing at that they'd let her over here like this and not told her to stay put? But then, how could you give advice to a big lumpen gowl of a woman like her? You'd have been as well off trying to advise the wind, because she didn't listen to him…. Look at how often he'd told her to stay where she was! She was hardly going to take much notice of what anyone else said to her if she didn't listen to him. Trevor got up after a while and had a quick bath. He had the place to himself, which didn't happen very often. He put on his brown Sunday suit, his white shirt and threw the rest of his work things into the bottom of the clothes press. On his way downstairs he met Madge who was going into her room; she'd already had a bit to drink if he wasn't mistaken; she must've started on the Christmas festivities early… since lunchtime, probably down at the Oxford Arms or in the Brighton.

'That room'll do fine, thanks very much,' Trevor told her. 'It won't take me too long to get a place, I think.'

'You're welcome, Trevor,' said Madge, giving him one of those impenetrable looks of hers. 'There's a double bed there already and a single, and I can change the bed-sheets on them,' she replied, and then, as if it had just struck her, she asked, 'How long have have you been married, Trevor?'

'Too long,' said Trevor, slightly gruffly. 'How do you mean?'

'Oh – nothing at all!' Madge replied, waving him off with a vague shake of her hand.

'I'll be sorry to see you leave; you've been here a long time now.' These words knocked Trevor off his stride: he wasn't too sure how to respond. Madge had never spoken like that to any of her lodgers although there were plenty of men in the house and all they needed was the word. That's if Trevor had read her words properly, that is – maybe he was just imagining there'd be a chance like that with Madge. He paused at the top of the stairs – then went out.

Down Arlington Road and into Parkway, then on towards the High Street. Nora's impending arrival wasn't the priority, not exactly; he had something else on his mind, he had something else to deal with, something more urgent. He sensed it as sure as day; he feel it in his bones. Tonight was the night that he and Christy Power would have it out and they'd finally know which of them was the best man. He was absolutely sure of it. Himself and the Jackeen. Tonight. He felt it in every fibre of his being. Trevor had an iron fist or steel knuckles, as he called them, in his pocket, a set that he'd taken from an Englishman who'd tried to use it on him in a fight in Peterborough one night. The steel knuckles made for a powerful weapon if a crowd ever attacked you, but the fight he'd have with the Jackeen would be different. Everything had to be fair and square so that neither of them could accuse one another of anything. Everything had to be above aboard. Trevor always had the steel knuckles in his pocket just in case, the same way that other men carried a knife. And it was also a sort of a trophy, a reminder. That Geordie he had fought outside the Bird in the Hand – that big Irish pub in Peterborough – had been a difficult customer, a right tricky son-of-a-gun and as tough as they came. Some people claimed that the Englishman wasn't much of a fighter (no more than he was a labourer), but Trevor had never given any credence to such assertions. There were plenty of Englishmen out there who were better than the Irish in a fist-fight, and – to give them their due – they were fair when it came to fighting, too, more so than Scotsmen. The Scots used razors when they were fighting, razors, broken bottles or anything else that came to hand, and the fight would turn savage, Trevor thought. The Jackeens weren't lacking when it came to the fighting stakes, the poorest of them especially. There was none of that 'Let me at him' or 'Hold me back!' that some country lads went on with, all that posing and shouting, and the suspicion all the while that the man in question hadn't the slightest intention of actually fighting. Trevor had seen two low-sized Jackeens give one another an almighty battering, outside Rowton House one night, men who had the courage of the slums in their veins and were as technical as any real boxer. Power would be even better in terms of technique than those two and he'd be stronger as well. After all, he must have been unbelievably strong to knock out Patrick Costello! And he wouldn't be lacking in confidence either.... Trevor knew that he'd have to match him in that department. The reputation of Galway and his own people depended on him and if Christy Power beat him, it would be a long time before they'd get over the shame of it. If Power won, he would be humiliated for all time. The Jackeen hated Connemara people, according to Mullen – in much the same way as other people hated blacks. And, truth be told, it was the same in reverse for Trevor. He preferred any other people – the Pole, the Scotsman or the black man – no matter how foreign any of them might have seemed – to the Dublin Jackeen. It was like something that he'd born with, a distrust and hatred of the city-born Irishman. All he needed was to hear their accent and he'd get angry. And out of all of them, he hated this Christy Power the most!

Maybe he could harness this hatred and turn it to his advantage? That might be give him the edge when it came down to it. It might drive him on, give him that extra power and determination when he needed it most. First off, he'd to make sure that the first punch he landed on Power rocked him from head to toe. It had to be a punch that he wouldn't forget. And who knows? Maybe if it were landed right, this one punch might win it for him? This was no time for fancy stuff or games anyway. He had to land a vicious salamander on the bastard as early as possible, a knock-out punch, simple as that. A punch that would make absolute shit of Power.

If he won, Trevor and his friends could go anywhere and they'd have drinks bought them whenever they walked into a pub. They'd never have to pay for a drink afterwards, probably. It would be their right from then on, as victors. People would always show him respect.

Someone offered Trevor a drink the minute he stepped into the Camden Stores, but he refused, somewhat abruptly. He wasn't in the mood for a chat tonight, he had more pressing matters to deal with.

The Camden Stores was crowded with Irish lads but it only took Trevor a few minutes to suss out that the Jackeen wasn't there.

Trevor threw back one quick beer and headed down to the Mother Black Cap, a massive pub that had a picture of a witch above its door and the words Wenlock Ales inscribed beneath it. The street outside was full of people, the road chock-a-block with big red buses and cars of every type passing by. All the shops had their Christmas decorations up and there was a festive atmosphere in the air with people rushing past him laden with presents. Not that Trevor took much notice. He was intent on finding the Jackeen and calling him out. The Mother Black Cap was mobbed, loud accordion music in the bar and the lounge at the back absolutely jam-packed. Trevor shouldered his way through into the backroom, oblivious to the shouts and greetings of different men but when there was no sign of the man he was looking for, he went straight back outside again. It was the same story in the Bedford Arms, in the Brighton, and in the Eagle. Trevor's intuition told him that he was getting closer, however. He could smell it. He turned down Greenland Street and spotted Mullen walking in his direction, all poshed-up in his blue suit, white shirt, walking that big loud showy walk of his – as much as to say that the street wasn't big enough for people like him! Mullen had a tiny piece of blood-smeared paper stuck to his face where he'd cut himself shaving. And… he was wound-up!

'Trevor,' he blurted. 'He's in the Hawley Arms!'

'Who is, you fucker?' Trevor said, even though he knew damn well straight away.

'The Jackeen, Trevor! I was just looking for you now. I knew that you'd be somewhere around, and just a few minutes ago, a Mayo lad in the Laurel Tree told me that Paddy McAllister's Jackeen is in the Hawley Arms playing darts and asking where he can find the red-haired man!'

'Let's go,' Trevor hissed, and they turned on their heels. The

Hawley Arms was an old pub set in a secluded avenue, an iron viaduct at the far end. The saloon was old with worn-looking carpets and a badly tuned piano, while the bar was as basic as you could get – bare wooden floorboards and nothing else. Over the counter, on the smoke-coloured wall, hung a yellowed drawing of a hurling team from long ago – but that was it. The Irish always gathered in the bar area whereas the local middle-aged or elderly people went into the saloon where they played old music hall numbers at the weekends while the Irish lads in the bar all played cards or darts and chatted about fights and work.

When the Irish were in the mood for music, they usually sang songs like 'The Valley of Knockanure' or 'Down Erin's Lovely Lee'; it was as though the only songs they knew related to emigration or the Irish War of Independence. There was little enough contact between the people at the bar and those in the saloon, and they usually sorted out the odd argument that blew up between themselves and never bothered with the law. Both lots kept to themselves for the most part. The Hawley Arms was heaving when Trevor and Mullen came in, the bar staff racing up and down behind the counter, pulling pints to beat the band. This bar always had a good crowd in, but tonight, it was difficult to get even standing room. Word of the impending fight had got around since people were clearly waiting for more than just a few pints. Trevor stood in the doorway, his eyes scanning the room, and he wasn't long picking him out. His eyes fastened on the Jackeen's and they gave one another a cold and vicious stare. The Jackeen was playing darts. He was in the middle of a game and, as Trevor looked on, he reached out to take a handful of darts from a Ballinrobe man that Trevor knew vaguely. Darts in hand, the Jackeen gave Trevor an evil stare and coolly turned to the other man, 'We'll finish the game first.'

Mullen was at the bar already, puffed up with pride; he was Trevor Nee's sidekick for the fight. He rapped self-importantly on the counter and ordered two pints of beer and two glasses of whiskey.

Trevor took a glass of whiskey from him but left the beer; his heart pumping as he knocked it back in one swallow. His eyes never left the Jackeen. No doubt about it, but this Dubliner had balls – to come into a pub like this one, where he'd hardly have any back-up. Then again, any man who'd knocked out Patrick Babeen wasn't easily frightened. Unless it was the hatred that your man had for all Connemara people that was behind it!

Hatred frequently got the better of good sense, they said, but he was certainly a brave man – irrespective of how good a fighter he was – to come into a place where, for all he knew, he could have been attacked from behind without warning. There was no way that Trevor would have gone in alone amongst a bunch of Jackeens like that. Trevor got a proper look at the Jackeen; he was taller than he'd initially thought and really well-built; he was very strong-looking, and for a sturdy block of a man, strong and agile.

Trevor loosened the knot in his tie and took another sip of whiskey. The game of darts was almost over; the Jackeen needed a ten and a double-five to win. The tension in the bar was palpable; any moment now, things would kick off…. But if the Jackeen felt anything, he certainly didn't show it. There wasn't a hint of fear in the way that he stood behind the mark, his eyes glued to the dart-board. He leaned forward – the small dart between thumb and forefinger – took his mark and threw. He got the double-five, right on the button and he'd won the game. An imperceptible sigh went through the crowd but there were no roars of congratulation for the Jackeen….

'I hope you're not planning on playing another game, lad,' Trevor called loudly across the room to where the Jackeen was replacing his darts in a small wooden holder as carefully as a surgeon re-arranging his instruments. He put the holder into his jacket, then placed it on the back of a chair nearby. His sleeves were folded high up on his arms, displaying his powerful muscles to the world. There was no trace of any beer-gut on this fellow either, even if – by all accounts – he hadn't been doing the hard labouring work that would have kept him fit. I'll have my hands full with this one, said Trevor to himself.

'The game that I'm going to play now won't be to your liking, take it from me, man,' the Jackeen said, giving Trevor a cold stare. 'I'm ready if you are.'

Trevor removed his tie and jacket and handed them to Mullen with a gesture so commanding that you'd have sworn he'd been his corner-man for years. Trevor's muscles bulged out from beneath his tight shirt and he rolled his shoulders now, warming up, and spat on his palms. He was ready. Whatever petty fears that had lingered in his mind earlier were gone and he couldn't wait to get down to battle….He glanced around him and saw all the Connemara people looking on. He saw hope in their eyes – in the faces that spoke of home – a place rocky and desolate, where its people spoke Irish and were their own tribe. He was their champion now and they'd placed their hope in him. A surge of courage and determination went through him. At last, all the waiting was over and it was time for action.

'Out of the way!' Trevor called out authoritatively. The Jackeen went out first, Trevor on his heels, and the crowd followed them beneath the streetlamps outside. The crowd fanned out and formed a big circle shielding the fighters. The youngest were buzzing, their faces lit up with excitement, whereas the older crowd seemed more detached. This fight had an awful lot riding on it.

'C'mon, ya boya, Bartley, make shit of him!' shouted one of the younger crowd. 'Up Doire Leathan.' Cóilín Pat Bobby had his hands raised in the air with all the authority of a real boxing referee.

'This man is a stranger who came amongst us and challenged Nee here, and let's give him fair play – that's all he's asking from us!' said O'Malley from the crowd.

'Oh, aren't you the right feckin' boss too, O'Malley?' shouted one derisive voice, not that anyone paid much heed to it.

The Jackeen gave a wry smile as much as to say that those words about fair play made no odds to him and that he wasn't fazed by the crowd one way or the other. He adopted a defensive stance, his eyes glued to his opponent.

'You took your time calling me out, lad,' said Trevor, circling him carefully.

'Sure, this is no big deal – what's the rush?'

So quickly that a gasp came from the spectators, Trevor launched himself forward, aiming an almighty punch at the Jackeen's jaw that would have rocked him to the core if it had only connected. The Jackeen was alert, however, and had slipped Trevor's punch fairly handily before replying, *Bang!* with a powerful shot of his own that landed full-square on Trevor's jaw and shook him. It was a left! The Jackeen'd caught him with the left instead of the right as Trevor had expected. This was a trick that Trevor would have to watch out for from now on. Instead of following up with a quick right as Trevor himself would have done, the Jackeen pranced around on his toes, craning his head insultingly at Trevor as if trying to draw him in, the way that a trainer would draw in an amateur. He was a cocky one, no doubt about it! Trevor shook his head to try and clear it and focussed on him again; he wouldn't give your man another chance like that, no way! There wasn't a gig out of any of the spectators. Silence reigned except for the dim echo of traffic in the distance and the footwork of the boxers as they circled each other, breathing heavily. The Jackeen bobbed his head, nodding towards Trevor and looking for an opening. Trevor moved closer, alert for the quick right, but the Jackeen let fly again with a powerful left hook. Trevor blocked this punch and while the Jackeen was off-balance, he caught him with a big slap to the chin.

'Atta boy, Trevor! Go on, make shit of him!' Mullen shouted, while other voices yelled their encouragement too. 'That's the man, Trevor, you have him, get him again! Give it to him, Nee! Good man! Hammer him, Trevor!'

Trevor's punch hadn't knocked the Jackeen off his stride, however. He still skipped around as athletically as a dancer, sneer slightly, as if annoyed that he'd been caught with that punch.

'A lucky one, culchie!' he muttered with contempt, then stopped dancing. He feinted, as if to throw the left again, then leaned the other way and followed through with the right, catching Trevor straight on the side of the jaw! It was a heavy one – like a kick from a mule – and he burst through Trevor's defence with two more punches and slammed him in the mouth.

'That's just for starters, culchie,' the Jackeen muttered through his teeth. 'That's nothing yet!'

The corner of Trevor's mouth was bleeding and he shook his head. No doubt about it – he was up against a very able opponent, a man who could master him in terms of skill. Still, Trevor had plenty of confidence in his own punching power, if he could only get the chance to land one of his own pile-drivers. The constant movement and agility of the Jackeen was a worry for him, however. Trevor backed off a second and the Jackeen rushed forward, cockily dropping his guard as if inviting Trevor on.... Trevor saw the opening and slammed him at speed with a powerful punch to the jaw that stopped him in his tracks. This was as good a punch as Trevor ever remembered throwing and for a brief instant, Trevor thought that he might have struck the winning punch! The Jackeen's legs seemed to weaken but he didn't fall. He must have had unbelievable powers of recovery, because he came back again a moment later, his defence held high this time. He dodged another right hook from Trevor and then responded with an attack of his own. The Jackeen had survived and now he bobbed and weaved, throwing off a few quick combinations. The speed of the Jackeen's punches was frightening and this was as perfect a demonstration of boxing skills as the spectators had ever seen. Trevor retreated from the onslaught and for the next few minutes, was on the back-foot, fending off the Dublin-man's hooks and combinations.

Bang! The Jackeen got through with the same left-hand trick as before and Trevor felt the top of his head explode in a ball of pain and one of his teeth go loose. He was dazed for a second but it would take one hell of a punch to knock out a man as strong as Trevor Nee; he withdrew behind his defence again and blocked a powerful left-right cross, then attacked once more. He got through this time and landed a haymaker of a punch that saw the Jackeen stagger backwards like a drunken man three sheets to the wind. It was now or never, Trevor told himself and he really went for it. He caught the stunned Dubliner with another powerful shot just beneath the ear and the Jackeen went down on one knee, his arms stretched out awkwardly in front of him like a big ungainly bird trying to steady itself.

Seeing him on his knees, the crowd went wild. 'Hit him again, Bartley, son. Don't let him up!' they bayed Trevor hesitated. He didn't want to ram home his advantage and finish the fight in this way. His pride held him back. He wanted a more spectacular finish than this: a clean knock-out akin to the one the Jackeen had dealt Patrick Babeen; that's what Trevor sought now, a win so comprehensive that no-one could ever deny it. And so he let the Jackeen rise up again despite the roars for blood he heard from all sides. And fair play to Power; he made the most of this moment's respite and got to his feet fairly quickly, his defence up.

'You lost your chance, culchie,' he said with a sneer. 'You'll regret that.'

Trevor went for the right-cross this time but the other man blocked it with his arm and caught Trevor with a powerful punch of his own. It was a clean shot and Trevor felt the back of his skull explode in a blaze of red light and pain. Everything around him seemed to go blank for a moment and the Jackeen was on him and pounding ferociously. He let fly now – left, right, left, right – hooks and crosses coming from every angle and forcing Trevor back so that he broke the circle of spectators around them; the watchers quickly shifting back out of the way.

'I'm nearly done with you now, culchie,' the Jackeen grunted, but Trevor's thirst for revenge drove him on and he charged forward again, his arms like flails and raining punches down on the Jackeen. He took them all, however, even while retreating slightly, and when the onslaught eased, he got through with two quick shots of his own, straight-on. Trevor shook his head again, angry that he'd been knocked off his stride. The Jackeen was up on his toes and playing games again, weaving in and out, feinting right and left. He caught Trevor with a number of stinging hooks and slipped out of the Connemara-man's range, mocking him. Trevor was on the defensive again but his confidence was still high because he knew that no matter what the Jackeen threw at him, he wasn't capable of knocking him out, not the way he'd creased Costello over in Kilburn, anyway. And if the Jackeen didn't have it in him to land that knockout blow, then Trevor had a great chance of winning. This was a slug-fest now and it wouldn't be decided on boxing ability or training: whoever was the toughest, with most staying power, would win out. The Jackeen was on the offensive again, that wild sneer on his face and hatred in his eyes. Trevor blocked a sneaky left-hand with his right, and caught the Jackeen a sharp one as he veered away. This was a solid punch – one that would have flattened a less powerful man – and Trevor went for it again. He followed this up with a straight right to the chin, a crunching punch that knocked the Jackeen's head right back onto his shoulders and wobbled him again. For a second, it looked as if the Jackeen was gone but he fell to one knee instead. He was definitely there for the taking now; a few more powerful shots and Trevor had him gone.

'You have him now Trevor! Finish him!' Trevor heard from the crowd, but he wanted this victory to be as polished as possible. He wanted this to be the ultimate performance and there was no way he wanted people saying afterwards that he'd clocked a man who was already half-way to the floor. Not when he could as easily knock the same man out while he was still standing. He gave the Jackeen a few seconds to recover and somehow, he got to his feet again. He wasn't the same man now, however; he was only just barely hanging in there. All the bluster and posing was gone: the only thing he had left was the cold ruthlessness of the trained fighter, the instinct to survive at all costs. Trevor read it in the Jackeen's face as clear as day; the only way left for the Jackeen was to use whatever ring-craft he had left in him and to hope that Trevor made a mistake. The next time there would be no mercy, Trevor said to himself, no more comebacks. He'd gone too far with this stupidity and it was time to make the Jackeen pay.

'Here you go, you bollix!' hissed Trevor, lunging forward, but the Jackeen slipped his attack and twisted away. Then, with Trevor off-balance momentarily, he landed a clean shot on the Connemara-man, right on his eye, which was already badly swollen. Trevor gave a low moan of pain and lashed out wildly in response but the Jackeen slipped his guard again, and connected with him again, left and right. One shot caught him four-square and blood spewed from Trevor's nose and covered his shirt. The Jackeen had got a second wind and the Doire Leathan man was in trouble again. Suddenly, Trevor looked tired and old, his lower lip busted, his nose pumping and his right eye almost closed. Any late arrivals to the fight would have thought that it was Power who'd been in the ascendant all along, given how bashed-up Trevor looked. The Jackeen seized the initiative and went after Trevor with an explosion of punches, left and right, as Trevor backed off and protected himself as best he could. The Jackeen's boxing training stood him in good stead now and he sensed that victory could yet be his. He had Trevor on the back-foot and he lurched forward and connected with a powerful salamander that made Trevor's legs go weak; he punched him again for good measure and Trevor wobbled.

The Connemara-man was on the brink, and in an effort to clear his vision, he drew the back of his hand across his bloodied nose. He was sorry that he hadn't finished the Jackeen off earlier when he'd had the chance; it was never good to be too cocky. Trevor was on the defensive as he attempted to fend off a slew of punches, the Jackeen throwing a series of combinations in succession. Trevor took some heavy shots but he was still standing – when most other men would have succumbed – and he was quietly convinced that he could take the Jackeen out. He had a better punch than the other man and the longer the fight went on, the more Power visibly tired. I've taken his best shots and I'm still standing, Trevor said to himself. I'm still in the hunt here. He bent his head low and tucked into himself, then surged forward again, now that the Jackeen had slowed down. The Jackeen was breathing heavily. Slowing down had proved to be a costly mistake on his part. He forgot to keep his defence up high and Trevor spotted the opening. He caught the Jackeen with a right bone-shaker, a punch that came all the way from Trevor's shoulder and then went for the penultimate attack. He caught the Jackeen right on the button and, sensing victory, a roar of joy went up from the crowd as the Jackeen staggered backwards with Trevor in close pursuit. The Connemara-man went in for the kill and caught the Jackeen with a volley of punches, a vicious combination to the head and the body. He slammed him in the rib-cage and saw the other man wilt. The Jackeen staggered; he was in big trouble; one of his eyes was bleeding heavily and the other was nearly shut; he was dazed and lurching from side to side. He didn't know where he was anymore. He reeled away from Trevor and tried to re-assert his defence, but it was no good; the Galway-man was on him straight away and moved in for the kill, rocking him with one big punch after another. The Jackeen was shattered and ready to go.

The strangest of feelings surged through Trevor now that his opponent was defenceless and ready to fall. The cold hatred for the Dubliner that had travelled his veins earlier just disappeared now that his opponent was defenceless and ready to fall. The intense hatred that had engulfed him earlier was replaced by a great surge of joy, and the pain of his injuries were as nothing compared to the wild ecstasy of this moment. It was better than anything he'd ever felt; this was the greatest victory of his life, no doubt about it. The Jackeen was still upright – just about – but he was very shaky, his legs looked as though they'd gone to jelly. He was so weak that he hadn't the energy to raise his arms or protect himself anymore. Both of his eyes were swollen-over and he barely knew where he was anymore. Trevor waited a split-second as the Jackeen staggered dangerously in front of him. 'It's time to put you down now, young lad. You won't get up from this one.' He slammed him with one final massive and bone-crushing right-hand. Christy Power fell unconscious onto the road, his prone form shrouded in the wan light of the street-lamps.

Chapter 17

It was Christmas Night, and Nano and Sheila sat on their beds, drinking mugs of cocoa. It had been one of the longest days that Nano had ever experienced. From when they'd walked to first Mass together that morning until she'd finished work hours later, it had really dragged. Nano had worked a split-shift that day, and the break of a couple of hours had seemed even more drawn-out than usual. Their Christmas dinner had been nearly the same fare as they had every other day of the year, and the supper was even worse. A cold blob of Christmas pudding and some strange stuff they called chutney. There'd only been a small crowd at supper when Nano had come off duty, and the paper-chains decorating the canteen walls already looked drab and dead. There was no life or atmosphere in the place and Nano had felt as lonely as she'd felt since the day she first left home. She couldn't wait for the rest of the holidays to be over.

'Aren't we the two sad gits stuck in here on Christmas Night with nothing to do and nowhere to go?' Sheila had said. 'If the pubs were open, now....'

'It wouldn't make much odds,' Nano responded, raising her mug for the toast, *'Sláinte!'*

'There's nothing so good for you as a cup of cocoa,' said Sheila, grimacing as she took a sip of hers.

'At least it's fine and sweet and there's plenty of milk in it. Where'd you get it?'

'Stefan gave it to me, that Ukrainian cook.'

'Stefan is Polish, Sheila.'

'Oh! Would you listen to herself, now! "Stefan is Polish, Sheila." Aren't you getting fierce knowledgeable about them all of a sudden!'

'Well if you were called English, now how –?'

'Oh! Whatever – sure I couldn't care less what they call me, sister. But, wait till you hear. Guess what your man said to me?'

'Who?'

'Who? You fool! The Polish fellow, Stefan; who else would I be talking about?'

'Guess what he said to me anyway?'

'How the hell would I know what he said to you – that you're good-looking, is it?'

'I know that myself; no, the fecker – he said to me that he'd a half-a-bottle of whiskey down in his room if I wanted to come down with him and we'd have a drink in honour of Christmas!'

'Janey, you missed your chance there, Sheila – you'd have had a great night!'

'I might be stupid but I'm not that feckin' stupid,' Sheila retorted. 'I wouldn't trust any of those feckers as far as I'd throw them.'

Nano reddened slightly with embarrassment but she didn't say anything else. Recently Sheila had been throwing little darts in her direction about the refugees in the place. Maybe she was secretly a bit jealous about Julius Kuzleikas; it was hard to know. There was no need for it, anyway, one way or the other.

Earlier that night, Nano had left the room and went out to meet Julius but she'd walked barely fifty yards when she'd changed her mind and her misgivings had re-asserted themselves. What did she do but turn on her heel and return to the room, mortified at her own stupidity. 'You weren't gone long?' said had Sheila to her in surprise. 'What brought you back again?'

'Oh… I don't know… a little bit of cop-on, I suppose,' said Nano sheepishly. 'It wasn't what brought me home, really, but what took me out in the first place, sister! I don't know what came over me, really.'

Recalling this later on that evening, Nano sensed that a part of Sheila was happy that she hadn't gone to see Julius in the end. One way or another, the previous night had been a restless one for Nano. She'd only slept fitfully and had had strange dreams that had left her on-edge that Christmas morning in case she met Julius somewhere between the wards and the nurses' quarters. It wasn't as if she needed to give him an excuse for not meeting him, if you thought about it. It wasn't as if she'd promised him anything. All the same, she'd felt as if she was under some kind of an obligation to him. It had been late afternoon on the following day – as she'd brought a series of medical reports to Sister Weston in Matron's office – that she'd run into Julius. She had blushed. Luckily, Julius hadn't been in the slightest bit awkward with her; he'd just calmly laid down the wheelbarrow of stuff he'd brought with him from the boiler-house and stopped for a chat.

'You didn't come in the end, Nano,' he'd said without a hint of accusation.

'I didn't say that I'd come, Julius,' Nano had replied, even though she knew he must have sensed how up-in-a-heap she'd really felt at that moment.

'I was expecting you, all the same,' Julius had persisted, piercing her with his green eyes. 'I waited a good while for you, in case you showed up.'

'Sorry about that,' Nano had replied, unsure of what to say. She'd folded the papers more tightly under her arm. 'I have to be going, Julius. They'll be looking for me back on the ward any minute.' Julius had given a gentle laugh that was difficult to read and taken up his barrow again.

'Yes,' he'd said, with a wry smile, 'don't let me keep you.' Nano was in a quandary for the rest of the day, unsure of her feelings. She didn't know whether she'd insulted Julius but was also slightly annoyed that he hadn't tried to waylay her a bit longer or asked her out again. They'd passed one another a few times since then – at a distance – and, while Julius had given her a friendly look each time, that was about it. She'd wished that he'd pursued her more. Then she'd seen him at the door of the kitchen, laughing and flirting with one of the Italian girls, the pair as relaxed with one another as if they'd actually been a couple. Unexpectedly, Nano'd felt a wave of jealousy and, for the rest of the day, this jealousy had rubbed away at her like a tiny, hidden sore, making her cranky. For a while after this, she couldn't set foot outside the door without being anxious that she'd see Julius again but unsure, at the same time, of what she'd actually say to him if she did see him. In fact, once or twice, she'd found herself taking her time on the short walk from the ward back to the living quarters, in the secret hope that Julius might suddenly appear around the corner. She hadn't decided what she'd say to him if he happened to ask her out again; all she knew was that she really wanted to meet him again. And even if she felt guilty and regretful in some ways, the truth was that Julius Kuzleikas was on her mind a lot more often these days than Máirtín was, the man that she should by now have been married to.

'Christmas Night,' said Sheila. 'It must be the most dead-boring night of the year.' Now, if the games-room had some sort of a shape on it, we could go down there for a while.'

'We're close enough to it as it is,' said Nano. 'Can't you hear them down there?'

Sheila listened carefully and she heard it, alright, the tragic notes of 'Kevin Barry' coming weakly down the corridor. 'Christ,' Sheila said. 'Wouldn't you think they'd get fed-up of that after a while?'

'I don't understand why you didn't go home for Christmas and take the holiday that's coming to you,' said Nano, after a few minutes. 'That's where I'd be gone.'

'Home, is it? That's the last place I'd go this time of year,' replied Sheila in a tone so bitter that it took Nano by surprise.

'Is it? Why's that?'

'Every reason,' said Sheila, as if she'd no inclination to say any more. Then, as if she'd changed her mind, she straightened herself up on the pillow and looked Nano straight in the eye. 'I haven't gone home any Christmas that it wasn't a bad one, Nano. This here is bad enough, but at least you've a bit of peace and quiet over here.'

'Sorry to hear that,' said Nano in a slightly uncomfortable tone. It was rare for Sheila to talk about home, and once again, it occurred to Nano that she knew more about some other women working in this place than she did about her own roommate.

'My father was the main reason for it: a right bastard of a man,' said Sheila. 'He'd always be at his worst at Christmas.' Sheila looked over at Nano as if she were trying to work something out. 'What sort of man is your own father?' she asked her.

'Oh, sure, he's a very nice man, Sheila, he wouldn't hurt a fly.'

'You were lucky, so, girl,' Sheila congratulated her. 'My father is the devil incarnate!'

'You shouldn't say that, Sheila, especially not at Christmas! We're all as God created us.'

'Well, if that's so, he did a bad job of my old lad, girl. He's a monster, and there's no other word to describe him.'

'See now, those savages and rednecks – the likes of McDermott and Geraghty and that whole gang. Aren't they always bitching about how bad life is in the hospital here?'

'Yep, they are of course,' said Nano, unsure where this conversation was going.

'Well, I was never as well fed in my life as I am in this place, girl! Almost every penny my old fellow made, he drank, the bastard; and I wouldn't mind if it made him happy, but it never did! Half the time he'd be hungover and cranky because of the drink and the rest, he was like a bear, he was so thirsty for more. And my poor mam trying to magic eighteen pence from every shilling he gave her. I don't know how in God's name she managed to put a bite into our stomachs or made sure that we'd clothes on our backs, Nano, to be honest. I know that she often went hungry herself trying to look after us, and she was so afraid of that b**x that she'd never talk back at him.' Sheila was finding it hard to open up like this and she was silent for a moment, as if the anger inside her had taken her words away.

'The drink, of course,' said Nano. 'There's many a…'

'"The drink", says you? Drunkenness shows the hidden badness of the person inside! There's many a man who was given to the drink but who didn't torment his wife and his family as he did. If that ignorance and badness hadn't been in him in the first place, the drink wouldn't have brought it out. If I was to sit here now and tell you about some of the things he's done, we'd be here for the next year, Nano, you don't know the half of it!' Sheila gave a rueful shake of her head. Nano had never seen her friend as wound-up as this; suddenly, it was as if she had a stranger in the room. 'You were talking about Christmas there; would you believe it but I saw him half-kill my mother one Christmas Day, girl? He punched her in the face with his fist, the same as if he was punching a man! Her mouth bleeding and she thrown down on the floor, and the children all screaming! Every man who drank a drop or two at Christmas wasn't killing his wife, was he? Your father didn't do that, Nano, did he?'

Nano didn't know what to say to this, so Sheila continued, 'She gave him the last crown that we had in the house one day, – the last crown that she had – and not a loaf of bread left in the house, not even one slice of bread to give the children! And guess what she said – and this is what killed me altogether! – guess what she said when he went out the door with the money in his fist. "Let's pray now," she said. "Let's pray now that he'll be in good form when he gets back from the pub!" That's exactly what she said, Nano, as sure as I'm sitting here in front of you!'

'The poor woman,' Nano said.

'You can say that again; because she was poor in every way!' If she'd had even a smidgen of spirit in her, she wouldn't have said something like that, now would she? And I just couldn't let her get away with that, young and all that I was…. "No mam," I said, "let's pray that he gets killed while he's at work, that something'll come off the crane and fall down on top of him!"' Sheila looked over at Nano as though she were worried that her story wasn't affecting her friend as much as it should. 'And do you know what he did then, Nano?' Nano shook her head but Sheila continued. It was as if something had triggered itself inside her and forced these painful memories to the surface again. 'If she only stood up to him, Nano, if she just fought the bastard back or watched out for her chance some night when he was asleep, she could've hit him in the head with a hammer; anything rather than letting him walk all over her for all those years like that! I'd do it, Nano, by Christ, I would! I mean, what did she ever have in life; what does she even have now – she might as well be in the lowest region of hell!'

'There'll be no hell for her or her like in the next life, anyway,' said Nano but regretted it just as quickly. What good did saying this do anyone?

'To hell with the next life, it's this one that I care about! But my mother didn't have the guts in her to stand up for herself. Even when the priest came to the house and tried to make peace, what did she do but send him away again and make out that everything was fine! Wait till I tell you, now, Nano, but the last time I went home – a year last August – she had a black eye. She was waiting for me at the station when I got there and she'd this stuff over her eye trying to hide the bruise. You wouldn't believe it, Nano, the shock I got, seeing the poor creature like that again. I knew then that he hadn't changed his ways, of course, even if I was delighted to be home, y'know. But I nearly died of shock, Nano, when I saw the state she was in, and all I wanted to do right then was turn round and come back here to England again. All the life just went out of me in that minute, the same as if you'd let the air out of a balloon.' Sheila gave a sigh and shuddered, trying to rid herself of this horrible memory. 'I was so excited from the time that we left Limerick Junction that I was actually saying the names of the stations we passed through in my mind: Rathlurk, and all the rest. It was my first time home from here – what am I saying? It was my only time home! And then, y'know, Nano, I arrive in on a high to see my mother, and there she is with a big black eye!'

Sheila shook her head again and Nano shuddered when she saw the tears in the other woman's eyes. Sheila O'Dwyer was the last woman in the world that Nano would have associated with tears.

'I brought my mother into a small cafe on MacCurtain Street as a treat. But I was in no rush to go home when I saw her eye, I can tell you. I was so proud of myself: back home with money on me, and all my fine clothes,' Sheila said with an exaggerated laugh. 'I was pretending I had a bit of an English accent, I was so proud of myself. It was all a bit ridiculous, really, I know! Well, we had tea and cakes, anyway, and then went home. My poor mam was so happy, you'd swear I'd just brought her to dinner in the Ritz in London. My father was getting out of bed to go down to the pub and the first thing he did was ask me for some money. I gave him a ten-shilling note, not out of any love for him but just so's he'd be out of our way for a while. He spent the rest of the day down in the pub and when he came home that evening he was in the mood for causing trouble. He wasn't long in the door when he started a row and went to try and hit *me*, if you don't mind! But, he didn't have my mother in front of him this time, that's for sure; this girl was ready for him, let me tell you! "Hit me now, Dad," I said to him, "hit me now or lay a finger on me, even and I'll go straight down to the Guards. You hit my mother again: look at the state of her eye, for God's sake. But you try and do that to me and you'll be the worse for it, I can tell you!"'

'He listened to you then, did he?' Nano asked, disgusted at this whole story.

'He listened this time alright, even if had gone within a whisker of giving me a belt. But even if he had tried to kill me right then, there was no way I was keeping my mouth shut any more. They say that hatred is stronger than fear, and I didn't ever hate anyone as much as I hated that bastard right then. But you won't believe what he said then to my mother! He turns to her and says, "You reared her up well, Lil," he says. "Oh yeah, she's a real credit to you, alright!" And what would you say to that, now, Nano?'

Nano was stuck for words. 'That was the longest fortnight of my life. I thought it'd never come to an end, and if it hadn't been for my mother and the younger ones, I wouldn't have stayed there even a day longer. And on the day that I left, when I said goodbye to my mam down at the station, I knew that I was finished with them for good. I won't go home again for as long as that bastard is still alive, Nano, not unless I have to; not unless my mother gets sick or something like that. There's only the two youngest left back there now, Pat and Tessa; a few more years and they can hit the road too. And maybe I'll bring my mother over here then; she'd get work easily, and at least she'd have some kind of a life over here, if she left that animal behind. But, she won't Nano; she doesn't have it in her to do that.'

Sheila gave a deep sigh and took up the mug of cocoa again. 'Damn it but my cocoa is gone cold with this rant of mine!' She hopped off the bed and went over to the mirror where she piled her hair up on her head. She turned her head right to left and examined herself closely in the mirror. 'I was thinking of putting my hair up high like this, Nano. What would you to say that?' She was the old Sheila again, and a lump came into Nano's throat that hadn't been there while Sheila was telling her story.

'It's really lovely, I swear.'

'You think so?' Sheila turned her head this way and that and all the anxiety seemed to disappear.

'Seriously! I wouldn't tell you a lie now, would I?'

'You have a real eye for style, Nano. Everything looks good on you,' Sheila said.

'You'd swear that I'd a full wardrobe of stuff or something,' said Nano.

'But I mean it! There's loads of them here that don't know how to dress properly; I mean, that Jackson is like something you'd see at the circus and even if Catherine Geraghty was wearing silk down to her toes, she still wouldn't look like anything; even McDermott herself hasn't much of a shape about her. But everything looks nice on you.'

'Thanks very much,' said Nano, laughing.

'Or do you think the twist might suit me? It's all the fashion, now that long hair is going out.' Sheila took up imaginary scissors to her hair and snipped the air with them.

'Mind that you don't do that. Don't ruin your hair, you idiot! You don't want to cut off all your hair like that, do you?'

Sheila's mind was somewhere else. She let her hair hang loose again and turned to Nano. 'As long as there's breath in this body, Nano Keane, no man will treat this girl here the way my dad treated my mam. I wouldn't stay two minutes with a bastard like that, it doesn't matter what the clergy might say!'

'I wouldn't blame you, sister,' said Nano.

'Oh God, it's not even nine o'clock yet! It's a pity that we don't have the radio here, isn't it?' Sheila asked with a sigh.

'That'd be nice, girl. A blast of music!'

'Someone could get Luxembourg here.'

'*Ceilidh House!*'

'*Din Joe,*' said Sheila, grimacing.

'*The Balladmaker's Saturday Night!*'

'*Question Time!*'

'*Fadhbanna Gaeilge!*'

'*Hospital Requests!*'

'*The Waltons!*'

'*The Angelus!*' Sheila finished and burst out laughing.

'Oh, you pagan,' said Nano, 'don't be so disrespectful.'

'Well, I don't know about you, but young Sheila here is going to bed even if it is Christmas Day evening itself,' Sheila said, and began to undress.

'I suppose we might as well,' said Nano.

Nano had her rosary beneath her pillow and once Sheila had turned off the light, she took it between her fingers and said a decade of the prayer to herself. She prayed for her relatives at home and for Máirtín and she prayed that she'd be strong enough to resist the trials and temptations that came her way. She was nearly asleep when Sheila spoke to her from her own bed. 'Nano?'

'What is it, Sheila?'

'I have just one thing to ask you, Nano, and please don't refuse me: come to the dance with me tomorrow night, will you? God knows, the night'll be no fun if you don't come!'

'But I don't want to go, Sheila, didn't I tell you…?'

'For God's sake, you're the only friend here that I can have the craic with!'

Nano kissed the rosary beads, then placed them back under her pillow again. 'Okay, so, I'll go.'

'Oh, you're my darling!' Sheila was back to her old self again. 'We'll have a great night altogether, wait'll you see, Nano!'

'Go to sleep now, you idiot, will you? Tomorrow won't be a picnic for either of us work-wise.'

****

The dance was in full swing and there was a good crowd in when Nano and Sheila arrived. It was in a big hall that had been a gym back when Norwood Hospital had functioned as a military hospital. But tonight, it had been all done up for the festivities. The music was loud. Onstage, a five-piece band was belting out 'In the Mood'; the heavy drum beats shook the windows, the deep bass of the saxophone echoed from the walls. The dancers circled the hall in lively fashion, the women in their long glossy dresses, and the better-off hospital staff – doctors and husbands of the senior nursing staff – in their evening suits. This annual dance was the only social event where all the hospital staff came together, from the matron down to the last girl employed as a domestic, and from the most qualified doctors to the men who looked after the hospital furnace. It was supposed to be an occasion where class distinction was set aside and no-one overdid the style. The idea was that anyone working there could socialise and dance with anyone else. In reality, the strict code that defined the workplace ruled here also. The various groups still kept to themselves and congregated between each dance. In fact, a slight tension could be felt among the gathering. This made for a strange atmosphere in ways, given the mix of different classes and nationalities, some of whom were still wary of one another. There were other Irish present, young men who'd been invited to the dance by their girlfriends from the hospital even if you could tell by them that this dance was a bit formal or genteel compared to the livelier and more spontaneous nights-out that they were used to. Some of these lads were tempted to shout out as part of the craic, and, needless to say, the women who'd invited them were very anxious that they didn't do anything wrong or out-of-place – the lads who had a drop or two on-board, especially! The last thing that the Irish girls wanted to hear the next day was a litany of complaints against them, especially from those who were already prejudiced against their nationality.

'I hope to God,' Mary McDermott had said to Nano earlier as they were making up some beds together on the ward, 'that none of the lads let us down tonight, Keane, I couldn't give a damn what they get up to down at the Irish Club but I wouldn't want them to give the crowd here an excuse to be down on them.'

No doubt, there were other men at the dance who, as did the Irish lads, felt equally uncomfortable in this environment, including the immigrants down from the old prisoner-of-war camp. The wariness and hesitancy that characterised the gathering faded as the night wore on, however, and there was to be no arguments or trouble that night.

The pair of them had gone to the hall after a quick drink in the Tudor Rose.

'Yerra, Nano, how could we walk in there unless we'd a quick drink beforehand? You'd want one small thimbleful anyway to get some jizz into you!'

'A glass of lemonade or orange juice won't put much jizz into me – but anyway,' said Nano as they'd got ready earlier. And even if she'd never have admitted it to herself, Nano was privately glad that they'd decided to go to the pub beforehand, as she secretly hoped that Julius Kuzleikas might be there and that he'd chat her up again.

'Fair play to you, Nano, we'll have a mighty night tonight!' Sheila had responded excitedly. The Tudor Rose was already thronged with workers from the hospital and men who'd come down from the refugee camp. They managed to find a place to sit. And, signs on it, Sheila brought her back a small glass of sherry and a glass of gin for herself.

'Now, here you go. A thimbleful of sherry and don't you say anything, girl. That wouldn't knock a stir out of a child, now, girl!'

'You know full well that I don't drink, Sheila; I never touch the stuff.'

'Oh sure, isn't it Christmas, for God's sake! A dropeen of sherry, you wouldn't even notice it on the palm of your hand, it's that small. Sure, if I wanted to get you drunk, wouldn't I give you the same stuff as myself?'

Nano shook her head ruefully but she didn't want to make a big deal of it.

'I'll be as bad as yourself, before long, you slapper!'

'Here now. Happy Christmas to you – what's left of it, and may all your best wishes come true for the New Year!'

'The same to you,' Nano said, taking the toast and a hesitant sip of her sherry at the same time. It didn't look like the New Year held out too much promise, she thought or rather, she shouldn't be expecting too much from it, anyway.

'Now, that wasn't so bad now, was it?' asked Sheila?

'Bloody rotten stuff!' Nano joked; it didn't taste too bad at all, she thought. It was nice and sweet and reminded her of something that she'd tasted before when she was a child. Maybe it was the small drop of porter or wine that her grandmother had always had a glass of around Christmas-time long ago – that and the handful of snuff she'd take from the box labelled Colman's Mustard

This half-buried memory disappeared from Nano's mind as she spotted Julius laughing with a group of his own people over on the far side of the room. Julius was wearing a black suit, a different one from that of the night he'd brought her here to the Tudor Rose. Instead of a tie, he had on a small black dicky bow; he looked really fine, very fancy, like some big-shot. A thrill went through her entire body, as if he could sense his effect on her and knew that she wouldn't reject him this time. And sure enough, Julius made his way over to their table before long.

'Look out,' said Sheila. 'Romeo's on his way over to you!'

Julius stood in front of them and bowed slightly, almost as if he were an actor in the pictures. He was as well-dressed as any actor too; his suit immaculate as if he'd been to the most expensive tailor in Norwold! He was one of the best-looking men Nano'd ever seen – no doubt about it! The love that she'd felt until recently for Máirtín Spillane was as nothing compared to the feelings that this man provoked in her. Her heart jumped with excitement and she felt as if she couldn't breathe.

'Hello,' Julius said to them, as confident as ever. He looked at Sheila for a second and then at Nano in a way that made her heart race.

'Hello yourself,' said Sheila, indifferently enough. 'How're you?'

'Fine, thanks very much,' he replied.

'Here, let me buy you both a drink for Christmas,' he said and Sheila accepted his offer readily.

'I'll have a gin-and-orange, please. How could I refuse!' she giggled.

'And you Nano, what will you have?' Julius eyes seemed to bore into her soul.

'I'm grand,' she said, after a minute. 'Don't mind me.'

'Oh, get her a small glass of sherry,' said Sheila. 'Anything's better than an empty glass,' and Julius went off to the bar.

'I didn't want another drink, Sheila, what did you do that for?'

'Ara, bullshit, girl! Take what you can get in this life. Isn't it great that it's on offer! I'm sorry now that I didn't get us two gins because I'd drink two.' She gave Nano a mischievous glance. 'You'll have a job shaking him off tonight, girl; that man's cracked about you.'

'Rubbish Sheila!' Nano said, embarrassed, but then she laughed the next second at the moon-face her friend directed at her. 'Go to hell, Sheila, I'm not on the market.'

'You aren't if you don't want to be.'

'Well, I don't want to be.'

'We'll see,' Sheila, giving her a sharp look, but Julius had returned with the drinks.

He placed the gin and the sherry on the table and turned to go again, as if he didn't want to impose on them too much.

'Your health!' said Sheila raising her glass. And whatever came over her then, Nano raised her glass too and uttered the word *'Sveikas!'*

'Sveikas!' replied Julius, proudly, his eyes melting into hers as he said something in his own language. 'I might see you over at the dance in a while,' he added before returning to his own group.

'Well, Sheila, I've often heard it said that it's the quiet ones you have to watch – but there's no beating you on that score, darling! Where'd you learn that lingo, girl?'

'Listen. It's only one word, Sheila,' said Nano, admonishing herself privately. Why hadn't she just kept her big trap shut?

293

But Sheila wasn't letting her off that easily. 'That's a word that you'd only learn down the pub!'

'God knows but you're worse than any solicitor,' said Nano, mortified. 'I might as well come clean about it, I suppose – you'll give me no peace otherwise! I had a drink with him here one night when I went out to post a letter. That was it – a half-an-hour or so was all it was – and then he asked me that night if I'd go out with him again sometime.'

'Oh, but aren't you the secretive one too that you didn't tell your auntie here anything about this?' Sheila joked, although Nano sensed a hint of resentment.

'Oh, well… sister, I was embarrassed about it, that's why! I was going to tell you about it once or twice but I just couldn't.'

'You're an easy one to embarrass,' said Sheila, laughing.

Nano looked over to where Julius was sitting a few times before they left the Tudor Rose that evening and there wasn't once that he didn't catch her glance and smile back at her. Sheila had noticed what was going on, however. 'You know what they say about love at first sight and all that, Nano?'

'I don't,' Nano replied, her cheeks reddening again.

'They say that those first looks are the prelude to love, girl.'

'Ara bullshit!' Nano said and they laughed. Once they had got to the dance, they took off their coats at the gym and made their way down through the crowd to the middle of the hall; Julius was there already; he'd left the pub earlier with his gang. It was so packed that it was difficult to make out anyone clearly but Nano trembled secretly with excitement every time she thought of him.

'They've a real band here, anyway,' Sheila said, glancing around. 'They'd a crowd of chancers here last year that you wouldn't have let out with the Wren.'

'It's way too loud,' said Nano, even though she didn't give a damn about the racket, really; they could have been banging saucepan lids together, for all she cared. Her attention was elsewhere, now.

'Uh-oh, Christ, look who's look come over!' said Sheila, giving Nano's elbow a squeeze. 'I was praying that he wouldn't come tonight.' Mike Shiels strode across the floor towards them with a real sense of purpose, his face lit up in a big smile. He really was a fine-looking man, Nano thought, if you liked his type. Nano was worried to see him here, however – almost as much as Sheila was. Wherever Mike was, the chances were that Peter Sharkey would be following along and there was nothing surer than the four of them would find themselves ensconced in a group for the rest of the night. Damn him, anyway! How the hell did she ever get stuck with that nerd in the first place, Nano thought to herself. This was unkind of her, she knew, and she regretted it immediately.

What sort of a woman was she that she could be so cracked about a foreign man and that such uncharitable thoughts went through her mind like this?

'Well, it's just as well that we weren't relying on the likes of yourselves to get an invitation here!' was Mike Shiels cheery greeting – as if to say that he wasn't bothered one way or the other. His cheeks were burning from dancing; he radiated an energy that was almost physical as he sidled up next to them. Mike gave Nano an inscrutable look and winked at her. 'Hello, Nano! Long time, no see.'

'It's been a while, alright,' replied Nano in a mopey voice.

'You'd think that Sheila'd bring you out the odd night with her or has the girl any nature in her at all?'

He thought a lot of himself, no doubt about it, Nano thought. He'd the swagger and self-confidence of a man who knows he's handsome.

'I'm not a child or an invalid that Sheila has to bring me anywhere! I've two legs of my own, haven't I?' Her response didn't bother Mike Shiels in the slightest, however; it was water off a duck's back to him.

'By God but that's for sure, girl – and you've a fine pair of legs on you at that! What about using them now to come out for a dance with me?' he said without batting an eyelid. The quickstep was about to begin, and Nano found herself on the dance-floor before she knew it, Mike's arms guiding her around the floor as smoothly as if they were long-time dancing partners. Nano looked over Mike's shoulder and saw Sheila stick her tongue out at her in jokey fashion; they were off, then, sliding in and out amongst the scores of other dancers. Everyone who wasn't on-duty or hadn't gone home for Christmas was at this dance, it seemed. Hilda Jackson was there with her new crazy-looking hairstyle, a headband encircling her forehead like a Red Indian and sporting a dress that only barely reached down to her knees. Fidelma Byrnes also looked really good in a black velvet dress, while Catherine Geraghty was enjoying the company of a big block of a man who was perspiring heavily. Mary McDermott was there as was Lena Murphy, all of them scattered around different parts of the hall, dancing and chatting – and not one of them going unnoticed to the matron who was standing on one side next to one of the doctors, those hawk-eyes of hers scanning the entire gathering. Nano hadn't spotted Julius yet anywhere, wherever he'd disappeared.

'Where's Peter tonight?' Nano asked Mike, partly to make up for her abruptness earlier.

'Peter's gone home for Christmas,' Mike replied. He stared at Nano intently for a second, then, as if unsure whether to say what was on his mind or not. 'He said he'd no business over here anymore!' Nano didn't say anything to this but, as she feared, Mike continued, 'Look Nano,' he said straight out; 'what would you say to seeing Peter again?'

'Again?' They'd circled the hall twice by now, twisting and twirling their way through the quickstep and Nano adapting to the dance-moves as readily as someone who'd been practising them all her life, but there was still no sign of Julius anywhere.

'You brought him home from the dance in the club that night, didn't you?' Mike asked her in as innocuous a tone as he could manage.

'I didn't ask him to go anywhere, Mike.' Nano felt a mixture of irritation and embarrassment at the way the conversation had turned.

She didn't like the cocky way that Mike had asked her straight out like that. And she was still embarrassed at the memory of that night and how she'd handled the situation. God knows what Peter had said about her to his friend; for all she knew, they might have been laughing at her behind her back!

Mike had turned serious in a manner that she had not seen previously, however. 'Is it that you don't like him, Nano?' he asked.

'What sort of a question is that, Mike?' Nano batted back.

'It's a simple question – either you like him or you don't.'

'You could say that I dont care about him one way or the other,' said Nano.

Was it just her imagination or had Mike winced slightly, in annoyance at her response?

'Peter's a very nice lad, Nano, as nice a lad as you'd meet anywhere!'

'Well, you like singing his praises anyway, that's for sure,' replied Nano, more prickly now that she'd spotted Julius Kuzleikas over on the other side of the hall, laughing and joking with that Italian domestic that she'd seen him having the craic with at the door of the hospital kitchen before – Raefelina or whatever the hell her name was. Next thing, the other dancers blocked her view and Mike was back plugging Peter again.

'He really has a thing for you, girl, he's always talking about you. When he was going home the other day, he said to me "If you see Nano at the dance, tell her I was asking for her".'

Nano didn't respond; she was touchy now, pricklier still because of seeing Julius. She couldn't wait for the quickstep to be over so that she could sit down for a while and gather her thoughts, without Mike teasing her like this.

'You might see him next week – he'd like to talk to you, anyway,' said Mike and suddenly the quickstep was over, and Nano had the chance to escape from him.

Sheila was just back off the dancefloor as well, her face aflame with the heat. 'Oh, if you saw the smasher that brought me out, Nano! He's going to ask me out again later,' he said. 'Isn't it an awful pity that Mike didn't stay away from us tonight?'

'Pity he didn't is right! He has me haunted,' Nano murmured and Sheila's eyes widened in surprise.

'No way...! He wasn't asking you out, was he?'

'"Asking me out", is it? No way! Trying to set me up with Peter is what he was at – that's all he was on about the whole time we were out on the dancefloor.'

'Oh!' said Sheila quietly, absorbing this information.

'Sure, why would you care anyway, now that you've this new smasher on the go?' Nano said, prodding Sheila with her elbow. Sheila gave a short laugh that had a hint of bitterness in it and shook her head.

'Course you know what they say, girl? It's better to have two notches on the stick than one!'

Nano started to say something but changed her mind; I mean, wasn't she as bad, really, messing around with lads here when she had her own man back home?

'Here he is now, anyway,' Sheila said as she glimpsed Mike making his way over to them. An old-style waltz was announced and Nano couldn't help but notice how enthusiastically Sheila joined Mike on the floor for this one – for someone who'd showed so little interest in him a few minutes earlier!

Her eyes scanned the room to see whether there was any sign of Julius anywhere. Wasn't it strange too how he hadn't come over and asked her out for a dance by now? He must know that she was there! Nano scanned the room until she felt a hand gently touch her elbow. She could barely hide her disappointment when she spun around to see who was there, however. It wasn't Julius at all but the pimply fellow who'd been playing the records. His face was lit up with a big self-satisfied grin and his eyes were huge behind thick spectacles. She went out onto the floor with him and the way the young lad carried on, you'd have sworn he was doing her a favour by dancing with her. He prattled on endlessly as they swung around the floor.

Suddenly, Julius was within touching distance of Nano, dancing with the Italian girl. The spotty lad kept blathering on about work and all the rest of it but Nano didn't hear a word of what he said, she was so distracted by the sight of Julius and the other girl and how happy they looked, the pair of them laughing together. So, this was the reason that Julius hadn't been over to ask her out! He was busy elsewhere chatting up this Italian girl, who wasn't half bad-looking, even if she was a bit squint-eyed. Raefelina – even her name sounded lovely! – was a good-natured, happy-go-lucky girl who was always laughing and singing when she was working in the hospital. You wouldn't have blamed Julius if he was taken with her because she was one of the nicest girls at the dance. Nano forced away this thought and tried to focus on what her dancing partner was saying. He was going on about a new club that was due to be built, if the authorities granted permission for it. There were so many people coming over from Ireland these days, he said, that they badly needed a new hall. Julius and the Italian girl skipped close by her again and this time, Julius stared intently at her, as much as to say that he wanted to talk to her. Nano's heart skipped a beat and she relaxed for the first time that night. She focussed again on the youth and his conversation.

Signs on it too, because your man who played the records tried his best to get a promise from her that she'd dance with him again later. Once the waltz was over, Nano eagerly escaped his clutches and went back to their seats.

'How did you get caught by that idiot?' was the first thing that Sheila O'Dwyer said to Nano on her return. Mike had gone to get another couple of orange juices for them from the drinks counter.

'Desperation, sister,' replied Nano, jokily. 'No-one else wanted to ask me out! Anything is better than nothing….'

'Don't believe a word of it,' said Sheila to Nano with a sardonic glance. 'Did you see Julius at all?'

'I saw him out on dance-floor, alright,' said Nano, praying that Mike would return quickly so Sheila couldn't ask her any more questions.

The fact that there no sign of Julius again bothered her. What was keeping him? It wasn't Mike Shiels who appeared next to her now, however, but Julius Kuzleikas, his face brightened by a big smile.

'I hope that no-one's already asked you out for the next dance, I was too late for the last two,' he said.

'Ara boy, this one is always snapped up quickly,' Sheila interrupted, 'you'd want to be at the top of the queue, let me tell you!'

'Better late than never,' said Nano as gently as she could muster; her heart pounding. Mike came over the next moment, three bottles of orange juice in hand, and a straw in each bottle.

Maybe she was mistaken but Mike looked surprised to see Julius there with them. If that was the case, he certainly hid it well, because he smiled at Julius, as friendly as ever. 'I'd have got one for you too if I'd known in time,' said Mike, handing around the bottles. 'Not that it's worth it!' he added, grimacing at the taste of the orange.

'Good job you didn't stick your nose in the door of the Tudor Rose a little while ago, then,' said Sheila, mischeviously. 'Julius got us a proper drink, didn't he, Nano?'

'Nothing wrong with this, that's for sure,' Nano said agreeably. No more than what they'd been drinking at Saint Bridget's club the other night. Mike wasn't a big drinker; and she could see now that he was clever enough in his own way, underneath all that playful, hale-fellow-well-met way of his. Nano had some intimation and felt anxious for her friend. Maybe Sheila wasn't as worldly-wise as she thought: maybe she wasn't as able for Mike as she let on. After all, they'd been going out together for a good while, even if it was off and on. It occurred to Nano that Sheila was a lot more cracked about Mike then he was about her. Nano hoped that she wasn't being too hard on him, but in truth she sensed that Mike was only passing the time with her until someone else came along. They were calling another dance now and Julius asked Nano out. Sheila took her drink from her. 'I won't touch a drop of it, Nano, I swear!'

'I'll choke you if you do,' said Nano with a laugh. They'd called a slow waltz this time and even though Julius wasn't as familiar with the steps as Mike Shiels, he was still ten times better at it than Nano was. Somehow, Nano felt like she'd come home. She loved the feel of Julius' hand in hers and the touch of his fingers on her back. Everything just felt right. They were so relaxed and comfortable together that they didn't even need conversation. It was enough to swing and circle the room with Julius this close to her. All her worries had disappeared and she was drunk on the moment. This was one night, just one night in time, a small voice in the back of her mind said to her, and it was important to make the most of it.

Julius' cheek was next to hers, stray locks of his hair caressing her cheeks. She felt his mouth against her ear as he whispered, 'Will you keep the last dance for me, whoever else you dance with for the rest of the night?' Nano gave his hand a small squeeze of promise.

***

Everywhere was quiet. The gymnasium lights had been switched off, and all the dancers had gone home. From the nurse's quarters and the wards, the faint gleam of the night-lights radiated across the night. Some of the girls were reluctant to go to bed. They didn't want the night to end. Thousands of stars sparkled brightly high in the black night-sky – a sure sign of frost. There was a bite in the air, but Nano Keane didn't feel it. She rested her head on Julius' shoulder and gave a sigh of contentment. His arms were around her and, as he kissed her gently, sweet shivers went through her body. It was a good hour since they'd left the dance but Nano had lost any notion of time. She longed to stay there with Julius behind the hospital, wrapped in his warm embrace forever. She placed her arms around Julius' neck, then pulled him to her, to kiss him. She whispered his name quietly and almost with reverence. She leaned into him and kissed him again for a long time.

Notes and Glossary

Hoors – Whores.

Fáinne – Ring-shaped badge, worn by many Irish-language revivalists, which indicated that a person spoke Irish.

Máirtín Thornton – Nicknamed the "Connemara Crusher," this Irish heavyweight boxer, well known in the 1940s, was a native of Spiddal, County Galway. Thornton fought Bruce Woodcock for the British Commonwealth Heavyweight title in 1945.

Bawneen – a woven white wool used for jackets, pullovers. – from Irish word "bán" (white)

Nearly landed – Nearly arrived/nearly there.

Signs on it – Sure enough/Indeed/It was clear from….

Arah, musha – Indeed/If so.

Streel – Older, nosy person who interferes in other people's business.

FCA – Army Reserve.

Knock a piece out of her – Try it on with her (vulgar).

There isn't a tap out there – There's no work available at all/everyone is out of work (may be originally a reference to a cobbler tapping shoes).

Sticking your arse out looking for it! – Doing something outrageous to try and find work/attract attention. May have its origins in the ancient Celtic custom of expressing contempt to your adversary by showing your behind: *póg mo thóin* (kiss my arse: Irish), *twll din pob Sais* (arseholes to the English: Welsh), and in *Braveheart*, the Scots demonstrate it to the English army just before battle.

Oxters – armpits.

Old wan – Old one/old woman.

Boreen – *small* road, lane – (from Irish word – "bóthar" – meaning "road"

Looder – idiot, fool.

Gamsa na ndoinín in arraí na geornan / An doinín gabóige chris sé a bhois – ("The gabbit rance in the farley-bield…") – meaningless gibberish words, sung as a bit of a "ditty")

Without a steer under him – legless/blind-drunk (staggering, swaying)

Wasn't a gig – Wasn't a peep/no word/keeping quiet.

I'm time enough – (I have plenty of time to do this yet/I'm on time/have time)

Gombeen – A derogatory or pejorative Irish term for a shady, small-time "wheeler-dealer" type – a businessman or politician, for instance

– someone who is always looking to make a quick profit, often at someone else's expense or through accepting favours or taking bribes. Its origin is the Irish word "gaimbín", meaning monetary interest. The term originated with moneylenders who exploited the starving during the Great Famine by selling food and other goods on credit at hugely-exorbitant interest rates.

Yoke – Slang word meaning "thing." *A "yoke" is literally any object that has no known name or that someone can't remember the name of.*

His back – Back-up for him. His "corner-man." Ensuring that the fight is organized fairly.

Jackeen – Dubliner, city boy.

The Far East – Official magazine of the Missionary Society of St Columban, founded in 1918 by Irishman Fr John Heneghan, who was killed by the Japanese in Manila in World War II.

Put it on the long finger – delay, procrastinate

Bulling – really angry, raging

The Holy Year 1950: a great Jubilee commencing at Christmas 1949. Pope Pius XII invited all the faithful to sanctify their lives in accordance with the spirt of the Gospel. A renaissance of humanity was deemed possible, were people to turn away from earthly secular things and focus on the eternal.

Shift – Kiss and cuddle/smooch/snog.

Donkey cart – From the Irish song, *An Trucailín Donn* (The Little

Brown Cart): 'One fine spring day as I trotted easily across the bridge in Mullinahone…'

In the heel of the hunt – When push comes to shove.

Dote – Someone who is cute/adorable.

Giving out to me – giving out/criticizing, admonishing

Well-on-it Tipsy/nearly drunk

Isn't it true for me – Isn't what I'm saying true?/Isn't that the truth?

Planking Beating/smashing/hitting someone hard.

Rip – a bitch, a hussy.

Knock a stir – wouldn't knock someone off their stride/ wouldn't bother them in the slightest.

A good run is better than a bad stand – An English equivalent would be: "It is better to turn and run away and live to fight another day".

Take his gig away – (take his "deal" or "advantage"/"job" away from him.)

Away on a hack – It will be plain sailing from here.

Fit to be tied – Livid, furious.

Blowing – (Slang) – boasting

Scrawns – Scrawny, skinny

Hames – (Slang) – a mess

Gowl – Idiot, fool.

Calling me out – Challenging me.

Up–in–a–heap – Upset.

Up–in–heap/up–in–a–heap Upset, confused, wound–up.

Let out with the Wren Wrenboys (and girls), also called 'strawboys', a band of mummers who go from house to house and pubs on 26 December to celebrate the wren, dressed up in masks, straw suits and colourful motley clothing, and performing music. In years past, they would have caught a wren and carried it in a cage (the tradition of 'hunting the wren' is also associated with Boxing Day in Wales). Nowadays, groups of Wrenboys (minus the wren) often raise money for charity.

as able for – Confident of achieving/capable of dealing with

PARTHIAN TRANSLATIONS

EXILES
Dónall Mac Amhlaigh

Translated from the Irish
by Mícheál Ó hAodha

Out October 2020

£12.00
978-1-912681-31-0

HANA
Alena Mornštajnová

Translated from the Czech
by Julia and Peter Sherwood

Out August 2020

£10.99
978-1-912681-50-1

Co-funded by the
European Union

Creative
Europe
MEDIA

LA BLANCHE
Maï-Do Hamisultane

Translated from the French
by Suzy Ceulan Hughes

£8.99
978-1-912681-23-5

THE NIGHT CIRCUS
AND OTHER STORIES
Uršuľa Kovalyk

Translated from the Slovak
by Julia and Peter Sherwood

£8.99
978-1-912681-04-4

A GLASS EYE
Miren Agur Meabe

Translated from the Basque
by Amaia Gabantxo

£8.99
978-1-912109-54-8

PARTHIAN TRANSLATIONS

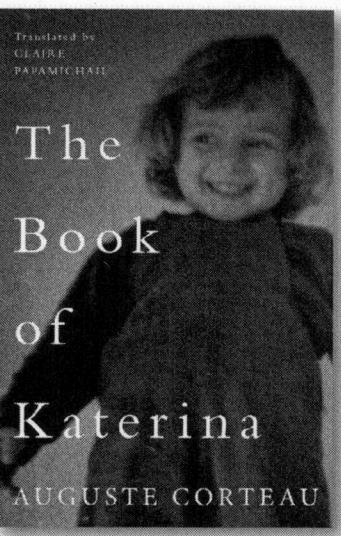

THE BOOK OF KATERINA

Auguste Corteau

Translated from the Greek by Claire Papamichail

Out 2021

£10.00
978-1-912681-26-6

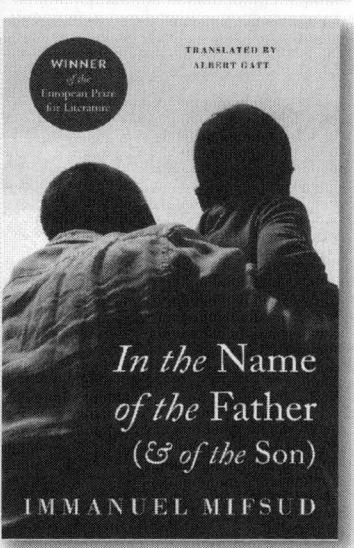

IN THE NAME OF THE FATHER (& OF THE SON)

Immanuel Mifsud

Translated from the Maltese by Albert Gatt

£6.99
978-1-912681-30-3

Co-funded by the European Union

 Creative Europe MEDIA

HER MOTHER'S HANDS

Karmele Jaio

Translated from the Basque
by Kristin Addis

£8.99
978-1-912109-55-5

WOMEN WHO BLOW ON KNOTS

Ece Temelkuran

Translated from the Turkish
by Alexander Dawe

£9.99
978-1-910901-69-4

THE HOUSE OF THE DEAF MAN

Peter Krištúfek

Translated from the Slovak
by Julia and Peter Sherwood

£11.99
978-1-909844-27-8